Praise for Sue Henry's previous Alaskan mystery
MURDER ON THE IDITAROD TRAIL

"DAZZLING . . . AN ADRENALINE-PUMPING DEBUT"

The New York Times Book Review

"THE ACTION IS PACKED AND FAST-PACED.
MS. HENRY DOES AN INCREDIBLE JOB "

Mostly Murder

"ENTHRALLING . . .
HENRY PROVIDES SUSPENSE AND EXCITEMENT
IN THIS PAEAN TO A GREAT SPORTING EVENT
AND TO THE POWERFUL ALASKAN LANDSCAPE."

Publishers Weekly

"EXCELLENT . . . REALISTIC AND CONVINCING . . .
WELL-PACED, WELL-CONCEIVED, ENGROSSING . . .
HENRY'S NOVEL MOVES ALONG LIKE A
HEALTHY, WELL-TRAINED DOG TEAM
ON A 1,000 MILE RACE"

Anchorage Times

WINNER!
The ANTHONY and MACAVITY AWARDS
for Best First Mystery

P9-DEK-996

Books by Sue Henry

MURDER ON THE IDITAROD TRAIL
TERMINATION DUST
SLEEPING LADY
DEATH TAKES PASSAGE
DEADFALL
MURDER ON THE YUKON QUEST
BENEATH THE ASHES
DEAD NORTH
COLD COMPANY
DEATH TRAP

Termination Dust

SUE HENRY

AVON BOOKS
An Imprint of HarperCollinsPublishers

AVON BOOKS
An Imprint of HarperCollins*Publishers*
10 East 53rd Street
New York, New York 10022-5299

First Avon Books paperback printing: May 1996
First William Morrow hardcover printing: May 1995

In memory of the thousands, wise and foolish, who, against enormous odds, toiled and trudged their way into the Klondike in 1897, where many died in the desperate winter that followed, when food could not be had for any amount of the gold they scraped from the depths of the iron-hard ground.

And for my brother, John, and his wife, Sue, for their unflagging encouragement and support.

Acknowledgments

Thanks are due to the following people, who assisted in the research and writing of this book:

Alice Abbott, Becky Lundquist, Phoebe Czikra and the Friday Night Adoption Society, for patience, proofreading, encouragement, and a most essential sense of humor.

The Alaska State Troopers, Scientific Crime Detection Laboratory, and the Yukon Royal Canadian Mounted Police, for generous technical assistance.

The Yukon Archives, Whitehorse, Yukon, for records and research on the Klondike Gold Rush.

The Lousaac Library, Alaska Collection, for research assistance on the Klondike Gold Rush.

James E. O'Malley, M.D., for assistance in understanding the implications and care of cold injuries, particularly frostbite.

Lieutenant Richard J. Tyler, a victim of severe frostbite on Mount McKinley in 1994, for the courage to share. My gratitude and best wishes.

Vanessa Summers for her wonderful maps.

Flo Foster and The Roadhouse, Whitehorse, Yukon, for bluegrass, enthusiasm, and shelter from the storm.

Charlotte Masarik for her cheerful company on the long drive to Skagway, Dawson, over the Top of the World, and back to Anchorage. Thanks, Thelma.

David Highfill, formerly of Avon Books, for faith and friendship.

TERMINATION DUST:

A term coined by early gold seekers
in Alaska and the Yukon
for the first snowfall on the mountains
that signaled an end to the year's prospecting season.

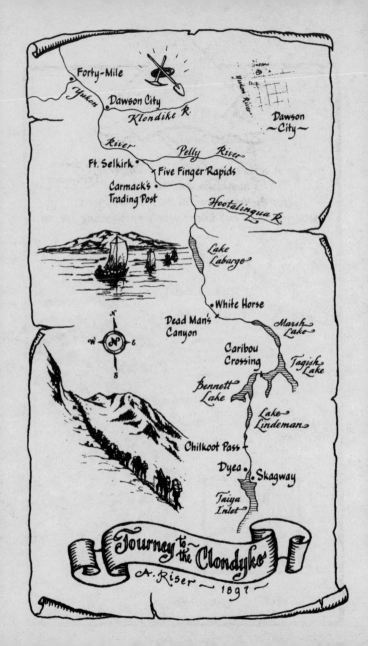

Forty-Mile

Dawson City

Klondike R.

Yukon

Dawson City

River

Pelly River

Ft. Selkirk

Five Finger Rapids

Carmack's
Trading Post

Hootalinqua R.

Lake
Labarge

White Horse

Dead Man's
Canyon

Marsh
Lake

Caribou
Crossing

Tagish
Lake

N
W — E
S

Bennett
Lake

Lake
Lindeman

Chilkoot Pass

Dyea

Skagway

Taiya
Inlet

Journey to the Clondyke

A. Riser — 1897

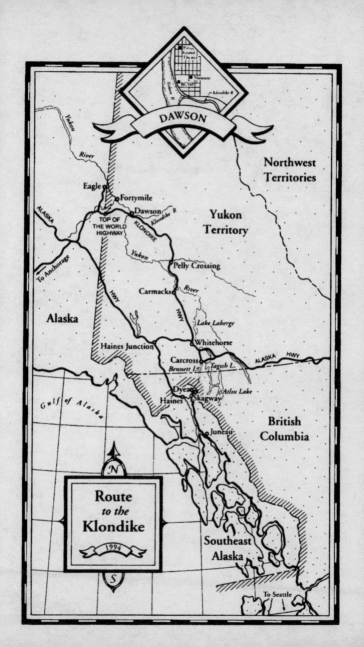

DAWSON

Northwest
Territories

Yukon
Territory

Eagle
Fortymile
Dawson
TOP OF
THE WORLD
HIGHWAY

Pelly Crossing

Carmacks

Lake Laberge

Alaska

To Anchorage

Haines Junction
Whitehorse

Carcross
Bennett L.
Tagish L.
ALASKA HWY

Dyea
Haines
Skagway

Atlin Lake

British
Columbia

Gulf of Alaska

Juneau

N

Route
to the
Klondike

1994

Southeast
Alaska

S

To Seattle

IN THE DARK ON THE ICE OF THE FROZEN river, small white crystals of snow swirled so thickly that it was impossible to see more than a few feet in any direction, let alone either bank of the Yukon. The colder the temperature, the smaller and harder moisture solidifies into dry, icy pellets. At over thirty below zero, these were so fine they flew abrasively on the wind and flowed across the ice like sand.

The early January night of 1898 was not one for traveling, rather for seeking shelter . . . any shelter. But in a blizzard on the upper Yukon, twenty miles north of the gold-rush city of Dawson, gray shadow among shadows, a lone figure moved on the river ice. One lurching step after another, it staggered against the wind that threatened to blow it over, hesitating to draw breath between efforts, but always stubbornly, hypnotically taking one more step, as it had done for hours.

A thick beard defined the figure as male, though this was so packed with snow its color was indiscernible. Ice, frozen from the moisture of his breathing, rimed it around the mouth and coated the mustache above it. A beaver hat came down low to the eyebrows, leaving only the nose and part of the cheeks exposed. Frost clung to the lashes of his eyes, narrowed to slits and circled darkly with fatigue in a face already gaunt from hunger. When he blinked, they sometimes froze shut and he would swipe at them with the back of the beaver mittens that sheathed his

1

hands and arms to the elbow. A tattered, gray wool blanket was draped over his angular frame and knotted clumsily at the waist, covering the shoulders of a knee-length parka, hand-stitched of wolf pelts, fur to the inside.

Boots over heavy wool socks covered feet he knew were still under him but could not feel. They had been numb for a long time, as had his hands and fingers. The exposed flesh of his cheeks exhibited the characteristic dead white of frostbite.

He had started this trek with a tiny amount of dried meat, now long since consumed a shred at a time. A bottle of water inside his coat had frozen despite his body heat. Snow, tongued from what collected on his mittens, melted into an unsatisfying hint of dampness and filled his mouth with a constant reminder of cruel thirst.

Earlier, he had towed a small sled packed lightly with personal gear. It lay where he had abandoned it when it became more than he could manage, perhaps five miles back. Simply dropping its rope, he had stumbled away without looking. Someone might find it. In clear weather a few freighters infrequently ran the river ice with their precious strings of dogs and heavy sleds. This night no musher would consider taking such a chance.

Many miles still lay between this man and the only possible shelter, and he would never reach it. Vaguely he knew that his journey was now measured in feet, not miles. Resigned, he concerned himself only with the next step and his ability to take it. He had known when he left Dawson that reaching the gold camp of Forty Mile alone was an impossibility, that he would almost surely die on the way.

It was his only option. Here, in the cold and storm of the wilderness, he would eventually lie down alone and go to sleep, perhaps momentarily imagining he was warm, if the tales were true. Here he would be able to die his own death, not that intended for him by his enemies. It would be less heinous than a crushed skull or being buried alive, which he suspected would have been his fate— as it had been Ned's.

His great despair was that his family might never know

what had become of him. Fear had made him reluctant to tell anyone of his departure. Secretly, carrying little, he had slipped away into the cover of the storm that obscured his trail.

With utmost caution, he had secreted the gold in the safest place he could think of, hoping they would assume he had taken it with him. But only a few nuggets were contained in a leather pouch in one deep coat pocket. In another, a tin held a carefully wrapped, waterproof packet holding the photograph of a woman and two small children in a narrow journal filled with his writing.

The next step forward became a stagger for balance on his wooden feet. Another, and he lost the battle to remain upright and sank to his knees in a spot where the wind had swept the thick ice almost clear of snow. Raising his head to look downriver, he suddenly saw a cabin with smoke rising from the chimney in the utterly straight line of totally still and windless weather. It sat solidly on the ice in midstream. There was the glimmer of light from a window. The wind blew snow into his eyes and the hallucination vanished. But for a moment he had seen and yearned toward it, thought for an instant he was saved after all. Now, once again he was conscious of the dark and the fierce cold. He was incredibly tired and sleepy. It was so hard to think.

Covering his face with his mitts to shut out the flying white, he leaned forward until his elbows rested on his knees, shutting his eyes. Rest for a minute. Only a minute.

No. Not here. Off the ice, on the bank. He had a personal horror of dying on the ice, which would melt in the spring and drop his decomposing body into the turbulent thaw, tumbling it apart among the ice blocks of breakup, rendering it unrecognizable even as a corpse, burying his bones in the silt of the riverbed. On solid ground he could sleep undisturbed. There was a slim chance his body might be found, someone know who he had been. He didn't suppose it was truly important, but it mattered to him. So, once again, he began the attempt to struggle back to his feet.

Twice, when almost vertical, he slipped and collapsed

into an untidy heap. There was a sharp pain in one knee, where it had slammed into the ice. But he could crawl, so he did, slowly, for long minutes, until he reached the snow-covered right bank. Floundering up it through the drifts and around a leafless stand of frozen willow, he at last found a level, somewhat sheltered spot.

There he lay down, pulled the blanket loose and over his face to keep out the snow, and was still. It was good to let go and rest, and it did seem warmer. The injured leg twitched stiffly. There was an ache in his neck, but he couldn't rouse himself to move. He dozed for a little, then semi-awareness returned.

He thought of his wife and shaped her name, Polly, at which his dry, chapped lips cracked and oozed blood that froze in his beard, though he did not know it. "Sorry . . . Polly."

They have murdered me, he told her in his mind. Sure as if they'd shot me. Ned, too. Bastards. What a long way to come for this. A thread of remembered anger floated through his thoughts and away.

He recalled her ironing his clothes in the kitchen of their small house and seemed to smell the hot starch of a clean shirt on the board as she smoothed the collar. Usually she ironed the sheets as well and you could smell both the freshness of the outdoors from the clothesline and the slight scent of the woodstove on them. He shrugged deeper into his soft featherbed, enjoying that smell. It must be Saturday, for he could feel a clean nightshirt and his hair felt cool and damp from a bath. Drowsily, he was aware of his mother's strong hands gently tucking the blanket up around his shoulders, smoothing the hair from his forehead.

Then it all drifted into comforting darkness and, as he slept, he was not hungry, was not cold—was not aware when a pair of wolves trotting up the river paused, sniffed, and listened carefully before slowly following his track across the ice and up the bank.

Chapter One

LATE-AFTERNOON SHADOWS REACHED LIKE fingers from the black spruce along the shore, darkening the smooth waters of a wide bend in the Yukon River. Undisturbed by rapids at this particular point, north of Dawson, Yukon Territory, the surface reflected a swirl of colors from surrounding evergreen, autumn-bronzed birch, and the faded-blue, pre-sunset sky. The raucous cry of a jay knifed through the air, turning the head of a bald eagle perched on a dead limb, waiting, patiently, silent, for a squirrel to emerge from its nearby hole. A dragonfly darted in Zs over the surface of the water, well above the reach of any ambitious fish.

A small, rhythmic splashing drew the eagle's attention once again from its objective, this time upriver of the south to north curve of dark water. Out of the shadows and into a last remaining streak of sunlight floated a red canoe with a single passenger, drifting with the current.

Raising a hand, the paddler shaded his eyes from the late glare of the sun, sighting ahead to make out the narrow line of a thin sandbar coming into view on the right. Protected by the bar was a bit of flat, pebble-strewn beach that looked just wide enough for a campsite. A trickle of a stream ran over it into the river, complaining quietly to the unevenness of its bed.

A strong, expert pull on the paddle corrected the direction of the canoe and sent it gliding toward the rind of beach. When the bottom grated gently on small stones, the canoeist did not move for a minute, but laid the paddle across the gunwales and leaned forward on his braced arms, assessing this choice. Judging it acceptable, he rose, stepped out, and carefully lifted the craft far enough from the river so there was no chance of its floating away without him.

Removing a floppy-brimmed hat and clasping a wrist behind his head with the opposite hand, Jim Hampton stretched to relieve the tension in his strong, muscular shoulders and arms, then ran a hand through the sand-colored waves of his hair and yawned. Pleasantly tired, he was pleased with his progress and appreciative of the wilderness he was discovering. It had been a good day of travel on this unfamiliar river.

Just under six feet tall, he was fit and even-featured, though his hair was beginning to recede slightly from his temples and a few gray strands silvered it. This secretly satisfied him, for through most of his thirties he had been embarrassed to appear younger than he really was. With the slight widening of his forehead and touch of gray, he knew he looked more his age and that it was not unbecoming. Even the creases developing around his eyes were not unwelcome, for they hinted at laughter and hours of looking over the glare of sun-bright waters.

Canoeing the headwaters of the Yukon River, gold-rush country, was a thing he had wanted to do for years. Working construction in the Denver area left him little extra time during the summer season, but this year he had taken it anyway. Late in August he had loaded the canoe in his truck and driven the long road north to Whitehorse. There he had left the canoe, driven three hundred and twenty-seven miles to Dawson, parked the truck, and caught a return ride with a trucker. Then for a week he had paddled the winding course of the river and the lakes it passed through, back to the famous gold-rush community.

When he learned that only two more days would take him as far as the Forty-Mile River and the termination of a scrap of road at the old settlement of Clinton Creek, he couldn't resist seeing more of a country with which he was rapidly falling in love. Arranging to be picked up there by a Dawson resident who knew the area, he extended his trip. Though it was late in the season, the Top of the World Highway would be open until it snowed, usually later in September or even early October. It ran over a pass as high as four thousand feet along a crest of the mountains between Alaska and the Yukon Territory, and the spectacular scenery alone would be worth the effort.

This night he was exceptionally glad he had yielded to impulse. The day had been gloriously sunny with a cool reminder of fall in the air, and the Yukon had changed character with the influx of several rivers and streams that broadened and added a deep feeling of power to its heavy waters. Though it was nowhere near the mighty, mile-wide Yukon it would become by the time it neared the coast of Alaska on its fifteen-hundred-mile run, it had already gained authority and the spirit of a major waterway.

Half a day in the town of Dawson, with its gold-rush atmosphere, gambling casinos, and dance-hall girls, had been amusing and interesting historically. It had also allowed him to add a few fresh groceries to his supplies, but it was good to be back on the river. He loved being alone on a new river more than any activity he could imagine. In the previous ten years he had been on many in the Pacific Northwest and British Columbia, but in this first trip on northern waters he found deep satisfaction from his own pleasure in it.

Swinging around to look back toward the river, he was just in time to watch the eagle launch itself in a deadly silent dive that ended with the faint shrill of the squirrel; dinner, deftly caught and clutched in razor talons as the raptor glided away into the trees. Turning back to the canoe, Hampton began to unload his gear. With little more than an hour of daylight left, he knew he would have to work steadily to have his camp organized as he wanted it and firewood collected before dark. His own dinner would be appreciated, though he had no intention of catching it.

With a little steel wool, twigs and dry grass for kindling, and a few splinters of driftwood, he quickly lit a small fire in a circle of rounded river rocks. Carefully feeding it until it was burning reliably, he dipped a kettle of water from the stream to balance over the blaze before he left the small beach to find more wood on the bank above it.

Most of the upward slope near the stream was crowded with yellowing willow. He scrambled through it, across a flat space and on into the larger trees beyond, where the grass thinned and he easily picked up an armload of good-sized deadwood. Carrying this and dragging a limb too long and awkward to lift, but good meat for his hand ax, he went back through the willow to the bank, where he deposited the collection and headed for a second load.

Taking a slightly different route through the willow this time, he was almost to the trees when he stumbled over something, lurched, and wound up on his hands and knees in a small open space. Curious, he looked to see what had felled him. Under his right shin was a dark, somewhat less than natural-looking object about the size but not the shape of his hat. Standing up, he brushed himself off and, squatting on his heels, reached for it.

It was hardened and uneven, stiff as leather that has been wet and dry numerous times. Looking more closely in the fading light, he frowned. It *was* leather . . . an old boot. A very old boot. Something rattled in the foot as he turned it over. Pulling on one side, he tried to straighten and open the cuff, which had doubled over and dried rigidly against the foot. It cracked and a large chunk came away in his hand, along with a knobby piece of something yellowish-white. Looking closely, he was startled to find he was holding a bone. Completely dry, fleshless and clean, it was some kind of knucklebone the size of the end joint of his thumb. Slowly, he upended the boot, so the torn hole in the ancient leather faced down, and out fell a small, pale heap of additional bones. Staring at them, contemplating their various shapes, he knew that he was looking at the complete bones of a human foot and ankle. Whoever had owned the boot had died wearing it.

Carefully, he picked up each pale fragment and dropped it back into the desiccated remains of the boot. Glancing around he noticed no other, but it was hard to see in the increasing shadows. Where was the rest of the skeleton? The man? The only other thing he found in the gathering dark was a battered tin so old and corroded that the lettering was long since departed. It was square, the size of a small candy box, and held something solid enough that he could feel it shift inside as he turned over the metal container. One end of the tin had been smashed at some time or other, so he could not get it open with his fingers.

Looking up, Hampton realized that the sun had disappeared behind the western hills and the light was almost gone. Hurriedly, he gathered another load of wood almost by feel, retrieved the tin and boot of bones, and went back to the camp beside the river, where the water in his kettle was just beginning to simmer gently.

Adding wood to the fire, he quickly went about arranging his bed next to the canoe and organizing the rest of his gear. It would be a clear night, so he did not pitch his small tent. A can of hash went sizzling into a hot skillet, soon joined by a couple of eggs. Three sourdough rolls, from the bakery in Dawson, warmed on a stick over the coals. A pot of coffee came to a rapid boil, speeded by some of the already hot water. Deciding it was strong enough, he poured in a little cold water to settle the grounds and set it to one side of the fire to keep warm.

Dinner ready, he sat astride a log, set the blackened skillet before him, and ate directly from it, using the bread to encourage bites of hash and egg onto a fork. As he chewed, he watched the dark and listened to the small sounds of the wilderness as it settled or woke for the night: a tentative birdcall or two, the soft murmurs and gurgles of the stream and river moving, the thump and crash of what could have been, and probably was, a moose in the alder thicket across the water.

There was no breeze, but with the sun gone, the air was progressively chilled and the warmth of the fire was welcome. A few stars pricked holes in the dark sky and he remembered that a pale, close-to-full moon would soon rise. The smell of woodsmoke combined with that of damp leaves, newly fallen, for a somewhat dusty, leathery, fragrant reminder of fall, with winter on the way.

Suddenly wishing he could share his pleasure in the moment, he regretted that Judy had not been free to come with him. Almost simultaneously, however, he remembered that though he enjoyed her company, some of his gratification with the trip resulted from being alone. That she recognized and accepted his periodic need for solitary journeys on unexperienced stretches of water was part of what kept them comfortably together. She could come next time, for there was no question that another trip north lay in his future.

Never married, Hampton had, for several years, enjoyed a close, exclusive relationship with Judy Rematto, a Denver divorcée with a teenage daughter, Megan. It was satisfactory to both, for they were as much friends as lovers, and suited each other well. Though independent, they shared interests, including a love of reading and the outdoors. He taught her canoeing. She encouraged an appreciation of history and travel in him. Though she sometimes accompanied him on canoe trips, this time her job as a social-studies teacher had held her captive, with school just starting a new year.

Lifting the last bite of hash to his mouth, he glanced at the boot that lay next to him on the log beside the dirty rectangular tin. Now and then, as he ate, he had looked at it curiously. But until he finished every scrap of food, scrubbed the skillet clean with sand, filled a mug with coffee, and added wood to the fire, he did not touch it. Then he sat down near his source of light and heat and, with the blade of the heavy hunting knife he carried on his belt, carefully pried at the aging metal till the flat lid popped off, allowing him access to some kind of package.

Though the body and lid of the tin had fitted tightly enough, a little moisture had slowly seeped in through the dented corner. The contents, however, had been additionally protected by a waxed wrapping of cloth over paper. As Hampton began to undo it, he could see that candle wax had been carefully dripped and smoothed over the entire package. Cautiously, with delicate strokes of the sharp blade, he flaked off enough of it to find and release the edges of the fabric cover. Slowly he unfolded it and the paper under it, like the four triangle flaps of an envelope laid to the center, overlapping. Some of the wax cracked and fell in crumbs into his hand, and he tossed them into the fire.

With infinite care, he lifted out the contents and laid the wrapping aside. In his hands was a narrow book, perhaps half an inch thick, with a rusty-black cloth cover, bound along the spine with dark leather that evidenced the discoloration and wear of significant use.

Because the leather felt dry and old, he was concerned it might break and fall apart as he very gently attempted to open it, but surprisingly, it was still in remarkably good condition. The extreme edges of the pages were brittle enough to splinter off small fragments, but he was amazed to find that they turned easily. There was handwriting on the pages, and it was readable, though the ink had faded to a sepia tone. A name was written at the top of the first page, Addison Harley Riser, and below it, carefully centered:

The Account of
My Journey
to the Gold Rush
from
Tacoma, Washington
to
Dawson City, Yukon Territory, Canada
1897

Facing this title page was a picture on photographer's heavy cardboard, which had been cut to size and glued to the inside of the front cover. From it the faces of a young woman and two children looked out. Seated in a straight chair in front of the sort of painted canvas background common to a photography studio of the day, she held the baby and smiled self-consciously. The little boy stood at her side, one arm laid across her knee, staring wide-eyed and serious at the camera. Across the bottom their names were written: Mary Riser, Thomas and Anna. Addison Riser's family, without a doubt.

A journal. Hampton could scarcely believe he had found the journal of a participant of the Klondike gold rush, but it could be nothing else. A very real man had recorded his small part of the incredible rush for gold in the Yukon almost a hundred years ago. He turned a page to see what Riser had written. It began with a date and a place: Sunday, September 5 Steamship *Al-ki*, Headed for Alaska Territory.

The writing was neat and not difficult to decipher, but small, two lines in each ruled section of the page, an indication that the writer had been concerned with conserving his supply of paper. Hampton turned some of the other pages delicately and the penmanship remained the same throughout, crowding as much onto each page as possible. At the back, half a dozen pages had not been filled and after them two or three leaves had been torn out, leaving ragged remnants where they had been.

Turning back to the first entry, Hampton frowned, considering his find. If he had gone to Dawson, how had Riser's journal found its way here, almost twenty miles beyond that community? Laying down the journal, he picked up the boot. Not only his journal, but Riser himself had apparently reached this location.

Carefully he emptied the bones into his hand. The individual yellowed pieces were so clean they seemed almost artificial, pleasing in their shape and smoothness to his fingers, divorced and distanced from their original function and purpose. It was possible to see how a few of them fit together as easily as they had in life, even without the tendons and flesh that had held them together and made them move. Though nature had picked them clean, some of the vanished tethers had worn reminders of their presence into the very bone itself, leaving evidence of their flexing, if one looked closely.

In their present state, they were not distasteful reminders of a death. Somehow, quite the opposite. They made Hampton wonder about the man who had walked through his life on these fragile supports. And here, beside his bones, in his journal, were his thoughts. Who had Addison Harley Riser been? How had he come to die in this unusual place? Where had he been going, and why? What had happened to his wife and children? And had they ever, almost a hundred years ago, known what happened to him? It seemed doubtful. How odd, after all this time, that he had stumbled, by chance and quite literally, over the lonely remains of Riser so near a river on which so many had traveled on their way to fortune or loss.

But there was also something dark and a little disturbing about Riser's bones . . . something that made him frown uneasily at the wrongness of it. This was not the way people were supposed to die and remain . . . aboveground, unburied, unmourned and lost. Why were his bones here and not in some peaceful, acceptable place with a stone to mark his passing, hold his name in remembrance? Something about this was unsettling and unusual . . . hinted of an uneasy dying, even, perhaps, a violent death.

Curious and hoping to have his questions answered, Hampton wrapped himself in his sleeping bag and sat so he could lean against the log by the fire, warm and near enough to poke in more wood, to read what the man had written.

Chapter Two

I BEGIN THIS ACCOUNT AS WE STEAM NORTH aboard a crowded ship, headed for Alaska Territory on the beginning of my great adventure to the gold fields, and on this day I am in a much more cheerful disposition. Upon departing Tacoma, the last of August on this steamer Al-ki, most of us, I think, felt a bit unhappy at the thought of leaving family and friends and embarking into the unknown wilderness. I was disconcerted and sad to leave my dear wife, Polly, and our children, Thomas and Anna, not knowing when I would be able to greet them again, and knowing that, until I can, she must care for all three. There were many of us on deck and most were quiet and thoughtful for a time, as we watched the island scenery slide by. But by the time we passed Vashon Island and docked briefly in Seattle, where we took on a few more passengers and a number of horses, a gayer mood prevailed and we were soon singing "Hot Time in the Old Town Tonight," and comparing our expectations of fortunes in shining gold in the future.

The Al-ki tied up at the Schwabacher dock, where the Portland came in from the Clondyke on July seventeenth with the two tons of gold that inspired this whole venture. I could not help but think of the headline in The Seattle

14

Post-Intelligencer. "GOLD! GOLD! GOLD! 68 Rich Men
on the Steamer Portland. STACKS OF YELLOW
METAL!" *And more than five thousand people waiting at
six o'clock in the morning to see those ragged miners
stagger off onto the docks with their strange assortment
of bags and containers so heavy they could scarcely carry
them. The handle pulled straight off one such case.*

*Hopefully, less than a year from now, I may come back
with such good fortune. How I long for that day. I know
Polly has forgiven me for throwing over my employment
at Jordan's Mercantile, and that she tries not to worry. I
simply could not be a clerk forever, watching Polly and
the children want for things they deserve to have provided. Had there been a position available for me to make
use of my training as a newsman, things might have been
different. The last few years of the country's depression
have been desperately hard and this is my opportunity,
the answer to our prayers. If I cannot find a rich strike,
I can, perhaps, write down my impressions and sell them
to a newspaper somewhere, possibly even a book.*

A book. Hampton stopped reading for a minute. Unfortunately, poor Riser had obviously never seen his
dream of publication come true. Too bad, for he seemed
a good observer and writer, his journalistic training apparent in the choice of words and colorful description.

What courage, or foolhardiness, it must have taken to
leave everything in hopes of a fortune in an unknown
place of such hardship. Hundreds of people had done it,
he knew, for gold fever had been contagious, especially
after the California strikes that mesmerized the American
public. Riser had probably invested everything he had in
this one chance and, from the evidence of his bones, lost
it all, including his life.

*Leaving Seattle, I took time to look about me and assess
the company and surroundings in which I was to spend
almost two weeks and travel more than a thousand nautical miles. This is a second Clondyke run for the Al-ki,
which is not a large vessel, having a single smokestack,
cabins and bridge toward the stern, and a rather long*

foredeck, where I have pitched a rain fly and deposited my bedroll between piles of cargo, wood for the steam engine, and the outfits of others going north. There are more of us without than with staterooms, since the boat was originally a freighter and not designed to carry the more than two hundred passengers that crowd its decks. I was surprised to find a few women and several families with children aboard. They are crushed into the few state-rooms, while most of us single men camp on the deck, where we do our best to stay dry in the mist and rain that accompany us up the coast. Temporary bunks have been hastily installed in the hold, but the air is close and stale below, rank with the seasickness of many unfortunates. I am glad to be up in the fresh air and do not much mind the dampness.

Imagine traveling all the way from Seattle to Alaska on the deck of a small steamer in September. Another of Hampton's ambitions was to explore the Inside Passage. With a friend who owned a sailboat, he had pored over maps of the route, dotted with uninhabited islands and hundreds of tangled waterways that cruise ships and fer-ries never penetrated. If they took his canoe aboard, they would even be able to slip through water too shallow for the sailboat's keel.

Quickly he read on, interested in the *Al-ki* and its pas-sengers but hoping to find more information on the coun-try through which they had passed. Riser discussed the steamer's crowded conditions and the problems presented by eating in shifts. His description of the passengers in-cluded many ordinary people, together with others more colorful. . . . *a couple of sharpers, one of whom runs a card game in a corner of the deck much of the time but has caused no particular problems and is balanced off by the young woman who leads a few souls in singing hymns in another corner. One arrogant young man from New York complains incessantly and runs his hired man rag-ged in the attempt to fetch and carry for this Eastern polka dot. Needless to say, I think he will get his come-uppance on the Yukon, though I gravely doubt he will make it that far. For the most part, however, my traveling*

*companions are pleasant enough and a polite camara-
derie, strangely lacking in class-consciousness, prevails.*

Hampton had to smile at the dated language, though
much of it was surprisingly contemporary in tone. Almost
a hundred years was not really so long ago, he thought,
remembering that his own grandfather had been born just
after the turn of the century. In the next paragraph, he
found what he was looking for about the waterway to the
north.

*Much of my time is spent at the rail, enjoying the scen-
ery, for the passage north is most amazing. Much of the
time we steam along between the mainland to the east
and islands to the west, which protect boats traveling this
route from the unpredictability of the Pacific Ocean and
its storms. Often the landscape is shrouded with heavy
fog and mist, and the shrieks of boat whistles and fog-
horns resound and echo back from the veiled hills. But
the few clear days have assured us that the land is truly
unsettled and a complete wilderness. Like a motionless
ocean of dark green, the tree-covered slopes roll back
steeply from the dark waters over which we speed. Only
once or twice have we crossed inlets through which we
could view the Pacific. The rest of the time we have
threaded our way through channels and passages that
twine between the islands like braided cords. Often eagles
soar overhead. Once we saw a bear. In one great open
sound, dozens of whales leaped from the water and blew
air and water from their spouts. How my little Tommy
would have enjoyed that sight! In the same place several
icebergs could be seen floating near the eastern shore.*

Much too short an account, Hampton thought, but tan-
talizing. Riser must have been more concerned with his
destination than with what he passed to get there.

In the next entry, dated September 11, he had reached
Dyea, Alaska, jumping-off point for the Chilkoot Pass and
the route into Canada. The *Al-ki* had made a brief stop in
Juneau before going on to the end of a long narrow passage, where he was . . . *unceremoniously dumped into the
mud* . . . of the beach with all his goods and gear. During
the trip, he had made a friend on the boat, one Frank

Warner, a . . . *streetcar conductor . . . with a red mustache and one walleye* . . . with whom Riser had decided to travel and partner.

He wrote that . . . *Dyea is like a hill of ants, with people moving constantly in all directions, but mainly toward the Chilkoot Pass. . . . In only a matter of weeks, wilderness has been transformed into a jumble of log cabins, frame hotels, saloons and gambling houses with false fronts, but nothing appears permanent, particularly the hundreds of tents scattered everywhere. . . . Everyone slogs knee deep in mud. Wagons mire up to the hubs. Transporting our goods up to and over the pass will mean many trips back and forth to ferry it all to the top, where we are told we must probably camp through the winter, build a boat, and wait for the spring thaw to continue our journey to Dawson City by water. Winter freeze-up has held off so far and, with a little luck, we may be able to make it downriver before the passage closes.*

As much as he wanted to go on with Riser's journal, Hampton soon found his eyelids growing heavy and frequent yawns began to interrupt the narrative. A day of strenuous exercise in the cool fresh air and a good dinner had made him, not unpleasantly but irresistibly, tired. When he jerked himself awake for the third time, he gave up and put the journal back in its tin. Scooting down into his sleeping bag, he levered the canoe over his bed, a hopeful discouragement to bears and a roof against unanticipated rain. As he slid into sleep, he wondered fleetingly if it would be possible to locate any of Riser's grandchildren and if they would be interested in his story.

By seven-thirty the next morning, Hampton had finished a satisfying breakfast of bacon, eggs, and pancakes with canned peaches. His gear, repacked in its waterproof bags, was in the canoe, which he had moved close to the water, ready for his last day on the river. Instead of pushing off, however, he sat on the log next to the dying fire, once again lost in the pages of Addison Riser's journal, the last dregs from the coffeepot growing cold in a mug beside him.

The bold flight of a camp-robber jay, swooping in to snatch a scrap of pancake from the edge of the fire, caught his attention and he lifted his head to notice that the sun had risen as he read and set the ripples of the river alight with gleams. Time to go, if he was to reach the Forty-Mile that evening before dark.

He closed the book, replaced its waxed wrapper, and shut it in the tin. Carefully he sealed it and the boot full of bones in plastic bags, packed them in his daypack, and placed it in one of the larger waterproof bags. Using the coffee mug to dip water from the stream, he drenched the fire and buried the remains with gravel and rocks. Glancing around his campsite, he made sure it was as close as possible to the clean wilderness condition in which he had found it.

Prepared, he suddenly found himself reluctant. Turning away, he decided to have a last look at the place where he had stumbled over the boot the night before and, making sure the canoe was secure, headed for the willow-crowned bank. The early sunshine backlit the yellowing leaves, turning them into a shimmering wall of glowing gold, which he clambered through again.

The clear space beyond seemed smaller than it had in the growing darkness of evening, but now he could see where the boot and square tin had shielded the scrub grass from light, inhibiting color, leaving pale spots in the places they had occupied. A third such spot caught his eye almost at once. He leaned over to pick up an object lying beside it, one he had probably struck and shifted as he fell. It was recognizably a small pouch of thin dried leather, so ruined and disintegrating that it fell to pieces as he handled it, allowing a few pebbles to drop into his palm. A closer, curious look told him immediately that they were not pebbles, but nuggets . . . gold nuggets. Fourteen of them, all approximately the size of his little fingernail, lay in his hand. Gold, by God. Riser had probably found it in Dawson and carried some of it with him. Could there be more?

A swift visual search of the area showed him nothing. But he went over it anyway, on hands and knees, moving aside any grass that might conceal a further prize. Nothing. Moving to the longer grasses of the uneven circumference of the space, Hampton conscientiously examined the roots of them as well, with no positive result.

Almost around to where he had begun, he parted one section of grass to find a white, rounded object the size of a small melon half embedded in the soil. Without touching it, he knew immediately it had to be Riser's skull. With extreme care, he dug around it, pulling away grass and weeds till it came loose without pressure.

As it came from the ground, it fell into two pieces in his large hands, the back of the cranium from the front section with the jaw attached. But it was complete, as if it had been held together until the flesh disappeared. Weathered and dirty, the top part was bleached white from exposure, the rest, which had been buried, was yellowish tan, covered with clumps and streaks of dark earth; still it was all but whole. The fracture that divided it ran across from temple to temple, and on the right, a hole clear through the bone. Several deep grooves marred its surfaces. Hampton frowned thoughtfully and narrowed his eyes at the idea of a predator. It certainly looked as though something had chewed and broken this skull. The hole would closely fit a tooth. Bear? Wolf? He laid the two pieces back together and turned the skull to face him.

"Well. Hello, Riser," he said to the empty sockets and teeth that grinned at him, silently guarding their secrets. "What happened to you, old man?"

And, as it stared dumbly back at him, "Never mind. I'll read the rest of your book soon."

Four hours later, on another sandbar, he was back at the journal, munching an apple, having gulped down a can of cold beef stew to save himself the time and trouble of heating it.

SEPTEMBER 21, 1897
LAKE BENNETT, YUKON TERRITORY

We have reached Lake Bennett at last, after more than a week on the trail. All that time to travel thirty-five miles, but the longest miles in the world. In actuality much of it was traveled not once but more than a dozen times, as we brought our outfits ahead one load at a time, then went back for another. And it is impossible to walk any speed but slowly with sixty to eighty pounds of goods on your back, over mud, rocks, roots, and all uphill. From the beach to the top of the Chilkoot Pass the trail rises, 3,740 feet in a series of steep, step-like ascents, interspersed with level areas.

Knowing little about the Chilkoot Trail, Hampton was fascinated with the long and arduous process of getting to the summit, and it had not taken just one trip up. He remembered seeing pictures of an endless chain of heavily burdened men climbing steps hacked into a snow-covered hillside so steep it required a rope to hold on to for balance, and hearing that if one of those packers stepped aside to rest, he might wait hours to rejoin the upward climb. Once there, he turned around and went down for another load. This, it seemed, was only a small part of the Chilkoot experience, but Riser had evidently climbed through the pass before the snow fell that year.

The first nine miles from Dyea had been accomplished with the help of Indian packers and their canoes, with which Hampton could sympathize. Poling heavily laden canoes upriver was not his idea of a vacation. Riser, Warner, and the Indians had used not only poles but ropes to pull the unstable craft along from the bank. After that, however, they had been on their own.

Where they left us the real effort began. We divided our outfits into manageable-size loads and started early. It did not aid us that, after two days of good weather on the river, the skies opened and poured rain for the next three.

Horses, wagons, and packers all moving up the trail had turned it to a quagmire of mud and water. As bad as it was on the trail, it was worse off it where branches of spruce, cottonwood, and hemlock clawed at your pack and the rocks and mud were wet and terribly slippery. Without my rubber boots, I would never have made it and I was glad for the rubber-lined coat Polly insisted I bring. With the collar turned up, my broad-brimmed hat kept the worst of the rain from running down my neck and soaking me immediately. Still, we arrived at the first stop on that trail as wet as if we had been plunged into the river before starting our tramp.

Landmarks on the trail had names that amused and fascinated Hampton: Canyon City, Sheep Camp, Stone House, The Scales. Riser mentioned them as they were passed in the relays required to transport all his gear. At one of these locations, he described a rough building where they paid fifty cents to sleep on the floor and seventy-five more for a meal of beans, bacon, and tea, a fortune in those days.

Not all who started the trip finished it, according to Riser. He told of . . . *abandoned goods, where some had simply given up the fight and left what they were carrying to go back to Dyea to await the next boat going south* . . . and said he . . . *picked up two good wool blankets and some nails from one such pile that had been left with a scribbled note which read, "Help yersef if yer loony enuff."*

Days of uphill packing finally brought Riser and his partner to the summit, which . . . *was a maze of heaped up goods that looked like a city of low buildings with spaces between for streets*. Their last look from the top of the Chilkoot was to witness a disastrous icefall from a nearby hanging glacier. Its collapse released a flood of water that poured into the valley, sweeping away anything in its path, including the hundreds of stampeders still on their way up.

Riser's journal entry mentioned . . . *Arizona Charley Meadows and his wife, Mae* . . . who were caught in the flood and lost part of their outfit. Meadows, he said, was . . . *a flamboyant character in buckskin jacket and high boots, with a pistol at his belt, who was once a star in Buffalo Bill's Wild West Show as a rider and crack shot*

*with a rifle. His wife was a rider and chariot racer in
Meadows's own show, which they had left to go to Dawson. Among other things, they were transporting goods
for a restaurant, a saloon, and a general store. At each
stopping place, he would set up the bar and sell liquor to
the stampeders, at ever-increasing prices as they moved
away from a source of supply. The flood carried off the
saloon, her clothes, his favorite pistol and supply of western hats. She bought what clothing she could from those
leaving for the coast and the two came on to the pass,
through the knee-high mud, to join the rest of their party.*

As Riser described the trials of the Chilkoot, Hampton
wished he had gone to Skagway and Dyea before starting
his canoe trip. This was a part of the gold rush he would
like to see, perhaps even hike the trail. With her interest
in history, Judy would enjoy it as well, he thought. Maybe
this winter they could read up on the route to the Klondike
and come next summer to see it.

It would be a good idea to know more about it and
there must be books with pictures like the one of the snow
steps that he remembered. Judy would know.

As he read on, Riser and Warner went down the other
side of the pass and eventually carried all their gear to the
shore of Lake Bennett, where they made camp and prepared to build a boat, with hundreds of other people.
There, Warner met a man . . . *an old acquaintance of his
. . . with whom Riser was not completely comfortable . . .
His surname is Wilson and Frank calls him Ozzy, so I
think his Christian name must be Oswald. They worked
together in the lumber camps before Frank became a
streetcar man. I am not sure that I would have joined up
with him, but Warner took it for granted and I really had
no chance to refuse. Since it will be easier and faster to
build a boat with three of us, I think it will be fine, but
this Ozzy is rather taciturn and perhaps a little sullen
compared to the loquaciousness of his friend. I am probably just used to having only two of us and we will all
soon grow used to each other, but time will tell how we
shall fare. He is a large man, with arms and shoulders
that show the result of swinging an ax.*

Together, they built a scaffold and began to saw rough lumber for their boat with a rig called a strong-arm mill, an arrangement where . . . *one man up and one down pull the whipsaw through the length of the log from one end to the other . . . quite an efficient method of cutting boards, but the sawyer on the bottom gets a shower of sawdust on the downward stroke, which sifts into eyes, ears, and shirt-neck, and is a constant irritation.*

At this point Riser related a story that made Hampton laugh aloud, startling a squirrel that had crept close to inspect a bread crust laid out for his consumption. It went scampering off, but not without its prize stuffed in one cheek.

This sawing of lumber can cause disagreements as to who is and is not doing his share of the work. Yesterday at noon two fellows near us had such an argument they decided to split up their partnership. They carefully divided up their supplies, down to and including the half-built boat, which they cut exactly in two. One took the tent, the other the stove. It rained like blazes in the night, so the one with the tent was dry but couldn't sleep for the cold and the other huddled by the stove all night, trying to dry out his wet clothes. By morning they had made up their differences and put the vessel back together again, giving us all a good laugh.

The temperature was growing colder and Riser worried about getting started on the last of their journey to Dawson before they were frozen in for the winter . . . *Water on the lake is already looking slick in the mornings and a rim of ice can be found where it meets the shore. Like almost everyone else, I am growing a beard. It is not always convenient to shave and whiskers will keep my face warmer this winter.*

Hampton rubbed his chin and wondered about growing a beard himself. He had never had one. Maybe . . . well, maybe not. Leaving Riser at Bennett Lake, he got up to put his canoe back in the river. The squirrel watched from a safe distance, hoping for more scraps, but doomed to disappointment.

Chapter Three

꧁꧂ ONLY WITH RELUCTANCE HAD HAMPTON put the journal away. Miles of river lay ahead before he would reach the Forty-Mile, then three miles of upriver paddling to Clinton Creek. He knew the journal must wait. With the book returned to its protective coverings, he was set to shove the canoe back into the river, when the sound of an engine made him pause. Almost immediately, a powerboat appeared, headed upriver, making good time against the current. It was similar to many other boats he had seen in the area, though larger than most.

Two men rode in the aluminum craft, one at the wheel, another seated beside him, both too far away to see clearly. A pile of some sort of cargo behind them was covered with a blue plastic tarp. The second man rose and moved to the side to look when he saw Hampton, who smiled and lifted an arm. Neither responded in kind, though they both watched him closely as they passed. In a minute or two they vanished around a bend in the river, the roar of the engine dying slowly in their wake. The sound of their passing seemed an unusually loud and un-welcome intrusion, fragmenting the pleasant stillness of the uninhabited stretch of the wild river.

Their lack of response seemed decidedly unfriendly to Hampton. His impression of the people he had met on this trip was one of welcome helpfulness. It was strange to find men who exhibited none of the usual recognition and empathy of fellow-travelers. During the morning he

had passed two other boats, a smaller aluminum one and
an inflatable rubber Zodiac, and all those riding in them
had waved as they went by.

He had also passed several Indian families subsistence
fishing along the river. They almost always took a minute
from their set nets and fish wheels, or from splitting and
hanging fish to dry on racks, to nod or wave. One man
had even offered him a fresh trout when he swung close
to examine the construction of the water-driven wheel that
so effectively scooped fish out of the water and into a
wooden box. Three children had run along the bank, calling and waving until they passed from sight.

Before lunch he had spotted a sport fisherman on the
bank with a small, neat camp and riverboat. When Hampton waved, the man, Warren Russell, *hallooed* him in for
a cup of late-morning coffee, and they had spent half an
hour trading appreciation of the river and its surrounding
fall colors. What a contrast with the two who had just
passed in their powerboat.

Shrugging, he stepped into the canoe and pushed off.
The fall sunshine was thin but warm on his back and he
soon settled into a comfortable rhythm with the paddle. It
wasn't long until his thoughts returned to Addison Riser
and his journey.

It was incredible that hundreds of people like him had
simply walked away from whatever they were doing and
headed north when they heard of the discovery of gold in
the Klondike. Of course, the country was in the midst of
a depression and many were finding it difficult to make
enough to live on, or to find a job at all, but very few of
them had made the fortunes they hoped for by coming
here. Hampton had thumbed through a book or two about
the area that included information on the rush; now he
was determined to find more. There had been a bookstore
somewhere on the streets of Whitehorse. When he made
it back there, he would find it and see what they had to
offer. It would also be wise to have a copy made of the
journal, so he could read it without damaging the original.
Though it was in exceptional shape for its age and the
conditions under which it had suffered for so long, it was

old, and handling would undoubtedly do it no good. He would look up someone who knew about old books and ask how to preserve it.

Thinking of the journal, he suddenly realized that it was beyond his reach if he should overturn. He did not want to lose it in an accident, which was always a possibility, particularly on an unfamiliar river. The idea caused him to swing the canoe closer to the bank, into slower water, take the time to lift the pack and set it behind him, close at hand. Satisfied, he went back to the long easy pulls that sent him ahead faster than the current could carry him.

Before he reached the midriver flow, he once again became aware of engine sound. Twisting, he saw the same boat headed downriver in his direction. Both the men were standing this time, looking at him over the windshield. The boat was directed straight at him and coming fast.

A few pulls of the paddle swung him away from midstream, but, looking back, he found they had also adjusted course. For a second or two he waited, expecting them to turn away. They couldn't really intend to run him down? Why would they? The boat kept coming. He caught his breath and lifted the paddle for an enormous effort, knowing he must move swiftly out of the way or be rammed. Convinced they meant to crush his canoe with the prow of the heavier, stronger boat, he was bracing to throw himself into the water when the man at the wheel cut the power and veered off slightly, allowing the boat to drift close, rumbling in idle. They floated with the current, side by side.

Bastards, he thought. Like smart-aleck drivers who swerve to scare cyclists or dogs. They'd done it on purpose. What the hell did they want?

Swinging the paddle across, he held it ready to fend off the silver hull looming over him, but it came no closer, remaining perhaps a foot away, rocking slightly in the sudden quiet. Both men stood by the rail, staring down at him with sneers and self-satisfied looks on their faces, obviously amused at the effect of their maneuver and his reaction, like a couple of delinquent children. It crossed his mind that he might need the paddle as a desperate, but probably inadequate, weapon.

They were not unusually large, but both were well-built, outdoors men. The one who had been at the wheel looked older and taller, perhaps a little over six feet, though it was hard to tell while looking up at him. He wore a billed cap, dirty green, over long tangles of dark hair. A bushy beard hung midway down his chest over a soiled red-plaid shirt. The other exhibited a two- or three-day stubble of whiskers, and his light-brown hair hung in straight greasy strands around his ears, brushing the collar of a grubby blue denim shirt, sleeves rolled to his elbows, a three-cornered tear in one shoulder. He was a kid, really, perhaps in his early twenties, and thinner than his companion, whose beer belly bulged over the waist of his dirty jeans.

The bearded one leaned over the rail and showed his yellowed teeth in what Hampton could only describe as a grimace, for it was nowhere near a smile. *Wolfish* was the word that came to mind.

"Hey, man," he asked. "You're not from around here. Where ya think you're goin'?"

"Kinda out by yourself, aincha?" the other taunted.

Trouble, without a doubt. As Hampton waited and watched, saying nothing, they both eyed the neat waterproof bags in the front of his canoe.

"Whatcha got there?"

"Camping gear," Hampton told him, shortly.

"Where ya headed?"

"Forty-Mile. My ride is waiting at the Clinton Creek road." It wouldn't hurt to let this pair of vultures know that someone expected him, knew where he was and when he should arrive.

As he spoke, he slid slowly back in the canoe until he felt the daypack and sat on it, his feet braced for more leverage, while, with the paddle, he reached to push himself away from the larger boat.

Before he could do so, the dark, bearded man suddenly raised his hands from the concealment of the side of the boat and leveled a shotgun at Hampton. "Wouldn' do that if I was you," he said in a conversational tone. "Just sit still. I think maybe we'll have a look at that camping gear. You won't mind, will ya?"

The younger man stepped forward with a boat hook. Reaching, he heaved the three bags one by one into their boat. The aim of the shotgun barrel did not waver from the center of Hampton's chest.

"If you're only going to Forty-Mile, ya won't need this stuff, will ya?"

In addition to, and because of, his fear, Hampton was frustrated and outraged. He could feel that his face was hot and flushed, and he wanted more than anything to be able to get hold of one of them.

"You won't get away with this," he said furiously.

"Oh, I think we probly will."

"Hey, Will. There's something else. He's sitting on something."

"Yeah? Whatcha got there, man? Let's have it. Maybe ya got a wallet, too, huh? Cash? Gimme."

It was more than Hampton could tolerate. Keeping his eye carefully on the shotgun, he raised himself to his knees and reached behind him, as if to pick up the day-pack. Then, with a sudden lurch, he threw himself side-ways, away from their boat, expertly overturning the canoe while keeping a firm grip on the paddle.

As he went under, he heard the blast from the shotgun and knew, thankfully, he had not been hit. It was shock-ingly cold, from the glaciers of a thousand mountains, so cold he almost sucked water, caught himself just in time. And quiet—there was only the white sound of water against his ears, blocking whatever was going on above.

He did and didn't want to know what was going on. They were undoubtedly waiting and, if he came up, would more than likely have another shot at him. He kicked strongly, let himself go as deep as possible and came up slowly, checking for the surface as he came, gripping the waterproof daypack that he had grabbed with the paddle as he went over. It tended to float with a small amount of air trapped inside, raising him gently. His roll into the icy water had been disorienting and the bag told him which direction was up. Near the surface, he saw the dark, canoe-shaped shadow over him and slid carefully up inside the upside-down craft, finding air without revealing himself to the two in the boat. Quietly, he clung to a strut with fingers rapidly growing numb, and listened, careful not to bobble the canoe. The paddle he allowed to float, confined with him in the shell of the canoe. He could faintly hear them talking somewhere beyond it.

"Where the hell'd he go? You hit him?"

"No. Goddammit. Missed. Hit the kayak."

"Canoe. It's a canoe."

"Who gives a shit? Where is he? Can't stay under this long. Is he fucking drowned?"

"Maybe. Wanna get the canoe?"

"Hell, no. It's got a hole in it. Don't want to explain *that* to the old man. Shoot a canoe? He'd laugh hisself silly."

"He's not coming up and he'd have to breathe by now. He's drowned. Let's get outta here."

"Yeah. I'll get the boat going. You get his stuff under cover."

The engine roared out of idle. Hampton waited, holding to the bag with one hand, the strut with the other. If they had decided to ram and sink it as they left, he couldn't have been in a worse place, but they were content to take off with their stolen goods.

When he could no longer hear the engine's growl, he ducked from under the canoe on the side near the bank, into the fresh air, and looked both ways. Had they gone up or down the river? Who knew. But they were gone.

So cold he could hardly move, he knew he had to get out of the water immediately, before hypothermia set in. Ducking back under, he shoved the daypack under a strut along with the paddle and awkwardly rolled the canoe over. His body was moving stiffly and he could hear his teeth chatter, his jaw tense with the involuntary effort. Quickly rocking the canoe to splash out as much of the water as possible, he levered and half rolled himself in and lay, soaked, in what was left in the bottom. When he had caught his breath, he tried to use his wooden hands to bail, but quit when he realized water was running back in as fast as he scooped it out.

In the left side, about two feet from the stern and just at waterline, was a hole the size of his fist. Several smaller holes peppered the hull around it. When he moved, water washed in, enough so that it seemed he had a choice—paddle or bail. Alternating these, it took him ten minutes, around two bends and perhaps half a mile downriver, to reach the mouth of a small creek. A few feet up it, behind a wall of willow, was a place wide enough to build a fire. If the deadly duo decided to come back and check on him, he wanted the kind of cover this would provide.

By the time he stepped out of the canoe he was feeling no colder and shivering less, as a result of the exertion, but he knew he had to get warm and dry or he would be in real trouble. It was very likely he wouldn't be able to go on to Forty Mile, and would have to overnight without his down jacket and sleeping bag. If so, it was imperative to have some dry clothes at least, and the ones he had on were all they had left him.

Quickly, he gathered the means for a small fire and got it started near a large log, with matches from a waterproof case in his pocket. Huddling close, he fed it twigs, small sticks, and finally, several pieces of dry driftwood. The heat brought his hands back to life and felt marvelous. He hung over it until his wet clothes began to steam.

Stripping off his boots, he poured the water out and took the laces off. Wringing out his wool socks, he used them to sponge out the inside of the boots, which he laid spread open toward the fire, but not too close. Once more he wrung out the socks and hung them on sticks he jammed into the ground near the heat. As he worked, he realized he was listening for the sound of an engine. Cover or not, if they decided to come back, the smoke from his fire could bring them directly to him. Still, there was no choice.

An experienced solo canoeist, Hampton never went unprepared into the wilderness. For this trip, knowing he could face any number of unexpected situations, far from assistance or rescue, he had packed with more care than usual. Besides the waterproof match case, he carried a multibladed knife in his pants pocket. His larger hunting knife hung from a wide belt with an inside pocket intended for cash. Instead, it contained a wire saw, two hooks, and fishing line. These he removed and laid the belt, with his jeans, near the heat.

The breeze off the river was cold on his bare legs, though the afternoon was still full of sunshine. Retrieving the daypack, he pulled the canoe over, nearer the heat of the fire, and examined the hole in its side. It was the size of a grapefruit, with ugly, ragged edges, and the sight of it brought anger roiling up again.

Wanting a traditional wooden canoe, he had built this craft himself: a winter's labor and careful workmanship; hours of fitting, molding, sanding, and painting. The finished craft pleased him enormously and the violence done to it was a personal injury and insult. That it needed patching, and that repairs were impossible now, was obvious, but it was mendable. He already knew how he would go about it in his Colorado workshop. During the winters there, when construction slowed, he carefully crafted fine furniture and other projects; he had a good collection of tools and material, for canoe building as well. For now, to get him on down the river, there was a roll of heavy duct tape in the daypack that would suffice when the hull of the canoe was dry enough. That meant tomorrow morning at the earliest, for he could not go in wet clothes. It would be a rough night, but not unendurable.

He shivered, grabbed the bag, and, turning to the fire, tossed on another piece of driftwood. Wood to last the night would have to be collected when he was warm. His hand ax had gone with the bags of gear. If he needed anything cut, the saw would have to do. For a few minutes he turned around by the fire, warming himself and coughing in the smoke. If he had been a salmon, by morning he would have been well preserved, he smiled.

The bag had leaked only a little through one small tear that had probably occurred when he overturned the canoe. Nothing in the daypack was soggy. The journal's tin seemed dry. He would check it later. This wasn't all bad.

At least he'd have something to read while he waited for daylight. The skull and the bones in the boot were slightly damp, but they had often been wet before. He dumped the rest of the pack's contents out on the ground and sorted through it. A pair of dry socks he pulled from a plastic bag and put on immediately.

All his fresh supplies had gone like his sleeping bag, but his emergency rations would get him through admirably: bouillon cubes, instant coffee, sugar, individual envelopes of hot chocolate, packets of Jell-O, a freeze-dried beef and rice dinner, two peanut-filled candy bars, a bag of dried fruit and nuts. It was all dry in the bottom of the pack, packed in plastic bags in a small kettle, along with a plastic bowl, spoon, and cup. Emptying the kettle, he filled it with stream water and put it on the fire to boil for a hot drink.

The first-aid kit he would not need, thank God. For the first time, he let himself consider the blast of the shotgun as he had thrown himself into the water, and shivered from something besides cold. The man behind it had shot at him, not the canoe, had meant to hit him, kill him if possible. It was incredible. If he had not lived through it he might have had trouble believing it. Muggers were supposed to live in cities, weren't they? If he had been hit, they would without a doubt have left him to bleed or die in the river. He tossed the first-aid kit back and forth between his hands, laid it down, and was thankful he could do it.

Taking off his wet wool shirt, he wrung it out and laid it over the log by the heat. Wringing out his undershirt and shorts, he put them back on. They would dry faster on his body, but he fervently wished for his stolen long underwear. Unfolding the final item from the pack, he wrapped a Mylar survival blanket over his shoulders and sat down facing the fire, holding the rustling, metallic material open in front to gather the heat and reflect it onto his chilled body. The result was immediate and satisfactory. He would soon dry out, and would definitely survive. He hoped his ride would wait and not take off for Dawson without him. With good luck and the duct tape, he could reach the Forty-Mile by noon tomorrow. It was two-twenty-five. Thanks to a waterproof watch, he could tell time.

Who were the guys in the boat? How could they think they could just get away with stealing his gear and trying to kill him? They looked local, maybe lived out here somewhere. Had they done this before? Who was the old man they had mentioned? He could remember one name, Will, the dark, bearded one, but knew he could describe them both. Had the boat had a number, a name? He could remember none.

He made a cup of hot chocolate when the water boiled and sat sipping it, trying to remember what kind of boat it had been. Open powerboat, twenty-five feet maybe, outboard, no canopy, fast, lots of horsepower. Not much else. Had they stolen it too? What had been under the blue tarp? Had they robbed, perhaps killed someone else?

As he grew warmer, he grew sleepy. Nodding over the last of the hot chocolate, he realized it was probably a reaction to his icy bath, adrenaline pumping through his system and delayed shock from the whole experience. His body was saying, enough already. While he waited for his clothes to dry, it wouldn't be a bad idea to recharge his own batteries, get some sleep before it got cold and he might not be able to. If they came back for any reason, the sound of the boat engine would wake him before they came close. Still sitting up, he let his eyes close and drifted off, rousing periodically to put more wood on the fire.

Just after five o'clock, he was still tired and sleepy, but awake enough to force himself to put on his damp-dry shirt and squishy boots, and gather a large pile of firewood, having already burned most of the readily available driftwood.

It took most of an hour of going back and forth and periodically pausing to warm himself, to carry dead branches down from under the trees above the beach. He had to walk quite a distance along the bank to find it, where the brush was thick and the ground uneven. With what he considered sufficient for the night stacked close to the fire, he put his boots and shirt back to finish drying, boiled more water, and reconstituted the chicken and rice dinner. He had meant to wait until after dark, knowing the night would be a long, cold one that dipped near freezing, but decided to pay attention when his stomach growled and he began to feel light-headed. When he had eaten, he made more hot chocolate, had a candy bar for dessert, and settled down to read another section of Addison Riser's journal, recovered enough to enjoy the smell of the woodsmoke and the crackle of the flames near at hand.

Absorbed, he started when a log burned through, allowing another to crash into the ashes and roll, still flaming, out of the fire against one of his boots. Jumping to snatch it away, he inadvertently dropped the journal, which fell, striking the rocky surface of the ground.

Returning the runaway log to the fire, Hampton picked up the book and examined it gingerly. The edge of the photograph was marred and a little loose along one side, part of its ancient, dried adhesive cracked away from the front cover at the corner. Damn . . . and he had taken such care reading it. Opening the cover to assess the interior damage, he was relieved that it was minor and a bit of glue would cure the problem later. What seemed to have saved it was that between the photo and cover, Riser had inserted some paper padding as extra stiffening and protection for the treasured picture of his family. A ragged edge told Hampton it was probably made from the pages that had been torn from the back of the book.

Pleased that there was not more damage to the journal, disgusted at his own clumsiness, and determined to take more care, Hampton settled down to read, more curious about Riser than ever. What had made him leave Dawson for Forty-Mile? Hoping he would soon find out, he continued to read the extraordinary account from where he had stopped when the log fell from the fire.

By the time the sun went down, his clothes were dry enough to put back on, though still somewhat damp and chilly. They would warm and continue to dry from his body heat and that of the fire reflected from the survival blanket. His boots, however, were still too wet to wear.

It grew dark quickly and he was soon nodding sleepily again over the journal. Putting it back in its tin, along with the disintegrating pouch and gold nuggets, he shoved it into a protective space under the log, though it looked clear and rain was not expected. Adding a reasonable amount of wood to the fire and reminding himself to wake later to feed it more, he wrapped himself in the silver blanket again, curled up with his back against the log, and fell immediately into a heavy sleep, exhausted.

Sometime during the night, half awake behind his closed eyes, he was aware that it was dark, that his head ached desperately, and that if he moved, he would regret it immediately and unpleasantly. He also knew he would be sick. So he didn't move, didn't open his eyes. Something was wrong. What was it? He didn't want to know. It hurt to think. He should put wood on the fire, but he was warm, the sleeping bag snuggled close around his shoulders, and exceptionally tired. He let oblivion pull him back into its comforting void.

Chapter Four

ALASKA STATE TROOPER ALEX JENSEN WAS not unhappy to be outdoors and away from any office on this sun-washed morning in early September. He felt enlivened by crisp, clear fall nights that seemed to sharpen the lines of the country, and the cool but brilliant days that followed them. Though the air in Alaska and the Yukon was always clean, unacquainted with smog, in the fall it almost seemed to sparkle. He felt more awake and aware of his surroundings as the far north was transformed into deep autumn golds that contrasted sharply with dark green spruce and the burgundies of shrubs and berry bushes on hillsides. So this location, on the Yukon River below Dawson City, did not displease him. The reason for his presence on this particular bend of that river, however, did.

A homicide detective for the State Troopers, Jensen had come to Canada on an assignment concerning a case of robbery and murder that involved both Alaska and the Yukon Territory, inseparably and amiably connected by the Alcan Highway that spanned their mutual international border. This morning's unexpected and unrelated investigation had required the use of a jet boat, in which he had accompanied another officer, Inspector Charles Delafosse of the Royal Canadian Mounted Police.

Jensen was the taller of the two, longer of limb and slightly more casual in bearing than his Canadian counterpart. Out of uniform, he wore a sheepskin coat over civilian clothes, with a tan western hat settled familiarly above attentive, but not unkind, blue eyes and a full, red-blond mustache. Just now, the weight of his lanky frame relaxed onto one leg, he was kicking repetitiously at a medium-sized rock with the opposite boot but, from his demeanor, would miss none of what transpired, as he listened to the inspector's inquiries.

Though he was not conspicuously muscled, there was an air about Canadian inspector Delafosse that hinted at physical strength and an ability to move quickly and with little effort, for he stood straight and confident, weight evenly balanced, shoulders square. Slightly shorter and of dark complexion, he wore a neat blue jacket, denim pants, and a pair of black, pull-on, waterproof boots. Face shaded by the wide brim of his hat, he looked down to read the driver's license he had picked up from the log where it had rested next to some cash and other papers from a wallet that lay beside them. They had evidently been put there to dry, for the wallet and some of the documents unprotected by plastic lamination exhibited signs of a recent soaking and were still damp.

Gently, but persistently, with his toe, Delafosse tapped the soles of the feet of a man facedown in a sleeping bag beside the log and near an almost extinguished fire.

"Wake up. Get up, please, Mr. Hampton. We need to ask you a question or two."

Groggily, the man in the bag began to show signs of waking. He rolled over, groaned, and opened his eyes, but closed them again immediately in the glare of late-morning sunlight.

"Hampton? James Neal Hampton? Denver, Colorado?"

The man in the bag laid an arm across his eyes, cautiously opened them again in its shadow and squinted up. He did not appear to recognize the face that loomed over him, but even out of uniform, it would not have been hard to guess from the attitude of polite authority that this man was definitely from the RCMP.

The two officers watched as Hampton sat up, immediately turned pale, and clutched his abdomen. Scrambling to his knees, he threw himself across the log next to him and emptied his stomach behind it. When it was over, he clung, looking as though he might black out, sweat beading his forehead. Closing his eyes, he held his head between his hands as if afraid it would fly apart. Exploring with his fingers, he pulled the hair aside so that a sizable lump behind his left ear was visible. "Water," he croaked. "Could I have some water, please?"

It took Jensen only a minute to fill and hand him a small kettle of filled with stream water, cold and clear. Hampton drank a few swallows and splashed most of the rest over his head and face. Pulling himself onto rubber legs, he twisted to sit on the log, panting. Still holding his head with one hand, he drank what was left in the kettle, rinsing his mouth. He looked terribly hung over.

"Have yourself a little too much party last night?" Delafosse asked in a mild tone.

Hampton glanced up with a confused frown. Alex could almost hear him thinking: Party? What the hell's he talking about?

He set the empty kettle down, then stared at the sleeping bag, still frowning. Next to it lay an empty Canadian Club bottle and its cap. He took it in, but didn't seem to recognize any of it.

"No party . . . ah, Constable," he said hoarsely. "It's not mine. I don't drink whiskey. You can see why."

"Inspector," the officer corrected him. "Charles Delafosse, RCMP. If the bottle isn't yours, you evidently drank it anyway. Mr. Russell's maybe?"

The younger man looked up sharply at the name, catching Jensen's silent attention.

"Perhaps you spilled most of it on yourself, Mr. Hampton?"

Glancing down, Hampton seemed to realize that much of the pervasive whiskey smell was coming from his own shirt, and that the sleeping bag was just as odiferous. Shaking his head, he opened his mouth as if to say something, but it remained open as he raised his eyes and focused on something beyond Delafosse.

Jensen turned to find what had drawn his interest, and

saw that it was a canoe, perhaps twenty feet away on the other side of the fire. Upside down, the part of the canoe that was intact shone bright red in the morning sun, but one whole side of the bow was caved in, with a large piece missing, as if it had hit something extremely hard, crushing the shell.

"Looks like you hit a rock, Mr. Hampton," said Delafosse. "Lucky to get off the river with a hole like that. In fact, we have already found the one you hit, back up-river a bit. Just made it this far without sinking, from the look of it. Think you might tell me exactly what happened?"

But Hampton was gaping in astonishment at the area around the fire. "It's all back," he said in a strangled voice.

Alex watched and considered thoughtfully as the canoeist looked over the area of his camp and a look of total bafflement replaced the surprise on his face. All seemingly in good shape and usefully arranged was a remarkably complete and compact camping rig; metal food box, duffel of clothing, rain slicker and down jacket, cooking gear, all of it looking as if he had taken considerable care to set it out neatly. Even a small tent was pitched and staked down.

Hampton's gaze suddenly hesitated and locked on the other end of the long log on which he sat. Grinning at him, round and pale, was a carefully balanced, broken skull and, next to it, a dried boot, with a variety of small bones carefully arranged beside it.

"Yes," Delafosse nodded. "We'd very much like to know about that, too. Wherever you got it, it's a poor joke, considering the other gentleman. What happened, Mr. Hampton? Wasn't it enough to steal his gear. Did he resist?"

At that point, with Hampton still speechless in shocked confusion, two constables came out of the brush, following the stream down to the narrow beach, pushing their way through the willow. They carried a stretcher between them, with what was obviously a body under a blanket.

Hampton stood up and stepped forward. "Wha . . . ?"

The inspector took his arm and walked him across to where the constables, headed for the jet boat that had been grounded on the edge of the beach, had paused at his command and set their burden down. He reached to remove the blanket from the top half of it, watching Hampton closely.

"Shotgun," he said.

Hampton's face abruptly lost any color it had regained and he swayed slightly, but there was a flash of recognition in his eyes, and both officers took note.

He knows this man, Alex thought. But he didn't expect to be confronted with a dead body.

The dead man's face *was* recognizable, but the back left side of his head was smashed and bloody, though most of it seemed dried and clotted in what was left of his hair. He had, without a doubt, and some hours past, died violently and not by his own hand.

For several minutes Hampton stared and didn't react at all. Then: "But . . . yesterday," the canoeist blurted out. "Yesterday morning. We had coffee. His name is . . . was Russell. He showed me four fish he had caught."

He turned away and staggered to the water's edge, where he threw up the water he had just swallowed. When he was finished, he couldn't seem to stop the contractions of his sour stomach and crouched, retching and trembling. He dipped his hands in the cold water and held his head between them. Slowly the retching eased.

"Please . . ." He stumbled toward Inspector Delafosse, who stood waiting, a repelled and calculating look on his face. "Antacid and aspirin in my first-aid kit."

Once again Jensen filled his request, and when he had swallowed the tablets, he went back to the log, slumped to a seat, and shivered, staring at the ground.

The two officers waited, attentively. Inspector Delafosse rekindled the smoldering fire and added the kettle filled with water. Then they sat, one on either side of Hampton, while water heated for the cup of tea he agreed he might be able to keep down. The constables who had carried the body were busy investigating the camp and beyond it, obviously looking for clues, taking pictures here and there.

The inspector calmly and formally cautioned Hampton with the usual rights, adding that he didn't have to talk at all, if he didn't want to.

They waited while he considered seriously, then listened as, with a few hesitations, he began, slowly, to relate a series of events he said had happened to him the day before. For over half an hour he carefully told everything he said he could remember and the order in which it had happened. He described a heavy, bearded man and a kid in detail; itemized their ages, height, weight, coloring, clothing, and the boat they drove; related his icy swim and the efforts he had made to survive.

Jensen listened intently without speaking as the inspector allowed Hampton to tell it in his own way, interrupting only once or twice during the narrative. When they were all sipping hot tea, including the constables, who were carefully going through Hampton's every possession, Delafosse asked a few more questions.

"If they took your equipment, how can it be here, Mr. Hampton?"

"I don't know."

"You do admit meeting Warren Russell late yesterday morning, but say you had nothing to do with him later?"

"Right. I liked him . . . had coffee with him. But why would I kill him, or take his gear? I have my own. Except for half an hour of casual conversation, I didn't even know him. It's crazy."

Delafosse showed him Russell's gear piled in the tent, some of it damp but not as though it had been drenched when the canoe hit a rock. He considered it.

"You know," he said. "All of his stuff and mine would never fit in one canoe. How could I have got it here?"

A hesitation, then, "The empty boat was found, Mr. Hampton. Almost to Forty-Mile. A native fisherman on his way from Eagle brought it on up to Dawson and started us looking for an accident, but we didn't expect a murder. I agree you couldn't have transported his stuff, *and* your own, *and* his body, all at the same time in the canoe. But you could have used his boat and let it go after you had gone back for your canoe, or towed it. We don't know yet when he died, do we? But perhaps you do . . . and where you found and killed him along the river.''

"I didn't . . . Then how did I bash that huge hole in my canoe? I didn't hit any rock, whatever you found. I barely made it here with a hole this big.''

As Hampton lifted his hands to illustrate, Jensen pushed back his western hat, gave half a nod, and leaned forward as if he were about to speak. But he hesitated and sat back, keeping the comment or question to himself, letting the inspector continue.

"About these two men *you say* attacked you and took your gear yesterday. I have to tell you, Mr. Hampton, there is no trace of them here. No tracks or evidence to identify anyone but yourself.

"We have only *your* word that you don't drink whiskey, that you ate only survival food last night because you had nothing else, though there seems to be plenty around, or that you didn't carry Russell's body up the stream and cover it with brush, where we found it.''

They wouldn't have left tracks on the rocky beach, Hampton said. "And there *was* a hole from the shotgun in my canoe. They must have run it against a rock to break that part out. Can I look at it?''

Delafosse considered. "Yes, it's already been printed and photographed.''

They walked across to the slender shell that still lay overturned on the narrow beach. Hampton dropped to his knees beside it and carefully examined the crushed section.

It was scarred and torn, and the damage could have been inflicted with nothing lighter than a rock. There wasn't a sign of a shotgun blast, not so much as a dent from a discharge. In or out of the water it could have happened the way they surmised . . . or someone could have run it hard or repeatedly into, or hit it with, a sharp rock, ripping off incriminating pieces, taking care to erase every trace of the pellets that had hit it. It looked as Delafosse had said, as if Hampton had slammed into the rock, then managed somehow to reach shore.

He shook his head and leaned it mournfully forward against the side of the canoe. As he blinked in discouragement and anger, something caught his eye. With one finger, he pointed, and Jensen, who was closest, leaned forward to see. Wedged between the hull and the wooden gunwale strip was a single shotgun pellet.

Delafosse thoughtfully extracted it with his knife and dropped it into a plastic bag, which Jensen witnessed. Though Alex supposed it was ridiculous to be grateful for one shotgun pellet, Hampton seemed to feel a personal vindication in finding the small object.

One of the constables, who were now slowly and carefully loading everything from the camp into the jet boat, called a question and the inspector went over to answer. Jensen walked Hampton back to the log by the fire. Before they sat, he laid a hand on the canoeist's arm and spoke directly to him for the first time. "Let me see that bump on your head."

Hampton turned his back and allowed inspection of the injury, which was handled with careful fingers.

"How did you get this?"

Hampton hesitated, then looked up.

"I don't know," he said. "It wasn't there when I went to sleep last night."

The other man returned his straight look with a thoughtful one.

"Well, there's no break in the skin, but you'd better have it looked at in Dawson," he commented. "You probably have a mild concussion. Having any double vision? Any symptom besides the headache?"

Hampton shook his head, plainly and immediately wishing he hadn't. But he seemed to find it less painful than before and said his nausea only whispered at him now.

"You don't sound Canadian," he said to Jensen.

The tall man smiled. "Because I'm not. State Trooper. Sergeant Alex Jensen from Palmer, Alaska."

He put out a hand that Hampton automatically shook

with a grip that was firm and solid, but felt clammy and cold. The sweat of fear or guilt could account for it, Alex thought, but so could shock and illness. He looked damp and feverish, and his stomach still cramped, from the way he clutched an arm across it periodically.

Jensen went on. "I'm here sort of by accident, not official. Since you're an American, and I'm here on another case, they invited me along. We work together sometimes, but the inspector's in charge. He'll ask most of the questions."

They sat back down on the log.

Delafosse came back across the open space and halted in front of Hampton. His attitude was impossible to read from the lack of expression on his face, but his glance was cold. He carried a shotgun, which he lifted to show Hampton. "It was under the body," he said and waited.

Hampton shook his head and stared back. "It isn't mine," he said miserably. "I've never owned a shotgun." When the inspector's appraisal did not waiver, he sighed heavily but remained sitting straight with his head held high, his face white and stiff.

Raising his eyebrows at Jensen, who shrugged, Delafosse took the gun back across to the jet boat, where he handed it to one of the officers.

Jensen frowned, looking down the log at the skull, which still sat facing them.

"Will you tell us about that old boot and the bones?" he asked, as the Canadian came back.

Hampton brought the items and obligingly told them both about tripping over the boot and finding the journal and the skull. The excitement of his discovery overcame some of his misery, enhancing the account, and was noted by both men as they listened. He pulled the tin box from under the log where he had stashed it the night before and showed them the fragile old book and the photograph of Riser's wife and two children. Carefully exhibiting the fragments of the leather pouch, he displayed the gold nuggets. Jensen was interested in all of it, handling the items with extreme care and handing them back when he finished examining them.

"I'd like to read that journal sometime," he said.

"Can I keep it?" Hampton asked. "I haven't finished it yet."

"We'll have to hold it while we check, but we could perhaps make you a copy," the inspector told him, with a manner quite departed from that of his inquisition. "You might want to consider the historical significance. The museum in Dawson would like to see it. I can't see that it had anything to do with this case, but we'll have to establish that for certain."

The journal and pouch were returned to the tin and, with the bones and boot, went into a plastic evidence bag that Delafosse provided.

At this point, Jensen leaned forward, at the inspector's nod, to ask one question.

"How did you chop the wood?"

"What?"

"The firewood. How did you cut it?"

"I didn't cut it. My hatchet was in the bag with my gear. All I had last night was the wire saw on the log over there, but I didn't have to use it. There was plenty of burnable stuff already."

Around the perimeter of the fire were several fragments left of the logs that had been burned. Two or three of them bore the definite, fresh marks of an ax, not a saw.

"I suppose you think I carried my wood, too, along with all this other stuff," he said, a bit bitterly. "Or pitched my hatchet in the river for no reason at all."

"No," Inspector Delafosse responded. "As a matter of fact, I don't think that. It's obvious that Russell was killed with a shotgun, and I can't think of any reason you'd have tossed such an essential piece of equipment into the river. But there's no hatchet anywhere here, though you say the rest of the gear is what they stole and returned sometime in the night."

Hampton shuddered, visualizing the shattered head of the friendly fisherman.

"And you really think I did that?"

"It's possible. The gun was there. We'll check. But he . . ." Thinking better of the comment he had been about to make, he broke it off. Alex knew he was thinking it might be important that Russell hadn't died at this location and would keep a discussion of it till later.

Hampton sat very still, concentrating.

Jensen observed with close attention as the younger man thought the situation through without speaking. It was obvious that he knew he was the prime suspect and that they were dubious of his denials and professed lack of knowledge. If the gear, as he said, had been stolen by the two men he said had been in the boat yesterday, then, for whatever reason, they had brought it back and set it up so it appeared it had never been gone. Why? They could have hit Hampton in the head as he slept, dumped whiskey over him, and somehow destroyed any evidence that they had been there. The stones and sand would leave no identifiable tracks.

As an attempt to blame the crime on Hampton, it would make his tales of theft and assault seem like defensive attempts to clear himself by accusing someone else. He could not prove that anyone had attacked him the previous afternoon. They might not have done a perfect job. There was the pellet from the canoe and they hadn't returned his hatchet and might still have it.

There were a few other small things he had mentioned; the way the tent was set up differently from the way he would have pitched it, for instance. But only he could know that. Pretty thin and he couldn't prove it. Someone in Colorado who was acquainted with him might know that whiskey made him sick.

Jensen curtailed his automatic analysis as Hampton turned to the RCMP inspector, who was also watching him so closely it would not have been surprising if he had already guessed Hampton's thoughts. Quietly and without defensiveness he spoke.

"I did not kill Russell. The only time I saw him was on the river yesterday. I talked to him, had coffee with him. We talked for close to half an hour, but I did not kill him."

They looked at each other and there was a long pause before Delafosse frowned and gave back his own truth.

"I'd say that there's at least as much possibility that you didn't kill him as that you did. There are odd things about this, but let's just say I'm reserving judgment . . . for the moment."

"Are you arresting me?"

"Not now. We will take everything here as evidence, so you'll be better off coming back to Dawson with us than staying here with no equipment or transportation. I'm offering you a ride. And, if you *didn't* do this, I'm asking your cooperation and assistance. I'd also like you to stay in Dawson a day or two."

"I have a ride waiting at Clinton Creek."

"We'll take care of it."

By midafternoon they were headed upriver toward Dawson in the jet boat. With little or no expression on his face, Hampton ignored the officers and watched the river's gold-splashed banks as they passed. Russell's body, a constant reminder of the man with whom he said he had enjoyed a few minutes of conversation, lay in a body bag inside a plain, utilitarian metal box. Surrounding it, beside the partially burned logs from his fire, were the two sets of camping and personal gear, including four fish in a plastic cooler that the old man might have exhibited with pride to a passing canoeist the day before.

Jensen thought it somehow interesting that Hampton had known exactly how many fish that cooler contained.

Chapter Five

DAWSON CITY LIES AT THE UPPER EDGE OF the Yukon Plateau, at the confluence of the Klondike and Yukon rivers. The Yukon was once a much smaller river, with headwaters near Dawson, that drained southward into the Gulf of Alaska. Two million years ago, when the St. Elias Mountains and others rose between the interior and the coast, the whole drainage pattern tilted inland. The glaciers of the Pleistocene Era blocked the southern canyons with ice, and smaller rivers were diverted north to the Yukon River drainage where, instead of running two hundred miles to the coast, they ran into the Yukon, swelling its volume. Also unable to reach the nearest ocean, the much-increased river created a new bed for itself, wandering in wide, meandering loops, fifteen hundred miles across what would become Alaska, finally emptying into the Bering Sea.

For centuries the area where the Klondike joins the Yukon was a seasonal fish camp for the group of Athabaskans called Han, People of the River. Most modern Han now live in Dawson City, where education is available for their children, but once they ranged over a much larger area that encompassed all the tributaries of the Yukon from the mouth of the Kandik to that of the Stewart. For at least part of the year, a few still live, or have subsistence fish camps, along the river between Dawson and Eagle, Alaska. The largest tribe in the area, the Han once had a well-deserved warlike reputation, but they were decimated by epidemic diseases brought into the country by fur traders, explorers, missionaries, and prospectors in the eighteenth and nineteenth centuries.

With the discovery of gold, Dawson City quickly became a boomtown with an itinerant population of almost thirty thousand, the largest city north of San Francisco and west of Winnipeg, if less stable. Unlike some other gold-rush communities, however, it did not become a ghost town, but survived, though on a much smaller scale, with continuing gold mining and a thriving tourist industry. Since it was a supply, service, and entertainment center for the surrounding mining area, only commercial buildings were originally built to last. The rest, made mostly of logs chinked with mud, were hastily erected, temporary shelter for miners who intended to leave as soon as they got their fortunes, and leave they eventually did, fortune or not, casually abandoning their shelters, which almost immediately disintegrated or were torn apart, the wood reused or burned.

After the rush, in the early 1900s, when profits from gold continued to come in at a steady if less substantial rate, more permanent buildings were constructed around the few remaining stampede landmarks, and Dawson became a settled community.

"Hey, Del, what's that?" Alex Jensen asked, twisting in his seat to get a better look at a large wooden building they were passing on a Dawson street. Over the double front door was a sign: GASLIGHT FOLLIES. Two more stories rose above it, with bay windows that extended enough to make small balconies with low railings. The edifice was impressive and made an unusual appearance with its dark, diagonal planking.

Delafosse smiled. "That *is* an oldie. The Palace Grand Theatre, in all its enormous restored glory."

"Gold rush?"

"Yes, and almost got torn down in the 1960s, but the Klondike Visitors Association saved it and National Historic Parks returned it to its original 1899 splendor. During the last of the rush it was the biggest opera house in the north, used for everything from Wild West shows to operas. Guy named Arizona Charley Meadows built it by tearing apart a couple of beached sternwheelers for lumber. Now the Gaslight Follies pull in the tourists with dance-hall girls, cancan, melodrama, and all.''

The two law enforcement officers rode together in Delafosse's pickup, heading through the historic town toward the Dawson RCMP Detachment Office. They had left Hampton on the dock, to be escorted along for a statement by the pair of constables who were also responsible for the gear and evidence they had collected at the site, and Russell's body, which would be flown to Whitehorse the following morning, destined for the Coroner's Office.

''What's your take on Hampton, Alex?''

The trooper hesitated thoughtfully, pulled a briar pipe from his pocket, and went about the ritual of filling it with a fragrant tobacco blend and lighting it with a kitchen match before he puffed smoke out the half-open window.

Well aware that the inspector was in charge and content to have it so, Jensen still found it unusual to defer to someone else. On Alaskan home territory, he was almost always the responsible officer on a homicide case. Several times on the riverbank he had all but bitten his tongue to remind himself that he must watch and listen until he had a chance to discuss the situation with the Canadian.

Del Delafosse was more than competent. Most of Jensen's questions had been answered, if not in the order he might have asked them himself. There were, however, enough nagging inconsistencies to lower his brows in a frown as he considered the strange circumstances in which they had found Hampton. The inspector's question was, he knew and appreciated, designed as much to invite him to participate as it was to solicit his ideas and opinions.

''Well,'' he said slowly, ''it's not a particularly open-and-shut case, is it? Lot of contradictions.''

''Such as?''

''Well, for one, I can't understand why a man who supposedly just hauled a stiff down the river, dragged it up a stream, and covered it with brush would set up an extremely organized camp right beside it, cook and eat dinner, and then proceed to get so drunk he didn't even hear your jet boat. Slept through almost an hour of investigation by the four of us. Of course, your Canuck whiskey may be more potent than ours, but I think it had more to do with that bump on his head. Somebody hit him pretty hard with something that didn't break the skin. Sap, maybe?''

"It's not that potent." Delafosse grinned briefly before becoming serious again. "It's been too long to know how much, if any, he ingested last night. That bump on the head *could* account for his somnolent state. *If* this was done by the two he suspects, and *if* they hit him while he slept, he wouldn't remember a thing. From where it was placed, it would have been hard for him to inflict it himself. What'd you sort out of the rest of it?''

"Well, it's your case, Del, of course, but I got as many questions as answers, just like you did. There any reason, other than the possibility it's a setup like he says, to think he's telling the truth? Any other robberies or suspicious deaths on the river this summer?''

"Nothing significant . . . the average tourist accidents. A drowning when a boat hit a rock, tipped over, and floated off. One stolen camper and a missing trailer, but the sergeant here in Dawson says it's been quiet downriver to the border. Our biggest problem has been those stolen vehicles. Along with the others stolen farther south—two trucks, one commercial, one rental, and a large RV between here and Whitehorse, but nothing on the river, no boats or gear reported.''

Jensen had come to the Yukon from Alaska a few days earlier to coordinate investigations with the RCMP on a series of vehicle thefts that had occurred on both sides of the Alaska-Canada border. It was believed that these had been stolen by a ring of thieves and drivers, and run south on the Alaska or the Cassiar highway into the more populated areas of the provinces or lower forty-eight states. By comparing cases and working together they hoped to gather enough evidence to stop the game, especially since two of the latest had resulted in the homicides of the driv-

ers: one a long-distance Canadian trucker, the other a retired American tourist on his way to catch a ferry in
Haines, Alaska, in a brand-new recreational vehicle. The
tourist had evidently suffered a heart attack as the result
of rough handling, but the trucker had been shot. Not that
it mattered. Both deaths were still murder on the books.

The two killings had brought Jensen into the cooperative effort. A homicide detective from Detachment G in
Palmer, forty miles east of Anchorage, he was not unhappy with the assignment, since he was already friends
with Inspector Delafosse of the RCMP General Investigation Section, or GIS, acquainted from past professional
and social events. They had come to Dawson from Whitehorse to check the background on one of the missing
trucks. Delafosse would stay to fill in for the officer in
charge, who had gone to Toronto where his wife was to
have surgery. With their work complete, the case at a
standstill, Jensen had been prepared to return to Alaska.
He had changed his plans when Delafosse asked if he
would like to come along on the trip down the Yukon
River.

An apparently abandoned boat had been towed into
Dawson the evening before, inspiring the idea that its
owner was in some trouble, possibly drowned. Early the
next morning, as it grew light, they had sped down the
Yukon's bends in the jet boat, easily locating and stopping
at Hampton's camp, where they found Russell's body not
far from the sleeping canoeist. The boat had turned out to
be Russell's.

"There's something off center about the whole thing,"
Alex commented, as he turned again to look with interest
at a turn-of-the-century building on a corner in the middle
of town. "Is that hotel authentic?"

"Well . . . sort of. It was built just after the gold rush,
but burned sometime in the twenties and was put back up
exactly like the original.

"Yeah, off center is a good way to put it. We still don't
know where Russell died either. It wasn't where he was
found. Not half enough blood there for a shotgun wound
and the lividity says the body's been moved."

Jensen knew that when a dead body lies for hours in one position, the blood drains to the lowest possible level, causing purple bruiselike marks under the skin. Shift a corpse from that original position, the marks remain. Examination of Russell's body showed he had evidently fallen and remained on his face after he was killed, but he was found curled in a fetal position under the brush above Hampton's camp. The lividity staining the front of his body said that he had died elsewhere and been moved. Or, Alex, had mused, he had been killed and immediately put into the boat facedown. It was just possible. He frowned again, considering. Neither the boat, nor Hampton's canoe, had exhibited any sign of blood. It would have been easily washed out, however.

"I think I'd be looking for evidence of homicide at some other location, starting with the spot Hampton says he had coffee with Russell. Who is Russell, anyway? You sounded earlier as if you knew him."

Frowning, Delafosse shook his head. "I don't know him, really, just *of* him. He hasn't made himself too popular with the native community along the river lately."

"Canadian?"

"No. A retired Alaska senator from Fairbanks. He's an avid sport fisherman, who drives over infrequently during the salmon run every year. The problem is that he has some political clout and campaigns actively and hard that subsistence fishing should be limited, or done away with, in Alaska and the Yukon, and sport fishing more solidly supported, especially when the runs are minimal, as they have been in the last few years. He believes there's no need for a subsistence life-style these days and other ways for those who adhere to it to make a living. Since the local Han Athabaskans, and others, feel the fishing is their historical right and use what they catch, his attitude doesn't sit too well, particularly when he comes to do his own recreational fishing in this area. There's been a clash or two. He's a feisty old man."

"Why doesn't he fish somewhere else?"

"He does, but he insists on coming here once or twice a year. Stubborn, I guess."

"I recognize the name, from the Anchorage news, but I haven't paid much attention. The murder of a retired legislator will get some press, you know."

"I anticipate that. Have to get a release ready, and get the investigation's wheels turning."

"Maybe I can help some with the Alaska press."

"That would be appreciated all right, but we've done enough for now. As soon as we get Hampton's statement we'll give it a rest for the day, eh?" Delafosse asked. "I renewed our reservation at the Midnight Sun and we can get a good dinner on the next corner at the Downtown Hotel, which should satisfy your interest in historical preservation, by the way. They might even have a shot or two of that *potent* Canadian whiskey."

Jensen chuckled. "Isn't all this downtown?" he asked. "Dawson isn't big enough to have anything else."

"Well, you're right, of course. But you should see it in July, packed full of tourists and Winnebagos. Not a room to be had and you wait in line for any kind of food. I try to stay in Whitehorse, though it's not much better." He turned a corner of the neat, even city blocks which indicated that someone long ago had had the intelligence to line up wide streets in an orderly fashion.

Jensen swept an interested gaze over what he could see of the variety of structures that comprised a small community in a constant state of flux over almost a hundred years. Though independence of thought and materials was evident, most of the buildings, new or old, looked as if they had been built with nineteenth-century plans, displaying frontier interpretations of the original Victorian influence, meant to fit in and attract the summer tourist crowd on which most of the local economy now depended. A modern service station they passed looked decidedly out of place among the boxy false-fronted frames.

"That sounds like another good chance to see the inside of some history. I need to clean up and make a phone call or two before dinner, too."

"Make them from the office." Delafosse glanced across and raised an eyebrow. "May I assume that you might be checking in with someone besides your dispatcher at this time of day?"

Alex chuckled and nodded. "Yep, told Jessie I'd let her know when I was headed home. I'd better remind her I'm not there yet and may be a while longer."

At the Detachment Office, the inspector shut down the engine and turned to Jensen before getting out.

"I think I'll call the hotel for another room for Hampton. We could keep an eye on him, take him with us to dinner, if he'll come, see if he'll volunteer anything useful. Okay with you?"

The idea startled Alex a little, coming from Delafosse. All day he had been careful to remain in the background, allowing and observing the inspector's right of investigation on the case. His methods interested and slightly amused Jensen with their reticence and a low-key style of interrogation. It was not the first time he had studied the Canadian differences. Though they were far from the stiffness of the English, and would probably have been considered rough at the edges by them, there was still a subtly polite tone to their procedures that could only be termed civilized. In Delafosse's case, it disguised a steel focus and effectiveness that often got results in less time than a more heavy-handed and impatient method.

Jensen liked Del Delafosse and was pleased to be working with him. A friendship based on respect for each other had grown over several years' acquaintance. He was comfortable with the Canadian's quiet sense of humor and appreciated his commitment to his profession. Their differences were mostly a matter of style, for they were much alike in their concentrated problem-solving approach to homicide.

The suggestion of a more than usually informal way of relating to a suspect was unexpected, but might be more effective than formal questioning. He nodded, thoughtfully, and Del continued.

"You know, Alex, I've got a nasty feeling about this one. I can't tell you exactly what, but Hampton's story of those two guys on the river is ringing faint bells. Trouble is, the particular bell I think I recognize is supposedly locked up tight for a robbery he pulled four or five years ago. He could be out by now, I guess, and I keep thinking that he pretty well fits Hampton's description of the bearded one.

"If you haven't got too much waiting for you back in Palmer, how'd you like to stick around for another couple of days and help me feel it out? With both victim and suspect Alaskans, I think it's warranted. Also, Hampton might be more willing to talk to another American."

Jensen rolled down the window to knock the dottle from his pipe before slipping it into a shirt pocket. "I'll have to check," he cautioned, "but I don't think there's anything that can't wait. I'd like to take another look at this. There's something almost out of focus about it. I'd also like a copy of that journal Hampton found. Can you make me a copy when you make him one?"

"Can that relate?"

"Doubt it. I'm just interested in the gold rush. All summer Jessie and I meant to get over here and look around, but never got time. A personal account by someone who was here while it was going on should be fascinating reading."

Chapter Six

 "...WHEN YOU HEAR THE BEEP." FOR THE
second time, Jessie Arnold's recorded voice came back to
Jensen from the Knik end of the telephone line. He had
tried once to reach her from Delafosse's office, where he
had also called his Palmer detachment for approval to ex-
tend his stay in Canada. When she hadn't answered, he'd
hung up, not satisfied to leave a message. Now, clad in a
towel, damp from the shower, he tried again from the
hotel room. Steam roiled from the half-open door of the
bathroom, where Delafosse was using his own share of
the hot water.

Beep. Damn . . . well. "Jess? It's me. Del and I are still
in Dawson. It's . . . ah . . . sort of turned into a different
case. One we didn't anticipate . . . involves a couple of
Americans, and . . . ah . . . It's hard to explain. I wanted to
talk to you . . . should have waited till later, but . . ."

Abruptly the receiver was lifted on the other end, interrupting him. He could hear a dog barking. "Shut up,
Sadie. I'm here, Alex. Sorry. I heard it ring from outside
and had to hustle. Down, now, it's not for you. Good dog.
Are you okay?"

"Yeah, I'm fine. I wanted to talk to you, not that idiot
machine. Look. I'm kinda hung up here. Won't get back
for a few days."

"What's the story? Sounded pretty straightforward
when you called last night."

"Yeah, I know, but . . ." He launched into an abbre-

viated version of the day's activities and the new justifi-
cation for his continued presence and involvement, while
she uh-huhed on the other end of the line, occasionally
asking a quick question.

He knew she was really listening, so he didn't cut his
account particularly short. In the six months since they'd
met, he had found her not only interested in his work,
when he could share it, but a good sounding board. She
presented opinions of her own when she had them and
often asked insightful questions that stimulated his thinking. She could also be relied upon to keep the discussions
to herself.

Arnold was a talented dog musher, well known and
respected as a top runner of the famous Iditarod Sled Dog
Race. She operated a kennel twenty miles north of Palmer,
breeding and raising dogs for her own pleasure and use
and for sale, when she wasn't out on the trail with a team,
training or racing, depending on the time of year.

They had met the previous March, during a particularly
hazardous running of the more than one-thousand-mile
Iditarod race, when a musher had attempted to better his
standing by eliminating several competitors . . . permanently. Jensen had been in charge of the team of troopers
who worked the case as the race progressed. He arrested
the perpetrator almost at the finish line in Nome, but not
before Jessie was attacked by him and caught a bullet in
the shoulder—although she still managed to take second
in the race. Despite the circumstances, their interest in
each other had continued to its present exclusive and mutual satisfaction and respect.

"You mean someone else may have killed the guy and
set Hampton up?"

"Yeah, something like that . . . at least it's possible. It's
a real confusing situation, with a lot of questions we don't
have answers for. Both Russell and Hampton are American citizens, so the powers that be have decreed I should
give Del a hand with it."

"So," she said. "I think it's a pretty sneaky way to
get to spend time in Dawson without me, trooper. Who's
going to catch the bad guys here, huh?"

"Well . . . so I take a day or two off. The crooks in Palmer won't mind."

"And what if I mind?" she teased.

"Hey, I love you too, lady. Why don't you come on over?"

"Naw. I'd like to, but I've still got some serious training to do here with Ryan. And for your information, I'm watching large white flakes float past the window. We got the first four inches of winter last night . . . more on the way. It'll probably melt off, but we got ambitious and took some of the mutts for a quickie run this morning. It was kind of thin.

"Just finished feeding the whole gang of forty and am about to feed us. Then I intend to curl up and enjoy the comforts of my big couch and a roaring fire, with a mug of peppermint tea, Carolyn Hart's latest Henry O mystery, and the company of Ryan, Sadie, and all four of her new pups. Yes"—smugly—"she didn't wait for you . . . had them last night."

Ryan. Alex hesitated, frowning, then forced himself to laugh. "You are a glutton for punishment if you've got Sadie and her kids all inside. She'll lick you to death in gratitude. You're a credit to mushing to take a team out at the first sign of snow. Better have a second sled ready when I get back. Ah . . . Ryan still there, huh?"

Jensen had spent part of the spring, when there was still snow on the ground, learning to drive some of Jessie's sled dogs. They planned to take some overnight trips with two teams as soon as snow cover allowed for it this fall. That he liked mushing enough to take out a team of his own pleased them both as much as her interest in his detective work.

"I'll do that, and, yes, he'll be here another couple of days."

Ryan was a musher friend of Jessie's who had come to pick out three or four of her dogs to buy for his teams. The two of them were trying out different combinations in his strings of experienced dogs that had worked together before, seeing how the new ones fit. He was also looking for a new leader, which was more important than team dogs. He and Jessie had been running the Iditarod together six months before when a moose stomped through his team, killing several of the dogs, injuring others, and putting Ryan in the hospital with broken ribs and a scalp wound over a concussion. Now he needed replacements and Jessie was glad to help.

Jensen knew he wasn't so glad, since he wasn't there. Ashamed of his jealous reaction to Ryan's presence, he tried not to let her know, afraid she would feel he didn't trust her.

"You okay there with everything?"

She hesitated a second, then, "Sure. Don't go protective, Alex. You know I can't survive without periodic doses of independence."

"Whoa. It's not interference, Jess. I miss you a fair amount."

"I think that's more than fair."

"Yeah, you're right . . . a lot more."

"Me too. Everything's fine here, Alex. Really. Call me tomorrow?"

"Sure. Here's the hotel number, or you can reach me through Dawson RCMP." He gave her that number too.

"Yes, sir."

In the receiver, she heard relief, acceptance, and satisfaction in the smiling sound of his breath as he puffed pipe smoke into the air, and was glad it was familiar enough to recognize. And he thought she didn't know he was bothered.

"Hey," he heard her, quietly. "I love you, trooper."

"Me, too, lady. Home soon. Pat the new pups for me. And . . . tell Ryan I said . . . hello."

As he hung up the phone, Delafosse came out of the bathroom, *showered, shaved,* and *shiny,* as he put it. "She got any sisters?" he asked, with a grin. "Sounds like a pretty good thing you got going there, if the nightly phone calls are any indication."

Jensen grinned back, pleasantly satisfied with his long-distance conversation, but irritated with himself because an unreasonable thread of concern still sat heavily in the middle of him.

"Get dressed and let's go get dinner. I'm empty as last year's bird's nest. Besides, you should be paying attention to that knockout redhead in your office. She's obviously trying to attract your attention."

It came as no surprise when Del grew exceedingly red in the face and sputtered an immediate denial. "Clair? Not . . . I m-mean, not . . . not a chance. She's way out of my league. What would she have to do with a policeman anyway?"

Alex had to laugh. "Man, you are *blind*. Every time you come into the room she registers you like a motion detector—all but sets off an alarm. Don't tell me you haven't noticed."

Delafosse stopped with his shirt half-buttoned, clean denims hanging unzipped around his hips, waiting for the shirttail to be tucked in, and stared at Jensen.

"You're not serious," he said. "She's like that with everybody."

"Bullshit. She thinks you just about walk on water, Del."

"No-o. You're going to get me in serious trouble, Alex. She's tied up with someone. Anyone that little and pretty's got to have some enormous bruiser around to take care of her." The Canadian jammed the shirttail in and zipped his pants with exaggerated care and attention, avoiding Jensen's eyes.

"Nope."

"How would you know?"

"Had a long talk with her the other day, when you were on the horn to Whitehorse."

"And she talked about me?"

"Well, no, not directly. But she let her appreciation show pretty clear. Fragile, you say? Looking, maybe. Did you know she coaches a softball team? Told me she built her own log cabin too. We got into a discussion on the relative merits of continuous foundations as opposed to piers, and the benefits of grooving and insulating logs as they're placed instead of chinking later. She knows what she's doing, Del. I'd take another look at just how fragile she is."

"She built that cabin by herself?"

"She must have had *some* help, but I bet she told them what went where, and why. Even you and I'd need help to get the logs up, but she cut, peeled, and grooved her own logs from the sound of it. Must swing a mean chainsaw. Better put her out of her misery and ask her to dinner, huh?"

"Easy for you to say. No risk involved for you. Besides, we want to feel out Hampton, remember?"

"Well, I didn't necessarily mean tonight."

"Oh." He crammed his billfold into his back pocket, grabbed his jacket, and escaped through the door, discussion over. "I'll think about it. Sometime. Maybe." The last words echoed back from the hallway as he reached the head of the stairs. "Come on."

Jensen shrugged and followed, checking to make sure he had his key and that the door was locked.

In the dining room of the Downtown Hotel, Jensen, Delafosse, and Hampton found a vacant table against one wall and settled in three of the four chairs. Patterned wallpaper, lace curtains, and period furniture decorated the large room in a comfortable old-fashioned style. Electrified versions of gas lamps lined the walls and elaborate turn-of-the-century fixtures hung over the antique tables.

Before their dinner choices, Jensen and Delafosse both asked for the Canadian whiskey they had joked about earlier, but Hampton, turning slightly green when it was offered, requested a beer.

"I honestly can't stand the stuff," he stated, then frowned in embarrassment at the defensive sound of it. "Sorry." He was obviously nervous and uncomfortable with the two law enforcement officers, aware that they were sizing him up.

"Look, Hampton," Alex commented, when their drinks had been served. "The situation is not conducive to much in terms of relaxation here. You're in a tight spot. Can we declare a truce for the meal at least? We're not for or against you at this point, but we're not ganging up on you. Let it go long enough to enjoy your dinner. Okay?

I, for one, would just like to get to know you a little better. It might help.''

There was an honesty in the appeal from the tall trooper that Hampton couldn't help responding to. He found himself wishing he had met Jensen in some other—any other—circumstances. He nodded and took a healthy swig of his beer.

"What do you do in Denver, Jim? Been there long?"

"All my life. Carpenter. Construction . . . foreman." The words came out stiffly, in jerks.

"That canoe looked handmade. You build it?"

"Yeah, last winter. I got a basement shop."

"Handsome. Ever build them for sale?"

"My first one. Furniture. I build furniture. Refinish some. Work construction in the summer."

"I did a little summer construction for college money as a kid. Liked the outdoor part of it. Denver had really changed the last time I was there. Looked like Los Angeles smog and traffic jams."

"Where you from?"

"Idaho, until eight years ago."

"Hey, I really like the North Fork of the Salmon River. Ever run it?"

"You have good taste. Salmon's my hometown. My folks still live on the land my grandfather homesteaded, up across the North Fork near Shoup. Old two-story log house. Have to go across the river on a cable or in a boat—no bridge. Run it? Hell, we used to innertube it in the summer. Well, parts of it."

Delafosse was quietly listening to the developing conversation and slowly sipping his drink. Alex knew that Del appreciated and was impressed with the casual, more easygoing manner most Alaskan law enforcement officers exhibited. There was something about Jensen that made people want to please him, an artlessness that encouraged trust. He meant what he had said about the temporary truce in the conversation, for he avoided reference to the incidents on the river, channeling the conversation onto topics anyone newly acquainted might discuss.

Del had told him more than once that he wished he

could cultivate a similar attitude himself and be more out-going, less correct. Part of what he enjoyed about working with Alex was that the Alaskan trooper made it easier for him to be less formal. Though Alex was never pushy or familiar, he could somehow manage to be totally unthreatening, unless he consciously chose to be otherwise.

Americans were simply more informal. Canadians were harder to get to know. Alex and Del had had enough prior contact to erase the barriers between them. But Hampton was a new equation. In this instance it was easier for Jensen to initiate a friendly conversation with him than it would have been for Delafosse.

Alex knew that Del did not feel excluded; that he was watching and listening closely, gradually gathering an impression of Hampton that he would balance with the canoeist's account of the past two days. By the time their dinners arrived, and the discussion of Rocky Mountain rivers and their canoeing potential flagged before their hunger, he was amused that the Canadian had still not ventured a word into the discourse.

He also knew that Hampton was not unaware that it was intended to put him at ease, and was grateful for the consideration. He had glanced a few times at the comfortably silent Canadian officer but had soon lost some of his uneasiness in that direction also. When coffee arrived, along with three slices of homemade apple pie with ice cream, Jensen was pleased that Hampton had relaxed enough to bring up the issue of Russell's death himself.

"You know, I keep wondering if there might be anything at the spot where I met him yesterday to help find out who killed him. If he wasn't killed where I camped . . . and it seems to me you don't think so . . . that's the next most possible spot, isn't it?"

Delafosse raised his eyes from the bite of pie he was about to lift onto his fork, glanced at Jensen, then nodded. "Thought we might go back down in the morning and take a look. Would you be willing to go along and help us locate that place, Mr. Hampton?"

"Sure. It'll be pretty easy to find. I stopped there just after I passed a fish wheel, about half an hour after the

Zodiac passed me. There's a rocky bluff just around the corner above that flat space that you can see for a long ways.''

"Zodiac?'' Alex asked. "How many boats did you pass on the river yesterday?''

Hampton frowned, concentrating. "Only three, I think, not counting the one that attacked me. One—an aluminum hull—zipped by right after I left camp in the morning. The Zodiac about ten o'clock, because it was before I stopped and had coffee with Russell. While I was reading Riser's journal and eating lunch, another aluminum boat went by. The last one—the guys that came back and stole my gear—went by, going upriver, just as I was pushing off after lunch, about one.''

"Anyone on board the first three you'd recognize again?''

"The first boat had a blue canopy and whoever was driving wore a baseball cap and sunglasses. The Zodiac had two, both native, a man and a woman. The one at noon wore some kind of hat. I don't remember what. He also had sunglasses . . .''—he paused a second, then continued—''. . . tan vest over a green plaid shirt. All of them friendly, waved as they went by.''

Jensen turned to the inspector. "Sound like anyone you know, Del?''

"The blue canopy sounds like Rickie Taylor. She helps run the *Yukon Queen* for tourists between here and Eagle all summer, but has her own boat for extra trips now and then. Was she going fast?''

Hampton nodded. "Fastest I saw, but I couldn't tell if it was a woman.''

"Bet it was Rickie. The *Queen* takes four hours downstream and six hours up, but she can make it a lot quicker on her own, and does. Any number of the native fishermen have Zodiacs . . . and wives. Couldn't say on that, or the other . . . noon . . . boat. Most of the boats on the river are aluminum look-alikes.''

Happily full of pie, Alex yawned and pushed his chair back from the table. "I'm for an early night,'' he said. "Think I'll take a quick walk, then bag it for the day.

What time do you want to go tomorrow, Del?''

"Eight'll give us time for breakfast. Eat here at seven?" As he shrugged on his coat, Delafosse stopped to take a handful of paper from its pocket. He handed half to each of the other men. "Here're copies of that journal of Riser's you wanted. Something to read yourselves to sleep."

He and Hampton headed for the Midnight Sun Hotel a few steps down the street. Jensen, pipe in his teeth, hands in his pockets, walked slowly in the opposite direction, assessing the antiquity of the buildings he could see in the streetlights. When he reached the riverbank he stopped and stood watching the dark gleam of wide water moving past almost silently in the night. Something crunched under his boot. Glancing down, he noticed that along the edge, among the pebbles of the shore, a rime of frost and ice was collecting like lace against the dark water.

Abruptly, he thought again of Jessie having dinner with Ryan in her compact log cabin in Knik. Though he was aware that there was a space for Ryan's sleeping bag on the floor near the large wood stove, and that Jessie would retreat alone to her big brass bed in the only other room, he couldn't stop his thoughts. Damn, he told himself. You have no reason to think there's anything to worry about on that score. Right? Right! Still . . .

Sensing something overhead, he looked up to find the sky streaked with the first northern lights of the year. Pale wisps of greenish light pulsed in slow motion above, some, almost curtain-like, seemed to flow in folds and swirls that brightened and faded as they drifted across the star-filled dark. Almost hypnotic, the glowing patterns held his attention long after his pipe had gone out and his toes grown numb with cold from standing still.

When he finally turned to walk back to his home-for-the-night, he found his uneasiness relieved. Once again he was pleased he had become an Alaskan, and that Jessie . . . was Jessie. Right under his feet and over his head were unexpected and extravagant compensations for living in an icebox half of every year.

Chapter Seven

BACK IN THE HOTEL ROOM, ALEX FOUND Delafosse already in bed.

"Light bother you if I read?" he asked, climbing into his own with the copy of Riser's journal. Assured it would not, he settled comfortably against a couple of pillows and, with anticipation, started the first page. He was soon deep in Riser's account of the terrible winter of 1897, though a part of his consciousness went on turning over the discrepancies of Russell's homicide. A time or two he was aware of people coming and going from the bar next door, as voices called out in the street below the window and cars came and went. After half an hour or so, Del began to snore softly, but not enough to be a real distraction.

In his room next door, Hampton had also tried to spend time on the journal, but did not get far. Exhausted by the day's physical and emotional stress, he was half asleep within a few paragraphs, and had soon laid it aside and turned off the light.

Allowing various curious aspects of a homicide to run through his mind while he was doing something else was not unusual for Jensen. When he was trying to put the pieces of a case together, he tended to let the unanswered parts work in the back of his mind, a little like letting a spinning gyroscope find its own balance, without spending much conscious effort. Often facts had a way of fitting their important relationships together if left pretty much alone, and he had learned to trust his intuition in this mental shuffling of puzzle pieces.

... the Al-ki ... is not a large vessel ... single smoke-stack ... long foredeck ... originally a freighter and not designed to carry ... passengers ... no private place to write ... a curious assortment of persons ...

Curious, he felt, was a good word for this case. Many of the details of it seemed backward. Bodies were usually discovered, then a search for the killer started. In this wilderness it seemed strange somehow to have found Hampton first—if he were the killer—and Russell's body afterward.

... landscape ... shrouded with heavy fog and mist ... motionless ocean of dark green ... slopes ... channels and passages ... icebergs ... vessels ... sunk or wrecked ...

Another curious bit was that they were so close together. Killers didn't usually remain near a body they had hidden—tried, in fact, to absent themselves as far and fast as possible, though they sometimes came back for one reason or other. But there had been Hampton, too soundly asleep, with his camp set up in an orderly fashion. *Asleep!* As if he had nothing to do with Russell's death at all. As perhaps he didn't ... said he didn't.

... Juneau ... small, bustling community ... keg of nails ... Frank Warner ... Dyea ... jumble of log cabins ... hundreds of tents ... knee deep in mud ... water ...

It was possible. He had certainly looked the part of someone who had half drowned in the river, as he claimed. His clothes were wrinkled and slightly damp, as if they had been wrung out. His boots had obviously suffered a soaking. But other things, his and Russell's gear, that should have been wet, were not. The pattern of what was wet and what was dry did not seem to fit the supposition of Hampton's moving the body.

... Indian packers ... to Canyon City ... rain ... quagmire of mud and water ... Sheep Camp ... so-called hotel ... icefall ... water poured into the valley ... Arizona Charley Meadows ...

There was also that single shotgun pellet, which Alex

thought was probably important but inconclusive. Was there another way the pellet could have become lodged under the rim of the canoe? Unless the craft was upside down it would not fall into that narrow gap . . . or if it was in the process of tipping over away from the gun, as Hampton had said it was. The impetus of the blast would be enough to wedge it there, hidden from the eyes of anyone battering pieces from the shell to conceal damage done . . . the hole it would have made.

. . . Bennett Lake camp . . . haste to build a boat . . . Ozzy Wilson

The logistics of moving the body and gear were also bothersome. It would be a lot of trouble and a high risk of being seen. There had to be a strong reason for it to be done. If Hampton had done the murder, why not hide Russell wherever he had died? Throwing suspicion on Hampton would be motive enough for moving it, if someone else had killed Russell.

Moving both men's gear would have required a second boat. If there was another, then the idea that Hampton had been stranded by his wrecked canoe made no sense.

. . . rumors of shortage of provisions in Dawson . . . ice on lake shore . . . hurry to leave . . .

Curious . . . yes. But who else could have arranged it all . . . set him up? Who, and why him? A complete stranger was unlikely, but who would Hampton—a stranger—know? The two Hampton said had stolen his gear were the most probable . . . *if* it had been stolen at all. If it had, why bring back his whole outfit, risking detection? Why was setting him up that important?

. . . tar soap . . . matches . . . evaporated potatoes . . . oakum . . . miner's candlestick . . . sheet-iron stove . . .

Just who was Hampton anyway? Was there a reason besides his stated vacation trip for him to be on the river in Canada? They needed more information on him. Alex made a mental note to start the wheels rolling in that direction with a morning phone call to the Denver police.

Part of what made Jensen very effective at his job was his willingness to use whatever worked in solving his cases. A stickler for following established procedure that collected and cross-referenced physical evidence, he was likely to follow his own patterns of thought and action when dealing with the less tangible.

He believed strongly in using both conscious and subconscious in collecting impressions, noting reactions, classifying feelings, and finding the patterns in them, if given the opportunity and encouragement of time and freedom to do so. Sometimes, he knew, the worst thing to do was force facts to fit some preconceived idea or conclusion. Often the process of relating them could not be hurried but should be left alone for answers to work their own way out, or some new fact to free them.

Alex was aware that he was becoming more willing to think Hampton innocent, but aside from the puzzles within the evidence, he could not have explained all the conscious and partly subconscious reasonings for this instinct. There was an inclination to accept the man as being as honest as he appeared . . . to believe he was telling the truth, though it complicated things considerably. Logic had little to do with it, though; as Delafosse had said, there was as much reason to assume he had not committed the crime as there was to think the opposite. Care was indicated. His instinct was not infallible, after all. He had been wrong before.

Then the journal took his concentration completely as Riser continued his trip into the Yukon. Briefly, he wondered how far Hampton had read and looked forward to comparing notes with him in the morning. What a find, an incredible personal account.

By midnight Jensen had finished a sizable chunk of Riser's account. Enthralled, he remained focused on the handwritten entries as the story unfolded, and the high points stuck in his mind.

On the first of October, Riser and his companions had arrived in . . . *White Horse City . . . aside from a few log structures . . . largely a tent-filled wide spot on the east bank of the river.*

While building their boat at Lake Bennett, Riser had met Ned McNeal, a Scotsman from New York, who joined their party. A former fisherman, at home with boats, he was not only a help with theirs but a relief to Riser, who was . . . *glad to have him along for another reason. There is something about Ozzy I can't quite cotton to, though he has done nothing to me personally to cause me to actually dislike him. He talks little and, when he does, says almost nothing about his background or where he came from. He has a temper and is unreasonably suspicious of others, seems to expect a slight or ill deed. There seems to be a suppressed rage in the man for some unknown reason. Midway through the boat building, he suddenly accused the perfectly honest pair of fellows working next to us of stealing our nails. They, astonished, declared their innocence, but Ozzy brushed it aside with an angry retort and picked up his ax, apparently ready to physically resolve the issue then and there, which concerned me greatly. I resolved never to be in the way if he becomes truly angry.*

At that point, Frank called out that he had located the missing nails in their keg under a canvas he had tossed over our supplies. Ozzy immediately laid down the ax and returned to his work, but never offered apologies to our neighbors, which to me seemed in order. They departed two days later, seemingly with relief, as they had watched Ozzy rather closely following the ruckus, and kept an eye on their goods.

Their boat completed, the four traveled down Lake Bennett, through Caribou Crossing into two more lakes, and onto the Lewes River, which took them to Miles, or Dead Man's Canyon, as it was less than fondly called.

Alex remembered stopping outside Whitehorse with Delafosse to see the wild Miles Canyon rapids before coming to Dawson. Confined between sheer stone cliffs, the water narrowed into a chute full of roiling currents, whirlpools, and a few hidden rocks, a stunning sight. While they had stood above, looking down into the churning water, a speedboat had battled its way up, against the flow, not having any particular trouble but not having an easy time of it either. He couldn't imagine what it must have been like in a homemade boat, racing with the current in the opposite direction. Riser soon told him.

... Tightening down and covering our gear, we rode through like an arrow from a bow. There was no time to even think, once we were in the clutches of the current and headed downstream at a speed faster than we could have imagined. It seemed much worse from water-level than it had from above, but we were committed and, with only a stroke or two of the oars to put us in midstream, were swept away by the boiling waters. Faster and faster we sped down the corridor of stone, past the whirlpools that we closely missed, rocking and careening atop huge waves that pounded against the walls, rebounded and hammered the boat in their fury to escape the confines of the canyon.

Just as we were coming close to the end, the boat was caught by one tremendous wave and thrown around almost crosswise of the current. A torrent of water washed in and threatened to swamp us. Frank scrambled toward the stern and seemed about to abandon ship, but Ned quickly threw his weight on an oar and shouted loudly for us to "r-r-row, boys, bloody r-r-row." His efforts, and some of ours, straightened the boat enough to allow the bow to once again point in the correct direction. Then, with Frank and Ozzy bailing for all they were worth while Ned and I manned the oars, we remained afloat. By the time we miraculously flew out the far end into calmer water we were drenched by both sweat and water, and panting with exertion. Both my hands had blisters, when I could force my fingers to uncramp from the oar I had wielded. We made it to shore and sat in the boat, shivering like dogs from fear and cold.

Strangely enough, in the midst of all the confusion, I remember clearly seeing the wreck of some vessel, splintered planks and shreds of canvas, sucked into a whirlpool as we passed it. What focused my attention was the white face of a man who was clinging to it, and the certain knowledge that he was a goner for sure, with no hope of rescue. When I had caught my breath, I mentioned it to Ned, who frowned and shook his head, but said nothing, for what could he have said?

Vaguely, Alex seemed to remember that a tramway had

been built to bypass the rapids, for a price. At the time Riser and his partners went through, it must not yet have existed and stampeders were still either running through or packing all their outfits around, an effort that would have consumed days instead of minutes. Miles Canyon was definitely a sight he wanted to make sure Jessie saw, when they came to the Yukon together.

He yawned and, laying the journal aside, shifted to reach for his pipe and tobacco. As he packed and lit it, he considered that he was beginning to feel involved in two mysteries, the first in finding who murdered Russell, the second contained in Riser's words on paper. Why had the miner, with a wife he obviously cared for and two young children, stayed in the Klondike—or Clondyke, as he had spelled it? What had brought him from Dawson to the place where Hampton had found his remains and journal?

Jensen was tempted to turn to the last pages of the account and find out, but the story was compelling enough to keep him from doing so. In fact, every time he had even thought of turning out the light and going to sleep, something in Addison's entries had held his attention.

He picked up the journal once more. Just a few more pages, while he smoked this pipe.

Riser's account continued after their departure from . . . *White Horse City* . . . and went swiftly down the Lewes River. He described the Yukon as . . . *a young, broad-shouldered country with terraced hills rolling back massively where glaciers once worked their way. The river flows through a wide valley from which canyons branch deep into the wilderness.* He mentioned moving between . . . *light-colored cliffs a hundred feet high . . . beyond them we could see rough mountains and timber-covered slopes.*

With the weather growing colder, he calculated that they would, hopefully, arrive in Dawson in about a week . . . *The thought of being frozen in somewhere along the river is not a pleasant one, although I imagine we could build a rough cabin and hold out with our outfits and food until spring. This, however, would mean missing the winter's mining on the Clondyke, so we proceed with all speed.*

As he read about the next part of Riser's trip, Alex was reminded of one of his favorite poems, for on October fourth they came to Lake Laberge. This was where Robert Service had set his humorous, fictional verse of the Dawson trail, about the prospector who cremated his dead partner in the boiler of the derelict boat *Alice May*. At least he attempted to, for when he looked to see if the job was done, he found Sam McGee ". . . looking cool and calm, in the heart of the furnace roar," saying, ". . . close that door . . . it's the first time I've been warm . . . since I left . . . Tennessee."

Wishing he had a copy of the poem to read again, Alex's focus soon returned to the journal, where Riser's description grew rather poetic.

. . . the riverbanks suddenly disappeared to right and left and we . . . were afloat on the waters of a broader body of water. . . . We could see for miles over the water. A large dark island covered with spruce trees stands out to the northwest and mountains rise all around it.

To a bird in the air the lake must seem a jewel in a sea of green that spreads out for hundreds of miles without the suggestion of a road or settlement. Such wilderness is almost impossible to imagine, and here we are in the middle of it, in a small shell of thin wood, floating along. The more I consider, the more I feel like an insect in a puddle, compared to the uninhabited space around me.

At this point, Jensen came to an entry in the journal which caught the complete attention of his law enforcement mind. Riser witnessed a theft by Oswald that, from the way he wrote, bothered and frightened him considerably.

Thursday, October 7, Thirty-Mile River, Yukon Territory: I must find a way to talk to Ned alone somehow. Whenever I suggest going for wood or leave the camp for any reason, Ozzy follows me, watches me. He knows I saw the watch fall from his coat pocket when he took out his mittens and that I know it is the Swede's watch and believe he stole it.

Late evening before last, when we were all but asleep, a boat full of shouting men pulled in, drawn by the light of our fire. Five Swedes jumped out and asked to camp with us as they desperately needed a quick fire. One of their number had accidentally fallen overboard while lowering the awkward sail they had contrived and was all but frozen. Stripping off his wet clothing and wrapping him in blankets, we built up the blaze and began to get hot liquid into him, along with a shot or two from Ned's whiskey bottle. Rubbing his extremities brought the color back to his skin and saved him from frostbite, but he was pretty well done in.

Ozzy wrung out the Swede's wet clothing and hung it to dry around a second fire. It steamed and was still damp yesterday morning in spots that had frozen as the fire burned low. The party elected to stay there another day, until all was dry and they were sure he was not to have pneumonia. They waved us off early yesterday.

I remember the victim of the drenching asking about his watch before we left to go on down the lake, and when they could not locate it, he decided that it must have been lost in the lake. Later, when we were well onto the Thirty-Mile, Ozzy pulled his mittens from his pocket and out fell the watch into the bottom of the boat.

I simply stared at it, and when I looked up, he was watching me. He picked it up and said it was his, but we both knew better without saying so. He even showed it to me and said something about having had it all along. I know it is a lie, for he has, several times on this expedition, asked me for the time. Would he have done so if he had a timepiece of his own? I think not, but cannot prove it. There were only the two of us, no other witness. Unless we meet up with the Swedes again there is no way to say positively. But I know. And he knows that I, at least, suspect.

What shall I do? Nothing, I suppose, for now. As I say, he has followed me everywhere, without seeming to. I have not been able to speak to Ned once in confidence.

All last night, when we camped on the river, he was there, slyly close at my elbow. Either he stays with me, or with Ned, so I cannot speak to him alone. . . . I am somewhat afraid of him. . . . he has a cruel streak, a way of expecting things to turn against him and, therefore, to feel the need to protect himself any way he can. I do not like this man Oswald, or trust him.

Riser was undoubtedly right, thought Alex, as he lowered the journal and yawned a huge yawn. Ozzy Wilson sounded like a bad case and likely to be dangerous. He felt glad that Addison Riser had a friend in Ned McNeal, and smiled to himself at the depth of his own involvement in a story that was almost a hundred years old and where participants were long dead. Riser made everything seem very real and interesting. Hampton had made a fascinating and unique find, a firsthand account of a famous trip. A couple more years and the communities along the route that the rush for gold had taken would be holding centennial celebrations for the Rush of 1897-98. Dawson itself was planning events in 1996 to commemorate the *discovery* of gold. It would be a summer worth visiting the Klondike community.

He raised the journal to read one last paragraph, for, glancing ahead, he had already noted its topic.

For the last few nights we have witnessed the Aurora Borealis, or Northern Lights, in bands of glowing greenish-white in the dark sky. They move and pulse in swirls and curtain-like formations, and one can see the brightest stars through them. Almost ghostly in their silence, they yet seem almost alive in the rhythm of their movement. Beautiful and alien, one could watch them for hours, their fascination is completely compelling.

Well, Jensen decided, that's enough for one night. Laying the copy of the journal next to his pipe, he turned out the light and slid down comfortably in the bed. Riser's last description seemed to fit his own experience earlier on the river bank. The aurora seemed to have the same awe-inspiring effect on almost everyone who saw it. It made him feel connected, both to Riser and the country he had passed through.

He fell asleep remembering Jessie tell of watching the aurora during the nights on the Iditarod Trail. She had said the lights were so bright she could see the shadow of herself and her dogs on the snow.

Chapter Eight

☙☙☙ "I HAD TROUBLE PUTTING THE DARN THING down," Alex commented to Jim Hampton the following morning, as he poured more syrup than necessary on a generous stack of pancakes. "Have you read the whole journal?"

Hampton looked, if anything, more exhausted than he had the night before. Dark circles under bloodshot eyes said he hadn't slept much, or well. Jensen had watched him swallow three aspirin while they waited for their food.

"Afraid not. And I didn't get much more read last night. Couldn't keep my eyes open, but kept waking up all night. How far did you get?"

"They were well on their way to Dawson, just past the incident with Oswald and the watch, when I conked out."

Hampton stopped chewing the sausage and egg he had just forked into his mouth and stared at his plate. The frown that wrinkled his forehead said that was more than he had read, and that he was feeling an unexpected jealousy that someone else should get to read his discovery first.

He glanced up to find Jensen looking across the table at him, eyes wide, brows raised quizzically, and responded with a rueful grin at the expression. Still as a statue, the trooper remained, knife and fork poised over his plate, waiting.

"Sorry," Hampton told him. "I just realized that I feel pretty possessive about that journal."

"I read more than you did?"

"Yeah, but I'll catch up with you. Don't worry about it. I just never found anything like it before."

"Don't imagine many people have. If you want to know, I'm envious as hell that you ran across it and I didn't. Hurry up and finish reading, then we'll talk about it. Okay?"

They returned their attention to the breakfast on their plates.

"You know," Jensen said, after a minute, "you might be able to find out more about Riser at the Yukon Archives in Whitehorse. Ever been there?"

"Never heard of it."

"It's all sorts of records. For instance, in 1898, what was then the Northwest Mounted Police established a checkpoint on top of the Chilkoot Pass and required everyone to have a year's worth of supplies before they could go on into Canada."

"I remember that from somewhere."

"The names of everyone they let through, and the date, is on a list in the Yukon Archives, along with another, earlier list of the people who took boats on Lake Bennett and Tagish Lake. Mounties took their own boat out and actually wrote down the names, ages, and where they were from. Somewhere on down the river they had a post and kept a journal every day of who came and went, what kind of weather there was, stuff like that. That's in the archives too. So is a journal or record from the Dawson post."

"Hey. That could be helpful, if they kept it in 1897."

"Don't remember the years, but it'd be worth checking. They were there in 1897. You might find Riser, and the rest of the names, in there somewhere."

"Report from Eagle that a Zodiac was stolen on Sunday or Monday sometime," Delafosse shouted as they made time down the Yukon with two crime-scene investigators, one piloting the jet boat.

The day was overcast and cold, so they sat as low in the boat as possible, huddled in their coats, and yelled at each other to be heard.

"Could be the one you saw Tuesday morning, Jim," Jensen called to Hampton, before turning to Delafosse. "Any description?"

"Yeah, but they all look pretty much alike. Have to check details to tell them apart."

Coming around a curve, Hampton stood up to assess the riverbanks they were passing. "There," he pointed. "See that bluff? And there's the fish wheel. We're almost there." A wide sand and gravel beach opened up to the left: the place he had stopped to talk to Russell.

Pulling the boat in toward one end of its curve, they climbed out and tied it up. Looking carefully where they stepped, Jensen and Delafosse led the way along the edge of the water, looking for signs, which they soon located. Deep lines from the hard keels of at least two boats were clearly visible. In another place, scuff marks that could be those of an inflatable Zodiac were fairly easy to spot.

Hampton identified the first mark as where Russell's boat had been when he stopped for coffee, and showed them a much lighter, slimmer mark where he had landed his canoe.

"Don't know about the other mark, or the inflatable," he told them. "The marks either weren't here, or I didn't notice them. But there was only his boat and my canoe when I stopped."

Delafosse took a number of pictures. Then, while Jensen drew a sketch of their placement, the other two measured the distance between the marks, calling out the number of feet.

"How can this make any difference?" Hampton asked, when they finished and the inspector had retracted the tape he had carried in one pocket.

"Probably won't, but you can't ever tell. We'll collect everything we can find and see if anything falls together."

Higher on the beach, Hampton showed them where Russell had set up his tent, and the remains of his fire. In the edge of the water, weighted down with a large rock, a constable located a plastic bag holding a few empty, unburnable cans and plastic containers.

"Garbage," Hampton muttered and started to reach for it, when Delafosse stopped him.

"Unlikely, but still evidence," he said, lifting it carefully out of the river, dripping water. "Grist for the mill. At least he knew enough to drown the food scent in case of bears."

The bag went into the boat, along with some other small bits of trash that Alex picked up, scattered near the fire: four screw-on bottle caps, a piece of rag, and a green ballpoint pen that had been all but invisible between two rocks. "Wasn't too careful with the small stuff," he frowned, dropping it all in an evidence bag. "Doubt he'd leave this kind of stuff on the floor of his house. Shouldn't leave it here, either."

Hampton nodded, appreciating the irritation that matched his own.

Beyond the blackened stones of the fire, Del stopped and squatted to examine the ground. Resting on his heels, he moved a rock or two, then asked Jensen to bring a trowel from the boat.

He watched while the trooper carefully scraped away a layer of earth where the rocks had been. In just a minute, a patch of dark rust-colored sand was exposed. Halting his exploration, Jensen glanced at the inspector and cocked an eyebrow.

Delafosse nodded. "Blood, and not frozen immediately or it would have retained a brighter color, so it must have been shed during warmer hours. Now, look from here to there." He pointed along a line from the stain to a section of the brush surrounding the beach. Something, more than likely some *body*, had been dragged across the stones, eroding the thin coating of sludge deposited at high water by the river, and disturbing the sand between them.

"Russell?"

"Be my guess, but remarkably little spatter or tissue for a shotgun."

When they followed the drag marks up into the brush, however, and lifted away some broken branches, they found not evidence of Russell but another body exposed to their inquiry; flat on its back, a green billed cap covering the face, surrounded by tangles of dark hair and full beard, a red plaid shirt made rusty by a massive amount of blood that had soaked, then frozen to it.

"Damn it." Delafosse lifted the cap with two fingers to expose a single bullet hole above the dead, staring eyes. Laying it back, he stepped away and turned toward the beach.

"Hampton. Come up here, but don't walk on those marks."

When he had joined them, the inspector lifted the cap once more.

"This the guy that held you up on the river?"

Hampton took one long look and turned away, once again pale and swallowing hard. "Yeah. The one with the shotgun. Will."

Jensen empathized with his reaction. No matter how many times he was called on to examine the body of someone who had died violently, it always made his own stomach turn over at first sight. Later, concentrating on the investigation allowed him to distance himself and regard the body as a source of the information he needed to work on a case. The waste of a life always made him angry, but that anger was useful. It intensified his determination to identify the perpetrator and established an odd sort of bond with the victim, who must helplessly rely on him for justice.

Being sickened at the sight of a murder victim, however, did not, in itself, indicate innocence. Many who killed, he knew, were not sadistic or cold-blooded enough to tolerate their own handiwork; they simply did not anticipate the result.

"You know this guy?" he asked Delafosse. "This the one that rang bells for you?"

The inspector sent Hampton back to the boat, before answering.

"Yes. I thought he was still in prison. He's old man Wilson's grandson. Mean as hell, but obviously met somebody meaner, or very lucky."

"He's been shot more than once."

"The body shot may go clear through, but he was alive afterward, judging by the amount it bled out. Looks like the head shot killed him. I'd like to turn him over, but we'd better get the team to work first."

When the investigation had started, he turned and walked away from the body in the opposite direction, along the line of brush. Jensen followed, taking care to watch where he stepped, but they were soon beyond the crime area.

Above the far end of the beach, Del stopped and stood looking out across the river, frowning, deep in thought. Alex halted a few feet behind him, rested one booted foot on a log and leaned both forearms on his knee, comfortably waiting until his friend was ready to share whatever was occupying his thoughts.

A light wind had come up and rustled through the dry leaves and twigs with a chill breath that crept into coat sleeves and down collars. As he filled his pipe, Alex glanced skyward. In the last twenty-four hours the temperature had dropped considerably. The sky had turned a flat white, signaling the possibility of snow. The surrounding hills were white most of the way down, ending in a horizontal line that had descended slowly during the last few days. Sourdoughs, he knew, still called these first powderings, which signaled the end of the year's prospecting season, "termination dust."

Termination was a good word for what had happened to the two men whose bodies they had found along this river. Both had been shot, but the MO did not appear to be similar. Who had put an end to their living season? The same person? And why? Several people had had the opportunity, and probably more that they didn't know about, since the river was like a highway for those who lived and worked along it. At the rate northerners in both the Yukon and Alaska carried firearms, most of them had the means, also. But who would benefit from the deaths of two such different people? A retired politician and an ex-convict. Had they even known each other? Or whom had they both known? What connected them?

He was about to ask, when Del turned around and spoke.

"How do you feel about Hampton now, Alex?"

"Well, not much different, I guess, but . . . Why? You see something I didn't?"

"No. I just can't get over the fact that he is connected to both these killings in one way or another. I just can't understand why. He has no obvious motive, unless he killed this one to get back at him for the theft of his gear, and that doesn't fit well, does it?"

"Nope."

"There's too many people involved somehow, damn it. All the tracks on the beach are unidentifiable, scrapes on rocks and dents in the sand. Looks like an army held maneuvers down there. Not much to go on." He sighed and shoved his hands into his jacket pockets.

Jensen took his foot from the log, straightened up, and continued his own thoughts out loud.

"This Wilson wasn't killed with a shotgun, Del. Would the same shooter kill two people with different guns? Possible, yes. But a man usually sticks with his weapon of choice, given the opportunity. Could we have more than one killer here? One who blasted Russell and one who, it seems, shot Wilson in the back, then finished him later with the head shot?"

"You mean Hampton might be involved?"

"No . . . I don't think so . . . somehow. But . . . I haven't thought far enough for the *who*, just a possible *how*. Another thing. Why would enough time elapse between the two shots to allow Wilson to bleed out on the beach? From the way the blood is spread down there, it looks like he was conscious enough to move around some. Plainly he was still alive, so why wasn't he shot again right away? There must have been a reason to delay shooting him the second time. Time to talk? . . . To try for information of some kind?

"Was the senator killed here too? If the blood we found is Wilson's, Russell's could be around somewhere close. That shotgun would leave a massive amount of evidence."

"Right. We'd better get looking."

Though they searched the beach and surrounding area thoroughly, they found no sign of the results of a shotgun, but one of the constables picked up a battered slug that had probably gone through Wilson. Since his body had been moved from where he had evidently been hit, there was no way of telling from which direction it had been fired. Finally giving up, they assisted in bagging the first patch of bloody sand for lab analysis, and collecting or photographing everything they could find of importance. When the two Canadian officers had finished with Wilson's body, they examined its back.

"Entrance wound all right," Jensen confirmed. "He *was* shot in the back?"

"And whatever the reason, it put him down pretty good, but didn't kill him. You're right. From the way he bled, the head shot wasn't made for a while afterward. That *does* make me wonder why."

Jensen turned to look down at the marks the boats had left at the edge of the water. "Have you considered sending someone along the river to talk to anyone who might have seen the boats Hampton described, and the Zodiac?"

"Meant to do it last night, but I was tired enough to let it slip. Get it going when we get back to the post."

"You know, the other thing that interests me is that both this man and one of the stampeders in Riser's journal are named Wilson. I know it seems crazy, but could they be connected somehow?"

"Pretty common name, but we could check. Old man Wilson's lived around here for a long time. I suppose it's possible."

"Yeah . . . common. Probably not related."

Alex went to help the constables lift Will Wilson into a body bag they had brought from the boat. There was no metal box this time, since the one assigned to Dawson had already gone to Whitehorse with Russell. As they lifted the bag to transport it across the beach to the river, Alex looked toward the boat and saw Hampton huddled dejectedly on a seat in the back.

Everything he had told them so far had seemed sincere,

but Jensen's experience told him to wait, watch, and give it time. People who were innocently involved in a crime had different ways of perceiving it than did those who were guilty and trying their best to hide it. Given long enough, a cover-up could hardly fit all the facts revealed in a case, would eventually slip to expose fabrication and duplicity. Lies lead to more lies, some of which would prove to be insupportable by evidence. So far, the inconsistencies in Hampton's situation did not add up to falsehoods, but it wouldn't hurt to let time prove them one way or the other.

Hampton watched the proceedings from his seat in the boat, feeling depressed, discouraged, and queasy. He had caught Delafosse's questioning look when they found Wilson and correctly assumed that the inspector was reassessing his suspicions. Would he be arrested? Should he call his father in Denver? He would have to call soon, anyway, for he had not checked in since he left Dawson for Forty-Mile and didn't want either his father or Judy to worry. When he was traveling alone he called before he started a specific stretch of water to say where he was headed, how long it should take, and when he would call again. It was a system that worked well and prevented worry for all involved. At the moment he wished he had his father along to talk over the situation in which he found himself.

The thought of Judy made him wish for her. If she had been with him, maybe none of it would have happened. Suddenly, he ached for her practical rationality and support, missed her terribly. He realized that, partly because he could not, he was more than ready to head home for a number of reasons, one of which was there waiting, and some of which were currently scouring the beach for clues.

Consciously putting the two deaths from his mind, he made himself think of his canoe, anticipating the repairs he would attempt as soon as he could get it into his basement workshop at home. It would never be as smooth and unblemished as it had once been, but he thought he knew

how it could be mended. That was where he would like
to be, in Denver, starting the work.

Wind whistled down the river, reddening his nose and
stiffening his fingers. Tucking his hands into his armpits,
he hunched over and allowed himself a couple of minutes
of perfect misery. If they arrested him, what the hell
would he say to Judy? What would his father think?

His head hurt again in the cold. Closing his eyes, he
tried not to think, but the events of the last night intruded,
though he found only half-remembered sounds, motion
. . . vague anger . . . all things he wanted to let go.

A shuffle of footsteps roused him. The four law enforcement officers were bringing Will's body down to the
boat. He stood and watched them approach like people
he'd never met and didn't trust, and felt a strange and
unreasonable combination of shame, anger, and guilt slip
in along with his despair.

Chapter Nine

AS THEY CAME THROUGH THE DOOR OF THE small RCMP office in Dawson, the ears of the three men were assaulted by an angry, whining voice, raised in outrage.

"Couldn't you have at least waited till I got here? It would have been decent, damn it, to let me see him at least once before your legal butchers got hold of him. What was the incredible . . ."

"Ah-h . . ." The response of Clair McSpadden, trying to break in.

". . . rush to send his body to Whitehorse? He wasn't under arrest . . . wasn't going anywhere. My God, he was dead. Right?"

"Please, Mr. Russell. You'll have to . . ."

"Why wasn't someone sent to find me? You left a message with a friend in Eagle, hoping I'd come in sometime in the next month? Don't you . . ."

"How could we know . . ."

". . . have to have some kind of release to slice him up? You didn't get one from me. And . . ."

"Listen, Mr. Russell. You'll have to talk to Inspector Delafosse, but I assure you . . ." From the sound of it, she was about to lose some of her patient politeness, suggesting she didn't have red hair for nothing.

"Sean, Russell's only son," Delafosse said in a low voice, stepping forward quickly into the room to rescue Clair.

"No, Mr. Russell. Actually, we don't need your permission when the death is clearly a case of homicide. The body remains in police custody until the inquest or until we have completed our examination and investigation of it."

The scowling man who was leaning over Clair's desk to bring his florid face and jabbing forefinger closer to her stormy gray-green eyes swung around to confront the inspector, redirecting his litany of complaint as well.

Except for the flush of anger, he was one of the most colorless people Alex could remember seeing. Not that he was an albino, or particularly pale. His skin evidenced time spent in the outdoors. It might have been a better description to say that he was more or less of one color ... beige. Eyes, hair, skin, well-trimmed beard, shirt and pants, boots and jacket were all light tan, though his hair and beard held a hint of red ... well, pink. Nothing about him seemed to contrast. Undercoat, Alex thought. He looked undercoated and still waiting for finishing color and definition. For all of that, he was not bad-looking.

"So. I have no say in what happens to my own father's body?"

"Not yet. No," Delafosse snapped. "We'll let you know when it's released. You can claim it in Whitehorse, sometime next week, I expect."

"*Damned* if I will. You can bring it back here to Dawson. I had nothing to do with it leaving here, so why should I pay for bringing it back?"

"Sean. You must realize ..."

"Realize? *Realize*? Goddammit. I realize all right. I realize my father's *dead*. And from what I understand, murdered by some bastard tourist that you haven't even bothered to arrest."

Delafosse's voice was professionally clipped and full of authority as he answered. "Now, wait just a minute, Mr. Russell. We will arrest whoever is responsible when we have finished investigating and accumulated evidence to secure a conviction. Until then, we have only suspects, no perpetrator. There is no obvious case against the gentleman to whom you are recklessly referring."

"*And pigs fly*. You are full of it, Delafosse. Meanwhile, this guy goes free as a bird. What's to prevent him from taking off back where he came from? Or killing someone else?" Sean Russell was practically shouting in frustration now.

"That's our responsibility. Not yours."

"Well, all I can say is, you'd better watch him like a hawk, or I'll have your tail in court . . . or get him myself."

"I wouldn't try that if I were you, Mr. Russell . . . Sean. There's no proof Mr. Hampton had anything to do with either death."

"Either? You mean there's another one? Who? What the hell's happening? What have you found out so far? I have a right to know."

Damn, thought Jensen, doubting that Del had intended the slip. He glanced around. Hampton had prudently stepped back into the hallway, out of sight . . . perhaps out of the building, if he was smart. Clair McSpadden sat still in the chair behind her desk, watching every move either of the men made, eyes wide and angry. Evidently, activating her temper also exaggerated her Celtic heritage, for a light dusting of freckles showed clearly over the pale skin of her cheeks, and her bright hair, loose in shoulder-length waves and curls, seemed to crackle with static electricity. Her hand rested on a square stone penholder, as if she didn't mean to go down without a fight.

Delafosse ignored the question. "No, you don't have a right to know. Not yet. Let it go, Sean. Have you ever known me to be less than thorough, or unfair? No. We'll check every detail, get it right. Don't worry. Calm down now and give us time to do our jobs and credit for doing the best we can. Your father deserves it. Will you do that? I promise I won't keep you hanging for any longer than is necessary."

The younger man stood still, frowning at the inspector for a minute, then nodded slightly. As Delafosse laid a hand on his shoulder and turned him toward the door, Jensen noticed for the first time that his face was covered with tears. Whether of grief, anger, or frustration, it was impossible to tell, and probably all three had their part in his current feelings.

Russell mopped awkwardly at his cheeks with the sleeve of his tan jacket and went where the inspector led him, out the door, toward the parking lot.

Clair heaved a great sigh of relief, let go of the heavy penholder, and leaned back in her chair. She smiled a little shakily at Alex. "Isn't he great?" she asked, obviously not referring to Russell. "I'm sure glad he turned up. I thought for a minute that Sean might smack me."

"And you'd've *hated* to have to flatten him," Jensen suggested, shattering her illusion of helplessness.

The accuracy of his comment drew her laughter, and she was smiling when Delafosse came back into the room without Sean Russell. Admiration for him still glowed in her eyes and Jensen could tell from the way Del shifted his shoulders slightly that he was not unpleasantly aware of it and her exceptional good looks. His ears seemed to have more of a rosy glow than a trip to the cold outside would normally elicit.

"Seem a little defensive?" he asked.

"Oh, I don't think so. Just his usual leap first, look later. He's okay, just a pretty impatient sort when something gets in his way. Probably a lot of transference of the anger he couldn't get rid of toward his father. He's upset and, I think, feeling a lot of guilt. Said he and Russell had another go-round last week over the subsistence issue, when the old man stopped in Chicken on his way here. What's mainly on his mind is that the last words he had with his father were angry ones."

"Finally had enough, do you think?"

"Angry enough to kill Russell, you mean?"

"Possible? Seemed like he was trying to find out everything he could, see what you knew. Lot of demanding going on there. Did you find out where he was when Russell died? Wilson?"

"Says he was downriver working on a village site. He's an excellent photographer and dedicated anthropologist. For the last few years he's been working hard at recording and preserving as much as he can of the old Han culture and traditions before they disappear. The village was abandoned long ago, but it seems to be one of the oldest in the area. He says he was there working and has at least one native helper as a witness. I think that's pretty straight, but we'll check it out.

"He and his father have fought over everything you can imagine for as long as anyone can remember. Russell thought Sean was wasting his time 'picking over old bones,' as he called it. Has no use for creative, artistic endeavor, either, so he hates . . . hated the photography. He wanted his only child to be an attorney and follow him into a political dynasty. Sean refused . . . years ago. Why would he kill the old man now, over the same things? Doesn't make a lot of sense."

"Something new, maybe? Well, you know him better than I do, but to me it felt a little histrionic. He was gauging your reaction all the time, seeing what he could get. Hiding something."

Delafosse frowned, considering. After a minute, he nodded. "You could be more objective than I am. I'll send someone down to Eagle to verify his statement. Can't hurt."

"What about his mother?"

"She's been dead a long time."

"So, Sean inherits?"

"Ah, I see where you're headed. Don't think so. Russell wasn't reticent about letting it be known that he'd willed a lot of his money—and there's evidently a fair amount of it—to support the subsistence battle, not Sean. Unless he complied with his father's dictates the will evidently cut him off with very little. Better check that out too, I guess. It could have been just talk. Should let Hampton know to keep clear of Sean Russell. Where is he?"

Jensen grinned. "I imagine he already knows . . . caught that loud and clear when he heard the unarrested bastard tourist part of the conversation. I bet he headed back to the hotel and didn't dawdle on the way. He's no coward, but no dummy either, Del. Not the type to go looking for unnecessary trouble, I think."

Delafosse turned with a hand on the telephone, to give Jensen a questioning and speculative look. "You really don't think he had a hand in these deaths, then?"

"I'd be surprised."

"Why?"

"Well . . . call it intuition . . . partly his personality, I guess . . . but also a lot of little things that don't add up. Mostly because I can't find any kind of a motive in the tangle. Somebody else must have cut the wood for that campfire, for one thing."

"Suppose he *did* do that himself *and* tossed the ax in the river?"

"Why?"

The inspector had to admit he couldn't come up with a reason, but wasn't completely satisfied with Hampton's innocence, not yet. "I think *he's* got something he's not telling us. He thinks a lot . . . and watches." Abruptly, he changed the subject.

"Listen, I'm going to call Whitehorse, then fly down with Wilson's body and stay for the autopsy, if they'll agree to do it today. I also want to see what I can get out of the coroner about Russell. You mind staying here? I'll be back in the morning and I'd appreciate your keeping an eye on Hampton."

"No problem," Jensen nodded. "I'd like to do some checking on the coincidence of the Wilson name. Clair can help me with that, I bet." She smiled at him and nodded. "Anything else?"

"A couple of small things. Before I leave, while they get the plane loaded and ready, we'll take a quick run upriver to notify Will's grandfather. But while I call, will you touch base with Hampton, just to make sure he understands about Sean Russell?. You could grab us something to eat, too, and meet me at the boat."

"Sure. You make your calls. I'll head back to the hotel. I want to put on another pair of wool socks before we go boating again anyway. See you there in"—he glanced at his watch—"half an hour?"

He left Delafosse dialing, but wished momentarily that he could be a mouse in the corner, to see if his friend would get around his own inhibitions and make a date with Clair.

Back at the hotel, he changed socks and knocked on the door next to his own, which was almost immediately opened by Hampton, obviously settled in for an afternoon of journal reading. The appealing scent of a half-eaten hamburger and fries, next to a milkshake and two apples on the table, made Jensen's stomach rumble.

"Where'd you find that?" he asked. "I'm hungry enough to eat a wolf raw."

"Little place called the Ninety-eight Drive Inn, two blocks up on Front Street," Hampton told him. "And there's a grocery store almost next door. Want a fry or two?"

"No, thanks. Think I'll hike up there. Listen, you heard the mood Sean Russell was in, but I think you disappeared before he threatened to take care of you himself. I'd stay out of his way, if I were you."

"Intend to. He's hot. I'll be right here, warm and indoors while I read some more of this journal. Can't let you get any farther ahead of me."

"Good. I'm going with Delafosse to carry the bad news to Wilson's grandfather, old man by the name of Duck Wilson—and wouldn't I love to know the story behind that handle. I'll check with you when we get back. Okay?"

At Hampton's nod, he closed the door and headed down the stairs with the 98 Drive Inn in mind, intending to take the most direct route he could to get his mustache over a bacon cheeseburger.

Chapter Ten

❦ ALEX JENSEN'S MUSTACHE WAS SINGU-
larly impressive. As full as regulations would allow, it
glorified his upper lip with a thick, red-blond reminder of
Vikings, old-time baseball players, and early American
mountain men. The ends he allowed not handlebars but
only a suggestive half curl. Men envied its flourish,
women speculated about being kissed beneath it, little
children automatically reached curious fingers to verify its
awesome reality.

Though he was not inclined to clutter his life with ex-
cess material baggage, two shelves of a bookcase in his
home displayed a fine collection of mustache cups given
to him over the years by family and friends. Several were
ornate antique examples of the china of the previous century, when hirsute lip decoration had reached epic proportions along with its shaving paraphernalia. Contained
within these was an assortment of appropriately shaped
combs, a variety of waxes, several trimmers, and other
mustache maintenance oddments that he almost never
used but kept in amused recognition of his own conspicuous vanity.

The mustache had become so much a part of his look
and personality that he had almost forgotten the shape of
his face without it. Lately, he was not unhappy to find a
thread or two of silver among the gold, for, in the back
of his mind, he carried an image of himself as an old man,
well turned out with a pure-white "soup strainer."

Jim Hampton watched the door close behind the tall trooper, thinking how much he resembled pictures of some of the Klondike stampeders he had seen in a book of photographs in Whitehorse, particularly one of a mounted policeman on the shores of Lake Bennett. Many Klondikers had grown beards that covered their chins as well, but it seemed clean-shaven had been regulation for the Canadian law enforcement officers, except for their upper lips, for many had sported full mustaches above their distinctive red coats.

Hampton liked Jensen more the longer he knew him and wondered idly if he was making a mistake in that confidence. He was glad to have someone with whom to share the journal. Jensen was clearly as interested in the history of the gold rush as he was and seemed to know quite a bit about it. He wished they could have met each other some other way, but was still pleased to know him.

As he finished his hamburger and fries, he speculated about Jensen's background. Knowing he was from Idaho gave his western hat and the extent of his mustache more credence. He reminded Hampton a little of his two brothers. Jensen was taller, broader in the shoulders, and lighter in coloring, but the confident, watchful eyes, slim-hipped economy of movement, and self-contained demeanor were similar. It seemed he didn't miss much and kept a lot to himself.

Finished with his lunch, Jim tossed the containers and scraps in the wastebasket, plumped the pillows against the headboard of his bed, and made himself comfortable to read Riser's journal. In a little while he reached the entry where Alex had quit reading the night before. There he paused and absentmindedly picked up an apple to munch as he considered the information about Oswald and the Swede's watch. It was obvious Oswald had stolen the timepiece. How unfortunate that Riser and McNeal could not have simply left the other two. But sharing a boat meant that they all had to stick together at least until they reached Dawson. He hoped things would change when they did.

On Saturday, October 9, the party of stampeders were

on the river above Carmacks Trading Post, in miserable
rainy weather that soaked them through and chilled them
to the bone. It was a relief to reach the trading post, where
they stopped for the night. Riser described their appreciation of the shelter.

*Having had enough of the rain, we pulled in and spent
the night in one of . . . three small log cabins. For the first
time in weeks we slept inside four walls, with a roaring
fire in the stove to dry out our clothes and gear, and cook
a meal on the rarity of a flat surface. What a luxury. I
had almost forgotten what it is to be completely warm.
We heated water and washed ourselves, then trimmed
each other's hair and beards. Soon we will be among
civilized people again and it seemed right to improve our
appearance as much as possible. . . . Snug in our wooden
tent, we slept warm and well.*

*When we awoke this morning the temperature had
dropped and the landscape was a sheet of ice. Freezing
as it fell, the rain had covered everything in sight with a
crystal coating that gleamed in the early sunlight like Polly's cut-glass bowl on the windowsill. Each tiny branch
of the bushes and trees was encased in ice. Walking was
treacherous, as at every step your feet threatened to fly
out from under and hurl you to the ground without warning. We moved like decrepit old men, ferrying our belongings from cabin to boat half a load at a time.*

*On the next to last load, Ned lost his footing where the
bank slopes to the river, and, feet and arms up, slid down
on his back to fetch up against the bow of the boat, his
burden of dry clothing scattered the length of his wild
ride. It was fortunate he was uninjured, for we doubled
over with laughter at his plight and would probably have
been unable to keep from doing so had he been broken
in pieces. The helpless waving of his arms and legs, and
his great howl of indignation, reduced us to kneeslapping
roars. In two minutes, however, we were all sliding like
children on pieces of sacking and having a gay time of
it. Even Ozzy made a trip down the incline, though he
growled that it was nonsense and a waste of time, impatient to get under way.*
                                       •

For the next few entries, Riser talked about their trip on the river and the appearance of its surroundings. They went through Five Finger and Rink rapids, which, he said, ... *were nothing compared to those above White Horse.*

Hampton recognized the places Addison mentioned and was pleased that he had run the same river in his canoe. Not long after passing the community of Carmacks, he remembered coming around a wide loop and seeing the Five Finger Rapids ahead to the left, just as his map showed them. They had indeed been easy to negotiate, adding character to the calm face of the river.

The land had lifted away to the right in a steep bank high above his head, and he saw that a long wooden staircase had been built to allow those passing on the highway above to stop and come down to view the unusual formations of rock that divided the water into the distinctive five fingers from which it derived its name. Looking up, he had noticed a gleam of light reflected from someone's binoculars and had raised his paddle in a salute to the person he knew must be watching him go by. A minute later something white, perhaps a scarf or large handkerchief, had been fluttered from above in answer.

Farther on, he had noticed an eagle tracing circles in the pale blue of the September sky. What a view it must have commanded. On the drive to Dawson to drop off his truck, he had pulled off to look to the east, where a viewpoint on a hill allowed a sight of the Tintina Trench. He contemplated this fine example of plate tectonics in the middle of a bowl-shaped valley, aware that it extended hundreds of miles across Alaska and the Yukon. Here was a visible proof of the movement of the plates that cover the earth's surface and grind against each other, producing earthquakes and bringing mountains and valleys into being.

As he stood there, looking out at the trench in the distance, Jim had wondered at the rugged newness of this northern country. The sharp peaks and ridges of the mountains spoke clearly of having had little time, geologically speaking, to wear into the softer rounded shapes of older, more mature mountains. And there, far below him,

had been indisputable evidence that the earth had not finished carving the landscape into yet more extreme sculp-
tures and unique designs. It had the same clean sharpness
he liked so much about the Rocky Mountain country, but
this had seemed even younger and more interesting, probably in part because it was less inhabited.

Leaning back on the bed, he now closed his eyes and
thought pleasantly of his canoe trip of the week before.
What a great venture, but compared to Riser's experience
through the unsettled wilderness country, his modern gear
made the travel a pleasure, not an ordeal to be undertaken
with much care and hard work. He thought of Riser's
many trips back and forth in the Chilkoot Pass, just to get
his goods and gear to the summit and down to Bennett
Lake. Then to have to build his own boat . . . not only
build it, but create the lumber with which to build it.

Replete with lunch and thinking of sawdust falling in
showers down the neck of a sawyer under a log they had
been required to cut, he yawned and drifted into a dream
full of rough-hewn planks and hot pitch on the bank of a
wide lake. Soon he was snoring slightly, the unfinished
journal rising and falling gently on his chest.

Almost two hours later, he woke with a stiff neck and the
groggy feeling of having slept through half the afternoon
in an unusual position. Splashing water on his face from
the bathroom sink, he remembered that he had wished for
a map while reading Riser's account of the long river trip.
The one he had used while canoeing was still at the
RCMP office with the rest of his gear, but there would
undoubtedly be one somewhere in the shops that catered
to tourists on the streets of Dawson. If he could find a
cup of coffee, it would wake him up, as would a walk in
the cold air.

He decided to go looking. It shouldn't be difficult to
keep an eye out for Sean Russell and avoid him if he
showed up. He could finish reading the journal later.
There wasn't much more to complete and, anyway, he
hated to come to the end. Might as well spread it out a
little more now that Riser had almost reached Dawson,

the objective of his long journey. Maybe he could also locate a map that showed what the town had looked like when the rush was going on. It would be interesting to compare it to what Dawson was like now. The Visitor Reception Center might have one. It was worth a try.

Stomping his boots on and grabbing his coat, Hampton stuffed the journal in his pocket and went out the door. Checking to be sure it was locked, he turned toward the stair and thought he saw something move out at the far end of the hall, but the light was too dim to see and he was in a hurry. Putting it from his mind, he clattered down the stairs, headed for the outside. Jensen and Delafosse should be back soon, so he wouldn't stay away long.

Passing the empty registration desk, he stepped out the front door onto the boardwalk and turned left. The Visitor Reception Center was only four or five blocks away on the street that faced the river. A large, two-story log building, it was a replica of the Northern Commercial Company store which had been built in 1897 and stood until it perished in a fire in 1951. Typical of several buildings hurriedly built during the first year or so of the rush, it was a symmetrical, rectangular box with four windows on each floor across the front and a door perfectly centered between those on the ground level. Wherever possible, boardwalks and porches had been built back in the days of the rush to allow pedestrians to escape the ruts and the mud that, when not frozen solid, was churned into a deep swamp by passing horses and wagons.

As Hampton approached, he admired the forethought that must have allowed goods to come straight from the steamboats almost directly into the mercantile area. Once inside he noted that though the roomy interior was largely empty now, one wall had been set up with a counter and shelves to simulate the commercial enterprise as it must have looked. The rest was spaciously decorated with racks of brochures, posters on the walls, and a counter where requests, questions, and reservations could be filled, answered, and made.

He found two maps that showed how Dawson had looked in 1898, but none in 1897, and none in much detail. A woman behind the reception counter suggested that he check at the museum, and he left with a handful of information on the gold rush, the town, and the goldfields, but not precisely what he had come looking for.

Halfway back to the hotel, he found a small café where he purchased a paper cup of coffee to take back to his room, along with a cinnamon roll of epic proportions and satisfying amounts of pecans. Balancing these, he headed on down the boardwalk past a saloon. Just beyond the door, a slightly familiar voice stopped him with a bark.

"Hey, you."

He swung around to find Sean Russell glaring at him. Damn. And he had looked carefully down each street to ascertain the absence of this very person before hurrying along it both coming and going from the Visitors Center.

"I want to know what you've got to say about my father," Russell demanded, stepping forward aggressively. He had obviously seen Hampton passing from inside the bar and come out in a rush, for he had left his jacket behind and stood in his shirtsleeves in the cold, both hands doubled into fists. "What've you got to tell me, huh? Huh? Police ought to have you in a goddamn cell."

A few beers had not improved his hostile attitude. He stomped up so close that Hampton could smell the alcohol on his breath and notice that one eye seemed slightly larger than the other. Though he stepped back, Russell followed closely, crowding him against the side of the building.

"Look," Hampton tried to say, "I only met your father once. I don't know . . ."

"Lying bastard! Who else would have killed him? Huh?"

Russell brought up one of his fists and the container of coffee went flying into the street. Before Hampton could react, the cinnamon roll followed it.

Three or four people had followed Sean Russell from the bar and stood near the door watching, but did nothing to interfere or interrupt the harassment.

"Bastard," Russell hissed again through clenched

teeth. "Son of a bitch tourist." He swung a fist that, because Hampton had no room to maneuver, connected solidly with his left cheekbone and snapped his head back to thump against the wall; then he followed it up with a left jab that split an eyebrow.

Hampton, his anger and resentment growing, had suddenly had enough. He stopped looking for a way to slide out of his position between the man and the wall, to avoid the confrontation, and buried his own fist in Sean's belly. Russell was so close he couldn't see the punch coming and the air went out of him with an explosive sound. Without moving his feet, he sat down hard on the boards of the walk, holding his midsection and struggling to catch his breath.

The canoeist, aware that his shoulders and arms were stronger than normal, had pulled the punch at the last second, but it still easily felled Russell. He stepped away from the building and stood for a second or two, looking down at the gasping man.

"I didn't kill your father. I don't know who did and I'm sorry he's dead. Now, leave me alone and get yourself together. And I warn you, don't try to hit me again. I won't hold back next time."

He stared a challenge at the group by the bar door, but none of them stepped forward to take it up, so he turned on his heel and walked off toward the hotel, the sounds of Russell's labored attempts to catch his breath fading behind him.

Chapter Eleven

"AT THE RATE WE'RE PROCEEDING, there'll soon be nobody in Dawson to so much as write a traffic ticket," Delafosse commented. "They'll all be working on this case."

Jensen half laughed. "Aren't they already?"

The hills surrounding the Yukon seemed to close in as they swept past them on their way upriver in the jet boat, though Alex suspected it might be a perception partly due to his tendency to hunch his shoulders against the chill breeze created by their forward motion. The whole country seemed to be turning inward against the coming winter. With the sudden drop in temperature, the rich gold of the deciduous trees that had stood out so sharply against the dark evergreens a few days before was fading into a more muted shade. Many large and small branches were now naked silhouettes against the gray sky, their wealth of leaves spread in a colorful patchwork over the ground.

He thought of Jessie, as she had pictured herself in their conversation the night before, in the big couch in front of a fire in her wood stove with the front that opened like a hearth. In cold weather, she loved to curl up there, with a new or favorite book, sip tea or hot chocolate, turning inward along with the season.

The couch was huge, wide enough for them both, if they sat facing each other from opposite ends, and expansive enough for Alex's long legs. Jessie had coveted its amazing bulk at a moving sale in Palmer, brought it home in the back of her truck, layered it with quilts, afghans, and fluffy pillows in several sizes. Jensen liked it so much that she humorously accused him of enjoying her furniture more than her company. They frequently relaxed there in the evenings, pausing now and then to throw a log on the fire or share a passage, if they read separately, but more often reading aloud in turns.

Watching the fall colors sweep past as the boat fought its way upriver, and clutching his collar close against the wind, he was not displeased with the idea of going home soon. Jessie and her enormous couch were both warm, comfortable anticipations in his mind.

Wilson's place was on the other side of Dawson from the murder site, so for almost half an hour they ran against the current, around the loops and curves of the famous river. The two officers watched the landscape unfold, wild and, for the most part, unmarked by the remarkable rush it had witnessed almost a hundred years ago and determined efforts to mine it since. Here and there, however, they passed small houses and cabins visible from the water.

"You use this boat like a squad car," Jensen observed.

"There's a fair number of people who elect to live along the river and it's the only way to reach them. Some live here permanently, a few have summer cabins. I have one myself not too far from here. It's a great escape with no telephone, but I seldom get to spend much time at it."

"Fish?"

"Off and on. Mostly it's an excuse to get out. Mainly I cut more wood than ever gets used, but it cleans out the deadwood and widow-makers on the property."

"Know how that 'getting out' feels. I like fly fishing, but on smaller waterways than this. Got started as a kid in Idaho. Some great camping spots there along the Continental Divide and a panful of brookies is the best breakfast I can imagine."

"We should go together sometime," Delafosse said. "I've always wanted to learn fly fishing, but never found the time or opportunity. I just periodically plunk a line in the water and hope it snags something with enough fight

to make it fun.'' He turned to look forward as the river
fell back on itself in a deep loop. "We're coming up on
Wilson's place."

The first thing to be seen was a battered dock with three
boats tied to it. One nearest the shore was only half visible
as most of it was sunk below the surface and the rest was
glued to the freezing mud of the bank. The other two rode
uneasily without fenders, banging against the rough-cut
pilings and planks. Obviously, their condition was not a
high priority of the owner.

"Pretty shabby way to treat a boat," Jensen observed.

"No different than he treats anything else he owns.
Wait and see. For a man in his seventies, he's one of a
kind."

"Where'd he get the name Duck?"

"Something about a bar brawl years ago. If I remember
right, somebody yelled 'Duck!' and he did, and the guy
who was about to punch him caught a bottle in the face.
The name stuck."

As Delafosse slung a rope over the sturdiest-looking
piling, the subject of their discussion came hurrying down
the path from the bank onto the dock, a shotgun in one
hand.

"Hold it right there," he roared as he rocked, rather
than walked, toward them. The uneven gait of a crippled
leg tipped him back and forth like a small boat in a high
wind. He halted at the end of the dock and stood scowling
down at the officers.

"Whatcha want?"

From under the crumpled brim of a hat of indetermin-
able color, long yellowish-gray hair flew in all directions,
joined by a grungy chest-length beard. Over sharp, dark
eyes, his scraggly gray eyebrows were just as unmanaged,
or unmanageable. Beneath dirty denim that flapped in the
wind, his legs looked bird-scrawny, shrunk to cords of
muscle that ended in half-laced boots. The filthy down
jacket he wore had once been green. Here and there it
leaked feathers from a hole or burn, a couple of which
were patched with the same duct tape that seems to hold
half of everything above the fifty-fifth parallel together.

"Just stay right where you are and state your business," he demanded, with a twitch of the gun in their direction.

Delafosse looked up at him for a long minute without answering. Indifferent to who was in charge, Wilson stared back at him, waiting.

"Back off, Duck," the inspector told him. "We came to tell you about Will."

"What about him?"

"We found his body this morning, downriver on a bar. Shot twice."

There was no flash of shock in the old man's eyes, just the cold, unwavering stare.

He already knew, Jensen told himself. How?

After a minute, Wilson frowned even more, before he opened his mouth to comment. "Ha! Always knew the dumb bastard'd get hisself killed someway. Who done it?"

"We don't know yet, but we will."

"Doubt it. Haven't got the brains of a chicken. Never had. Goddamn cops. Where do I git him?"

"Nowhere, until we finish with the autopsy. Sometime next week you should get in touch at the office."

"I got anything to say about that?"

"No, Duck. You don't. You have a kid named Charlie here? Younger than Will, in his twenties. Brown hair, no beard. Not a local."

"No."

"Do you know him? Has he been here with Will?"

"Don't have no kid."

"Well, then, do you have another, newer boat? Bigger than these two, windshield, outboard?"

Wilson shifted his weight from his crippled leg.

"You see what I got," he growled.

"I see what you have . . . *here*."

It was plain he was avoiding the question. As his silence strung itself out and Delafosse waited, another figure came out of the trees, down the bank, and made a small sound as it stepped onto the dock.

Wilson whirled to face the girl, who halted and looked

defiantly at him, then at the officers in the boat. "Will?"
she asked.

She wore dirty, ragged tennis shoes, denim pants with
a hole in one knee, and a tattered red jacket much too
large for her thin frame, as though she had grabbed the
first coat to hand as she followed Wilson outdoors. Still,
her long blond hair and face looked clean. She clutched
the jacket around herself and waited for an answer.

Delafosse was nodding when Duck Wilson lurched toward her, roaring inarticulately. Faster than he could possibly move, she climbed up the bank she had come down
and stopped to look back.

"Dead?" she called to the inspector.

"Yes."

She whirled and disappeared so quickly they could not
gauge her reaction to his confirmation.

Wilson shouted after her. "Get back to the house, you
useless bitch. I told you to stay put and you'll do what
you're told or answer to me. Goddammit."

Looking after her, Alex caught glimpses of the red
jacket as she ran toward a low log cabin half hidden in
the trees. The place was poorly kept and depressingly clut-
tered with discarded mining equipment, snow machines,
and boats, most broken and never repaired. In the open
door, another, older, female figure waited to pull her in
and slam it shut. Old as he was, Duck Wilson obviously
had his family cowed, except, perhaps, this girl.

"Daughter?" he murmured to Delafosse, as Wilson returned to his threatening position on the dock.

"Will's wife, Cherlyn, poor kid."

"Now git out of here," Duck demanded, once again
gesturing with the shotgun.

"Where's Charlie, Duck?" Delafosse tried again. "He
was seen with Will."

"Don't know nothin' about him," Wilson insisted
stubbornly.

"I can get a warrant and search this place, if I have
to."

"Like to see you try."

"We'll be back, if we don't find him. Better think

about it, if there's anything you know about Will's death, and I think you do.''

"Git, I said. Wouldn't tell you what time it was if I knew, but I don't know . . . nothin'." He reached to lift the rope from the piling with the barrel of the gun and deliberately dropped it in the water rather than toss it back into the boat.

Disgustedly, Delafosse hauled it in, coiling it neatly into place on the deck, where it would certainly freeze and be difficult to handle by the time they reached Dawson. Without another word, he waved a hand at the constable pilot and the idling engine roared to life, pushing them back into the mainstream of the river.

Duck Wilson stood crookedly on the dock, staring his belligerence after them until the bend in the river swept him from sight.

"Bastard," Delafosse allowed himself, and settled on a bench to wait out the trip back to Dawson.

"He already knew Will was dead," Jensen commented, a minute later.

"He did."

"How?"

"I don't know. Charlie, probably."

"I'd sure like to know where *that* one is. Talk to him."

"So would I, but he won't come walking into the office. I saw him once on the street with Will. Looked a pretty tough case. Maybe a prison buddy."

"You think there's another boat, don't you? The one Hampton says Will and Charlie were in when they blasted a hole in his canoe?"

"Yes. You noticed how he avoided my question? Why? Does he know where it is, or is it missing?"

"Interesting question. Charlie have it, you think?"

"Well, if we could find Charlie, it's my bet we'd be able to locate the boat. I'd also like to find out who it belongs to. Duck? Will? Did they steal it?"

Jensen gnawed at the edge of his mustache with his lower teeth and watched the bank fly past. Traveling with the current toward Dawson made the trip a much quicker one.

"You know," he ventured slowly. "I wonder if the Wilson family—and Charlie—might have anything to do with the stolen trucks and RVs. There haven't been any more of them since this whole thing started. Maybe Will and Charlie switched to stealing boats and gear instead."

Delafosse thought about it. "Could be, I guess," he said. "Wouldn't be the first time they were involved in theft. Boats wouldn't make them as much as trucks and would be harder to transport . . . well, maybe not. Less identifiable, anyway."

"You going to get that warrant?"

"No. Not for the moment. Think we should let him stew for a while. He'll have to come into town for Will's body in a few days anyway. Let him worry about how much we know. I'll put a patrol on the waterfront while we do a little more digging in that direction."

Delafosse turned to watch the wake of the boat roiling out behind them. Finding Will's body bothered him. Something connected him with Russell. That seemed totally unlikely, but they had been killed in the same spot and within hours of each other. Could the subsistence issue have anything to do with it? Had Sean Russell and Wilson somehow been the link? He wasn't comfortable with that either. Charlie—the kid was the unknown factor in the thing. Hampton? Could Jensen's reluctance to fasten the killings on him be intuition alone? Or did the fact that he was another American enter into it?

With that thought, he felt immediately guilty. There was absolutely no reason to believe Jensen would unfairly protect a fellow countryman. The trooper was as committed to law and order as he was, whoever the culprit. Oh, hell. They needed more information, obviously.

And there was something disturbing about this case, something that made him frown uneasily at the wrongness of it.

He leaned against the side of the boat and shrugged his collar up closer around his neck. The air smelled like snow, and from the looks of the sky, it was going to be soon. Was there something more at either site on the river that needed checking before it was buried under a white blanket for the winter? He couldn't think of anything.

What he would really like to be doing was relaxing indoors near a warm wood fire, with, perhaps, a snifter of good brandy and coffee—after a good dinner—without a care or a case to fill his mind. Perhaps with Clair? He remembered the look she had given him that morning, appreciating his handling of Sean Russell. Maybe she *wouldn't* say no if he asked her. Maybe he should . . . Well . . . maybe *after* they solved this one . . . when things quieted down and he could focus on it . . . keep himself from making some enormous and embarrassing social blunder.

Clair was more than just attractive, with that wonderful cloud of red hair. Smart, too. Had a good sense of balance and humor. He was pleased that Alex liked her. It validated his own taste. He just might . . .

"Well," said Jensen, raising an eyebrow, "you ask her yet?"

Chapter Twelve

Seeing Delafosse off to Whitehorse and driving his truck back to the hotel alone felt strange to Alex, after several days of the cooperative partnership. He stopped in the lobby, intending to call Hampton rather than climb the stairs.

"Haven't seen him," the hotel clerk told Alex, when an empty ringing of the telephone indicated he was not in his room. "If he went out, he didn't leave his key. But I was up in fourteen fixing a leaky faucet for over half an hour. Just came back down. You could check the bar."

Alex was turning to do so when the door opened and Jim Hampton walked in, snowflakes in his hair and on the shoulders of his coat, one cheek swelling and a thin line of blood trickling from an eyebrow.

"Hi," he said, with a rueful grin.

"What the hell happened?" Jensen asked. "Where've you been?"

Hampton stopped, startled, and the grin faded from his face.

"I didn't realize I was under house arrest."

"No," Jensen told him. "No, you aren't. I'm just concerned about that hothead, Sean Russell. Evidently, I have reason to be. At least I assume he may have something to do with your somewhat battered condition."

Chastened and a little resentful, Hampton nodded. "I only went out for a minute, to the Visitors Center, looking for a map of old Dawson. I thought I'd been careful, but he came out of a pub and caught me coming back.''

"What does *he* look like?''

"Nowhere close to this bad. I stopped him with one punch that took the air out and left him sitting on the boardwalk. He'll be sore in the middle, but I didn't hit him very hard.''

"Any witnesses that he started it? Just in case.''

"Oh, yeah. Half a dozen barflies stood and watched the whole thing. They didn't cheer, but they didn't help either.''

"You want to do anything legal about it?''

"No. No. Definitely *not*. He's got good reason to be unpredictable and upset right now. I'm okay, or will be as soon as I clean up some.''

The refusal seemed a little too enthusiastic to Jensen, whose questioning look brought an embarrassed glance that dropped immediately to monitor ineffectual swipes at Hampton's bloody shirt. "I probably shouldn't have hit him, but he had me backed against a wall.''

The clerk, not wanting his floor dripped on, had come out from behind the counter to hand Hampton a couple of tissues, which he immediately held to his face. "Come in here,'' he suggested, opening the door to a small lavatory. "I've got a first-aid kit. You going to need stitches?''

"Just some disinfectant and a Band-Aid, I think. It's not really bad, just bleeds like a sucker. Hope Russell's hand hurts right along with his belly.''

"You finish the journal?'' Jensen asked, watching the repair process.

"Nope. Took an unexpected nap. Got them almost to Dawson though. Where's Tweedledee? Thought you and the inspector were inseparable.''

"Quick run to Whitehorse,'' Jensen told him, feeling strangely uneasy giving him the information that Delafosse was out of town.

A rakish Band-Aid plastered over the cut, Hampton turned from the mirror and came out dabbing at the blood that had stained his clothing on the way back to the hotel.

It had rinsed off the jacket's waterproof fabric, but his shirt was now a streaked ruin.

"Any way I could get some clean clothes from my gear at Delafosse's office?" he asked. "Sure hate to go to dinner in this mess."

"No reason you shouldn't. The clothes're not really evidence. I need to talk to Clair anyway. Let's go."

Without going upstairs, they left the hotel and headed through the new snow toward the RCMP office. A thin layer of white was already blanketing everything in sight and was coming down more heavily all the time. As they walked toward the river, then turned west along the main road between it and town, Jensen thought of dogs, sleds, and told Hampton about the overnight trips he was looking forward to this winter. The opposite bank across the wide stretch of the Yukon could hardly be made out behind the veil of falling flakes.

"There's a graveyard of old paddle wheelers downstream from the ferry dock on the other side of the river," he said, gesturing in that general direction.

"Steamboats?" Hampton questioned with interest.

Jensen grinned. "Only the largest steamboat graveyard on the Yukon. It's got five of the grand ladies that used to travel the river in the old days. All of them are gradually disintegrating."

"Wow. Is it okay to go see them?"

"Sure, but most of them have pretty well fallen apart." Alex recited the names he had found in a brochure at the hotel earlier. "The *Victorian*, the *Schwatka*, the *Tyrrell*, the *Julia B.*, and the *Seattle III*. They were all hauled out and put up on ways years ago, when they became obsolete and no one wanted them. They just decay and collapse a little more every season. Parts of them are just piles of broken boards. If you really want to see what they looked like when they were still working, take a tour of the *Keno*."

"That the one on the riverbank close to downtown?"

"Right. Last one to run the Yukon, brought down here from dry dock in Whitehorse in 1960 and permanently docked on the riverbank to be restored. It's not really an old one, built sometime in the twenties, but you can get a pretty good idea how they were put together. The others were built in the late 1890s, during or right after the rush.''

"You seen them?" Hampton asked him.

"Just from the river. I'd also like to get a look at the goldfields up around Bonanza Creek. Haven't seen them either. Del . . . the inspector says there's still a big dredge up there—the Yukon Gold Company's Number Four— out on Claim Seventeen Below Discovery. Closed for the winter now, but it's been restored and they open it for tourists in the summer. It was the largest wooden-hull, bucketline dredge in North America. Chains with links a yard long. Supposed to be pretty impressive.''

"Seventeen Below Discovery? What's that mean?" Hampton frowned, puzzled.

"Well, claims at the site where gold is found are traditionally called 'Discovery.' The first to stake a new claim gets two, the original and one more by *right of discovery*. The rest are staked above and below the first, and are called by their numbers away from it: One Above Discovery, One Below Discovery, and so on. The names were, of course, shortened to Four Above, Ten Below, like that, depending on how far away they were. The dredge is on Seventeen Below.''

"How far from Dawson are they?"

"Not far if you're driving. But back during the rush it was a three-hour walk to Discovery Claim. Long way if you're carrying everything you need on your back.''

"How big were the claims?"

"They measured five hundred feet along the creek bank and drove in four-foot stakes with the name of the miner and claim number. They usually ran a hundred feet from the creek.''

"That's a good size.''

"Yeah, but they staked them in a hurry and some were pretty rough. When they were surveyed later, some were long, some short, and scraps and wedges showed up between some of them and were claimed by others who hovered like vultures while the survey was made. One fraction was only three inches wide, and they called the greedy owner 'Three-Inch White' for the rest of his life.''

Hampton chuckled as they climbed the steps to the door of the office. Jensen went to talk to Clair, while a constable helped Hampton find the bag that contained his clothes, in the evidence storage room. He quickly changed shirts, discarded the blood-soaked one into a wastebasket, and collected a change of under- and outerwear to take back to the hotel.

"Well," said Jensen, when Hampton joined him at his desk, "you look spiffy enough. Let's go find some dinner. Clair's coming along to introduce me to the curator at the museum on the way. She thinks he may be able to answer a couple of my questions."

They waited at the door until Clair came out of the back room, pulling on her coat, then walked out into whirling flakes of snow, now falling like feathers through the early dark.

"O-oh." Clair raised her face to catch a flake on her tongue. "First big ones of the year. Pretty early. We don't usually get this until October."

As they turned off Front onto Church Street, Alex bent to scoop up a handful of snow, which he quickly molded into a snowball and tossed at the back of Hampton's head. For a minute or two, the resulting barrage between the two was fairly spectacular, but quickly resolved into a game of skill in hitting power poles that lasted until they reached the museum.

Hampton was suitably impressed with the well-kept Neoclassical Revival building, which was two stories tall, occupied most of a city block, and was painted two attractive shades of gray. It had, Clair explained, been constructed in 1901 as the grand federal Old Territorial Administration Building, and had been turned into a museum in the sixties. "Has the largest collection in the Yukon," she told them proudly. "You should look for a map here, Jim. Fewer injuries involved. It's also a place to look for the names in that journal. They have a great archive of people who were here during the gold rush. The curator won't have time tonight, but he could help you tomorrow."

"Hey, that would be great."

The museum was closed for the season, but Clair led them around to a side door and pounded on it. Through its panes of glass, they watched a figure pop out of an office halfway down a long hallway inside and hurry along to open it for them.

Robert Fitzgerald was a small man with an unruly mop of fuzzy gray hair that stuck out from the sides of his head. The top was bald and shone dully under the light over the door as he stuck his head out.

"Come in. Come on in," he said, peering over a pair of reading glasses. Obviously, he was pleased that someone needed his assistance and expertise.

Clair introduced the three of them, then suggested that, rather than waiting, she and Hampton go on to claim a table for dinner while Jensen asked his questions.

"You won't be long and I'm ready for a sit-down," she smiled. "How about you, Jim?"

"Well . . . considering that I lost my afternoon snack . . ." He grinned sheepishly at Jensen. "It *was* as good a reason to deck someone as any. A competition-sized cinnamon roll that he batted out of my hand and into the street." He followed Clair back through the door into a whirl of snow. "See you later."

"Come back tomorrow, Mr. Hampton," the curator called after him. "I'm sure we can find you a suitable map."

Jensen followed Fitzgerald to his office and sat down on the straight chair the curator offered with a casual wave. The office was remarkably neat, not the clutter he had anticipated from the manager of a museum. He was almost disappointed, as he had imagined it full of artifacts and piled with paper. Chiding himself for prejudgment, he watched as the curator pulled open a drawer and removed a file with a self-satisfied flourish.

"Wilson, you want? Oswald? I know that one all right. One of the few from the gold rush who stayed around afterward. Yes, his family's still here. Bad bunch, then and now, but part of the history."

He sat down and opened the file between them on his

desk. Along with a handful of papers, it contained a photograph of several men on what was obviously a mining claim. They were posed around a sluice box with water running through it, holding shovels and picks, as if they were working.

"Here," he said, pointing to a large man with a full dark beard and a wide-brimmed hat shoved back on his head. Four of the five miners pictured smiled at the photographer, but Wilson's expression was more of a glare. "Oswald Wilson. From the records, people around him tended to disappear. Guy he came with went missing the next spring, 1898."

"So Oswald and Duck Wilson *are* related?"

"Duck . . . real name's Samuel, but . . ."

"Yeah, I heard the story about his nickname."

"Oswald was Duck's father . . . Will's great-grandfather. I hear he's been shot."

Jensen nodded.

"Oswald came to Dawson from Wyoming in 1897 with another man, name of Franklin Warner, who evidently went back where he came from, wherever that was. Wilson stayed."

"Tacoma, Washington."

"What?"

"Warner came from Tacoma, Washington."

"Now, how would you know that?"

Alex described Hampton's find on the Yukon riverbank and its identification of the three men with whom Addison Riser had traveled.

Fitzgerald listened intently, obviously excited at the idea of the discovery. He asked several questions about the bones and, particularly, the journal. Though he shook his head at the name of Riser, he frowned at that of McNeal. "Now that sounds familiar."

For a minute or two, he flipped through the files in two or three drawers, but came up with nothing.

"I know I've heard that name . . . run across it somewhere . . . but I'd have to do some digging to recover it. Sorry. Should remember a fellow Scot. It's not as if there were that many of them here then."

"Well, don't go to a lot of trouble," Alex told him. "It's Wilson I was wondering about and you've solved that particular puzzle for me." He got to his feet. "I'm keeping you from home and dinner. I'd like to see the museum, but I'll come back sometime when I can really enjoy it."

"Just let me know when and I'll give you a private tour." The curator walked him to the door, still ruminating over the Scot's name as Jensen thanked him for his help.

"Anytime at all. I'll think of where I saw McNeal. It's here somewhere. Will you be in town long?"

"A couple of days, I think, but . . ." Alex pulled a card from his wallet and handed it to the much shorter man, who peered at it through his reading glasses. "I'd be glad to know if and when you find it."

"Gladly. And I'd like a look at that journal. Can you get me a copy?"

"Better than that, I think. Del's got the original in his safe. I'll ask him to let you at least take a look and copy it."

On that agreement, they shook hands and Fitzgerald let Alex out into the snowy night.

Chapter Thirteen

JENSEN TRUDGED AWAY FROM THE MU-
seum, making new footprints in the snow that had per-
ceptibly deepened during his time with Fitzgerald. The
blanket of white hushed the world around him so that
every sound seemed softer and far away. For the most
part, the few vehicles and pedestrians he saw moved almost as silently as shadows, except once, when the growl
of a snow machine in low gear crossed a side street ahead
of him and was gone. Houses he passed seemed cozy
refuges in the storm, doors shut tight, windows cheerfully
lighted. He caught glimpses of their inhabitants: a family
seated round a dining table, an old man comfortably relaxed with a newspaper in front of a glowing fireplace, a
cat on a windowsill watching the feathery snowflakes fall.
A television set or two flickered with the strange white
light that makes them hard to miss.

His steps slackened to a saunter as he appreciated the
frosted fantasy of it. Sometime in the first few white days
of every winter he would find himself walking through it
alone, conscious of the world shutting down for the cold
season. The landscape seemed to take a deep breath and
relax into contemplation, readying itself for a few months'
nap. Snow silvered everything, softening shapes and lines.

The last few days had been very full of people and
problems. For a few minutes it was pleasant to walk alone,
without making the effort to speak or answer anyone. He
lit his pipe and went along slowly, stem clenched between

his teeth, hands in his pockets, satisfied to be exactly where he was, pleased with the interesting idea of the relationship between Ozzy and Duck Wilson.

To have met the son of a stampeder, however obnoxious, made the whole rush to the goldfields seem much more real. The journal, interesting as it was, still seemed like a story, almost fiction. Duck's existence made it come to life in a new way. What an old curmudgeon . . . and wasn't that a great word? He wondered where it had come from. Have to look it up in Jessie's enormous dictionary, if he remembered.

Concentrating on the Wilsons, he almost walked past the door of the Downtown Hotel, caught himself, and went up the front steps.

In the dining room, Jim and Clair had settled at a table by a window, where, in warmth and comfort, they could watch the snow fall outside the glass. Their drinks had arrived, but they had waited for him to show up before they chose dinner. When they had all ordered, he sipped slowly at his whiskey, still feeling separate after his solitary walk and disinclined toward conversation. He was perfectly content to listen as Clair answered Hampton's questions about the famous mining country around Dawson, a conversation that lasted through to coffee and dessert.

With Clair on her way home, Jensen walked with Hampton back to their hotel. Though it wasn't late, he realized that a day in the cold air followed by a good dinner was making him drowsy. When they were about thirty yards from the hotel door, a figure in dark clothing came out and turned toward them. Then quickly it reversed direction and walked rapidly away.

The swiftness of the reversal, as if avoiding confrontation, caught Jensen's attention and pricked lightly at the automatic alertness he had developed over years of practiced observation. Following the figure with his eyes, he relaxed and mentally tossed out his suspicion as the individual turned into the bar next door. Yawning for the third time, he stumbled over the top step as they reached the first landing of the stairs. A phone call and sleep were what he wanted, in that order.

Climbing beside him, Hampton seemed more awake. Briefly, Alex wondered about the woman Jim had mentioned a time or two in passing, but was too pleasantly relaxed to ask and risk starting a conversation. Had he called and told her about what had and was happening?

Reaching the top of the stairs, they had turned toward their rooms when Jensen noticed that both the doors were ajar. Knowing he had left his locked, he was suddenly wide awake himself; he stopped and threw an arm in front of Hampton to impede his forward motion.

"Wha . . . ? Hey, I didn't leave that open."

"No. Neither did I. Be quiet and wait here."

Pulling his hands from a search for his key in his jacket pockets, Alex moved quietly toward his door, which was nearest. As he went slowly and carefully down the hall, he regretted, not for the first time, the lack of the .357 Magnum he carried in Alaska but had not been able to bring across the border into Canada without authorization. In this case, it made him feel somewhat naked and vulnerable. Stopping to listen outside, and hearing nothing, he stood to one side and pushed the door open with his knee.

The room was empty, but nothing was the way they had left it. Drawers had been dragged from the chest and upended, mattresses and bedding pulled from the beds, both men's bags emptied and the contents scattered across the floor. He stepped next door to Hampton's room and repeated his listening and opening procedure, with the same results. No one was there, but the room was in chaos.

Bending, he examined the doors in turn. Both had been kicked in, probably with one blow of a heavy boot, for a dark streak remained on his door where the perpetrator's foot had slipped slightly and the frames were both splintered.

"What the hell happened?"

Hampton, sensing from Jensen's reactions that no one was there, had come down the hall to look in over his shoulder. He started angrily toward his room, only to be stopped by Jensen.

"Don't. We need a constable to take fingerprints."

"But . . ."

"Look. Can you step in and, without touching anything, see if you can tell what if anything's been taken?"

"Yeah. But you really think whoever made this mess is going to leave fingerprint evidence?"

"Probably not, but that's the drill, and sometimes we get lucky."

"But a hotel must have a thousand."

"Still . . ."

Hampton reported nothing missing from the general tangle of his few possessions. Jensen, turning slowly to examine his own room, noticed only one thing gone, the copy of Riser's journal, which he had left on the table by his bed. Gingerly he lifted the mattress, the only place he could see that anything could be hidden. Nothing.

Why would someone break in to steal the journal? A copy? Not even the original?

After everything he could do alone, and a quick, careful phone call to the RCMP office, he retreated into the hallway where Hampton, who had taken off his coat and gloves, stood watching. Jensen walked back to the stairs and sat down at the top to wait.

"You going to stay here?"

"Yeah, better watch the place till someone comes with the equipment to check it out."

"I think I'll go down to the pub next door for a beer. That okay?"

"Sure, Jim. I'll come and let you know when they're finished up here, or if we have any questions about your stuff. Here, give me those clean clothes you picked up at the office. I'll put them in your room when they're through."

Hampton nodded, handed him the tidy bundle, and was gone with a thump of boots on wooden steps.

Actually relieved to be alone to think, Jensen settled, leaning an elbow on one knee, chin in his palm. It was irritating to lose access to the room and bed he had been anticipating. However, the shot of adrenaline he had experienced on discovering the break-in had had a stimulating effect, and he was back in the game, wide awake, his mind already turning over possibilities.

Del Delafosse had left a constable, Mel, in charge of the post in his short absence, but he would depend on Alex's careful assessment and conclusions. Besides, he was now alone, not constantly sharing the case. It gave him a sense of autonomy and challenge that had been lacking before and he did not resist it.

Who would want to know what was in the journal enough to risk breaking into the rooms to get it? And why? Was it somehow connected to the murders? What was in the rest of the journal? Now he wanted to read it all, see how it ended. If the present Wilsons were related to the Wilson in Riser's account, did that fact have a connection to the theft? The murders? From the afternoon's encounter with Duck, there seemed to be very little chance of getting information from him, and Will was dead. What about Will's parents? Who and where were they? Why was he with his grandfather? What a tangle.

Okay. Who'd had the opportunity?

Charlie, the kid Hampton had seen with Will on the river, about whom Duck had undoubtedly lied? It seemed he was probably still somewhere in the area, especially if Duck's lies were any indication. He could have slipped in and torn the rooms apart till he found what he wanted, and was it the journal? But why? What reason could there be to his killing either Russell or Wilson? According to Hampton, the kid and Will had tried to kill him. Was it more than the robbery it appeared? Who else?

Duck Wilson? Pretty thin, he thought. Be harder for him to go unnoticed in the hotel. Why would he break in? No reason occurred to Jensen, as he pictured the old man ka-thumping his way up the stairs. Had anyone in town seen him? Questions would have to be asked. Did the journal hook him up to Hampton somehow?

Standing up, he went back to his room and, careful not to leave or destroy prints on the phone, called the desk and asked the clerk to come up. But the man could contribute little when he arrived.

No one had asked for either of the officers or Hampton during the afternoon. He had seen no questionable person go up the stairs. Only those staying at the hotel. But, yes, he had been away from the desk several times during the day. The repair to the faucet in fourteen, twice to the dining room, couple of rest room visits, helping carry down some luggage from the second floor. Every day was like that . . . not all spent in the lobby. Anyone could have come and gone, if they were careful not to be seen. He had not heard the doors being kicked in, but scowled as he examined them without touching. He would give them two other rooms and have the doors repaired tomorrow. Still grumbling over the damage, he disappeared down toward his desk.

Sean Russell had been in town since his appearance in the RCMP office. Alex couldn't think of a reason he would have broken in, or wanted the journal. Did he even know it existed? Would he care? Could he have been looking for information about his father's death? If so, what? There was something about Sean's behavior that made him uneasy, but it was hard to tell with people you didn't know. Their watchful distrust of law enforcement was enough at times to make it seem they were hiding something.

Could taking the journal be a cover for something else? Nothing else appeared to be missing, unless Hampton had lied about his room.

Jensen paused and frowned. Hampton *had* been alone all the while he and Delafosse were on the river. He had *not* stayed in his room as he had indicated he would. He *had* asked for clean clothes after his confrontation with Sean. Could it have been to keep Jensen from going upstairs? To allow more time, widen the window of opportunity? Nothing from his room had been taken, *he said*. He could have done it before he went out to the Visitors Center. Could the fight with Sean Russell have been staged, or at least instigated?

Though his concentration was interrupted by a consta-

ble coming up the stairs with a fingerprint kit, he had one
last, unrelated thought.

They had not searched Hampton's truck when it was
brought back from Clinton Creek.

Chapter Fourteen

⟡⟐⟡ FIFTEEN MINUTES LATER, JENSEN WAS BACK on the snowbound streets of Dawson, heading for the RCMP office where Hampton's pickup had been parked in the lot following its return from Clinton Creek. Leaving the constable to play dippity-dab with his black powder and tape, Alex headed straight across town, long legs covering ground in steps that had no relation to the casual walk he had enjoyed earlier. It had stopped snowing for the moment and the temperature had dropped. He noticed the difference and added to it by creating a windchill in his hurry.

Retrieving keys to the vehicle along with a flashlight from a constable in the office, he walked across to where it was parked at the back of the lot, near a second access gate. In approximately four inches of snow that rose around its tires and covered the body, the pickup looked as if it had hunkered down protectively in the dark, resenting the weather. The snow-blanketed windshield darkened the cab too much for Jensen to see anything inside through the driver's window.

Brushing away flakes with a gloved hand to reveal the slot for the key, he unlocked the door. A small cascade of snow fell from above the door as he opened it, but the interior remained dark as the light that should have blinked on did not. Taking the flashlight from a pocket, he thumbed it on and directed it into the cab.

Someone had been there before him. The seat was partially dusted with snow that had fallen or blown through the wing window, which flopped broken and half missing where that someone had reached through to unlock the door on the passenger side. The glove compartment gapped empty of the contents that had been pawed out onto the floor. The cab, like the hotel rooms, had been thoroughly ransacked: tools, water bottle, maps pulled from behind the seat and dumped in a disorderly pile in the middle of it. The visors both drooped down over the windshield like sleepy eyelids. A forgotten empty Coke can and a set of socket wrenches had been pulled from under the seat. The overhead light had been purposely smashed, scattering fragments over the seat.

Jensen stood still for a long minute or two, assessing the condition of the cab. The pickup had not been moved. He knew it had been refueled when it was brought in from Clinton Creek and now he found that the gas gauge still read full. No hot-wiring effort was obvious. Whoever had broken in had not wanted the truck, but whatever they were looking for in it. What? Who? The same person who had torn apart the hotel rooms seemed likely from the look of it.

Knowing there had been no tracks on the driver's side, Jensen half closed the door gently to keep more snow from avalanching off the cab, and walked around behind the bed, with attention to where he put his feet. Standing beside the rear wheel he could see that the snow on the ground below the passenger window had been disturbed, but long enough ago for new snow to partially fill the tracks. Whoever had broken in had moved around enough to flatten a space perhaps eighteen inches across. From it a series of depressions showed where an individual had come and gone from the street, hidden from the RCMP office window by the body of the truck.

Cautiously, Alex moved to these tracks and knelt beside two that seemed particularly distinct. Gently, he waved a gloved hand above one of the depressions, taking care not to touch, and blew a puff of air directly into it. The new uncompressed snow was light enough for the air to lift most of it from the print, leaving only a thin layer clinging to what had been solidly packed by the weight of the person who made it. Though it was too indistinct to make taking a print for identification worthwhile, Jensen could see the shape of the boot that had made it. It was a type he recognized, often wore himself, with a pointed toe and a riding or bulldogger heel that left a deeper impression than the rest. Western. No boot could have been more familiar to a man who had grown up seeing it every day on the feet of ranchers and cowboys in his home state of Idaho.

After a long look, he moved to the second print, obviously of the opposite foot. There he repeated the procedure and found more clues. The print was clear enough to show what looked like a crack in the sole of the instep on this left foot. The back of both prints indicated wear at the heels, and the toes curved up slightly, as the type tends to do with long wear and poor care. The boots were not new.

With a satisfied grin completely lacking in humor, he stepped back next to the bed of the truck and stood calculating the length of the space between prints, which told him the person who made them had been of average height.

Striding off across the lot, he went to find a constable with a tape measure. As he went through the office door, he was conscious of the whine of a snow machine passing on the side street and grinned to himself. Lovers of winter recreation in Canada were evidently as overjoyed with the first snowfall as they were in Alaska. Several times in the last hour or two, he had heard and seen snow machiners exuberantly zipping through the streets of Dawson.

Interested in what he had found, an RCMP recruit accompanied him back to the truck. Pausing first by the driver's door, Alex showed the young man the chaos of the cab and they talked for a minute of the remote possibility of any recoverable fingerprints. With that, he led the way around the back of the truck once more, and stopped cold as he approached the tracks in the snow.

Beside the singular set of prints, coming and going from the vehicle, was a fresh line of disturbed snow. No individual footprints were apparent, but something had been dragged from the street to the truck. It led to the passenger door, but, except for one short space, did not cover the tracks he had previously examined, almost as if the perpetrator had purposely avoided them.

The two men followed the mark, which continued through the gate and stopped at the street. A piece of a cardboard box lay discarded in the snow next to the obvious tracks where a snow machine had pulled off the street and parked. In the short time he had been inside the office, someone had approached the truck and returned to a snow machine, destroying the evidence of footprints in the retreat with the cardboard.

His absence had allowed a very narrow window of time, only a few minutes. But of course, if whoever it was had been watching him examine the truck and prints, they might have assumed he would not come back. Why would anyone risk being caught this close to the RCMP office? And why had this person been so careful not to obliterate the first set of prints? The quick answer was that it had been a different person, who had wanted the first to be identified while remaining anonymous himself. Coming to the truck and destroying unavoidable footprints that would identify and implicate implied a reason important enough to negate the risk of discovery. That reason had to be significant.

Jensen stood for a minute, looking up and down the street, though he was sure the snow machine and its rider were long gone, remembering the whine of the engine he had heard as he went into the office earlier. The street *was* empty, but as he looked the way he thought the sound had gone, he thought he saw something move in the shadow of a spruce a hundred yards away. For a few seconds he gave it close attention, but the suggestion of motion was not repeated. When the lights of a passing car showed only the shape of the tree itself and nothing resembling a human figure, he let it go and turned back to the puzzles at hand.

Slowly, he traced the track back to the truck, followed silently by the recruit, who seemed hesitant to interrupt the American officer's concentration, but was carefully watching every move he made. Good lad, thought Alex, and was immediately amused at the Canadian phrasing of his thought.

With keys for two new rooms, Alex quickly climbed to the third floor and turned toward the old ones that the constable he had passed on the stairs had assured him were completely photographed and fingerprinted. As he neared the doorway of the one that had been his, a small sound from within arrested his forward motion. Another shadowy figure? The light was on, but had the thief returned? Cautiously, he leaned around the door frame to take a quick look.

"Did a thorough job, didn't they?" Delafosse commented, looking up from where he was retrieving and refolding his scattered clothes.

"Hey, Del. Thought you were going to be gone till tomorrow."

"Planned to, but the weather report says there's more snow on the way that could have grounded me in Whitehorse for an extra day or two. So I took advantage of a short break in the storm to hightail it back up here. We just made it. Pilot wasn't too happy to be flying at all and isn't going to be able to get back out of here tonight. Anything missing from this mess?"

"Just that copy of the journal you gave me, unless you've got something else gone. Hampton says all his stuff is accounted for. But you'll be interested in what else I found tonight."

While they cleared up the confusion of their belongings, Jensen detailed what he had discovered in and around Hampton's truck, including the obscured track.

Though Delafosse frowned, he also nodded thoughtfully at this revelation, took several printed pages from a pocket, and handed them to Jensen. "Here. The coroner's report on Warren Russell, and it is strange, to say the least."

The trooper righted an overturned chair and sat down to read it.

The first page of the coroner's report of the autopsy on Warren Russell was pretty much as he expected it to be. He flipped to page two, where the information was mainly about the head wound that had caused Russell's death. Halfway down the page he found what had concerned Delafosse. Russell had indeed been blasted with the shotgun, but the evidence from the autopsy indicated that before that he had been hit with something else, something sharp and heavy enough to penetrate the skull. Beneath the destruction caused by the gun was the shape of what the coroner speculated was most likely an ax or hatchet.

"Damn. So a hatchet was used to kill him. Hampton's? Explains its not showing up." He looked quizzically at Delafosse, who was appreciating his reaction from a seat on the mattress he had lifted back onto the bed frame.

"Well . . . don't assume. Interesting, yes?"

"Doesn't make a lot of sense yet."

"Read on."

First Jensen turned back to the front page to find the time of death. Allowing for the cold temperatures of the night of Tuesday, September 7, Russell had died sometime between noon and four o'clock in the afternoon.

Back on page two, he found even more confusing and conflicting evidence. Incredibly, both the shotgun blast and the blow from the hatchet-shaped thing had been declared postmortem. A blow *had* been the cause, but not the *hatchet* blow. During the autopsy, hidden in the hair, the coroner had located a bruise and resulting hematoma on the front right side of Russell's brain, the side opposite the shotgun damage, indicating that the blow had been a result of the trauma of his head hitting something, not something hitting his head. The skull was fractured, but split, not depressed as it should be if Russell had been hit *with* something.

Jensen knew that the brain's protection is the liquid surrounding it inside the bony sheath of the skull. When the cranium *hits* something, the force throws the brain to the side of the skull farthest from the impact, causing what is called a "contracoup" bruise or injury on that opposite side. On the other hand, when the head is hit *with* something, it causes what is called a "coup" bruise on the surface of the brain immediately nearest the impact. Though an impact of either kind is not necessarily, or even usually, fatal, Russell's had been and he had evidently died before either of the other external wounds had been made. Whoever made them must have known that for they had been made quite some time after Russell was dead.

Jensen frowned and leaned back against the bed frame, staring at the ceiling in thought.

"If Russell was already dead, there wouldn't have been much blood from the shotgun blast, which accounts for our not finding it. But then, why shoot him at all? To cover the hatchet blow? But why? And why hit him with the hatchet? What did he hit his head on? Did he fall somehow? Did whoever killed him push him? What the hell?"

He laid down the report and sat, thinking hard, trying to make sense of what he had just read in terms of what they had seen and found in both locations on the river.

"Three distinctly different head injuries, Del? One on top of the other? Any one of them almost certainly fatal. Whoever hit him with the hatchet and whoever used the shotgun—if it was the same person—had to know he was already dead from whatever his head hit to begin with. The only thing that works at all is a cover-up, but why cover up something that could easily be viewed as accidental death, even if it wasn't. And why inflict a second cover wound with the shotgun, over the hatchet blow? Either or both would be evidence of violence."

"Where is the hatchet? Why leave the shotgun and get rid of, or carry away, the hatchet?" Delafosse mused. "And why? To frame Hampton? Who had the opportunity, for that and for the break-in here and at the truck? The same person?"

"Well, who've we got? Unless he's slicker than I think he is, I can't imagine Hampton leaving evidence pointing to himself, but he had the chance at the rooms, with us gone up to Wilson's, and could have gone to the truck— though why trash his own truck?—with me busy here.

"Those tracks in the snow are confusing, and probably meant to be. Either one person made them . . . but then why not wipe out both sets? Didn't want it known they came back again? Why come back? Or a second, different person was satisfied to point suspicion at the first, while wiping out their own prints.

"We don't know where Charlie is—whoever Charlie is—but if he killed Russell, he could have wanted badly to implicate Hampton. He could have done any or all of it, but I don't understand why he would want the journal copy.

"What about Sean Russell? And how about the boot prints by the truck? I haven't seen Hampton wearing western boots, and we don't know about Charlie. Was Sean?"

"Don't remember, Alex. But I'm beginning to wonder if he *was* downriver, as he says he can prove. The constable I sent called from Eagle to say he couldn't locate the native man Sean says can give him an alibi. He wasn't at the village, or in Eagle."

"So, that's three possibles and a whole pile of unexplained details. We're collecting suspects like flies. Got any more you want to throw in? Who's next?"

A knock on the door brought an immediate answer to the factitious question.

Chapter Fifteen

‹❦❧› OPENING THE DOOR, DELAFOSSE FOUND THE constable he had sent down the river. Looking half frozen, the younger man stood looking in, snow still clinging to his hat and the shoulders of his coat from his walk to the hotel. With him were two native men, both dressed for cold weather in heavy boots and down jackets.

The older man was shorter than anyone in the room, probably in his fifties, though it was difficult to tell, as his face, now watchful and serious, held the lines of a lifetime of the weathering effects of outdoor living. His son was slightly taller and had his father's dark, intelligent eyes. He seemed more nervous than his father, who maintained an impressive outward dignity and calm.

"Henry," Delafosse greeted the older of the two with pleased surprise. "Come in. Take off your coats and get warm. Alex, this is Henry Kabanak, leader of the local Han Athabaskan tribal council, and his son, Henry junior. Sergeant Jensen is a trooper from Anchorage, Henry." As Jensen stepped forward to shake hands, he turned to his constable, "Bill. You find something?"

"Yes. More than you expected, I guess. On the way back from Eagle, when I stopped to talk to Mr. Kabanak, he was pulling a deflated Zodiac out of the river near his fish wheel. I think it may be the one you're looking for. Let him tell you."

Delafosse swung around, eyes wide, to Henry Kabanak, who nodded. Neither of the native men had removed his coat, and they stood, somewhat stiffly, waiting for the inspector's reaction.

"Please," he said. "Sit down. I will listen."

They nodded and lowered themselves into the room's two chairs as he offered them, but only unzipped their coats. Alex leaned against the windowsill. Delafosse sat down on one of the beds.

"Bill, would you phone down for some coffee? I can see you're all cold. Ask for some brandy while you're at it. You look like you could use it and even the Royal Navy gets its tot of rum. Now, what happened, Mr. Kabanak? What did you find?"

"The Zodiac boat. As he says, I pulled it out by my fish wheel, where someone had cut it to let the air out, then sunk it with rocks."

"You know Mr. Russell is dead?"

"Yes, your constable told us."

"Did you see him this week, Henry?"

"Once in his boat, but not to talk."

"When?"

He shrugged. "Monday? Noon? After noon? Early sometime," he said vaguely.

"Tell me about the Zodiac."

"Nothing to tell. I saw something dark in the water and pulled it out."

"I got there just as he was getting it into his boat, Inspector," the young constable said. "I can vouch for where it came from."

"Good, and I remember where his wheel is."

Silence hung in the room for a second or two. Delafosse looked down at the carpet, thinking hard. When he looked back up, he was frowning. He shook his head, but spoke straight to Kabanak, though Jensen could tell he respected him and didn't like to do it.

"I *must* ask this, Mr. Kabanak. Did you put it there? Do you know who did? You have been known to say bad things about Mr. Russell. Did you, or anyone you know, have anything to do with his death?"

The eyes of the Athabaskan leader narrowed as he stared at Delafosse without answering. Then he made a sound in the back of his throat that conveyed, better than words, several feelings at once. Resignation was among them, as was a thread of contempt and confirmation, both mixed with disappointment and some anger. When he spoke, his eyes were cold, sad, and full of pride.

"And I *must* answer you. I have said bad things about Mr. Russell. Yes. I would say them again. He was a fool, with foolish ideas about the way my people should live. But I did not kill him and hide the boat, whatever it has to do with his death. And I do not know anyone who did, or who knows about it. The rubber boat was there, where someone had put it, near my fish wheel. I pulled it out. That is all."

"Did you see anyone in such a boat on the river Monday?"

"I don't remember. There are several Zodiacs used by my people and others. There may have been one or more on Monday, or it may have been Sunday, or Tuesday. I come and go from my wheel less than I did when the fish ran heavy in July and pay less attention. Who can remember?"

Another knock on the door announced the coffee and brandy. The constable poured for them all, though Alex refused and lit his pipe instead. He was aware that the confrontation was almost painfully formal and difficult for everyone involved, and was not unimpressed with Delafosse's handling of it, noting that the inspector left the traditional, polite native silences after each of his questions and did not press for answers. Both native men accepted brandy with their coffee, though the young Athabaskan gave his father a searching look before taking the mug of hot liquid. They sipped in silence for a minute before the conversation resumed. Alex noticed that Delafosse waited, patiently, for Kabanak to speak first.

"You have some reason to think Russell's death was caused by one of my people?"

"No. Your finding the boat makes it necessary for me to ask you these hard questions. But we are already watching three other men, all white. But you and Russell were not friendly . . . had threatened each other and spoken in anger in the past. If you had been killed, I would now be asking him, if he found a similar boat.''

Kabanak nodded his understanding without speaking, though he did not seem fully convinced. Jensen thought, not for the first time since coming to live in the north, that it was unfortunate there was no one standard of behavior for everyone. No matter how evenhanded the law was supposed to be, and usually tried to be, suspicion of offense was much more likely when the suspect was non-white. The Athabaskan leader's disgust was come by honestly and he was right not to trust easily.

Del was trying hard to avoid making unfair judgments and to give the benefit of the doubt. But Jensen knew that some natives, and others, were smart and quick enough to use that very reluctance to allow prejudice to be a shield for their misdeeds. He did not know Kabanak. Was he one of them? Could his half smile have more meaning than it seemed to? The chief could be hiding a lot behind his impassive face. He was answering the questions he was asked, but volunteering little else. Something about the way he sat and spoke gave Alex the feeling he wasn't telling all he knew . . . keeping something back. What? His refusal or inability to remember when he saw the Zodiac seemed out of character. Jensen shifted slightly on his windowsill perch, and returned his attention to the conversation, which was ending with the two native men setting aside their cups and standing to shake hands with the inspector.

"I will wait to hear from you," Del was telling Kabanak. "We will let you know if we find out who was involved in these murders."

Kabanak hesitated. "Murders? More than one?"

"Duck Wilson's grandson, Will, is also dead."

The two Indians glanced at each other and the son's eyes narrowed, with concern or fear, when Kabanak nodded to him. "Tell him what you saw on the river."

The young man spoke quietly, but with assurance.

"I saw that one on the river on Monday, in a boat I did not recognize, with blue plastic over something in the back. He was driving it recklessly in the river with two men that I did not see clearly, but I knew that Wilson. Mean.''

''What time, exactly?''

''I don't know. Sometime after noon. They came by going too fast and threw a couple of beer cans in the river as they passed. They did not notice me. They were laughing and shouting about something I couldn't hear.''

''Three men?''

''Yes.''

''You're sure there were three? Not two?''

''Does it matter?''

''It might. Would you swear there were three?''

He hesitated. ''I . . . no, I could not swear. They went by very fast and the glare from the water was in my eyes.''

Delafosse held out a hand. ''Thank you.''

He shook hands again with Kabanak.

They left with the constable, who would make sure they got home.

''Jesus! What the hell is this turning into?''

''Well,'' Alex grinned, in an attempt to lighten the atmosphere, ''it seems almost complete. I was waiting for an Indian. We have most of the rest, don't we?'' He quoted, ''Rich man—Russell . . . poor man—his son, Sean . . . beggar man—Duck Wilson beggars the imagination . . . thief—Will and Charlie . . . doctor—I'll throw in the coroner . . . lawyer—well . . . The Indian chief we just got. If we stretch it and look at everyone involved, I guess we still need the lawyer . . . or, hopefully, someone will.''

Delafosse groaned. ''If an attorney walked in and *confessed*, I think I'd resign, Indian or no Indian. I really hated putting Kabanak through that kind of questioning.''

''Could he have done it? He . . . they . . . certainly have motive over the subsistence thing.''

Delafosse emptied his coffee cup and set it back on the room-service tray. ''I don't think . . .''

''Might have been the last straw, having Russell fishing on the Canadian Yukon one more time. He certainly saw the boat—described it down to the blue cover in the back.''

''Possible, I suppose, but I can't really take it seriously. He's well respected and has too much to lose, for himself *and* his people. Charlie, now. Him and Will I can take seriously. Interesting, though, that the stolen Zodiac from Eagle shows up on this part of the river. Says that Sean Russell could have come up in it, do you think?''

''Says also that Hampton couldn't have had anything to do with the inflatable. Not humanly possible. Eagle's a long ways away down the river.''

''Right. Where *is* Hampton, by the way?''

''In the bar next door. I told him I'd let him know when we were through up here, so I'd better go down.''

''Well, wait for me. I'll go with you, get out of this mess for a while and finish it later.''

''Can you wait ten minutes? I haven't called Jessie yet and it's getting late.''

''Sure.'' Delafosse sat down and unfolded the coroner's report again as Alex went to the phone, eager to be in touch with Jessie Arnold. Before he dialed the number, he turned to Del for one last comment. ''You didn't ask Henry junior where *he* was when he saw the men in the boat.''

Chapter Sixteen

⟨⟨ornament⟩⟩ THE PHONE RANG ONLY TWICE BEFORE IT
was picked up in Knik.

"Hello."

Expecting Jessie, Jensen was startled for a moment by
the male voice.

"Hello?"

"Ah . . . Ryan?"

"Yeah. Who . . . Alex?"

"Yes. Is Jessie there?"

"She went out to check on Sadie and the new pups.
Be right back. Hey, how's Dawson? Heard on the news
that you guys are catching snow too."

"Oh? Yeah. Snow."

Alex could feel his whole body stiffen in resentment
and confusion. In thirty seconds he had gone from a warm
anticipation of Jessie's voice to a jolt of unjustifiable jealousy that shamed and turned him cold.

Del, flipping through the pages of the report across the
room, looked up with a startled expression at the tone of
his voice, a question in the lift of his eyebrows.

A door slammed in the background on the other end of
the phone line.

"Hold on," Ryan said. "Here's Jess."

Jess? Jess was his own affectionate shortening of her
name, and Ryan's use of it somehow gave a tone of jus-
tification to his flash of hurt and anger. Wait now, he told

141

himself . . . slow down . . . take a deep breath . . . count to
ten . . . all the clichés for "watch out."

He hardly heard the receiver change hands, bringing her
bright voice and quick breathing into his ear.

"Alex? Are you psychic? How do you always know
when I'm outside, near enough to hear the phone, far
enough to have to run to get it?

"I was just taking a final peek at Sadie and the kids.
Oh, you're going to love these pups, Alex. They're good
ones, every one. Not a runt among 'em. They'll all make
runners, a leader or two maybe, with Tank for a father.

"How are you, love? Any closer to a solution?"

Her flood of words gave him a chance to regroup a
little, but his voice was still a croak. "Fine. I'm fine. . . .
How're you?"

"Great! What a day of running! We caught a foot of
snow last night and went over halfway to Susitna and
back on the old Iditarod Trail today. God, I love the first
run of the season with a fresh team. Makes me wonder
how I got through the summer without snow. The mutts
were like little kids—and I wasn't much better, as I'm
sure you can tell. Babble, babble. I'll shut up. What's
going on in the Canadian wilds?"

"Ah . . ." He swallowed a lump and forced himself to
reply. "Same old stuff. Hunting bad guys," he said, with
forced enthusiasm. "Nothing half as great as first runs"—
a hesitation, then he heard himself say helplessly—"with
Ryan."

For a long moment there was complete silence on her
end of the phone, while he felt like an idiot. Damn! Damn
and damn!

When she spoke, her voice held a painful stillness.

"Alex?"

"Yes?"

Pause. "Did I hear that right?"

Misery, mixed with irritation. He could hang up now.
Just hang up and it would go away. She would go away.
It could get worse. He drew a deep breath, "Yeah. I'm
sorry, I . . ."

"Wait. Hold on."

Listening closely, he heard her tell—not ask—tell Ryan to go water the dogs—that he knew had been watered hours ago—*all* the dogs. *Please*!

"Alex," she said, quietly a minute later, "that wasn't fair. I feel like we just had a six point five on the Richter scale. Not enough to bring down the house, but enough to shake us up pretty good. Where did that come from? Can you tell me?"

He looked up at the sound of the door closing behind Delafosse.

"No . . . well . . ." Where *had* it come from? Why hadn't he kept his damned mouth shut. "I'm not sure."

"But it's there. Right?"

"Yeah, but . . ."

"No buts. Honesty. Can we figure it out? Did I do something? Not do something?"

"No." Not to welcome Ryan as her friend and fellow musher wouldn't have been the answer, to insist he stay elsewhere. These professional sled-dog racers took care of each other. Hospitality was taken for granted, single or not. In fact, most of bush Alaska was that way.

"Sorry."

"If you're jealous, it's fear, Alex. How can you be afraid? I'm not going anywhere, you know. I wouldn't intentionally hurt you, but I can't live hostage to that kind of unfounded fear. I know what it's like and I won't."

She had put a courageous finger precisely on a nerve. Yes . . . well. Afraid? Of what? Not that she was a friend of Ryan's. It hadn't much to do with Ryan, actually, or Jessie either, had it?

Suddenly, for the first time in a long while, he thought of Sally and realized, with the thought, how long it had been since the last time he remembered her. Until he had met Jessie last spring, Sally had been regularly in his mind. After eight years, he had still felt cheated by her death.

Now, with the thought of her, he recognized that he was afraid of Jessie leaving, too. Had been since the first.

And he was . . . was beginning to want something more permanent with her, though not yet ready to suggest marriage. He had a feeling she would probably refuse to consider it yet.

Yet? Damn it, just listen to yourself, he thought, as if with the idea of it he had suddenly found himself on his knees with a ring in his hand. However . . .

She was waiting, quiet as an Athabaskan, for him to speak first.

"Can you forget it?" he asked her.

"No. Can you?"

"No, you're right. But I know where it came from."

"Do you?"

"Sally."

"Ah-h. I think I see part of it."

"We can talk about it when I get home, if you're okay with that."

"Okay, if you are, but we will need to talk it out. And . . ." She hesitated.

"What?"

"Alex. I am *not* sleeping with Ryan."

"It's not the point . . . doesn't matter."

"It's not exactly what you're focused on right now. It does matter, but it's just another subject we haven't got clear. You guys tend to get unrealistic ideas in your heads, I think."

They talked for another ten minutes, reestablishing themselves with each other, before Jessie said, with a smile he could hear in her voice, "We'd better stop. If I don't tell Ryan to come back in, he'll freeze. He's probably crawled in with Sadie by now."

Alex agreed, chuckling at the image of the long-legged musher curled up in the doghouse Jessie used as a puppy nursery, insulated and heated with a light bulb. "Don't tell him I was . . . stupid, okay? No need to make him uncomfortable."

"I won't. Love you, trooper."

"And I, you. A lot, Jess."

"Well, get the damned case solved then, and come on home, or *I'll* be bunking with Sadie for company, if not warmth."

Chapter Seventeen

꘏꘏꘏꘏꘏ DELAFOSSE KNOCKED BEFORE HE OPENED the door and stuck his head in to see if Jensen was still on the telephone and he should go away again, but his face held a confused irritation as well as concern.

"Storm warning's canceled," Alex told him. "Sorry about that."

"Need an ear?"

"No. I just got a little torqued and made an assumption or two that were out of line. It's okay. Jessie, thank God, takes her time coming to a boil."

"Good. I won't ask over what. Listen. Which bar did you say Hampton was headed for? I looked here and next door, and couldn't find him either place."

"Did you ask?"

"Here, not there. Bartender's on a break. I also got sidetracked by Sean Russell, who stopped me on the boardwalk outside the hotel to make a few more demands. He evidently saw Kabanak and his son leaving here, and is now convinced the Hans are somehow connected to Russell's death, but doesn't like accusing his friends. He'd had more than a couple of beers and was pretty upset. Kept saying he should have at least tried not to get into arguments with his old man, even if they didn't agree. The fight they evidently had when he saw the old man last is tearing at him some. Says he's going to stay in Dawson till he gets what he wants—his father's body or somebody's arrest, or both."

"You ask him about attacking Hampton?"

"Yes. He's mad and upset about that too. Wouldn't say much, but I told him what he would be up against if he tried anything like it again. He's getting to be a real pain."

"Well, guilt or guilty, let's go track down Hampton. He said next door. Maybe you missed him in the men's room."

Snow was falling hard on Dawson, making it look straight out of the gold rush. False fronts on most of the buildings were reminders of shapes commonly constructed a hundred years earlier. The few figures that hurried between doorways could have been frozen miners. Seen through the veil of flakes, their modern clothing was not apparent and the silence of their steps, muffled in the inch or two of white carpeting the wooden walkways and unpaved streets, gave them a ghostlike unreality. Alex thought that all it needed was a rinky-dink piano and some rowdy Klondikers spilling nuggets or gold dust on some bar to complete the illusion.

Opening the door of yet another saloon, a block from the hotel, supplied the piano and a rousing rendition of "A Bird in a Gilded Cage," but no sign of Jim Hampton, though they hunted through every pub in town. Returning to the bar next door to the hotel, they went in, stomping the snow off their boots and shaking it from their jackets and hats. The bartender, returned from his break, met them with conspicuous politeness at the end of the long bar near the door, distinctly aware he was in the presence of the law.

"Help you . . . gentlemen?"

Delafosse described Hampton, a skill he had perfected in the last half hour.

"Oh, the canoe guy from Colorado."

"He *was* here?"

"Drank one Bud, then they left."

"They?"

"Yeah. He and that grubby city kid, the one that was around with Wilson before . . . well . . ."

"Charlie?"

"Never got his name. They talked, sort of growled at each other for a minute or two, your guy wrote a check for the beers, and they left."

Jensen frowned. "Check? Personal?"

"Traveler's."

"He had cash at dinner. Let's see it."

The bartender rummaged in the drawer under his till and finally fished it out and laid it on the bar between them. Fifty dollars, signed by James Hampton, dated in Dawson, Yukon Territory. Alex turned it over to find something scrawled across the back. In the poor light, it was hard to read. The bartender handed Jensen a small flashlight, retrieved from somewhere below the bar.

"Charlie—the kid!" it read.

The officers looked at each other, then at the bartender.

"Better keep it," Delafosse said, pocketing the paper rectangle.

"Hey, that's fifty dollars you're walking away with. The boss'll take it out of my pay."

The inspector wrote a quick receipt on a page from his notebook, while Jensen asked a few more questions.

"Any idea where they went?"

"Nope. Didn't say anything. Just wrote the check."

"The city kid say anything?"

"Huh-uh. Looked like somebody worked him over pretty good. Eye going black, nose had been bloody. But for that matter, the canoeist looked like he'd gone a round or two with somebody. I got the feeling he wasn't too happy about the kid showing up, or leaving with him either, but he said it was okay when I kind of let him know, you know, subtle-like, that he had help if he wanted it. Just shrugged and pointed at the check. Hey! Maybe he knew you'd be in looking for him?"

"Maybe. How long ago'd they leave?"

"Better part of an hour, maybe more."

A constable Delafosse had sent to check on Hampton's truck caught up with them on the steps of the hotel, where they had paused to consider their next move. It was still snowing heavily, covering everything in sight with several inches of clear and lovely white, so thick in the air that it all but hid buildings just across the street. Streetlights were vague glows in the distance.

"It's gone," he said, breathless from hurrying, "and not long ago, because there's not much snow over the bare ground where it was parked before the storm started again."

"Where the hell would Hampton have gone with Charlie?" Delafosse wondered aloud. "Doesn't seem like he would have willingly gone off with the guy he says held him up and tried to kill him on the river."

Jensen kicked reluctantly at the small drift that was building up along the edge of the boardwalk. "Maybe he did or didn't go willingly. But Will was the one he said shot at him, not Charlie, and Kabanak's son *did* say once that he saw *three* men in the boat."

"You mean he's been having us on, all this time?"

"I don't know, but it sure looks questionable, doesn't it?"

"Yes. Very. If they were in it together, a lot of things about the whole thing would make more sense." He turned to the constable, still waiting for his instructions.

"Call Carmacks and let Johnson know to watch for that truck headed for Whitehorse. They have to go through there if they've gone south. No, damn it. They could take the Campbell Highway to a couple of kilometers before Carmacks, but it's two hundred and twenty-five kilometers to Ross River, and another three hundred and seventy to the Watson Lake junction with the Alaska Highway, with no way off on the full length of the road. Have Johnson get up to the Campbell turnoff. If they're going either way he can stop them there."

"Could they possibly have gone north?" Alex ventured. "Over the Top of the World?"

Astounded, Del swung to face him. "Not a chance. It'll be howling a blizzard up there. No one would even entertain the fantasy. Not in a hundred years, on that road. Some spots are so exposed I swear you could fall for minutes at a time, down thousands of feet, before anything got in your way. And when it blows, like it has to be blowing now, there are places you can't see even a suggestion of the road, or any of the drops, for that matter.''

"Does either Charlie or Jim Hampton know that? It's a road on a map to outsiders, isn't it?''

The inspector's expression grew troubled. *"Merde."* He swore in French only when his emotional state was extreme, as it was just then, in a combination of irritation and concern. "You're right, or course. We'll have to check it out. But, no . . . they'd have to cross the river first, and the ferry's closed for the duration . . . or should be . . . but I suppose . . . Damn it, Jensen. Come on.''

Even with his longer legs, the trooper had to practically sprint to keep up with Delafosse, as he headed for his truck at the RCMP office. Once inside, windshield wipers thrashing on high speed to swipe the snow from in front of their faces, the inspector headed directly for the ferry dock, on the riverbank east of town.

Alex recognized the shape of the steamboat *Keno* through the falling snow as they quickly passed it. One of a fleet that had played an important part in opening the Klondike, it was similar to those that transported gold, silver, lead, and zinc from the mining country during and after the gold rush. Another thing he wanted to have time to thoroughly explore.

At the river, they got out of the cab and stood staring into the curtain of white. At the bottom of a gently sloping gravel ramp, where the ferry should have been securely tied up, was an emptiness. Barely visible, rapidly being obscured by the falling snow, were parallel tire tracks, leading directly to where the small ferry should have been. It was impossible to see across to the far side of the river.

The inspector now swore profusely in his second language. Jensen wasn't disappointed not to understand all Delafosse had to say concerning tourists, murder investigations, the Yukon River, snowstorms, and how late it was. He ended his volley of invective by kicking the tire of his pickup, but had the grace to look a little embarrassed when he noticed Jensen's grin.

Back in the truck, they drove to the RCMP office, where Jensen called the Alaska State Troopers in Tok, to let them know someone was attempting to cross what was currently and without a doubt the most dangerous highway between Canada and Alaska, though there was little chance they would make it. Delafosse put on a pot of coffee and they set about making a reasonable game plan.

"We can't go after them until it stops snowing . . . tomorrow morning at the earliest. I think our best bet is to get in the air with a helicopter as soon as it clears and find out where they've gone off the road, as they certainly will. Then we can decide how to reach them . . . take the big plow truck, or snow machines, depending on the circumstances and distance."

"Hampton's from Colorado. He'll be used to driving in snow. They may get farther than you think."

"That's true, and his driving ability may be the only thing that saves them a lot of grief. But that Charlie is a Californian, who has probably no more than heard a rumor of snow a time or two in his whole life. He'll think it'll be like it was here before they left . . . have no idea what a real blizzard can be. I hope they *don't* make it far. After they climb the first hills, for a long ways it's pretty flat and all they could do is slide off into a drift. After that, if they get out along the ridges, it'll turn really mean, windchill will be more than I'd want to risk.

"If Hampton's driving, which is the only thing that makes sense, if he didn't go willingly, as you suggested, and the city kid hijacked him *and* his truck, he may have the smarts to sort of accidentally-on-purpose put his rig in the ditch and wait to be found."

"But he won't know we've figured out where they are."

"True."

The door opening put an end to their speculations for the moment.

Jensen did not immediately recognize the woman standing just inside the door, which closed itself behind her. If it had not been for the too large, tattered, red jacket that he had seen briefly that afternoon, he might not have known it was Cherlyn Wilson, Will's wife, from up the river. She once again clutched the jacket around her thin body, with fingers blue from the cold, cradling an arm against her body. Her ragged tennis shoes and denim pants with the hole in one knee were familiar, but her face was beyond identification without careful scrutiny. Swollen and bruised around the cheeks, her lower lip oozing a little blood from a split clearly caused by some blow, she stood looking in at the two officers through eyes puffed half shut.

"*Mon Dieu*," Delafosse exclaimed, it definitely being his night for French, and Alex came swiftly to his feet at the sight of her. Drawing her quickly into the warmth of the office, they sat her down close to the light to examine her injuries. His lips tight with anger, the inspector asked her assailant's identity. "Duck Wilson?"

She nodded wearily, tears escaping to run down her ruined face, but there was no mistaking the fury in her voice and the slits that were her eyes when she mumbled her response past the damaged lower lip. "Old bastard's mad about Will. Took it out on me . . . son of a bitch."

"How'd you get here?"

". . . drank himself to sleep . . . took his boat . . . 'll miss it tomorrow."

Motioning Jensen to care for the girl, Delafosse stepped to the phone. In quick succession he called a local doctor—"That lip's going to need a stitch or two, I think"—and Clair McSpadden—"Please, Clair, I need your help."

They arrived at almost the same time, no more than a quarterhour later. Clair had plainly been roused from sleep, for her tousled auburn hair was piled haphazardly atop her head, wisps and tendrils escaping a hasty pinning. Jensen caught the appreciative look on Del's face at the sight of her, and smiled to himself, but she was all business and concern for Cherlyn, who, it seemed, she already knew.

"Men," she stated tersely, with an arm around the younger woman's shoulders, while the doctor examined the split lip and bruises. "Especially dirty old ones."

"You do need some repair on your lip to avoid a scar," the doctor acknowledged, ignoring the slur on his sex.

"And I want to X-ray that arm. Let's get you over to my office."

Cherlyn straightened in the chair and looked up at Delafosse.

"Got to tell you first," she said. "Something funny about Duck and Charlie."

"Charlie? The kid that was with Will?"

"Yeah, Duck kicked him out . . . this afternoon . . . beat him up good. Duck knows all about Will getting shot. I think he did it . . . or Charlie."

The doctor interrupted, frowning. "Can't this wait? I'd like to get started on this before it swells any more. She needs some medication for pain; that's got to hurt a lot the more it warms up."

Delafosse started to nod, but Cherlyn shook her head stubbornly.

"*No.* Got to tell you. Think I'm going to be really sick and you've got to know . . . *now*. This time I want you to get him."

"Okay. Okay. But make it short. Then we'll fix you up and find you a place to stay."

"She's coming home with me," Clair said, in a tone that would brook no argument, but with an anxious glance at their medical authority. "If the doc'll let her."

He frowned, then nodded. "Probably."

"Good."

Delafosse pulled another chair up close and glanced at Jensen, who was ready to take notes. "Now, tell me just what you need to, Cherlyn. We'll take care of Duck Wilson. You don't need to worry about that, if you'll sign a complaint."

She nodded slightly and told him the rest. From her sentence fragments and interpretation from the inspector, the information was quite rapidly given and recorded.

". . . said if I told anybody, he'd get me. Will and Charlie . . . working for someone in Whitehorse . . . stealing trucks and campers. Someone got hurt . . . died. Came home to hide out."

Del glanced again at Alex. "You were right."

"Charlie came after you were there . . . afternoon. Said

something about some bones. . . . Duck beat him up . . . said to get the tourist to tell where he found them. Something about the bones . . . made him crazy mad. Somebody stole his father's gold and Duck wants it back. . . . ''

"Father? Whose father?" Jensen interjected a question.

"Duck's . . . Ozzy . . . in the gold rush."

"Oswald Wilson again," he murmured.

"Don't know . . . whole family . . . looking for years. Some journal . . . he wanted Charlie to find out about. Lot of gold . . . somewhere."

"The break-in at the hotel, Del?"

"Has to be. Where's Charlie, Cherlyn? Do you know?"

She shrugged and shook her head. "Somewhere in town, I guess. Went after the tourist . . . like Duck said. Mad . . . though. Said looking for hundred-year-old gold was nuts . . . he was getting out of this damn icebox . . . may have gone. Don't know."

"Do you know for sure that Duck shot Will?"

"No . . . Knows something about it. Charlie too."

She was visibly slumping in the chair with exhaustion and pain.

"That's enough. Anything else can wait till morning. Right?"

The doctor began to help her up, when Jensen stepped in and carefully lifted her. "Where's your car, Doc? I'll put her in it."

"I'll be right behind you. She can stay at my place. No one, even Duck, would think of looking there, or would get around the shotgun my father taught me to use." Clair followed them out the door and in minutes they were gone, leaving only Delafosse and Jensen at the office to sort out the information Cherlyn Wilson had insisted on giving them.

"Nothing weak about that one, is there?" Jensen commented, as they sat back down with fresh coffee.

"Yes. She'll use that shotgun, too, if she has to."

"I meant Cherlyn, Del." Alex grinned, but refrained from the obvious comment. "How did she *ever* wind up

married to Will? And is everyone in Dawson getting beat
up tonight? What is it? A full moon?''

"I don't even want to know. I've no idea how Cherlyn
and Will got together, but it was a distinct mistake. Clair
met her a year or so ago, when she was in town for some
reason, and has worried ever since about her being out
there all alone with Duck and his shadow of an old
woman, with Will in jail. Not that he made anything but
trouble when he was at home, but the old man likes to
hit on, or just hit, whoever's handy, as you could see. I'll
send someone out to bring him in tomorrow. Like to get
a whack at him myself, the old buzzard."

"Somehow I just can't think that Duck would shoot his
grandson. Charlie may answer several questions for us,
when we catch up with him."

"Well, at least we get a break on the vehicle theft. Get
Charlie and we can put some pressure on to find out who's
running the thing out of Whitehorse. At least we know
where Charlie is, don't we?"

"Oh, yes. Totally out of reach for the moment. I hope
Hampton's okay. It's going to get cold up there tonight.
Miserable place to be stuck, and they are surely stuck by
now."

Chapter Eighteen

HAMPTON AND CHARLIE WERE NOT STUCK, but would be in a very short time. For the moment, they were still in motion on the Top of the World Highway, headed west toward Alaska at a slow speed, in the middle of one of the worst blizzards Hampton had ever experienced.

He was driving, or attempting to. Though the windshield wipers were going full speed, they scarcely made a difference in the snow that seemed to come from every direction at once as the wind whipped across the stark, treeless hills beyond the beams of the truck's headlights. It was growing darker, deeper, and colder by the minute. Earlier, when the storm paused now and then to draw breath, he had seen glimpses of nothing but endless white drifts in an empty landscape that sloped away from the top of the ridge the road seemed to follow and cling to.

"Can't you make this thing go any faster?" Charlie whined, not for the first time. "We're not hardly moving. They'll be after us."

"How do you expect them to come after us with the ferry on our side of the river?" Hampton asked. "You can see the road as well as I can, or rather, not see it. You want to drive?"

"No way, man. This is unreal. Just get us out of it and to somewhere I can catch a plane to anyplace warm." He gestured with the Smith & Wesson .44 in one hand. "Get it going, man."

"Oh, shove it, Charlie. Shoot me and you've got no one to drive. I'm going as fast as I can, unless you want us in the ditch."

In fact, as Delafosse had correctly guessed, Hampton had been contemplating how to ditch the truck for quite some time. Only the fact that he had no idea what Charlie would do with the gun if he didn't keep the truck in some kind of forward motion kept him from twisting the wheel and plunging them off the road on one side or the other. It was clear that Charlie was desperate. So he used the barely perceptible depressions of the barrow pits on each side of the road as guides and kept the truck moving between them at a snail's pace on the snow-clogged gravel surface. He didn't like the idea of being shot here, where medical assistance was guaranteed to be unavailable, and watched his traveling companion closely as he drove. Hampton was tired, furious, increasingly cold and worried. He resented Charlie's having kidnapped him from the bar where he waited for Jensen, but the pressure of the .44 in his ribs had been enough to keep him still and make him go along with the kid to his own truck, where his anger was reinforced by evidence of the break-in.

Though the temperature on the pass had fallen to just above zero degrees, outside the windchill dropped it to somewhere around minus fifty. Winds above forty miles an hour have little additional effect on lowering the temperature. The temperature of that truck's cab now hovered close to freezing as the wind found every tiny opening through which to suck out warm air the instant it escaped the heater, turned as high as it would go and still practically useless.

Moisture from the breath of the two men had frozen on the windows until the side and rear were completely frosted over and only the lower half of the windshield could be kept clear where the heater melted two spaces just large enough to peer through. Driving with his nose almost against the top of the wheel helped him see, but bent him forward in a position that made his neck and back ache as if they were broken. Anger and concern added tension to the discomfort.

His only relief was not having to worry about any other vehicle on the road. No one else would be idiot enough to use it, he thought, flexing the chilled fingers of one hand at a time. His leather driving gloves didn't even come close to the kind of protection he needed to keep his hands warm. He longed for the pair of insulated ski gloves he had left in Denver, but said nothing, afraid his traveling companion would demand even the inadequate gloves for his own bare hands.

Charlie, mumbling to himself, put the gun between his legs and buried a hand in each armpit inside his jacket, trying to warm his stiff fingers. His feet in western boots were propped close to the laboring heater. The truck rocked as a blast of wind hit it, and a sifting of fine snow leaked in through a thin opening in the wing window to fall to the floor at his feet. He stared at it and snuffled. He was catching a cold, his nose running a stream in the icy air, so he either snuffled or wiped it on his sleeve.

"Goddammit. How much longer is this son-of-a-bitching snow going to keep up?"

"All night, I'd guess," Hampton answered. "The weather report was for blizzard conditions till tomorrow."

"How long till we get to Alaska?"

"Well, it's a total of sixty-six miles from Dawson to the border and over a hundred after that to the Tetlin Junction with the Alaska Highway. We'd have to turn off and go a ways to make Eagle, so the only community on the road between here and there is Chicken, on the Alaska side."

"Chicken? There's a town named Chicken?" Charlie grinned in spite of himself.

"Chicken used to be a common local name for a kind of grouse called a ptarmigan. The story goes that they wanted to name the town Ptarmigan, but nobody could spell it, so they settled for Chicken."

"What's a . . . Chicken, huh? The stupes." Charlie obviously didn't want to admit he had no idea what a ptarmigan *was*, let alone how to spell it. He changed the subject. "So . . . a *hundred and sixty miles*? How fast are we going?"

"More like a hundred and seventy-five or eighty miles and, right now, we're moving six or seven miles an hour."

"Shit. That means we won't get there for . . . for . . ." He paused and frowned as he tried to figure it out.

"Sometime tomorrow night, if this weather keeps up and we can't pick up some speed. We've already gone almost thirty miles. It wasn't so bad till we got up here on top. We made better time coming up from the river."

Charlie scowled, thinking hard. "How much gas we got?"

"Pretty close to a full tank when we left and an extra ten gallons in the can in back."

"That enough?"

"I hope it's enough to get us somewhere and that's the least of many worries. Shut up, Charlie, and let me concentrate. It's getting worse."

The truck was now almost continuously rocking in response to the gusts of wind. It was clear that the road began a series of turns through a group of barely visible small hills, where the snow had blown across it in growing drifts, obscuring any trace of the way through. Hampton took his foot off the gas and allowed the vehicle to coast to a stop, its bumper and front wheels buried in the first drift.

"What the hell'd you stop for?"

"Charlie. I've got to tell you. There's no way we're going to make it even as far as the border. What we should do, right now, is turn around and go back to Dawson while we still might make it."

The kid jerked up straight from his slump in the passenger seat. "No way, man. Don't even think about it."

"Look at that." Hampton pointed to the drifts ahead. "Just how do you expect me to find the road in that?"

Charlie peered out at what little he could see in the headlights. "Just drive. The road's gotta be there."

"And go right off and get stuck. It's a series of curves, dummy."

"Don't call me no dummy, you bastard. You're just try'na make me think we should go back." He waved the gun in Hampton's direction. "Get moving."

"Where? You tell me exactly where you want me to drive."

Charlie was yelling now and waving the weapon. "How should I know. I said get moving, you son of a bitch. I'm not going back and you're not either. You know how to go in this stuff. You're from Colorado where they got lotsa snow. Go on."

Hampton sighed and shook his head. "Look. I'll try it, but only when we know where the road is. One of us has got to get out and walk ahead to make sure we're on it."

"Not me."

"Okay. But if I go it'll take longer. Since you won't drive, I'll have to walk ahead, come back and drive that far, walk ahead again, come back and drive again. Take twice as long and be twice as cold. If you walk, I can drive right behind you without getting in and out, opening and shutting the door, and leaving the truck to sit here while I walk."

"No. Not a chance, man. You'd turn around and leave me."

That thought had, of course, crossed Hampton's mind, but he wasn't admitting it to Charlie.

"Just how fast do you think I could turn? You could be back before I was halfway around, if I didn't get stuck in the process." Unfortunately, it was true, he realized, and gave up the idea of leaving Charlie *and* his gun.

"Yeah . . . well . . . Not me. You walk."

"And take the extra time?"

"Yeah . . . No . . . Oh, hell." He yanked hard on the door handle and threw his weight against it to push it open, letting in a cloud of blowing snow, letting out even the tiny bit of heat. The wind slammed the door behind him. As if it had lain in wait, it caught him as he moved forward, one hand on the fender, and threw him against the truck. When he recovered and stepped away from it into the headlight beams, it blew him to his knees. Snow packed into his clothing and hair till he looked like someone had sprayed him with flocking for a Christmas tree. Getting up carefully, he looked back and shook a fist at Hampton in the truck, but walked on into the drift, feeling with his feet for the roadway. The drift soon deepened, reaching his hips, as he struggled through it, wiping his nose.

Suddenly, with no warning, he sank farther into the snow. Waving frantically, he lost his balance and toppled over, momentarily disappearing. Wallowing his way back onto the road, blanketed with white, he shouted profanities Hampton could not hear and only saw the shape of before Charlie moved on.

Easing down on the gas, Hampton gave one thankful thought to the four-wheel drive and the heavy lug tires he had on those four wheels—though he would rather have had snow tires with studs—and drove forward, keeping away from the place where the road ended and Charlie had sunk out of sight the first time. Then, for a long, slow five minutes, he followed as the kid staggered forward through the drifts, hands tucked in his armpits. The truck wheels spun frequently, but somehow they always grabbed and made it.

When they were almost to where he thought the curves ended, either he or Charlie grew careless and assumed the road straightened faster than it did. With a sick sense of inevitability, he suddenly felt the truck, moving without his guidance, drop the right front wheel, then the rear, over the edge of the road. Desperately, he swung at the steering wheel, trying to pull it back on the roadbed, to no avail. Slowly the pickup canted to the right, slid, and came to a tilted rest, irrevocably sunk in the ditch. He knew instantly that there wasn't a chance they could get it out without a tow.

Charlie came floundering through the snow, back to the door on the driver's side, which he wrenched open in a paroxysm of rage.

"You bastard," he shouted. "You silly son of a bitch. Now you've done for yourself. Did it on purpose, didn't you? Well, get out of there. I'm gonna do you, I swear I am." Then, with a wail of contradiction, "What are we gonna do now?"

He pulled the gun from his jacket pocket and tried to

point it at Hampton, but his hands were so cold he dropped it in the snow, where it disappeared under the truck. Throwing himself on his belly, he scrabbled after it, found it, and, getting up, put it resignedly back in his pocket.

Hampton leaned forward, resting his head on the steering wheel, and said nothing. It was hard to keep himself from sliding down into the passenger side on the steep pitch of the seat. In a second or two, he raised his head and looked at the kid, covered with snow, stomping his feet and wringing his hands.

"Check to be sure the exhaust isn't buried in the snow, so we don't die of carbon monoxide, and get in, Charlie, before you freeze to death."

Surprisingly, without a word, the kid did as he was told, pawing snow away from the exhaust pipe and muffler with numb hands, then climbing into the tipped truck through the driver's door, where Hampton allowed his tired body to slide slowly down to rest against the passenger door to make room. The door shut, they sat in silence, listening to the wind howl outside and the tiny, whispery sound of grains of snow hitting the windows.

Hampton felt there was little to say that was not self-evident about their predicament. It was likely to be a considerable amount of time before anyone found them . . . if anyone did. They had enough gas to run the truck, off and on, to keep from freezing for quite a long time, if they were careful. But they had absolutely nothing to eat or drink, nothing to melt snow in, and nothing but what they wore for protection against the cold. He wished for his heavy boots.

"Better start the engine and get it as warm in here as possible for a little while," he said to Charlie, who followed his instructions without comment. The sound of its running decreased the empty, isolated whine of the wind a little. The truck still vibrated in the Arctic blasts that howled over the ridges, almost as if it were angry at not being able to reach them with its bitter breath.

Charlie clung to the steering wheel, trying to avoid sliding down across the seat into Hampton.

"You can't sit that way for any length of time," he told the kid. "Turn your feet down here across my legs and brace yourself against the door, but kick the snow off your boots first."

With one side of the truck buried in a snowbank, less wind found its way into the cab to steal their precious heat. As Hampton watched, snow began to drift across the windshield, covering more of the exposed surface of the truck. It would be some insulation, he realized, slightly amused that every obstacle seemed to hold at least one positive, encouraging element.

In ten minutes, when they could once again feel their fingers and toes, and most of the snow had melted off Charlie's clothes, leaving him damp but warmer, Hampton turned off the engine and the storm's howling seemed to increase again. He pulled the collar of his jacket up around his ears, put his gloved hands in his pockets and slumped down in the seat, knees against the dash.

Would anyone follow them? he wondered. Could they? Would anyone even know, or figure out, where they had gone? Would Delafosse and Jensen have found the clue he had left on the check? Slim chance. It would be suicidal to try anything but wait here in the truck and hope. Thirty miles in any blizzard, let alone this one, made any thought of walking out ridiculous. He remembered Riser's journal. How he must have tried to walk the river from Dawson to Forty Mile. Riser hadn't made it. Neither could they. If they were lucky, someone would find them here. If not, when they ran out of gas and grew cold enough, they would just go to sleep, as he probably had. The only difference was a metal shell of protection and a little comforting heat to hoard and use infrequently.

Charlie shifted slightly and Hampton looked up to find him watching with frightened eyes. He cleared his throat and snuffled again.

"Are we going to die?" he asked in an uncharacteristically small voice.

Hampton hesitated for a minute, deciding what to say. That this kid knew nothing about wilderness or extreme weather conditions was unmistakably plain. He panicked at things that should be mere irritations, brazened his foolish way into real dangers. "I don't know," he said, finally. "I hope not."

Charlie really looked like a little kid, he thought somewhat sympathetically, then, with a start, remembered that this was the same shit who had helped Will rob him on the river, almost killed him. Who had kidnapped him at gunpoint—well, gun-in-pocket-point—from the bar in Dawson and forced him to drive his truck, run the ferry to get them across the river, and drive to this godforsaken snow-buried location on the roof of the world where they could, with very little trouble, freeze to death . . . who had set him up to take the blame for Russell's murder and probably killed Will.

He looked at Charlie, who looked back.

"Why," he asked, "did you bring my gear back, almost destroy my canoe, and set me up for Russell's murder?"

The kid frowned. "Back?"

"Yeah. Why set me up like that?"

"How? Look. I'm sorry Will shot your canoe. Sorry we took your stuff, too. It was stupid. Okay?"

"Then why set me up?"

"Whaddaya mean? We never set you up. We just took your stuff."

"Oh, come on, kid. It's a little late in the game now. I'd just like to know, why me? It didn't really work, you know. Didn't take them long to decide I probably hadn't had anything to do with it. They're looking for you because of Russell."

"Who's Russell? I didn't have nothing to do with any Russell. Never saw him, don't know him. Ask Duck."

"You mean you and Will never brought my camping gear back to where I camped after you took it? Never set it up and left Russell's body in the brush, so it looked like I killed him? Never bashed up the end of my canoe with a rock? I'm supposed to believe that?"

Total confusion filled Charlie's face. "No. Shit no. Why'd we bring your stuff back? We was gonna sell it." He frowned and shook his head in absolute denial.

Hampton stared at him, thoughts whirling.

If Charlie was telling the truth, who *had* set him up? And who had killed Russell . . . and Will, for that matter? But the chance he was telling the truth was certainly slim.

Chapter Nineteen

༺❀༻ "SAYS SHE HASN'T HEARD FROM HIM SINCE last weekend and has been worried since she heard about Warren Russell. He didn't even call to tell her his father was dead."

Early the next morning, Delafosse had telephoned Sean Russell's wife, Marilyn, in the small mining town of Chicken, Alaska, where she and Sean ran a small gold-dredging operation when he wasn't doing research and photography on the Canadian Yukon. Though their main objective of the day was to locate and retrieve Hampton and the kid, the inspector had agreed with Jensen that it wouldn't hurt to look a little closer at the other suspects on their list.

The snow had stopped sometime before dawn, but on the ridges of the Top of the World the wind was still blowing too strongly to allow the safe flight of the helicopter Delafosse had put on notice the night before.

"Let's give it an hour or two," he suggested. "It's supposed to calm down soon. Then, if we still can't fly, we can fire up the big plow truck."

While they waited, he and Jensen had both made phone calls.

"Evidently Warren Russell stopped by their place last Saturday on his way here to fish," the inspector continued. "Marilyn says he left in a temper when he and Sean had another confrontation over the subsistence issue and his son's life-style. He had evidently promised to help

Sean buy a new boat that he badly needs, but slammed out swearing that Sean, or anyone else who would use his money to fight for a cause he disagreed with, wouldn't get—and I quote Marilyn, quoting him—'even enough of it in change to rub between two fingers.' She says he called Sean worthless and told him again that he was wasting his life, when he should be doing something respectable."

"Pretty strong stuff," Jensen said. "Had he ever completely disinherited Sean before?"

"Every other week, from the sound of it. Sean has tried for years to please Warren and still live his own life. They've always had conflict, but it wasn't so bad while the mother was alive. Marilyn was upset over this one, though. Seems Sean was more than usually depressed and angry. She hasn't seen or heard from either of them since, but Sean didn't leave for his village photography site until the day after Warren had gone—Sunday. I told her if I saw him I'd tell him to call her."

"Not much of a recommendation of innocence, is it?"

Delafosse shook his head. "Still, it's not exactly new information—more like old news."

"Well, here's another piece of news, old and new, that may interest you."

Jensen shuffled notes he had made while talking on the other telephone line. He had followed up on a couple of calls to the Denver police to find out more about Jim Hampton, with an unexpected result—Hampton had a record. Approximately ten years earlier, he had been arrested for assault in the aftermath of a brawl in a bar, but the charge was later dropped. The man he fought with had ended up in the hospital with a broken arm and jaw. The arresting officers had both left Colorado and no one presently on duty remembered the incident.

A second startling, and perhaps more damning, item, however, was that another assault charge was currently pending against him. The officer who had investigated informed Jensen that Hampton had punched out a fellow workman on a construction job in late July, knocking him against a cement truck and giving him a concussion.

"Some sort of disagreement over quality of work," he told Jensen. "We weren't even on the scene. The guy came in to file charges after it was all over and he'd seen a doctor. Said Hampton attacked him for no reason at all. I'd take that under consideration, since the supposedly injured party's a troublemaker, with a record himself. The contractor has slapped a lawsuit on his company for substandard materials and breach of the subcontract."

"Was Hampton dismissed?"

"No. I'm sure he wasn't. But he must be a hothead, and strong. He's got some shoulders on him. Shouldn't hit people."

In the RCMP office, the two officers looked at each other in silence, both thinking hard. Finally, Jensen spoke, thoughtfully.

"Well, getting in a fight doesn't mean much without other evidence, but it's no wonder he didn't want to charge Sean with assault."

"What if he and Charlie knew each other and took off together on purpose. It could be just their bad luck and lack of knowledge that they drove right into more trouble, instead of a getaway."

"There's no indication they knew each other."

"I'm just playing what if with all the possibilities."

"He'd have to be a pretty good actor."

"Yes."

"Something's just not right about the idea, Del."

"Something's not right about all of it. Maybe—to make another bad pun—we have too many chiefs and not enough Indians—or too many suspects."

Delafosse had already sent the jet boat upriver with two constables to bring in Duck Wilson. Cherlyn had signed a complaint and he would be arrested as a result, as well as on suspicion of the vehicle theft, until they could put the evidence together.

Another assault charge, Jensen thought. Why did people insist on doing physical damage to each other? It seemed so senseless. If Charlie *had* forced Hampton to leave town with him, he hoped the canoeist was safe and unharmed. It would have been a cold and uncomfortably dangerous night wherever they were up there. He went over to the window to see what the weather was doing and found that the sun had come out through a dissipating layer of cloud and the crystals of new snow sparkled in its thin, tentative light. He thought of Jessie Arnold and her honest delight in the run she had made yesterday with her dogs. Less frustrated, he turned back to Delafosse, still seated at the desk.

"At least Duck Wilson won't be beating on anyone again soon. Can't we get going?"

The phone rang, commanding Delafosse's attention. After a brief conversation consisting mainly of single syllables on his part, he laid the receiver down and rubbed his ear thoughtfully, frowning.

"What?"

"Coroner. Found about what we expected with Will Wilson. It *was* the head shot that killed him. The odd thing is that he was shot with two different guns. The head shot from a thirty-eight at fairly close range—there was some carbon tattooing—and the other, the one in his back, probably a forty-four from a distance, tore him up pretty good. Took out a kidney and damaged his spleen. He bled a lot inside, but quite slowly.

"Damn it, Alex, how many people killed these two guys? Three types of injury to Russell's head. Now two different guns used on Wilson. One killed, then shot later. The other shot, then killed later."

"You ever read a book called *Murder on the Orient Express*?"

"Wasn't there a movie?"

"Yeah. In the end, every suspect turns out to have taken a whack at the victim. They were all in it together."

"You don't think that's what's going on here?"

"No, but it makes you think. We've got motives for more than one. More than one seem to have had opportunity. There's something we're not getting hold of, though."

"Well . . . whatever it is, we'd better be thinking about getting to those two at the top of the hill. Let's check the weather again. Maybe we can get that bird off the ground and find out where they are. I think we'd better pack a bag of survival gear to drop to them. It's more than likely we won't be able to land if the wind is blowing a ground blizzard the way it does for days sometimes. We could at least drop them enough so they can eat and stay warm enough to last till we can plow our way in there. Better pack two or three liters of water. They'll dehydrate pretty fast up there.''

"How about a couple of snow machines?" Alex remembered the amount of ground he had covered on one the previous spring to investigate two deaths during the Iditarod.

"We could take a couple in the back of the plow truck, with a ramp to get them down, but it'll be easier and warmer to ride inside and clear the road as we go, so we can bring Hampton's truck back. If we need to, we can use them off road when we get there, but they won't be stupid enough to try to walk out, I hope.''

It had grown light, but the two at the top of the hill, in the cab of the now all-but-buried truck, were both half asleep in the gloom of the snow-covered cab. The wind had died from what it had been at its worst, though it still shrieked across the barren landscape, but the snow, drifted and packed around the truck, shielded them from most of it. It was difficult to tell if the flakes that still flew on the wind were coming from the ground or the sky, but the temperature had not risen.

Through the night that never seemed to end, they had dozed off and on, waking, as the confined space grew progressively colder, to run the engine and heater. Hampton had twice cleared snow from around the exhaust and emptied the extra can of gas into the tank not long before it began to grow light. So far neither of them had frozen fingers or toes, but it would not have taken much.

He had traded places with Charlie, partly because whenever the kid went to sleep he relaxed, his knees buckled, and he slipped down the seat until he was piled up against Hampton, mashing him against the door. Now curled up in the tightest ball he could make of his lanky body, he had both knees under his chin, head against the passenger window, and was snoring with his mouth open.

The kid was having trouble breathing. The last time he woke, his face was flushed and his eyes feverish. He had shivered uncontrollably as he moved. When he spoke, his voice was raspy and thick with a sore throat.

Hampton calculated fatalistically that if they got out of this predicament there was probably no way he could keep from catching whatever it was Charlie had. The cab of the truck must be full of a million germs, all looking for a home, and he was an unavoidably convenient virus hotel.

There was no way to be comfortable in the limited space. Whatever position Hampton assumed, part of him quickly grew numb or cramped, and most of him was cold. He lay for the moment on his back, head on the seat below the steering wheel, wiggling his fingers inside his pockets, boots propped up beyond and over Charlie, braced on the top of the window, trying to straighten his legs for a change. Not quite asleep, he was thinking of Judy Rematto, that he should have called her, and what he would have said if he had. Now that he couldn't, and had time to think about it, the issue loomed significantly in his mind.

More than anything he could imagine, he also wished he had a lot of hot coffee—along with an enormous breakfast: steak, eggs, hash browns, biscuits and gravy, grapefruit juice. He particularly liked the clean tanginess of grapefruit juice in contrast to the flavor of fried eggs and hash browns, which he liked to mix together, especially if the yolks were slightly runny. He was mentally adding salt and pepper to his imaginary feast when he became aware of a muffled, rhythmic thumping sound.

"Charlie," he yelled, yanking his feet from the window and struggling to sit up. "Charlie, wake up. It's a helicopter."

The kid woke with a start and groggily shook his head. Hampton slid into him in his scramble to turn around toward the upside driver's door.

"A helicopter. They're looking for us." Levering himself up on the wheel, he reached for the door handle.

"Hold it."

Set to push open the door, he paused to glance back, only to find that the kid once again had the .44 leveled at him. Damn. He should have lifted the thing from his coat pocket while he slept and pitched it into a snowbank.

"Don't touch that damn door," Charlie told him.

"But they might not see us. The truck is almost buried."

"I know. Sit still and we might get lucky. They may go away."

"Charlie. Do you want to sit out here and freeze . . . or starve?" Clinging to the wheel, Hampton pulled his body to a sitting position behind it.

"It's daytime now. We can go on when they leave."

"You're nuts, kid. We're down to a whisper of gas in the tank. We have nothing to eat. You've probably got pneumonia. We aren't going anywhere without help."

"*You say*!" This comment came explosively through a bout of coughing.

Hampton had finally had it. His anger came, as usual, like lightning out of nowhere, in a flash of adrenaline and heat. While Charlie was distracted by his coughing fit, in a quick, desperate motion he grabbed the gun barrel and shoved it aside toward the floor of the cab. At the same time he let go of the wheel, allowing himself to slide toward the kid. With the gun barrel pointed at the floorboard, he punched him in the face as hard as he could from a sitting position. Without intention, but not caring, he connected solidly with Charlie's already bruised nose and felt something give under his gloved fist.

The resulting howl of pain filled the cab as Charlie let go of the gun and brought both hands up to cradle his face, from which fresh blood poured over mouth, chin, and jacket front. The .44 dropped to the floor under his feet.

"Oo-ooh. By doze. Broke by damn doze."

Concentrating on the helicopter, Hampton did not take time to try to find the gun. Lunging, he opened the driver's door of the cab and tumbled out into the snow beside it. The door slammed itself behind him, shutting off Charlie's muffled and anguished cries. The drift he had fallen into was a full three feet deep. Untangling himself, he stood up, wiped the snow from his face, and looked up.

They had not missed the truck, buried or not. The helicopter was there, moving north in an arc to come back over. It had stopped snowing. The sky was only lightly overcast, displaying a thin patch or two of blue. Most of the wind had died, but it was still blowing close to the ground, making it almost impossible to see. Fine crystals of snow flew like a fog, obscuring drifts and low spots alike.

As the helicopter came close and reduced speed to attempt to hover overhead, Hampton identified Jensen beside the pilot, Delafosse in a rear seat. The wind was still strong enough to keep the pilot busy fighting against it to hold the craft in place and it swung like a pendulum with the gusts that shoved it around the sky. The two officers opened a door on the sheltered side and leaned out to look down. Hampton waved both arms over his head and grinned. The roar of the rotors was too loud to hear voices, but he could easily read Jensen's first question, "You okay?"

He nodded vigorously, then hugged himself and jogged in place—cold—rubbed his stomach—hungry.

"Where's Charlie?"

He thumbed at the truck.

Jensen nodded and Delafosse signaled "wait" with one hand, reached back into the helicopter with the other and pulled forward a large duffel bag, which he proceeded to drop out the door. It fell perhaps twenty feet away and disappeared into a drift. He pantomimed eating and wrapping a blanket around his shoulders, then wrote in the air as if he had a pen and gestured at the bag.

Hampton understood. They had put a message in the bag with the supplies. But their next signals were disappointing. They couldn't land in the helicopter because of the wind and snow conditions. They would be back, but on the road. Jensen made the sign of a snowplow with the tips of his fingers together to form a V pushing forward.

"How long?" Hampton asked, pointing toward his watch arm.

Delafosse frowned and shrugged—he didn't know exactly. He held up two, then three, then four fingers—two to four hours—maybe.

With one gloved hand, Hampton patted the gas cap on the truck and gestured pouring something into it. Gas. He needed gas for the truck.

Jensen nodded and gestured a thumbs-up. They both waved and the pilot let the helicopter slide away with the wind, circling back toward Dawson.

Feeling abandoned, Hampton stood by the door to the truck, watching it go and wondering how difficult a time they would have getting a plow up the road and how long it would actually take them. At least he and Charlie would have food and whatever was in the bag to keep them warm. He hoped they had thought to put in some of the hot coffee he had been dreaming about earlier.

As he turned his head to look toward the spot where the bag had disappeared into the snow, the truck door flew open and Charlie lunged out with an arm raised. Before Hampton could begin to move, the kid hit him hard in the head with the butt of the gun he had recovered from the cab floor. Coming from above, the blow was forceful enough to drop Hampton into the snow like a sack full of old clothes. Should . . . have . . . got the gun. As his awareness faded, he remembered the contemptuous sneer he had seen on Charlie's face during the attack on the river . . . then it was gone.

The kid stepped down from the truck and stood looking at him with hardly any expression at all, then shoved the gun into his jacket pocket, swiped gently at his injured nose, and, without a second look, wallowed off through the deep drifts toward the place where the bag had fallen.

A thin trickle of blood ran through the unconscious man's hair to drip into the snow, staining it a red that held its crimson color as it quickly froze.

Chapter Twenty

CLAIR MCSPADDEN LOOKED UP FROM HER desk in anxious question as Jensen and Delafosse tromped into the office after their flight. Delafosse nodded and her expression turned immediately to a smile. "You found them."

"Yes," Delafosse told her, stopping at the desk as Alex disappeared toward the back, "and they're stuck all right. We couldn't land. It's blowing like a son . . . sucker up there. We did get the survival gear dropped, though. They'll be okay now until we can get to them, even if they've run out of gas for the truck. You could camp out in that survival gear for three or four days at fifty below and Hampton's an outdoors man, he'll know how to use it. We'll have some time to plow them out and bring Hampton's truck down without worrying about somebody freezing to death."

"But you're not going to take your time?"

"No. We'll go right away, as soon as we can arrange for the plow truck. Can't take a grader; there's not room for us all."

"I already got in touch with Willard Ely. He's coming in to meet you in an hour."

"Good. We'll pick up something to eat and get a couple of snow machines gassed up. Have we got any cans around to carry gas for the pickup?"

"If not, Howard will have some at the station. I'll call him *and* get the food. What do you want?"

"Something we can eat in the truck . . . sandwiches, coffee . . . whatever. Get enough for Willard too. Thanks, Clair. You're really . . ." He paused, looking at her.

She looked back for a long minute, then smiled and blushed bright pink.

"Listen," he said. "When this is over . . . m-maybe you'd like . . . ah . . . maybe . . . ?"

"Yes, I would."

"Yes?"

She nodded happily, and he started to say something else, but the sound of Jensen coming back stopped him.

Alex walked into the room, immediately aware, from the way they were smiling at each other, that his friend had finally found his nerve, with a positive result.

"Well," he said, almost sorry to interrupt. "You get a plowman?"

Clair turned toward the phone, but swung back holding a slip of paper toward Jensen. "A friend of yours called from Alaska. Jessie Arnold? Is she the Iditarod musher?"

Alex nodded.

"Wow. She asked if you would call her back when you got in."

A look of concern followed Alex's quick glance at the note, which held only Jessie's name and number.

"No message? Did she say if anything's wrong?"

"Nope. She sounded cheerful, not like an emergency. Just asked for you to call her when you had a minute."

"How's Cherlyn doing this morning?" he asked when he had dialed and was waiting for the phone to ring in Knik.

"She was still asleep when I left. Whatever the doctor gave her really wiped her out and she slept all night. I left the pain pills and a note to tell her where to find the makings for an ice pack and breakfast. She'll call when she gets up. Not home?" she asked, at the sight of his frowning response to the phone.

"Not answering at least. May be out in the dog lot. I'll try again before we leave."

"What's going on with Duck Wilson?" Delafosse

asked, with a glance at the closed door to the holding cells.

"Nothing . . . now. He wouldn't stop yelling obscenities, so I shut the door and left him to his echoes."

The two husky constables had picked up Wilson before daylight and, after a wrestling match in which all three suffered bruises and abrasions, physical and vocal, had brought him, under restraint, to Dawson in the jet boat. Formally arrested for assault, and held on suspicion of felony theft and murder, he now prowled the cell, reminding Delafosse of a caged bear as he shuffled back and forth, howling in indignation and demanding his rights.

"Ignore him. His wife must be relieved with the golden silence at home. He'll have legal advice soon. Let him yell at his . . . mouthpiece."

Clair laughed. "I intend to do just that. What a piece of work." She made a face. "I never saw clothes any filthier, let alone him. Somebody should turn on a hose. How often does he take a bath? Once a year, whether he needs it or not? I'm not going in there with his lunch, by the way."

"That's okay. Tell Mel to do it when he gets back from having that loose tooth checked. Duck whacked him pretty good this morning." He turned to Jensen with a chuckle. "We're about to see the attorney you said was missing from that bit of doggerel, Alex. Now we've got them all."

On the Top of the World Highway, Hampton slowly regained consciousness to find himself facedown in the snow beside the truck. Once again his head hurt so much it made him nauseated to raise it. But what concerned him most was that he was terribly cold, his hands and feet so numb he couldn't feel them. The cheek that had been in direct contact with the snow was also numb. Just how long had he been out? he wondered, struggling to his feet and leaning against the back of the truck.

He vaguely remembered Charlie behind him just after watching the helicopter carry Delafosse and Jensen out of sight toward Dawson, and knew the kid had hit him, but he was now nowhere to be seen. Carefully, quietly, he limped forward until he could peer in the driver's window. The cab was empty. No Charlie. Where the hell was he? Well, it wasn't the most important thing now.

Fumbling with the door handle, he finally got his wooden fingers to work well enough to open it and crawled into the cab. Starting the engine was another challenge of determination over ability. The key was still in the ignition, which he had been afraid to consider closely. If Charlie had intended to kill him, it would have been easy to toss it out into the snow, losing it effectively until spring, if then. But if Charlie had wanted him dead, it would also have been simple to shoot him where he lay senseless.

His pegs for fingers were almost useless, but by bracing one hand with the other he finally turned the key and got the engine started. With it running, he sat sideways in the tilted seat, shook his hands and stomped his feet against the passenger door, waiting while the heater warmed up enough to blow something besides cold air. Head throbbing, still feeling sick, he pulled off his gloves with his teeth, managed to partially unzip his jacket and tuck his hands into the warmth of his armpits.

By the time he could feel the temperature rising in the cab, he had some sensation in his fingers. Turning, he took his hands from inside his coat, held them out, but not directly in front of the heater, and let the warm air play over them. Bending forward made his head swim, but it couldn't be helped. In a few minutes, he almost wished his hands numb again, for the pain of their thawing was intense enough that he couldn't hold still but sat shaking them and whining through his nose. Gritting his teeth, he ignored as much of the hurt as possible, curling and uncurling the fingers to get the blood circulating. It was an agony and his thoughts of Charlie were all dark ones.

Soon his feet began to let him know they were still alive, with the same shooting pains. Pawing at the laces, he managed to undo them and push off his hiking boots. Holding his feet in the warm air and wiggling his toes,

he endured ten minutes of sweating, while he alternated
whines of pain with a truly creative assortment of swearing at Charlie the kid. The short time it took to warm his
extremities told him he had probably not suffered any
serious frostbite. Gradually warming his hands in water
might have been easier to take, but stressful as it was, the
process did work. It was not good, he knew, to warm
frostbite up in direct dry heat, but he had little choice for
he couldn't leave the truck running too long. He was also
tempted to rub his hands and feet, but remembered reading somewhere that this was damaging to tissue already
traumatized.

Examining his fingers and toes carefully, Hampton had
found that, aside from a small patch or two of the dreaded
white of frostbite, they seemed okay. The side of one
pinkie finger showed a pale spot, as did two toes on his
left foot. Any longer outside the truck, without heat, and
he would have been in real trouble.

Cursing Charlie made him wonder where the kid was.
His next thought was for the supplies dropped earlier from
the helicopter. Though his feet had swollen some, he
forced them back into the boots, after warming the in-
sides, and replaced his gloves on fingers that were also
slightly fat. They could get worse, he knew, and must not
be allowed to be so cold again, if at all possible. If there
was anything outside that would keep him warm and feed
him, he must get it now.

Leaving the engine running, he opened the door and
climbed out as quickly as possible to conserve heat. Just
before he slid down from the driver's door, which was
tilted higher than the rest, he noticed a track in the snow
that led away from the truck. It went west, toward the
border and Alaska, many miles away. Charlie had taken
off, as he had threatened when the helicopter arrived.

With little optimism, Hampton saw that the snow had
been torn up between the truck and where the duffel bag
had landed. Charlie again. When he reached the spot, his
anger took a decidedly different turn. If the kid had been
within reach, he knew he would have made an effort to
break something besides his nose. He was too furious to

swear, too coldly outraged to say or do anything. He felt his face grow hot and his whole body stiffened in anger till he was almost hyperventilating.

Charlie had evidently sorted through the bag, throwing out or dropping the few items he didn't want to carry. He had clearly taken everything he thought he *might* even be able to use, leaving Hampton with almost nothing at all.

One wool blanket lay where it had been tossed and was now blown full of snow. A pair of wool socks and a down vest lay beside it, also snow covered. That was all, except for two plastic liter bottles of water, half frozen into slush. Nothing else remained—not a scrap of food, not any of the other survival gear Hampton knew would have been dropped. There had to have been insulated clothing and sleeping bags, probably two sets. He knew there had been food, and hot coffee or soup in unbreakable thermoses made sense. The thought of food made his stomach turn over in something besides nausea. A first-aid kit would have been included. He could have used some aspirin, the way his head felt. Whatever there might have been was history now. He didn't even try to imagine what else the bag had contained.

He just stood, staring at the items in the snow, until he gained control over the hot lump of rage in his chest and slowly began to think rationally again. Then, without a word, or an uncontrolled action, he picked up the blanket and shook it hard to get most of the snow out of it, took the socks, vest, and water bottles, and returned to the truck. Once there, he tossed in all but the blanket and took out the jack handle from behind the seat.

Thinking of Charlie, he held the blanket in one hand and used the jack handle to beat it with the other. By the time he finished, most of the snow had fallen away, leaving the blanket pretty much freeze-dried. He didn't know if it would be dry enough when it warmed up inside the cab, but he had little choice in the matter. At least it was wool, which wouldn't turn soggy on him and was of some warmth even when it was damp. Either he used it or froze—and might anyway. There wasn't enough gas left in the tank to keep the heater going, even sporadically, until the officers arrived with the plow. Of that he was sure.

The other thing he was sure of was that Charlie would not get away with this. Somehow he would find that kid. Twice he had come close to dying at the hands of that particular piece of garbage. Once had been too many. Twice was intolerable. Yes, he would definitely see Charlie again. And since it was unlikely the kid would ever make the border, and the law would probably go after him when they came, Charlie would see him sooner than he expected.

Hampton got back into the cab and let the heater hum until he felt a little warmer. While it ran, he had started to wrap the vest around his lower legs and ankles, but stopped to empty the pockets when he felt something the kid had overlooked. In one pocket were two plastic envelopes that grew chemically warm when you bent a trigger inside. These he slipped into his jacket pocket for later. In the other vest pocket was a treasure, four Snickers bars. There was no trace of the message Delafosse had promised. Whatever it had said had gone with Charlie. Hampton now had no idea what the officers were planning or what they expected of him, if anything. He would just have to wait it out until they showed up.

He checked his boots to make sure they were not too tightly laced and that his socks were still dry. Wrapping his ankles in the vest, he put the socks on his hands over his gloves; cocooned himself as snugly as possible in the slightly damp blanket, and settled back to eat two of the Snickers bars immediately.

Between bites of candy he drank large gulps of the ice water from one of the bottles he had placed near the heater to thaw. Aware that every time he exhaled, his breath released precious moisture, he knew that, though it would have been better warm, liquid was what he needed to prevent dehydration that would encourage hypothermia and frostbite. When the water thawed some more, he would tuck a liter of it under his coat, next to his body to keep it from freezing again, and drink as much of it as possible. The increase in body fluids would keep his blood pressure up and circulating more efficiently. Given his present situation, every small opportunity to better his circumstances, inside and out, might make a difference in the long run.

Hopefully Delafosse had overestimated the time it would take to reach him. Till then he would try to stay quiet, wiggle his fingers and toes often, sleep if he could, and conserve heat and energy. The whole cab smelled of damp wool. His swollen feet and hands ached and itched, his head felt as if the back of it was about to come off, and his stomach growled in indignation at having only a token dropped into it. Well, he was alive ... very much alive, and intended to stay that way, if only to settle the score. At least, he thought, curling up on the seat to conserve his body heat, there's more room without Charlie, and had to grin. Once again, every cloud had its silver lining ... so far.

Across the river from Dawson, Delafosse and Jensen were heading up the highway in the cab of the large truck that was used to plow the route open until so much snow fell that it must be closed for the season. Equipped with an enormous blade, the powerful vehicle bulled its way through most drifts as if they weren't there. Its driver, Willard Ely, knew the way so well that he now cleared a strip the width of two cars in the center of the road, even around the bends and turns, without slowing down.

Ely had started the truck and let it run while they loaded two snow machines into the back bucket, tied them down, and put in cans of gas for Hampton's truck. With an extra-efficient heater, it was now warm enough so both officers had removed their coats, gloves, and hats, and were focused on the sandwiches they had brought for lunch.

"Want one of these, Willard? We've got extra."

"No, thanks. Mavis fed me last night's leftover pot roast before I left. I'm good."

"How long will it take to get up there?" Delafosse mumbled around an impolitely large bite of ham and cheese.

"Er, har-r-rah ... well, depends. Have to wait till we get up top and see what winter has dumped on the road before I can make a guesstimate. About thirty miles, you say? I'd guess maybe an hour and a half, maybe a little longer if it's drifted irregular and we have to slow down for the deep spots. Have to see which way the wind's blowing too. Takes more time to go against it because I can't see enough to make much speed. Har-r-rah-t-t.'' He cranked down the window just enough to spit a stream of tobacco juice expertly through it and whipped it back up with a practiced twist of the wrist.

An icy whisper of cold stole in to finger the back of Jensen's neck, widening his eyes and sending a shudder through him before it was cut off and died in the blast of the heater. It smelled overly hot and he leaned forward to be sure nothing had fallen against it to scorch. He thought longingly of the thick wool scarf packed in a duffel back with the snow machines.

Also in the bag were warm snow machine suits, along with an assortment of face masks, heavily insulated mitts, and other items to fend off the worst the winter had to threaten those daring or foolish enough to ride ''iron dogs'' in weather like this. But the scarf was uppermost in his mind, as he turned up his collar and wondered how often Willard would expectorate during a plowing run. He hoped the *har-r-rah-t* he had heard before the window went down would be enough warning to allow him to protect his neck.

Delafosse, noting the shudder, looked sideways at him and grinned, guessing his thoughts. ''Willard's our best plowman,'' he commented. ''He's been doing this for years. We plow to the border and your folks do the other side.''

Clair had gone for their food, bringing back two enormous sandwiches each, plus a thermos of hot soup and two of coffee, one with cream and sugar, one without. ''If you don't eat it all, Hampton and what's-his-name will,'' she said. ''All the survival gear in the world is not going to make it anything but uncomfortable up there.''

Now Delafosse put his second sandwich back in the bag and sighed contentedly. ''Can't find room. How about some of that coffee, Alex?''

"Sure. Want some of the soup?"

"No, thanks. Maybe later."

Jensen was also satisfied with a single sandwich. He put the paper bag out of the way of their feet and poured coffee for them both. Handing Del a cup, he grinned. "You asked her to dinner?"

Delafosse grinned back. "Yes. No. Sort of."

"You did, or didn't?"

"Yes, I asked her . . . but we never got to the for what part. She just said yes."

"Whatever. At least you finally did something."

They sipped their coffee in mutually pleased silence.

"Be dark before we make it back," Willard said. "You want to bring the pickup back to Dawson, right?"

"Right," Delafosse affirmed. "Can't leave it up there all winter and this may close the road."

"They go off on the right side, or the left?"

"Right, I think."

"Won't take but a minute to jerk it out with this rig."

Conversation lagged, as they watched the hypnotic flight of snow across the windshield in front of them. It had almost stopped falling, but seemed to blow up from the ground and ride the wind a few feet in the air. When it hit the truck, it flew higher still. White grains also blew back from the blade, as it scraped them from the surface and rolled snow back to the side of the road. At times it seemed they traveled through a constant white curtain of disturbance. Jensen was glad to be traveling in the warm protection of the truck, with plenty of gas and Willard's driving expertise. It was going to be dangerously cold when they reached the truck and got out to work in what was left of the blizzard.

About half an hour into the rescue mission, the radio crackled to life, attracting their attention. Jensen, warm and relatively comfortable, was half asleep, his long legs stretched forward, arms folded across his chest. He had been wondering again what Jessie wanted and wishing he could have spoken to her. The phone had remained unanswered. Must be off with the dogs, he had surmised.

The voice that came through the truck radio was that of Clair McSpadden, from the RCMP office in Dawson.

"For you." Willard caught the microphone in one giant paw and handed it to the inspector with a grin. He had evidently figured out just who the inspector and Jensen had been discussing earlier.

Though the transmission was filled with static and broken here and there, all three of the men in the cab were used to communicating on a radio and understood what she said clearly enough. Jensen was amused to hear her put on her public voice, since she knew she could be heard by more than just Delafosse.

"Inspector?"

"Yes, here."

"Henry Kabanak is here in the office. He says he wants to confess to killing Warren Russell. What would you like me to do . . . ah, sir?"

A moment of silence, empty of any reaction, fell in the cab of the truck. Astounded, Jensen heard the blade hit a fairly large rock and felt a slight vibration as it rattled along the flat, metal surface before being hurled to the side of the road.

"Inspector? Did you copy?"

"Yes, Miss McSpadden. I think so. You said Henry Kabanak was there?"

"Yes, sir."

"Ah . . . Kabanak senior or junior?"

"Ah . . . well, both, sir. But Henry . . . senior . . . is the one who wants to confess. Henry . . . junior . . . is in the cell next to Duck Wilson. Mel caught him and another native man—the one who works with Sean Russell—with a hatchet, sir."

"Did you say 'hatchet'?"

"Yes, sir."

Delafosse turned to look, wide-eyed and confused, at Jensen.

They both hesitated. Delafosse frowned and shook his head as if to clear it.

"And . . . Henry . . . senior . . . wants to confess, Miss McSpadden?"

"Yes, sir. Says he won't leave until he does and he'll only confess to you. He won't talk to Mel."

"Hold on, please."

The inspector turned back to Jensen with a frown. The silence in the cab of the plow truck was loud enough to make them ignore the howling wind. He stared at Jensen, who stared back. Both their minds were recalculating the situation with such intensity that nothing came out in words. When, finally, Jensen spoke, it overlapped Delafosse's first words.

"Na-a-aw!"

"What the hell is he trying to do? But . . ."

"Maybe . . ."

"Something's going on that we don't know. He's trying to protect the kid from whatever it is. Otherwise he wouldn't confess to it, if he didn't do it, and I do not think he did."

Alex nodded and sighed at the disappointed look on his friend's face. "Yeah. His son . . . with Hampton's hatchet?"

"Right. Has to be. Damn it."

"Cl . . . Miss McSpadden?"

"Yes, sir?"

"Ah . . . will you ask him if he will wait, please? Explain why I can't get back for four or five hours. I'll see him then."

"You want him to remain here, sir?"

Knowing he could be heard in the office, Delafosse elaborated only marginally.

"Yes. But until I see him he is not technically under arrest. Tell him I trust him to wait. There shouldn't be a problem, since he came in on his own and wants to speak to me. Ask him."

After a pause, she came back on the line.

"He will wait, sir."

"Tell him thank you."

"Yes, sir. Anything else, sir?"

"No, Miss McSpadden. Not at this time. Call again if you need me. Ah . . . thank you."

He hung the microphone back by the radio and scowled. "Damn it anyway."

"Well," said Jensen, who had been analyzing the situation from this new angle. "It could fit just about everything concerned with the two deaths, with a few details left over that could be worked out pretty easily."

"I know. But it doesn't feel right, Alex. What's this bit with the journal copy disappearing, for instance? I'm going to have trouble with it. Think I should have locked him up?"

Jensen pictured the dignified Han Athabaskan chief and shrugged as he shook his head. "Why? Where would he go? You've already got the thing that will keep him there . . . his son."

Chapter Twenty-one

WHILE HAMPTON HUDDLED MISERABLY, cold and angry, in his buried truck, a mile or more to the east, Charlie wallowed and stumbled through a world white with endless snow. There were no trees; nothing that provided even a modicum of shelter hindered the wind or broke the expanse of drifts that rolled away as far as he could see through the ground blizzard.

He had put on one of the bulky, coverall snow machine suits he had found in the duffel. But under it his clothes had already been packed with snow. Now his body heat had melted some of it, leaving him damp and chilled. At least his hands were covered, for he had also found thermal mittens, but they were not warm and were growing gradually colder.

In the bag, besides the mittens, had been sandwiches, one of which he had wolfed, not caring what it was. When he was well away from the truck, he had washed it down with half the contents of a thermos of hot soup. This he followed with a couple of swallows of coffee from another, but he didn't care for coffee and unfortunately didn't drink much. Both thermal containers were now back in the duffel, which he carried on his back. It was heavy and awkward, slipping when he walked and causing him to lose his balance often. His nose ran constantly and he had begun to cough in tight, hacking spasms that added to his exhaustion.

With Hampton unconscious, Charlie had gone in search

of the duffel and quickly sorted through it before leaving. Dumping half the contents into the snow, he had looked for anything he could leave to lessen the weight, including the water bottles, but decided to carry most of it as far as possible in case he needed its critical items. He had not intended to leave anything but the water, but when he had put on one of the down vests and the snow-machine suit, he thought he heard a sound that might have been Hampton coming to. Zipping up the bag, he had abandoned a blanket, the second vest, and a pair of socks and taken off, seeing as he passed that the other man still lay by the truck.

Now he was tired, and knew the load was too much for him. Stopping, he immediately grew more chilled as the sweat from exertion and some fever, along with the damp inside his suit, grew clammy. Dropping the bag, he coughed until he felt light-headed and his throat was on fire. With a stocking cap he had located in a pocket and put on, he wiped at his hot face and dripping nose. Snow crystals abraded his cheeks like sand with the force of the wind, including two pale spots of early frostbite. Half blind, he turned his back to it and stood, panting and dizzy, until his breathing slowed. It was so damn cold and he was so hot and tired.

When he looked back along the wandering line of his own tracks, he could not see the truck, or anything beyond a few dozen feet. Clouds had piled up, the thin sun had disappeared and the world gone darker. There were no landmarks, nothing to aim for, and without the tracks he would have been totally disoriented.

Slowly he settled to his knees and, pulling off his mittens, unzipped the bag. Though he hated the idea of undressing, he decided that he needed to get on the dry suit, with or without shelter from the storm. Reluctantly, he removed his boots, the snow-machine suit, the vest, his own inadequate gray jacket, shirt, and jeans. Shivering uncontrollably in his shorts, he fumbled into the tops and bottoms of one pair of insulated underwear. Brushing ineffectively at the clinging snow, he climbed into the second snow-machine suit. His own socks were now wet with snow, so he pulled them off and, standing on the discarded suit, yanked a dry pair onto his feet with fingers so cold he could hardly feel them.

Tossing aside the clothing he had worn, back to the wind, he pulled on his thin, inadequate western boots and danced in place. His feet had hurt earlier, but were now quite numb and not painful. Clumsily, he retrieved the gun from a pocket of the abandoned snow-machine suit and put it into the one he had on, along with a half-empty box of shells.

Another extended bout of coughing caught and left him breathless and bent as an old man over the duffel at his feet. He couldn't decide if he felt warmer or not, for snow had blown into everything he put on, leaving him once again damp from the inside out as his body warmth melted some of its fine grains.

His head ached. He felt deafened from the howling of the wind. Digging out a thermos from the duffel, he drank the rest of the soup it held and tossed aside the container. Numbly, he also threw out everything but one sleeping bag, the rest of the sandwiches and coffee, and a first-aid kit. One wool blanket he unfolded and wrapped around his head and shoulders like a giant babushka. Pulled forward around his face, it kept out some of the flying snow. Picking up the bag, he zipped it shut and, clutching it under one arm, staggered off again, not noticing that he had made a quarter turn to the right. Alaska had to be out there somewhere, with people and airplanes and warm places to go.

Dreamily, he thought of lying in the sand of a favorite California beach, letting the sun bake his back and splashing into the water periodically to cool off. One foot felt tight in the boot and he began to favor it, limping slightly, not aware that, with every step, he was bearing farther and farther to the right. Soon he had established a curve that, if viewed from above, would have revealed that in the not too distant future he would find himself very near the truck in which Hampton huddled, furious and miserable, ready to pound him to a pulp on sight. On he limped, longing for Alaska ... shelter ... anyplace he could lie down and go to sleep. Without his knowledge, patches of white spreading from the tips of his fingers were joined by the dead white of all his toes.

"You know," Jensen said to Delafosse after a long silence, during which the plow truck cleared a temporary track on another couple of miles of the Top of the World Highway. "When you think about it, most of this case hinges somehow on the relationships between sons and their fathers."

Delafosse turned a listening face toward him and held out his cup for more coffee. "Like Sean and Warren Russell, you mean?"

"Yeah, that's the most obvious one, with their constant disagreements and conflict. It's a power struggle; if one wins, the other loses, and neither wants to lose. Sean wants his dad to approve of him, like we all do, but he also needs to live his life the way *he* wants to, with respect for his own values and talents. It's interesting how some guys will go along with whatever their parents want, and wind up with a profession they don't really care about. Too many fathers try to live vicariously through their sons. Maybe they went along with their father's ideas and want their sons to live the ones they gave up. Fathers and sons compete and the fathers are often, realize it or not, jealous that the son is a younger, stronger, more attractive man.

"But think about it in terms of the others involved here. Kabanak wanting to confess got me started. He must have some good reason, other than that hatchet, to think his boy had something to do with Russell's death, so he says he did it to save his son. We don't know his reasoning, but the value he puts on his son is pretty impressive, if he's willing to take his punishment." He poured black coffee into the inspector's cup and recapped the thermos.

Delafosse sipped at it carefully to avoid burning his mouth before he spoke.

"Duck and Will are certainly another thing entirely, though that's got to be a power struggle too. Says

something about Duck's own son, Will's father, and that
situation as well.''

"What happened to him?''

"Died in Vietnam.''

"A Canadian?''

"Yes. While you had protesters coming north from the
States, we had a few who went south to join up with your
army. He was one of them. Made Duck furious that Tom
was that desperate to get away from him. From what I
hear, he hasn't allowed his name to be spoken since. Fastened all his attention on Will and pretended his son never
existed, especially after he was killed. His reaction to the
death was that it was Tom's own fault and it proved him
right.''

"What happened to Will's mother?''

"Oh, she took off years ago, after Duck made her life
a hell, but had to leave Will with the old man. He raised
him to believe she left him because she didn't want him
and that he was worthless like his father. Will never had
a chance. His whole life was filled with hate and anger
of one kind or another, abuse and contempt. The meaner
he got, the better Duck liked it, but he wanted everything
his way, as you saw yesterday. Beat Will if he didn't go
along.''

"God, what a horror.''

"A vicious circle. Ozzy treated Duck the same way.''

"From what Riser had to say about him in the journal,
I believe it. We don't know much about Charlie, but I'd
be willing to bet there's a similar story there. Makes himself feel big by preying on others.''

"That Will Wilson's a rotten one. Killed my dog,'' said
the plow driver, rolling down the window to spit with an
energy that expressed his disgust. Alex noticed, however,
that he was careful not to let it go into the wind.

"When was that, Willard?''

" 'Bout five years now. Good hound too.''

"You report it?''

"Couldn't prove it . . . but I *knew*.''

"What a tangle of family ties, guilt, independence, fear,
anger, love, stubbornness, violence, and whatever else,''

Alex said thoughtfully. "Makes you wonder how any-body grows up normal."

"Wonder what Hampton's father's like," Delafosse considered.

"Haven't a clue. But I expect he's completely different from Wilson. Hampton seems pretty squared away."

"Yeah, seems like. What was yours like? Was he disappointed when you went into police work?"

"No, mainly encouraging. Only worried about it as a dangerous profession. He was—and is—infatuated with literature, Scandinavian and other, reads all the time. My mom, with her Celtic background, has always called him the melancholy Dane, because he's serious and studious. He taught English at the local high school until he retired. They always made me feel that whatever I did was okay with them, as long as it satisfied me and I was good at it. Still do."

"Mine, too. He'd rather I'd wanted to be a farmer and inherit his wheat ranch, but was proud of me and let me know it."

"Where are they?"

"Dad's dead, an accident with a combine. They had moved from Montreal to Swift Current. Ever hear of it?"

"Nope."

"Out in the flatlands of Saskatchewan. When he died, my mom sold the place and moved to Ontario to be near my sister and her grandbabies. I was eleven years in the Regina and Saskatoon RCMP before I came up here."

"Sas-s-skato-o-on, Sas-s-skatchewan," Alex tried it out. "What a great mouthful of a name. You can almost taste it. Exotic."

"Wasn't really. Ranching community above Montana. Flat, with sky that went on forever. Took me a while to get used to mountains when I came here."

"Ontario where you got your French?"

"And that two of my grandparents were French immigrants."

Alex grinned. "That was quite an exhibit of profanity at the ferry landing."

"Now, that I *did* get from my dad."

Chapter Twenty-two

⟨⟨⟨⟨⟨ As the light faded from the snowy world outside the truck, it began to look flat, lacking the definition of shadows in the drifts. Willard leaned forward, watching closely for clues to the road. "Can't be too far now," he said, and the two officers also turned their attention to the front.

It was almost dark when they caught sight of an almost buried, truck-sized bump in the right-hand ditch, and Willard slowed the powerful plow to a stop where the headlights illuminated the side of the pickup. There was no movement from the smaller truck. It sat silent and snow-blown, seemingly empty, the windows thickly covered with frost on the inside.

Putting on coats, hats, and gloves, Jensen and Delafosse climbed down the side of the high cab, shutting the door behind them.

"Must have run out of gas and hasn't had the heater," said Jensen, stepping forward to pull open the door. "Good thing they had that stuff you dropped. Good God!"

What he found in the front of the pickup was a stiff replica of the man he had last seen in Dawson. Clutching a half-frozen wool blanket around him, Hampton struggled weakly to sit up on the tilted seat, batting toward the door with a sock-covered hand that was obviously too cold to be of much use. A swift glance told Jensen he was in serious trouble, and Charlie nowhere to be seen.

Reaching in, he grabbed at Hampton's arm, pulled him up and over the edge of the seat, and lifted him out onto the road, where he collapsed into a heap.

"What . . . ?" Delafosse stepped forward quickly to help pick him up. "Didn't you find the duffel bag we dropped?"

Hampton was so cold he hardly shivered and could scarcely speak. A croak told them, "Charlie . . ."

"Where?"

Hampton gestured ineffectively toward the west.

Willard leaned out the passenger door of the plow truck and shouted down from above. "Ask him questions later. Get him up here where it's warm."

With Willard's help, they lifted the almost helpless man into the cab of the larger truck, leaving the frozen blanket in the road. Delafosse clambered in after him, leaving Jensen to inspect the pickup. He and Willard immediately peeled off Hampton's coat, gloves, socks, and boots to allow the cab's heat to reach him directly. The inspector was disconcerted to see the pale condition of his toes and fingers, though they did not feel frozen. One ear also had a pale look to the lobe, but his face he seemed to have buried in the blanket, where his breath kept it from freezing.

Willard took one look at the useless hands and, pulling open his own coat and shirt, put them on his bare belly, drawing his warm clothing back in place over them. "Not going to be fun when they start to come to," he stated, "but this'll help. Reach under that seat, Del, and you'll find my survival stuff. Get some dry socks out, warm them up a minute and get 'em on his feet, then put his feet against you under your coat. Need to get some heat on the inside of him too. Coffee or soup, and fast. There's a bottle of brandy in there, but none for him. Not good for what he's got."

Delafosse did as he was told, glad they had the full thermos of coffee with cream and sugar, still hot. Pouring a lid full, he held it against Hampton's now-clicking teeth and helped him take a swallow or two.

"G-g-god, tha-a-t's g-g-good," he gasped. "G-got any f-f-o-od?"

Tucking Hampton's feet inside his jacket, Delafosse glanced up. "Haven't you had anything to eat? We drop . . ."

"Ch-Charlie t-took it."

"All of it?"

"Kn-nocked m-me out. T-took it all."

"The ruddy bastard." Though it took a lot to get Inspector Delafosse's temper up, he was incensed and angry now. "The son of a bitch." He lapsed into a few choice phrases in French, which drew a chuckle from Willard and even the ghost of a smile from Hampton.

As he resumed warming Hampton's feet and legs, the canoeist began to groan and writhe as his extremities came to life again. "D-damn. D-did some of this b-before, a c-couple of hours ago. Hurts w-worse now."

"You bet it hurts," Willard sympathized. "Better be glad it does. Gonna have to put up with it for a while. Sorry."

"Th-that's okay."

"There's aspirin where you found the socks," he told the inspector. "May help some."

Delafosse found it and gave Hampton a double dose, washed down with more coffee. "Can you eat a sandwich? Soup?"

Hampton nodded, pulling his hands from Willard's belly to sit up and shake them helplessly in front of, but not too close to, the gentle warmth of the heater.

"O-o-oh. Son of a bitch. Both, please. Soup first, but you'll have to hold it."

His hands soon began to flush pink with a few small burgundy-colored spots. Delafosse poured vegetable soup into the lid of the other thermos and balanced it while Hampton slurped it down ravenously. He then fed him a sandwich, a bite at a time. It also disappeared in record time and was followed by the rest of the soup.

"Heaven," he sighed. "Thanks, guys. I had about decided you couldn't make it to the party."

"Now," said Delafosse. "Tell me about Charlie."

"I don't know much because, like I said, he knocked me out. Hit me in the head with that forty-four of his. See?" He turned to show the lump and cut where the butt of the pistol had connected with his skull. "I've been hit in the head more this week than in my entire life. I'm beginning to resent it."

"Where did he go?"

"Headed for the border, I think. Didn't seem to believe me when I told him there wasn't a chance of making it. Thought I was telling lies to keep him here. He threatened me with the gun before I got out when you were here in the chopper. I caught him off guard, broke his nose, and jumped out. That probably set him off. He hit me before I could get back in the truck, just after you left. Then he took off with almost everything you dropped and left me out cold in the snow. Don't know how long I was out, but long enough to get a good start on this damage." He held up his hands. "I already had a white patch or two. Damn, this smarts."

"So he headed west and has a forty-four."

"Right. At least that's the way his tracks go. I'd like to get my hands on him—though they're not much use to me right now. I'd pound the shit. I could have died out there if he'd hit me just a little harder."

Delafosse looked up at the plow driver, who was listening closely, taking it all in. "You take care of him, Willard? I'll go help Alex. Okay?"

"Hey, no problem. I got plenty of gas, so we'll stay toasty. You go on." In almost one motion he swiftly rolled the window down and back up. Midway through the process, a stream of tobacco juice went flying with deadly aim. Del was sure that if Charlie had been standing within reach, Willard could and would have hit him in the eye.

Outside, Del found Jensen pouring the second can of gasoline into the tank in Hampton's pickup.

"Even when this is out of the ditch, I doubt we're going to get it started without a jump from Willard's battery," he said.

"No problem. We'll do it when we get back and let it

run till it gets warm. One of us will have to drive it to Dawson behind the plow.''

"Right. I was going to unload the snow machines, but it'll take both of us to move that piece of wood you brought for a ramp.''

"Got to be done. Like it or not, we'll have to go after that damn kid.''

"Yeah, I figured as much, though I'm tempted to let him freeze for pulling such a stunt. Can you charge him with attempted homicide? Not much longer and he might as well have shot Hampton. How's his frostbite?''

"Not as bad as I first thought it was going to be,'' Del told him. "He'll be okay, I think, but better not get those hands cold again in a hurry. It's mainly light. He's got feeling in all his fingers and toes, so he shouldn't lose any; may blister up some, but he's damned lucky and it's through no fault of Charlie's. Right now he's suffering through the thawing out.''

"Hurts a bunch, but better than not hurting at all.'' Alex set the gas can down next to the pickup. "Let's get those sno-gos out and go find that kid.''

"Hampton said he's got a forty-four.''

"He better not even think of using it . . . just give me an excuse.''

Charlie, in his fuddled state, had by now forgotten he ever had a gun. Close to the end of his tether, he was still making what he thought was forward progress to the border, but it was very slow and increasingly unsteady. Actually, he was just a bit over a mile from the truck and headed straight for it, though he had no idea how far he had wandered.

He didn't know much of anything. His clothing grew colder and partially froze as the temperature fell with approaching dark, bringing his fever down even more as a result, but he was starting to hallucinate from dehydration and hypothermia. The wind had abated and no snow was falling, allowing him to see quite a ways, if there had been anything to see. He staggered through another in a series of large drifts and almost fell out the other side of it. Without realizing it was gone, he dropped the duffel from under his arm into the snow and walked away from it, hands completely numb to the wrist. Doggedly hugging the blanket around his head and shoulders, he did not see it fall.

Violent shakes seized him periodically, rattling his teeth. He breathed through his mouth, expelling twice as much moisture and hastening his delirium. In the next few steps he fell twice and crawled back to his feet. He couldn't remember when he had completely stopped feeling his feet and his hands. His ears and battered nose were also pale and bloodless. If he had poked them with a finger—if he had been able to feel with that finger—they would have felt inflexible.

The third time he fell, he lay there for a minute, thinking. It felt wonderful to lie down and not struggle for the next step. Huffing and puffing through his mouth because his nose was stuffed and swollen shut, he was having trouble breathing. His throat was so sore he couldn't swallow. He closed his eyes and thought about it. It was dark. Maybe if he napped for a few minutes he would have the energy to get going again. It seemed like a good idea.

Before he allowed himself to drift off "for just a little while," he forced himself to sit up and tug the blanket around so he could put his face on it when he lay back down. Glancing up, he noticed a glow of light some distance off in the direction he had been going. Well, he thought, the border couldn't be far away if he could see its lights. He would go there as soon as he had his nap. Just as he thought, the damned tourist had lied to him.

He lay back down and thought of the border between Mexico and California, with its multiple lanes for checking papers and the hundreds of people who crossed it daily, driving or walking. He doubted that this border would be quite that large—maybe only four or five customs agents, each in their own little kiosk. Hm-m-m. What had he done with his papers? Was his wallet in his pants pocket? Would he be able to remember any street Spanish? ¿Cómo está? Uno, dos, tres . . . cinco . . . diez. Taco . . . enchilada . . . Ensenada . . . Tiajuana . . . na . . . na. . .

* * *

The noise of the snow machines precluded any speech between the two officers as they flew through the drifts, following the increasingly well-defined traces of Charlie's meandering stumble over and around the ridge. One after the other, Delafosse in front, they swung around in the broad, three-mile circle prescribed by their quarry's floundering attempt to reach the border. Dressed in the insulated snow machine suits, face masks, heavy gloves, and boots, they were warm enough, though the temperature was dropping steadily as the dark thickened.

Two thirds of the way around they found his discarded clothes, including his jacket, by running over them. The duffel, Jensen caught a glimpse of and, slowing slightly, snatched up like the gold ring on a merry-go-round from the drift where Charlie had lost it.

Del almost ran over the kid when they finally reached him. He threw up a gloved hand to warn Alex and veered off to one side, shutting down the engine and slowing quickly to a stop. Behind him the Alaska State Trooper did the same. Looking up, Alex was somewhat amused to see the lights of Willard's big truck shining over the snow in their direction, easily within walking distance. If they had waited another half hour, Charlie would have come right back to them. But maybe not. He was lying very still, curled up in a blanket, as if he had simply collapsed and gone to sleep.

Turned over, the kid did not look good at all. His broken nose was frostbitten white. Blood from it had smeared when he wiped it, coating the lower half of his face and freezing on his upper lip.

"Here's our truck-burglar," Jensen commented, taking a look at Charlie's boot soles, where he found the left one cracked under the instep, as he had anticipated the minute he saw the totally inadequate western footwear. His feet were probably in bad shape, though they didn't pull the leather boots off to check.

Tugging one mitten off the kid's hand to take a quick look, Delafosse immediately put it back on and shook his head.

"Dead white and cold as ice. Hate to think what his feet look like. He's in real trouble. Damn tourist."

"Let's see if we can wake him up enough to get him back to the truck. We'd better call up that chopper. He's going to need medical treatment faster than we can get him to it on the road. The wind has died enough so they can at least hover."

"They still won't be able to land in this pile of snow—have to lift him up in the basket—but I think you're right." The inspector began to shake Charlie, first gently, then with increasing roughness as the kid didn't wake. He groaned and shook his head in irritation, but did not come to. Delafosse punched his shoulder with a mittened hand, not wanting to slap the disaster of his face, but got no more response.

When it was obvious they were not going to get co-herence from him, Jensen got back on his snow machine, and Delafosse lifted the kid to the seat in front of the trooper. They rode back to the trucks with him balanced between Jensen's arms, the inspector riding behind in case he fell off.

They arrived to find that Willard had already towed Hampton's pickup from the ditch, jump-started it, and left it running. The cab was barely warm, enough to keep Charlie from further hypothermia and frostbite without prematurely thawing his injuries, so they put him there and went to the radio.

When the helicopter had come, lifted, and carried him off to Dawson, the two officers and Willard stood in the road looking after it. Hampton, recovering rapidly with warmth and food, looked down at them from the cab of the plow truck, having refused to take the quick air trip. He wanted to be sure his truck got back to town okay and would ride in with Jensen.

Helped on with the snow-machine suit Alex had been wearing, he climbed into the passenger seat. Willard, with Delafosse, drove ahead to clear the road one more time and they went down the Top of the World Highway to Dawson in half the time it had taken them to go up.

Chapter Twenty-three

⟡⟡⟡⟡⟡ "WE HAVE TERRORIZED TOURISTS. WE have dead politicians and angry sons. We have dirty old men and abused daughters-in-law. We have frostbitten thieves. And we have stubborn Indians. Oh, lordy, do we have Indians."

Arriving back in Dawson, Jensen and Delafosse had dropped Hampton at the clinic for medical treatment, before going directly to the RCMP office. Though he seemed recovered from his mild frostbite, had full sensation and motion, several of his toes and the tips of two fingers had dark patches that might be more serious than they appeared.

At the office they found what Delafosse could have sworn was the whole Han Athabaskan tribe showing solidarity for their chief in a nonviolent occupation of the building. They had taken over the few available chairs, stood along the walls, and sat on the floor in tenacious, silent immovability. A few crowded the small porch, quietly smoking cigarettes as they watched the two officers climb the front steps to the door. There weren't actually as many as it seemed, but the front office was fairly small and four or five dozen eyes followed their every move.

Clair McSpadden, unable to convince them to leave and determined to retain some kind of control of the situation, had made and distributed several pots of coffee, then continued to occupy as much of the office as she could, which turned out to be her own desk. Mel, the constable on duty, had tried to move Kabanak to a room in the back of the building, but had given up when all the others began to follow him in. So the chief sat in the most comfortable chair, with his wife in a chair beside him. He looked up calmly at the two officers as they came in and inclined his head in greeting.

Signaling Clair to come along, Delafosse left Mel at the front desk and went to the back room to discuss the situation.

"It could be worse," Jensen could not resist commenting, in response to the inspector's half-frustrated, half-amused description of the population of the case. "They may be stubborn, but they seem well behaved and they aren't wearing warpaint. You okay, Clair?"

"Oh, sure. They came in quietly one or two at a time and sat down to wait. No trouble, they're very quiet, but they're rapidly depleting the coffee supply. How's Hampton? . . . and that kid, Charlie?"

"It looks like Hampton's going to be fine. Charlie's in bad shape. Froze his nose, ears, and both hands and feet wandering around in the snow up there. Doctor's still working on him."

"Kabanak say anything else?" Delafosse asked.

"Nope. Just that he was here to confess to Russell's murder and would be happy to wait till you got back."

"Just what we need, right, Alex? Before we talk to him, what happened with his son? He was with Sean Russell's Athabaskan helper, you said?"

"James Hasluk. You remember Eddie couldn't find him at the village site to double-check his statement, and nobody on the river had seen him?"

"Yes."

"Well, Mel was in the storeroom by the back door and heard something on the back porch. He went round from the front and caught them both on the porch. When he found out they had the hatchet, he locked them up till you could come back and question them."

"Where's the hatchet?"

"In the safe."

"Take the desk and send Mel back, would you? Tell him to bring it with him."

In only a minute or two, the tall constable came in, sat down as the inspector waved him to a chair at the table, and laid the incriminating hatchet on the table in an evidence bag. It was plain, the kind that could be purchased almost anywhere. The attention-catching details were the initials burned into the wooden handle: J. H. . . . James Hampton, without a doubt. But caught between the handle and the head were several gray hairs, stuck in what appeared to be dried blood. This was also smeared on a small part of the blade, though the rest of it seemed to have been wiped or worn clean.

Jensen frowned. It was obviously the hatchet that had been missing from Hampton's camp on the riverbank. But something about it bothered him.

"How the hell?"

He and Del looked at each other and both spoke at the same time.

"If the . . ."

"What did . . ."

With a grin, Jensen leaned back in his chair and laced his fingers together behind his head, elbows framing his face. "You talk, boss. It's your office."

Delafosse turned his question to Mel.

"What happened? What were they doing with it?"

He repeated the story Clair had told, adding a few details.

"They tried to run, but gave up when I let them know I had recognized them both and they might as well straighten it out now as wait for us to come and find them later."

"What the hell were they doing on the back porch?"

"Said they were leaving the hatchet. That they were turning it in—leaving it for us to find."

"Why? How did they get it?"

"I don't know. They won't either one say anything else. You know how closemouthed Athabaskans can be when they want. They both just sat and stubbornly refused to say anything other than their names and that they were giving the hatchet to us. I gave up and put them both in a cell. An hour later, Henry Kabanak senior came in and said he wanted to confess to you."

"Has he seen his son?"

"No. I thought I'd better keep them apart till you decided what to do about the whole thing."

The inspector turned to Alex.

"What do you think?"

"May give us a handle to know why he wants to confess."

"True. We'd better talk to him first, I think. Ask him back here, will you, Mel? Alone. But put this hatchet away first, please."

"I don't believe he's the scalping kind, Del," Alex joked, when the door had shut behind the constable. "But I think it's considerate not to confront him with it."

When Chief Kabanak was sitting at the table in the small room, across from the two officers, Delafosse leaned forward.

"You'd better tell us what you want to say, Henry."

Kabanak nodded, laid his hands on the table, and sat up straight in his chair. His expression was totally impassive, revealing nothing of what he felt.

"I killed Warren Russell. I confess it. That is all."

Delafosse looked hard at him and pursed his lips, then shook his head.

"No. That's not all, Henry. Where and when do you say you killed him? And how? We must know it all . . . especially why."

Kabanak frowned. "Monday. I killed him on Monday, on the beach where he was fishing in our river."

"Because he was fishing again?"

"Yes."

"What time did you kill him?"

The chief hesitated slightly, considering. "Not long after two o'clock sometime."

"How then? Tell me exactly how you murdered him in cold blood on that beach." The tone of his voice gave away his frustrated skepticism.

There was a longer pause this time while Kabanak

thought, glanced at Jensen, then at the floor.

"I shot him."

"Where?"

"In the chest."

"With what?"

"With this gun. You can see it has been fired."

He reached into a jacket pocket and pulled out a handgun, bringing both officers automatically to their feet. But he held it by the barrel toward Delafosse. "It is not loaded."

"Put it on the table," the inspector told him. "Lay it down."

Kabanak did as he was told and sat back again as Delafosse quickly checked to be sure it wasn't loaded.

It lay there between them, an old gun that had plainly, from the scratches and wear, been around a long time.

"This looks like one of the thirty-eights that Smith and Wesson made back in the seventies," Jensen commented. "Where'd you get it, Mr. Kabanak?"

"It belonged to my father," he said.

"And you say you shot Russell with it?"

"Yes. I shot him."

There was a long silence until Delafosse spoke gently.

"Henry, Russell was not shot with a handgun. He died from a blow on the head and was only shot after he died . . . with a shotgun . . . and never in the chest with any gun."

The Athabaskan chief sat completely still for a moment, but his eyes slid back and forth between the officers, seeking validation of the statement. There was a long silence. Then he sat up straight in the chair and stared at Delafosse. "You say a shotgun?"

"Yes."

"No one in my family has a shotgun . . . not since my cousin lost mine out of the boat last year."

"So you couldn't have killed Russell. Why did you say you did?"

For the first time they saw emotion on Kabanak's face—relief.

"I thought my son . . ."

"I figured as much. Why?"

"To you he said *three* men. Then again later to me, he said he saw only two: Will and the other one, his friend."

"Charlie. Will and Charlie."

"Yes. I didn't believe him. I was afraid . . . when he said he saw . . . Charlie . . . shoot Will. Then you put him in jail."

"You saw Charlie shoot Will Wilson?"

"Yes. From across the river."

"Tell me."

Chief Kabanak now sat quietly next to his son at the table, listening while the young man told the inspector what he knew about the murders.

"I don't know what time it was. I left my watch at home that morning. But it was after noon when I saw Will and . . . the other man, that Charlie, coming upriver in the boat."

"Just the two of them?"

"Yes. Only two. I went to check the wheel for my father. I saw that part of it was coming loose, so I sat down behind the box to fix it with wire. I was working there when I heard the loud voices. I looked up and saw them go by. They did not see me, but I wondered what they were doing when they made a turn in the river and went back down, going slower.

"So I got up and ran along the bank and heard the motor as they went around a turn and in to the shore. I went far enough to see them stop where Russell had his camp. I knew it was there. I watched him the night before. We know when he comes."

"Always?"

"Someone sees and comes to tell my father."

He continued. "They were out of their boat on the bank, walking toward the tent. Then someone shot from behind the willows on the high bank. Will had a shotgun and that Charlie had a handgun, but they couldn't see what to shoot back at. The one doing the shooting didn't seem to try to hit them, just to scare them away. They started back toward the boat, but ducked behind the tent.

Then that Charlie ran for Russell's boat, got in, and yelled for Will to come on and they'd take Russell's boat, since they couldn't get to theirs.

"Will started to go, but the hidden person in the willows shot at him and missed again. That Charlie shot at the bank without careful aim and hit Will, but I don't think he meant to. Will fell down and didn't get up. Charlie started to go up to him, but the other shots came again and made him go back to the boat. He really hurried getting in, tore his jacket when it got hung up on something, and ripped it loose. Finally got it started and left, went upriver very fast.

"When he was gone, I went back to the wheel. I waited there, not long, to think what to do. I had no boat and was afraid to go across anyway. A white man had been killed . . . near a man everyone knows we don't like. Who would believe me? And I was the only one who saw what happened. So I finished fixing the wheel, took the two fish out of the box, and went home."

"And didn't say anything to anyone?"

"I told my father and he said we should keep quiet. He said it must have been Russell shooting from the upper bank and to let the white men fight each other. Wilson would be found soon enough, and we would not be blamed. Then he found the Zodiac in the river and found out that Russell was dead too."

Delafosse turned to look at the chief, who nodded slightly in agreement. Yes, that was the way it was.

"So, Charlie shot Will?"

"Yes."

"In the chest, or back?"

"In the back. He was facing where the shots had come from, while he tried to protect himself and get to the boat. Charlie shot wild and hit him. He fell down right away."

"What kind of a gun?"

He shrugged. "Don't know. Too far to see. A handgun."

"And you thought he was dead?"

A nod. "Yes. He didn't move after he fell."

"You didn't see anyone else?"

"No. But there was someone in the brush on that upper bank. Someone shooting. Russell maybe, I guess."

"Did you see Hampton? The tourist in a canoe?"

He shook his head.

"How about Sean Russell? See him that day?"

"No."

"Duck Wilson?"

"No."

"Why did you say *three* men?"

"I knew there were three all together: Will, that Charlie, and Russell shooting at them. I just said three before thinking, then couldn't say two without it sounding . . ."

"Like you changed your story."

"Yes."

Jensen leaned forward and waited for Delafosse's nodded permission to ask a question.

"Could Charlie have come back and killed Russell?"

"Maybe. I don't know. I went home. I stayed home too."

Delafosse spoke to Kabanak senior. "And you were willing to say you killed Russell, so your son would not be suspected."

"He is a good son, but he is young and sometimes quick to act. Who knows if he would be believed? If he had been somehow involved, he might have tried to protect me by not saying so."

There was a long pause as the inspector collected his thoughts, then turned to Henry junior.

"Now, tell me about the hatchet."

The cooperative look on the young man's face changed to one of stubborn determination.

"We brought it here to turn it in."

"You and James Hasluk?"

"Yes."

"Why didn't you bring it to the front door?"

There was no answer. The young man looked him straight in the eye, but his face could have been carved from stone, his lips pressed tightly together.

"Where did you get it?"

No answer. He stared at the floor.

"You know who it belongs to?"

Silence.

"Henry. You must tell us what you know. Otherwise, we may have to assume that you had something to do with either or both of the two murders ... that you, or James Hasluk, took it from Hampton's gear."

The chief muttered a few words in Athabaskan to his son, who jerked his head around swiftly to look at his father.

"No!" he said, outrage in his voice.

Another mutter of Athabaskan, but the younger man would not look up again and only shook his head without speaking. At this, clearly a parental command disobeyed, Kabanak senior let his anger show.

"Why?" he demanded in English.

Reluctantly, his son responded. "Not mine to tell," he said.

"Whose, then?" Delafosse asked.

Again, no answer.

"Hasluk?"

But no matter who asked, or how, the young Kabanak remained determinedly silent.

Finally, Delafosse stood up and looked down at him. "It would be better for everyone if you told us the truth," he warned. "I cannot let you go until you do."

Opening the door, he called Mel to return Henry junior to his cell and, when he had gone and the door was closed, turned once more to the father.

"Henry, I'm sorry. Do you understand?"

His face a study in frustration and sadness, the chief nodded.

"Yes. I understand, but he did not kill these men. He is protecting someone else."

"I would like to think so too, but who, then? James Hasluk?"

The chief looked up at the ceiling, considering. "I think ..." he said slowly, "but maybe not. He thinks it is best to tell his own story, not that of someone else. It could be someone else. Who knows?

"You know ..." he said to Delafosse, frowning, trying

intently to help the inspector grasp something he was finding awkward to put into words. "The law is the law, but it has always been more your law than ours, and is hard to understand. Our ways are different and sometimes it troubles our people to know what to say or do, so they say nothing, do nothing—just be still—and sometimes angry. They are both afraid, I think, that it will be decided that they must be guilty of this crime because they are Indian. Do you see?

"Let it wait a little. He would not speak to me either. Perhaps tomorrow."

The inspector stood up and held out his hand.

"Well, let him think about it tonight. We'll take care that no harm comes to him and will see if we can learn anything from James Hasluk. Will you take your people home now?"

Kabanak rose and shook hands with the inspector, nodding. "Yes. I will come back tomorrow."

Without another word, he left the room, walked through his Han Athabaskan people to the front door and out into the night. Silently, the rest got up and followed him, one by one, until the room was as empty as if they had never been there. Only the paper cups they had used for coffee were left, placed neatly in the trash can.

Though Alex and Del spent another half hour attempting to wrest information from James Hasluk, immovably mute, he gave them no more than Kabanak junior. Only one comment slipped out in frustration, before they locked him up again. But it was one that Jensen would not be able to get out of his mind.

"You would not believe me," he spit out. "All Indians are liars, right?"

Discouraged and too tired to discuss the events of the day, Jensen, Delafosse, and Clair fumbled on their coats and left the office. The two officers accompanied Clair to her car, then walked on up the street toward the hotel.

"Hungry?" Del Delafosse asked.

"Pooped, but not really hungry; besides, everything's

closed by now. How about a big breakfast in the morning?'' Jensen suggested.

''Fine with me.''

The streets were quiet, the sound of the only passing car muffled by snow on the road. It was much colder than it had been the night before, though overcast. The air was so still that, going by a small log cabin, Alex noticed the smoke from its chimney rising straight up into the night in a tall column. Snow squeaked under their boots; a sound that was heard only at low temperatures. Briefly, he wondered how cold it was, but decided he really didn't want to know, since knowing wouldn't change it and would only make him feel colder. He yawned an enormous yawn that Del involuntarily copied.

''Stop that,'' he said. ''You'll have us both asleep in a drift in a minute.''

Jensen grinned wearily. ''Did you ever play that game in school—yawning to make the teacher yawn too?''

''Yes, but I had Mrs. Kolleran, who was so stiff her yawns hardly moved her mouth and who sneezed through her nose like a cat. She had the straightest back I ever saw on a human being and a most excellent aim with a ruler.''

It was late and they walked all the way without seeing anyone, even in the middle of town, though they heard the small sound of a jukebox still playing in one bar they passed. Turning down the side street, they quickly covered the remaining two blocks to the hotel and stumbled in the door.

Alex was wondering if he would have to do the two flights of stairs on his hands and knees, when a sleepy-looking, blinking figure stood up from where it had been curled in one of the antique armchairs of the lobby and moved toward them. He looked, then looked again, and was suddenly much more awake.

''Jessie?''

She walked right up and into his arms, ignoring Delafosse.

''Hi,'' she said, circling his chest with a hug, her face against his shoulder. ''Where you been, trooper?''

"Jessie. Where did you come from? How . . . ?"

She looked up and gave him a sleepy smile. "You invited me. This case is taking too long and I missed you. Ryan's feeding and running the mutts, but Sophie wouldn't let me sleep in her puppy nursery. So . . . here I am. Is it okay?"

"Most definitely okay."

As he swept her into a bear hug and kissed her soundly, Alex caught a glimpse of Del's broad grin.

Chapter Twenty-four

IT WAS ALREADY LIGHT WHEN ALEX opened his eyes the next morning and lay very still in the bed, savoring the warmth of Jessie curled up against him, sleeping with her head on his shoulder. Sensing the waking change in his breathing, she stirred, laid an arm across his chest, and wiggled her fingers in between his back and the sheet, all with her eyes closed.

"Morning. Welcome home, trooper."

"We're not home, Jess. Still in Dawson, remember?"

"Yeah, but we're *both* in Dawson. You know?"

"Hm-m. I do."

The bed was exactly the right comfortable temperature. So was Jessie, gone back to snoozing next to him. He had no desire to disturb either just yet.

He thought of Hampton as they had found him in the cold pickup on the Top of the World Highway the day before and was glad to have made it back with everyone alive . . . even Charlie. How was the kid doing? he wondered. If Del was right, he could lose fingers and toes. What a price to pay for stupidity. A flash of anger reminded him that it was not just stupid, but a maliciously selfish thing Charlie had done in taking—let alone wasting—the bag of survival gear, leaving Hampton unconscious in the snow with nothing to protect himself from the ravages of the northern weather. Unconscionable.

Jessie raised her head to look at him. "That bad?"

He stared at her. "What?"

"You huffed. What were you thinking about?"

After he kissed her, he scooted up to lean on pillows against the head of the bed and told her, briefly, about Hampton's near-miss with freezing and Charlie's part in it.

By the time he finished, she was sitting up, cross-legged, on the bed facing him. She wore purple socks and an enormous T-shirt, size 3X, that came down over her knees and, with her tumble of honey-blond waves and curls, made her look like an urchin, though she was taller than average and tough from driving dog teams. She hated gowns or pajamas that clung or wound up around her in the night and always wore a large T-shirt and sweat socks in cold weather.

"Did he do it on purpose?" she asked, when Alex finished telling. "If he wanted to kill Hampton, why didn't he make sure he finished the job before he left?"

"He just didn't care one way or the other, I guess. But we'll find out more this morning, when we have a chance to talk to him, I hope. He's in pretty bad shape. Much worse than Jim Hampton, who was doing okay by the time we dropped him at the clinic last night. They didn't keep him over. He came back here to the hotel. Delafosse bunked in the extra bed in his room last night so we could have this one. But the doctor evidently thinks Charlie's hands and feet may be a serious problem, and his face was a mess."

"Serves him right," she snapped.

"Aw, Jess . . ."

"Yeah, I know. You're right. Nobody deserves . . ."

They looked at each other and Jensen grinned. "I deserve," he said, reaching for her.

"*You*? You deserve . . . nothing," she told him and a wrestling match ensued, full of shrieks and giggles. "You made me come all the way to Canada to see you . . . considerably tarnishing my independent image."

She had just whacked him with a pillow, when a knock rattled the door. Jessie cracked it open to find Delafosse outside holding a pot of coffee and cups on a tray with two considerable cinnamon rolls, gooey and covered with pecans.

"Oh, you wonderful man," she told him, swinging the door wide. "Are you spoken for?"

The inspector turned extremely red in the face, but smiled and handed in the tray. "Hi, Jessie. Thought you might . . . ah . . . be ready for this."

Jensen roared with laughter from the bed. "He's already got a friend, Jessie. You'll meet Clair of the gorgeous hair later. Come on in, Del."

But Delafosse, on his way to the office, refused.

"Want to have a chat with Duck Wilson about that vehicle theft Cherlyn mentioned, and check on Kabanak and Hasluk. Wilson should have cooled off some by now. I'll meet you at the clinic, for Charlie, in an hour. Okay? Hampton's going with me to identify the hatchet."

Then he was gone, closing the door behind him.

While they ate, showered, and dressed for the day, Jensen filled Jessie in on everything that had happened since they found Hampton in his sleeping bag on the riverbank.

"What's all this about a journal and some miner's bones?"

"That's Hampton's story. And since he found them, I'm going to let him tell you, but it's pretty interesting. Besides, I haven't finished reading the journal yet and he has . . . or soon will."

"Okay. I can wait. It sure sounds like you've got yourself a real tangle this time, trooper," she said, as she ate the last pecan from the plate, licked her fingers, and picked up her coat.

"Yeah, but we got part of it last night and I've got a feeling the rest may be about to untangle soon. At least some of it."

Alex, waiting at the door, watched her tug on her boots and thought how glad he was that she had come. Tall and fit, Jessie was tanned and healthy-looking from the time she spent outdoors. In less than six months she planned another assault on the Iditarod.

And here she was, though taking time off was not part of her current schedule, in response to his unreasonable jealousy. But that was only part of it, he reminded himself honestly, knowing the rest was just as she had said last night: She had missed him, wanted to be with him. And she had cared enough to go to the trouble of coming all the way from Knik, on at least three different airplanes, not wanting a misunderstanding to become a problem. In itself that seemed even more astonishing.

But she would never have come if he hadn't asked her. They respected each other's work and were careful not to intrude. Hers was more accessible because she lived it every day and he was often included. His law enforcement work was mostly separate, though he talked to her about it regularly, as much as he could. She insisted that she not be protected and wanted to know what he was working on, assuring him she would worry more about what she didn't know than what she did. Besides, she was insightful and often made astute suggestions.

"Hey in there. Come out, come out, wherever you are."

He was startled to find her standing directly in front of him, looking up. Leaning down, he kissed her and folded her solidly into his arms, coats and all.

"I love you, Jess. I'm glad you came."

Smiling contentedly, his arm around her shoulders, they went down the stairs together, out the door and into the snowy street.

"Duck thinks Charlie shot Will, though the kid told him whoever was shooting at them did it. He went downriver with him after dark that night, but they didn't find Will's body, and every bit of gear was gone from the beach, including the boat Will and Charlie had been in. He won't say where it came from or who it belonged to, so I bet they stole it somewhere. They went back to Wilson's place and he beat hell out of the kid, trying to get the truth out of him, so he says."

Alex sat with Delafosse in the clinic waiting room.

Jessie had gone with Hampton for coffee so he could tell her all about Addison Riser and the journal. They then intended to head for the museum to see if the curator had an early map of Dawson.

"You guys talk to suspects. We're going history hunting," she told Alex as she left. "You don't need civilians hanging around. See you later for lunch?"

"Give me your reading on this guy?" he had asked her in confidence before they left the hotel.

"Sure. But you know my rules on that. I won't be put in the middle . . . won't snitch."

"No problem. Just an impression. If there *is* anything, he's not going to tell you."

The inspector had already talked to Charlie briefly, and was waiting for the medical staff to finish checking the kid's hands and feet, then allow him back into the room.

"What's the doc have to say about the kid's frostbite?"

"They're flying him to Whitehorse tomorrow. It's too soon to tell for sure. He was badly dehydrated and hypothermic, which made the frostbite worse. The altitude on the pass didn't help. The doctor said they're giving him lots of fluids. They thawed his hands and feet at the same time they warmed his whole body in a whirlpool bath. Bet that was painful. He looks awful, with huge blisters. Pretty obvious he's going to lose parts of his toes and fingers at least, maybe more."

"Poor guy."

"Yeah . . . well, if he'd stayed with Hampton . . . He says he never went near Russell's campsite, and swears he didn't shoot Will."

"Lies like a rug."

"Prove it?"

"Well, for one thing Kabanak's son said Charlie tore his jacket getting into the boat after he shot Will, remember?"

"Hm-m."

"And do you remember that scrap of cloth we found on that beach where Russell was camped?"

"Sure. Gray?"

"Wasn't there a gray jacket in that pile of clothes he abandoned up on the pass?"

"Yes. There sure was, and it was ripped too. Let's dig

that stuff out when we get back to the office."

"Other thing is that the bullet from Will's back should match Charlie's gun."

"The slug we picked up was too battered to use as evidence, except that its weight says it probably came from the forty-four."

"Charlie doesn't know that, does he? It could have stayed in Will's body. He never got close enough to him to see before he took off in Russell's boat, if what Kabanak's son says is true."

Delafosse was on his feet. "You're mean and nasty, Jensen. You don't play fair. I like the way you think."

Ten minutes later, confronted with Jensen's suggested evidence, actual or not, Charlie confessed to shooting Will Wilson. The officers stood away from his bed to ask their questions, wearing gowns and masks to avoid introducing infection, a serious risk in post-frostbite cases, while the doctor once again checked the ruin of his extremities.

"It was an accident," Charlie whined. "Will stepped in front of me when I was shooting at that guy in the brush that was shooting at us."

"You hit him in the chest or the back?"

Though he was listening to what was being said, Alex found himself filled with an overwhelming pity for the boy who lay in the bed. He *is* hardly more than a boy, he thought, whatever he's done. What a disaster. Ignorance. Nothing but incredible stupidity and anger. Hampton was damned lucky.

There were other possible words to describe Charlie's condition, but disaster it most certainly was.

"It hit him in the back and he fell on his face. But I swear I didn't shoot him on purpose," Charlie said, and slightly raised a hand that resembled a claw to make his point.

He was a miserable, pitiable mess. Open to medical inspection, the heart-stopping caricatures of his hands and feet lay uncovered on sterile sheets. Gauze bags would lightly cover his hands when the doctor finished and a prop would keep the weight of the sheets off his feet. Parts of his hands hand and the lower half of his feet were puffed to twice normal by the blisters Delafosse had mentioned to Jensen. They were much worse than he had anticipated. So full of clear fluid they looked ready to explode at the least touch, they extended from his wrists to perhaps two thirds of the way down his fingers. There they abruptly ended, leaving the ends, from the first or second knuckle to the tips, ordinary size. Their appearance, however, was anything but normal. Deep purple, almost black in color, they looked dead, slightly flattened, spatulate.

From something he had read, probably in furthering his first-aid training as a trooper, Jensen remembered that the lack of blisters signaled damage too deep and complete to have much chance of recovery. No blood would flow through the ravaged veins and capillaries. The dead fingertips would blacken, dry, and mummify, slowly separate from the healthy tissue until, weeks later, they finally either dropped off on their own, or were surgically amputated. The blisters formed only over viable tissues, where fluid from the blood found its way through the damaged but still functioning circulatory system.

Alex found he had clenched his fingers into fists, a half-conscious self-protection, he realized, in reaction to two things. First, the knowledge that Charlie would probably lose a significant part of his fingers and toes. Second, horror that the young man would have to spend weeks with the dead parts of himself still attached, horrible reminders, while the doctors struggled to save what they could of the rest. Amputating the gangrenous tissues too early could mean sacrificing more of what could be still viable. The idea was chilling and made the trooper swallow hard.

Charlie's face exhibited less damage and would heal almost completely. It had recovered its normal pink color, even his broken nose, which the doctor had put back into place. However, a burnlike blister had, almost humorously, doubled its size, covering it from just below the eyes to around the tip, making it look as if Charlie had laid it on a hot stove. It ran constantly from the head cold that, according to the medical staff, might lead to pneumonia. He couldn't wipe it with his ruined hands, but managed to dab his lip ineffectively against his shoulder and the sleeve of his hospital gown, much to its detriment.

The doctor finished his work and left, with a nod to the officers and, "Not too long now. He's due for whirlpool therapy."

Jensen thought he had never seen a sorrier sight, but remembering the murders and attacks in which the kid had been involved, suddenly didn't feel like telling Charlie that he hadn't killed Will—that someone else had shot him again later. Let him worry a little; the way he had treated Hampton, he had it coming, didn't he?

"And what did you stop at Russell's camp for anyway?" Delafosse asked.

"Just stopped. To see if anyone was there."

"You couldn't see anyone?"

"Nope. Seemed abandoned."

"So you stopped to steal his gear, the way you stole Hampton's?"

Soon he admitted that, too, and escaping in Russell's boat because he couldn't get back to Will's.

"What did you do with his boat?"

"Turned it loose below Dawson and caught a ride back to Wilson's."

Jensen nodded. That could fit.

"And where'd you get the boat you and Will were using that day?"

Charlie turned his head away and looked at the wall. Pressed by Jensen, he finally admitted it was stolen. "But I don't know where. Will went into Dawson one afternoon and when he came back he had it." He then confirmed that he and Duck had gone back, but found nothing on Russell's beach.

"Duck thinks you killed Will . . . and then Russell," Delafosse said with a straight face. Jensen wasn't the only one who could tap-dance around the facts.

"Did not. I swear I didn't mean to shoot Will and never saw Russell. Didn't kill him. I wouldn't know him if I saw him. Honest."

"Then who did? Killing people doesn't seem to bother

you much. You left Hampton to die in the snow.''

"I thought he'd come to and get back in the truck. I don't know who killed Russell. How would I know?'' He was yelling by that time and trying to sit up in the bed.

A starched nurse stuck her head in and scowled. "Gentlemen, law enforcement or not, the patient needs rest. It doesn't sound like that is happening here.''

"Okay. It's okay. He's just a little upset. Calm down, Charlie.''

She shut the door and went away.

"Mrs. Kolleran,'' Delafosse muttered under his breath.

"Charlie, why did you break into our rooms at the hotel and take my copy of Addison Riser's journal?'' Jensen asked suddenly, catching the kid off-guard. He stuttered slightly.

"W-what journal?''

"Look. Don't deny it. We found it in the jacket you left in the snow when you changed clothes up on the hill.''

"Oh, *that* journal. No big deal. Duck said there was some old gold hidden somewhere and wanted to know where. He heard somewhere that the guy in the canoe had found a journal and some bones. I went looking for clues and found it, but I didn't go back to his place, so he didn't get it, did he?''

Delafosse jumped back in, ready to take advantage of Charlie's cooperation.

"Okay, let's talk about the trucks and campers that have been disappearing this summer.''

A sulky, defiant look crossed Charlie's face. "What trucks and campers?''

"Don't get stupid now. Duck has told us all about you and Will stealing them.''

"Bullshit.''

"It'll be worse on you if you don't get it right, kid,'' Jensen told him.

Charlie glared at them both, then, without warning, burst into tears.

"You bastards. This hurts like hell and they're gonna cut off my toes and my fingers, maybe. Why don't you leave me alone? How would you feel if they were going to cut off yours? All right. So we lifted a few trucks. We didn't know that guy in the RV would croak. Will only hit him a tap and the old coot fell over and died on us. What's it matter now? They're going to cut on me. Don't you get it? Look at this.'' He raised the wreck of his hands off the sheet. ''I want a lawyer.'' He smeared his lip on the gown once more.

Delafosse rolled his eyes at Jensen in defeat.

''I think we've got all we need for now. The details can come later, Charlie. Like your trying to kill Hampton on the river . . .''

''Will shot at him. Not me.''

''. . . and your putting his gear back later to set him up.''

''Didn't. Never did. His gear got left at Russell's camp when I took the other boat. Never saw it after that.''

''Later, Charlie. We'll see you again later. Get some rest.''

''God. If he'd only stayed in the truck,'' Jensen exploded as soon as they were in the hall and out of Charlie's ability to hear. ''What a price to pay for stupidity.''

''Yeah.'' Delafosse held his hands out in front of him as they walked toward the door. ''I couldn't help thinking of all the things I need my fingers for. Working on my truck or my boat . . . turning knobs, screws. Getting lids off jars. Turning on lamps.''

''To say nothing of shaving, buttoning buttons, zipping zippers . . .'' Alex paused. ''And Jessie,'' he said, slowly.

Delafosse glanced at him and nodded. ''That . . . would be a pretty big loss.'' He shivered and hunched his shoulders. ''Gives me gooseflesh. I'd rather think of losing my computer keyboarding ability.''

''You'd never be able to play the piano again,'' Alex handed him the old saw, attempting to lighten the conversation.

''I've never . . . Oh. I get it. You're right. No more concerts.''

They grinned at each other and went through the door, headed for the parking lot.

"So where did Will steal the boat, and why hasn't someone reported it missing?" Jensen asked.

"Probably took it from one of the summer cabins and no one knows it's gone. If it was in a boathouse, or out of the water in storage for the winter, its absence wouldn't attract the attention of someone keeping an eye on the place for the owner, unless they went looking. I've got a couple of ideas, but that's the least of our problems."

Jensen pulled his pipe from a pocket, lit it, and puffed smoke thoughtfully.

"Had a chat with Hampton this morning," Delafosse told him, as they drove his truck toward the RCMP office. "We discussed the assault charges in Colorado."

"What did he say about them?"

"The one back in 1983 was a bar fight all right. Evidently some guy got drunked up and hit the bartender with a pool cue. Hampton, with support, didn't take kindly to it and jumped in with his fists. He broke the guy's jaw, but someone else broke his arm with the very cue he used to begin with. The whole bar stood up for Jim when he got arrested, and the charges were dropped. The guy he hit was convicted of the assault on the innkeeper, but that doesn't show up on Hampton's record."

"How about the pending one?"

"Just about what your informant from Denver told you. He did punch out a guy on the job. Evidently, he was pouring substandard concrete and Hampton found out about it. As foreman, he had a right to question the guy, but admits he shouldn't have hit him. The guy's head hit the cement-truck bumper and gave him a concussion. When the contractor initiated the suit against his company, the guy retaliated by filing charges against Hampton for assault, a week after it was all over. It will probably get tossed out, one way or another. Whatever. But your source is right. Jim shouldn't hit people. He's strong enough to do some real damage. Lucky he pulled his punch on Sean Russell."

"At least—if we believe him—we know it was justified, if not totally legal, in both instances.''

"Yeah. Maybe I've reached a point where I don't trust anyone anymore. You'll have to admit it's funny the way he seems to be involved with all the aspects of this case. Somebody hit Russell pretty hard with that hatchet and it was Hampton's. You don't suppose he could be a sleeper in the truck and camper thing, do you?''

Jensen laughed, but wrinkled his forehead in a thoughtful frown.

"I can't imagine it, but we've both seen stranger things. Right?''

"Right. And who was shooting at Will and Charlie? Was it Russell? Or was Russell already dead?''

"Now there's an interesting idea.''

"What if Hampton was more recovered than he claims, and set out to get his gear back and get even with Will and Charlie?''

"How would he have got up the river? That canoe of his wasn't going anywhere.''

"When we saw it it wasn't. But it didn't show shotgun damage then either. And there's still the matter of that Zodiac.''

"It was stolen from a long ways downriver. How would he have got hold of it?''

"I don't know, but he's under every rock we turn over. Maybe there's another dead person somewhere that we haven't found yet—who was maybe driving the Zodiac when it was stolen.''

"Maybe, but a stretch. There's also Sean Russell, whom we haven't seen for a while. Where's he in all this?''

"Hasluk was working with him at the village site and was supposed to give him an alibi, told the Eagle officer that the only time Sean left was when someone brought word his father was dead. If that's the case, we have nothing solid to put him at the murder site or Hampton's camp on down the river. But Eddie couldn't find him to confirm it, and now Hasluk won't say anything either way.''

"Pretty convenient for Sean.''

"Well, Hasluk's still being as stubborn as Kabanak.

Let's go back to the office and see if we can get anything more out of the two of them. I promised to tell Sean to call his wife. I'll send someone out to find him and send him in to talk to us again.''

''Can't hurt,'' Alex said, as Del started the drive back through Dawson. ''How about confronting the two of them with each other?''

''Mean *and* nasty. Just like I said.''

The snow had stopped, but the flat white of the cloud cover continued to give the impression that it could start again at any minute. The whole town looked clean and older than it had before the storm began. Reproductions of gold-rush buildings, as well as the newer ones that had been built in the same false-fronted style, now seemed close to how they must have looked in the last of the nineteenth century. Though the clothes of the pedestrians on the street were brighter, more modern in color than the black, gray, and brown worn by the stampeders, they could almost have been miners, storekeepers, bartenders from the rush.

''You know,'' Alex said, his mind shifting back to the problems at hand, ''Hasluk said last night that we wouldn't believe him. I wonder if he'd tell us about that hatchet if he thought we would. What do you think about telling him we don't think he had anything to do with Will's death? Since he's most likely the one who knows something, we might also mention that he's forcing us to hold Kabanak junior.''

''Hm-m,'' Del agreed. ''Could give it a try. I also want to look at that jacket of Charlie's.''

Chapter Twenty-five

⟶ As Delafosse and Jensen speculated on the case before them, in a café in the middle of Dawson, Jessie listened, fascinated, as Jim Hampton told her about the journey of Addison Riser from Tacoma, Washington, to Dawson, as his journal related it. He introduced her to Frank Warner, Ozzy Wilson, and Ned McNeal as they built their boat after scaling the Chilkoot, ran the rapids outside of Whitehorse, and made their way down the river. He told her of Riser's doubts about Wilson and the incident of the Swede's watch.

"Was Ozzy really the great-grandfather of this guy, Will, who was killed on the riverbank?"

"Yeah. Isn't that almost too much?"

"And you found the journal with some of Riser's bones between here and Eagle?"

"Right. Literally stumbled over them while I was getting wood for a campfire."

"How'd he get there?"

"I don't know yet—haven't quite finished the journal, but I hope it will have some clue. You want to hear some of it?"

"Yes, absolutely. I'd love to hear it. Where is it?"

"Right here." Hampton pulled the much-handled copy from his coat pocket and rolled it against the curl that had developed from carrying it around. Spreading it out on the table, he turned pages, looking for the place he had stopped reading. "I got them down past Five Finger

Rapids before I took an unintentional nap the other day. Here. Here it is.''

"Wait," Jessie told him, picking up their coffee cups. "Let me get us a refill before you start."

She reappeared almost instantly and set down the full mugs.

"Now. Read on, please."

Her enthusiasm was encouraging, and Hampton found he really enjoyed sharing the story with someone who obviously was as interested as he was.

Riser's account described the trip on down the river, and he soon found a time to speak to McNeal, who . . . *thinks I did well to keep silent and pretend the incident of the watch was forgotten. Reminding me that there is absolutely nothing to be done, he suggested that we wait until we arrive in Dawson. The Swede will catch us up there, he says, and it may be possible to have a word with him about the lost timepiece. I agreed. There is nothing to be gained by confronting Ozzy now. Neither of us, however, wants to work with him in Dawson. We will make sure that he is not included in any partnership we make. In Ned's mind this also includes Frank Warner, for he and Wilson seem to be an obvious twosome. So we wait and watch, but I feel better for his knowing what I witnessed.*

"I'm glad they decided not to go on working with Wilson and Warner," Hampton commented, as he paused for a swallow of coffee. "I don't like those guys any more than I liked Wilson's great-grandson."

"Sounds like they really did a number on you when you met them on the river," Jessie said. "What a rotten thing to do. You might have died."

"Jensen told you?"

"Yes, some of it. He doesn't tell me everything, obviously, but he was pretty put out over what they did to you, and about Charlie leaving you out cold in the snow on the pass."

"Well, it wasn't a lot of fun, but it seems that Charlie's sort of taking his punishment for that."

"Right. Go on. What happens next?"

As Hampton read, the party of four stampeders passed Fort Selkirk, and finally, midweek, arrived at their destination, Dawson City, completing the long, hazardous journey. Riser did not immediately write in his journal, letting a week go by before he put pen to paper to describe his impressions of the settlement and his reactions to it. Hampton could imagine his bitter disappointment at finding it crowded and extremely different from what he had expected.

The once mud streets of this so-called city are now frozen into ruts and ridges. Hundreds of men walk up and down them, most with nothing to do and nowhere to go. They simply cannot stay still in one place after so many miles of moving ahead as fast as possible to reach this place. All of us feel an incredible anticlimax.

There is no gold to be had for the taking in or around Dawson and little even to share work for. All the claims were filed long before any of us left on the long, difficult passage that brought us here. Indeed, Bonanza and Eldorado Creeks were completely staked, by men already in the territory, six months before the steamer Portland tied up at the Schwabacher dock last summer.

Thank God we brought our winter supplies with us, for there is almost nothing to purchase. We have had dozens of offers for what little we have and two days ago caught a blackguard attempting to steal from our cache, so we now keep a firearm handy at all times and watch through the nights.

Ned and I stick together in town, for Frank and Ozzy have hiked off to search for some opportunity in the goldfields, but the venture seems all but hopeless.

"Wow," Jessie commented. "Just think what it must have been like, knowing there wasn't going to be enough food for everyone for the rest of the winter. There must have been some pretty desperate people."

"And some with all the money they could imagine and nothing to spend it on."

"Think of all the people who didn't make it to Dawson that fall and had to wait out the winter along the river, at Lake Bennett, in Skagway, wherever. Those already in

Dawson knew the great horde would descend on them in the spring, having eaten most of their own food.''

''Well, there would be some supplies on the steamboats when the ice melted and they could get through.''

Riser's journal entries became more infrequent as he and Ned settled into an uneasy winter in Dawson. Moving into the rough cabin of a Scots miner that McNeal met, who was going ''outside'' for the winter, they began to burn a shaft for him in the frozen ground. The journal described this method of opening a passage to the gold-bearing ore far below the surface of the ground they stood on. It was difficult and backbreaking labor and, as Riser put it, *Its one redeeming feature is that it will require finger-warming fires to melt the frozen ground as we must first heat, then dig out as much as we can, making a deeper space to build another fire. Between times, we walk miles to cut timber for those fires, since every close tree was long ago reduced to ashes in the shafts of other claims.*

All the rubble we dig out is piled around outside the cabin to await sluicing when the spring melts enough water to allow it. The melted earth immediately refreezes into a solid mass.

The cabin, he said, *. . . was minimal shelter at best . . . the frigid wind whistles through like a sieve, whipping heat away from my stove, which we have set up in one corner, as fast as it is produced.*

But Warner and Wilson had found a place of their own somewhere near Dawson and were not a part of the effort. Riser, however, believed that Wilson had stolen . . . *portions of my beans, sugar, and rice, as we separated our outfits. Damn his eyes.*

Jessie found herself watching Jim as he read and thinking that he did not fit her idea of the type who would be involved in a murder. His disgust with the behavior of Oswald in the journal was apparent and seemed completely natural. It was also clear that he had immersed himself in the hundred-year-old account of the rush for gold. He really seemed to empathize with the people Riser described and to care about them. She watched his ex-

pressions change as he responded to the things they did
and places they passed, almost as if he were a part of the
effort.

Then she remembered Alex saying that before heading
for the Forty-Mile, Hampton had canoed the waterway
between Whitehorse and Dawson. No wonder he was em-
pathetic. He had just followed the route the four in the
journal were taking—seen it all and understood exactly
what Addison was talking about. She refocused her attention on the narrative he was reading aloud, unaware that
he had been conscious of her scrutiny.

Jensen had good taste, Jim thought. This was a confident, interesting, and very attractive woman. An Iditarod
musher. Amazing. He had never met one, and didn't know
exactly what the qualifications were, but he had somehow
expected large, burly outdoors men, or women in enormous parkas and boots. Could she possibly be strong
enough to drive a team more than a thousand miles to
Nome? Must be. She had come in second in the last race.
Unmistakably intelligent, too. Would have survived the
trip to Dawson with no trouble at all.

The situation in the Dawson of 1897 was growing desperate and could only become more so. The Yukon had
frozen earlier than expected, trapping thousands, with
boats frozen in at mining camps for miles downriver. No
supplies would arrive until spring opened the passageways
to the coast, and many who had not carried in their own,
expecting to be able to buy what they needed, would soon
be in serious trouble. To make things worse, the cold intensified, dropping far below zero. Riser and McNeal huddled inside their small, inadequate shelter and worked on
the shaft to keep themselves warm by moving.

On November 29, the temperature dropped so low we
spent two whole days wrapped in our blankets, shivering
though the fire was never allowed to subside. We know
now that it was sixty-seven below and trees cracked like
gunshots in the cold.

On Thanksgiving night half of Dawson burned down
when a lamp thrown by a dance-hall girl ignited a saloon.
But the most important thing to the two men was that, at

almost twenty feet down in the shaft they were sinking, they found gold and began slowly accumulating nuggets in a coffee can for the owner of the claim. It was as exciting as if it belonged to them, as in part it did. They were careful to take only their small wages from the buckets of ore they hauled to the surface and dumped into piles that froze solid as stone. Christmas came and went.

Hampton stopped reading and took a turn bringing more coffee.

"Had enough?" he teased, when he came back to the table.

"Don't even think about stopping now." Jessie threatened him with a metal-topped sugar jar. "There're only a couple of pages left, from the look of it. I want to know what happened to make Riser hike up the frozen river in the middle of that horrible winter. It had to be something pretty important."

Hampton flipped pages to find they had only three to go and the next entry was the last. He began to read again and soon sat up straight as he came to an incredible passage.

On Tuesday, January 4, 1898, Riser had left the claim to go for a load of firewood. When he returned, he found tragedy, his partner dead. . . . *His head crushed . . . by a large rock rolled in on him . . . certainly by Warner and Oswald. I . . . found Ned crumpled and half buried in the shaft, his bright blood frozen on his clothes and broken skull.*

Fascinated and horrified, Hampton glanced up at Jessie, who sat wide-eyed, her coffee forgotten, to hear what would happen next. Quickly, he completed the rest of the entry and sat back, stunned with the results of the murder of McNeal. He and Jessie stared at each other without speaking for a long minute. Now they knew what had impelled Riser onto the ice of the storm-swept Yukon in the middle of that terrible winter and what he had done before he left Dawson. Assessing his choices, the stampeder had decided that he had few, especially if he wanted to have any small opportunity for life. It was awesome. What a strange, and yet predictable, turn of events. If

Riser had not come to the Yukon. If he had not met Frank Warner, who in turn met Oswald Wilson. If he and McNeal had not found gold in the shaft they dug for the absent owner of the claim.

He stood up and began to put on his coat and mittens.

"Come on," he said. "I think it's time to take another look at the original journal. If I'm right, it has more to tell us than I thought."

Chapter Twenty-six

ANOTHER ATTEMPT TO GAIN INFORMATION from the two native men had ended in the same stalemate. Hasluk refused to talk, as did Kabanak, though he seemed almost apologetic about it after a night in jail.

"Let them sit awhile longer," Alex suggested. "Time is on our side, after all. They can't enjoy staying in here all that much. Let his father talk to them both, when he comes in."

Del opened the evidence bag and dumped out the items they had found on the beach where Russell was killed. The four bottle caps, green pen, and piece of gray fabric lay on the table in the back room of the RCMP office.

"You were right. There it is."

Jensen picked up the scrap of gray and matched it to the tear in the jacket he had also laid out on the tabletop. "Matches perfectly. He was definitely on that beach. There may also be threads on whatever he tore it on."

"We'll check it out, but we don't really need them with this, if we believe the Kabanak boy's testimony about what he saw on the beach and Charlie's confession. What I want to know is, where is the boat Will and Charlie were driving? Both Duck and Charlie admitted going back that evening and that it wasn't there. Why hasn't it turned up? It must have been used to move the gear and bodies down to Hampton's camp, whoever did it."

"Well, there must be a hundred places on the river that

a person could hide a boat that size between here and Eagle.''

"True enough," Delafosse nodded. "But I want to know where . . . and why.''

"Could have been sunk.''

"That, too.''

Jensen stood up and began to pace around the room as he considered. "Let's go back over the thing and what we know. There are several things that bother *me* about all this, including that boat. That hatchet is going to tell us something. Bet on it. We still don't know how those two got it, but I'll bet it wasn't on the river in Hampton's stuff. Seems wrong for them to bring it in here, not just ditch it somewhere we'd never find it, if they had anything to do with Russell's death.''

"I agree. Have to wait and see.''

"Would they both lie just to lie? I don't think so, but they may both be afraid we won't believe them, or there may be some other threat we don't understand yet.

"Here's a Sherlock Holmes-ish theory for you. You know, the one that says if you answer all the questions logically, whatever is left has to be the answer, even if it doesn't seem possible?''

"Yeah.''

"Well, there's still blood on that hatchet. That means there's no way it could have been used after it was used on Russell, so it must have been used before. The wood must have been cut before.''

"And transported down the river, you mean?''

"It could have been, along with all that other gear.''

"Why?''

"Maybe the killer knew he would need a fire and couldn't be sure of finding wood somewhere else. Sounds like he didn't know exactly where he was going, doesn't it?''

Delafosse grinned. "Or she?''

"Yes, it could have been a woman. But I'm not saying 'he or she' every time I refer to the killer. Let's agree on 'he' for the sake of argument.''

"What would need to be burned?''

Jensen took out his briar, packed it with tobacco, and puffed it alight, thinking hard. "Maybe not burned," he said slowly. "A fire would also be a source of light and there was a lot to do, setting up Hampton's camp to look like he had done it himself. Maybe he needed to see what he was doing."

"If the whole thing *was* a setup?"

"Right."

"Why would . . . *he* . . . take Russell's body and leave Will's? Why not leave Russell where he died, or transport Will too? Must have been more than just to frame Hampton. Pretty risky to take all that stuff downriver."

"Let's look at it from the viewpoints of the people involved." Jensen sat down, picked up one of the four screw-on bottle caps, placed it by itself in the middle of the table, and gave it a name. "If it was *Sean*, for instance, getting his father's body away from where he camped would solve more than one problem. He might be less likely to fall under suspicion; it would confuse clues and put someone else right in the middle of any investigation."

Delafosse placed a second bottle cap near the first. "And if it was *Hampton*, what better way to elicit sympathy and dispel suspicion than to make it look as if you had been set up—that someone else did it to you? That shotgun we found under Russell's body had Hampton's prints all over it. But either the person who knocked him out wiped it clean, and used his hands to make prints pointing to him and him alone, or he did it himself, once again to suggest a frame."

Jensen pushed another bottle cap to rest beside the first two. "Is Charlie that clever? Or Duck? Was Will?"

"Pretty unlikely, but anything's possible, I guess. The old man's not stupid. He *is* sly."

"There's that shotgun pellet we found in the canoe and the hole in it. Why wouldn't some of that gear be wet if Hampton crashed the canoe as badly as it looked when we found it?"

"True. But why would setting Hampton up be so important? If it was done, it took a lot of hard work."

"How would someone who set up Hampton know where to find him? Why pick him? If he did it himself, that question would be easy enough to answer."

"Maybe the killer wasn't looking for him. He may have been headed somewhere else and stumbled across Hampton, then took the opportunity that offered itself."

"I just can't see what Hampton would have to gain by killing anybody. He didn't know either of them." Jensen clenched the pipe he had lit between his teeth and frowned.

"Satisfaction? He must have been angry. But what did Russell's head first hit? Could the whole thing have been an accident and Hampton tried to cover it up in a panic?"

"That might apply to whoever did it."

"Right. And if 'whoever did it' was interrupted by Will and Charlie, it would explain why 'whoever' was shooting at them."

"Could have just stayed quiet in the bushes."

"Not if they were about to steal what he needed to get away."

"Does the timing tell us anything more?"

"I thought it might to start with, but half the people involved with this are the inaccurate, 'sometime-around . . . whatever' sort of timekeepers. Nothing agrees with anything else."

Jensen smiled. "Yeah. People in Alaska run on 'bush,' or 'Yukon River time,' too. Everything moves slower and everyone pays less attention. They aren't being intentionally vague—they really don't know—or don't often care exactly what time it is. If it's time to do something, minutes on a clock don't usually matter much."

"I don't think it matters a lot with this either. Any of them could also be lying, or mistaken. It's like the reports of boats on the river last Monday. Almost everybody who was asked said they remembered some, or thought they did. They see so many that no one pays attention. Everyone saw some, but it could have been morning, noon, afternoon, or not at all—two, four, or six o'clock, for that matter. There are more important things."

"Like the three different blows to Russell's head."

"Yes. There's got to be a reason for each of them."

Jensen reached to push across the last bottle cap.

"We can't eliminate Kabanak's son till we know what the boys know about the hatchet. I need another bottle cap here for Hasluk, but I guess we can count them both on this one, since we put the Wilsons and Charlie on that one. Do I need more?" He waved a hand at the line of four on the table.

"Not in my opinion. Why? You think of something else?"

"No. Just double-checking, but . . ."

The door opened to admit Clair, with a business card in one hand, the coffee pot in the other. "Wilson's attorney's finally making an appearance," she said, handing Delafosse the card and filling their empty cups. "Now take note here. Seems like I'm doing an awful lot of coffee the last couple of days. Don't get the wrong idea."

"Duly noted. As of tomorrow you're off coffee duty for a week or two. My turn. Okay? Thanks, Clair," Delafosse told her. He looked at the card and nodded. "Tell this guy we're having a meeting in the only interview room and have Mel let him into Duck's cell. I'd just as soon keep Wilson under lock and key. He can be a real pain and smells like something the cat drug in. Let his lawyer put up with it."

She laughed. "You haven't seen him since this morning. The guys got together and tossed him in the shower. He roared like he was going to melt—I could hear him howling clear out at the desk—but they didn't let him out till he scrubbed and shampooed. His dirty clothes have been bagged for fumigation, or the trash, and he's wearing a set of baby-blue sweats. You wouldn't recognize him—until he opens his mouth."

"Cherlyn?" Jensen questioned.

"Doing great. Still looks terrible, but feels better and has got a lot of her confidence back. She's going to either stay in town and get a job, or move to Whitehorse and go back to school. She'd like to be a teacher.

"Oh, Alex. I met your friend. She came in a few minutes ago. She's really nice. I think she and Hampton have something to tell you. They're both excited about something. Like a couple of kids.''

While she was talking, Delafosse had picked up the evidence bag and the items on the table.

"Let's go out there," he said, standing up. "I'll take the lawyer to Duck. I think I'd better have a word with him about the charges.''

In front, they found not only the attorney but Jessie, waiting in a chair near Clair's desk, with Hampton standing nearby. She stood up as they came in.

Delafosse invited the short, round, nondescript man, who wore a trench coat, carried a briefcase, and looked completely out of place, to come back to Wilson's cell. When they were almost to the door, he paused and returned to hold out the evidence bag and items he had removed from it.

"Put these away, would you, Clair? We're through with them for now. Oh, get a separate bag for the gray fabric and that jacket Jensen is carrying. Okay?''

She nodded and laid the items down on her desk on top of the original evidence bag. Jensen handed her the torn jacket.

Delafosse disappeared with the attorney.

"So," she asked Jessie, "how long are you going to be in Dawson?''

"A day or two, I guess. Depends on the trooper here.'' She turned to looked at Alex, her eyes shining and an anticipatory grin on her face. "You'll never guess what we think we've found out. Can we have a look at the original journal Jim found?''

"Why? What's up?''

"You tell, Jim.''

Hampton brightened visibly. "Hey, we finished the journal and you won't believe it, but Riser evidently hid the gold somewhere here in town . . . before he left for Forty Mile, after they killed McNeal. And he drew a map. What do you think? A map!''

"Whoa," Alex stopped him. "What gold? Who killed McNeal?''

"Oh, yeah . . . sorry. You haven't finished it yet. I forgot." He couldn't help grinning at Jensen. "Riser and McNeal were digging a shaft for a miner who went outside and left them his cabin for the winter. There was gold. Oh, hell." He pulled the journal copy from his pocket and opened it to the last entry. "Listen to this."

As he began to read, Delafosse came back into the room and stood listening with the rest.

TUESDAY, JANUARY 4, 1898
DAWSON CITY, YUKON TERRITORY

I am heartsick and frightened. McNeal is dead. His head crushed in the shaft by a large rock rolled in on him, certainly by Warner and Oswald. I came back to the cabin with a load of wood and found Ned crumpled and half buried in the shaft, his bright blood frozen on his clothes and broken skull. There I left him and walked to the next claim for help. We pulled him out and wrapped him in his blanket, but the two fellows who helped gave me odd looks and mentioned cautiously that two friends of mine had found him earlier and gone to Dawson for the law. Their description matched Frank and Ozzy, and I recognized their tracks in the snow.

So I am now hiding with a friend in Dawson, whom I will not name for fear this journal may be found. He has determined that Frank and Ozzy told the authorities they saw me leaving the cabin just before they found him dead. I could assure my innocence and provide witnesses of my character, but would I be believed? The deciding factor, however, is that I know they intend to kill me as surely as they killed Ned, and why.

They came to our camp last week, asking to share and claiming rights as our partners. When we refused, they insisted they would have it, one way or another, that the owner would not return and the claim should be ours and, therefore, theirs. Ned showed them the shooting end of his rifle and they left, making threats.

They will not leave me alive to witness against them, when my death would make all easy. I expect that if they had the chance, they would kill me and tell the authorities, such as they are, that I attacked them, tried to escape, or some other such nonsense. Whatever they said, it would be two against none, with me dead, and two against one, if I were to go to report it myself.

I have decided that my only course is to attempt to head down river for Forty-Mile. My friend agrees and has made me the loan of a wolfskin coat, beaver-fur mittens and hat. We both know it is more of a gift. Probably I will not make it, but, who knows? God being just, I may, and can return his coat next spring. It is better than waiting here for their nefarious and certain judgment. The first time it snows to cover my tracks, I will be off with a small sled and only enough goods for survival, probably tomorrow. I have buried most of the nuggets here in Dawson, in the best place I could think of that could not be easily located, and have drawn and hidden a map.

Dearest Polly, If I perish and this is found, know that I love you and the children. All I can leave you is this record and the gold, which does not really belong to me. If you will remember where you secreted the letters I wrote you before we were married, you will know where the map is hidden. I am only sorry things did not turn out differently, but it was not a bad idea to come here, all being considered. Events simply conspired against me, and against Ned, certainly. If we had been wintered in at Lake Bennett and forced to wait until spring, it might have been advantageous. But one can go crazy saying what if. Just know that I would never leave you with two children to raise unless it were as necessary as it seems to be. Either I die here, or try to make it there and perhaps die on the way. I like my chances better in not waiting here. Whatever happens, I send you all my love. In haste. Your loving husband, Addison Harley Riser.

"And that's how he wound up where I found him on the riverbank." Hampton paused to take a breath.

"So, there's a map?"

"Yeah. At least he says so. There's no way we could

ever find out where his wife hid his letters, but I was thinking. Remember that paper padding under the picture of his family? Could that be it? Can we at least look?''

Amazingly, it was.

Retrieving the original journal from the safe in the RCMP office, Delafosse handed it to Hampton, who carefully extracted the folded paper from behind the photograph and looked up at Jessie with his eyes dancing. ''A real treasure map.''

Crossing the room to a table, he cautiously unfolded the fragile pages and spread them out on the level surface. In the same ink used in the journal entries was a hand-sketched map in two sections that fitted together. They all leaned over to look at what was recorded. It *was* Riser's map of his trip to the Klondike, for Dyea and the Chilkoot Pass were labeled at the bottom of the drawing and Dawson City near the top. In between were the names of places Riser had mentioned along the route: Lake Bennett, Dead Man's Canyon, White Horse City, Lake Laberge, Cassiar Bar, Five Finger Rapids.

As they looked more closely, Jensen noticed that the Yukon River was drawn farther than Dawson on the map. At the extreme north, or top of what was recorded, Forty-Mile Camp was clearly labeled. So, Riser had tried to go on to Forty-Mile, or at least known it was there.

There was a small, separate sketch at the bottom of the second page: a detailed drawing, with streets and buildings, of Dawson, with a number of claims marked outside of town, including the most famous one, Bonanza, to the west. What a great thing Addison had done, leaving a picture of what it had looked like to him in 1897. And there, on what seemed to have been a vacant lot, was an X for the spot he had hidden the gold.

Looking at the detail of Dawson, Hampton unfolded the modern map he had found at the Visitors Center and compared the two.

''They didn't have one old enough to see the way it used to be,'' he told the others. ''Nothing quite fits with this new one. From Riser's map, the mark he made to indicate where he buried the gold could be anywhere in about a four-block area. How can you tell?''

It was true. Streets had been moved, buildings were marked where none currently stood, and new ones had been added that had not existed during the gold rush.

Alex glanced back and forth between the two maps and shook his head.

''Why don't you take this with you to the museum and show it to Fitzgerald. If anyone could make sense of it, he could.''

''Yes,'' Hampton agreed, enthusiastically.

''I'll bet he could figure this out with some of the old maps he has over there. Worth a try, at least. I'll give him a call and see if he can take a look at it.'' Delafosse went to the telephone and soon had an affirmative invitation from the curator. ''He said to bring it on over. He'll look at it as soon as you get there. You can take the journal for him to look at too.''

They all stood grinning at each other for a moment.

''How many people find an authentic treasure map?'' Hampton crowed.

''Not many,'' Delafosse agreed, then cautioned, ''but don't get your hopes up too high. The gold is probably gone long ago.''

''It might still be there,'' Jessie threw in. ''There's a chance.''

''Oh, sure, a chance. *If* this was the only map, and *if* he buried it deep enough, and *if* nobody dug a basement there, and *if* . . . Who knows?''

The glow of even partially solving the Riser mystery could not be doused by Del's cool splash of reason. Hampton and Jessie, with the journal and map, headed for the door, excited and pleased with themselves.

''It may take some time,'' the inspector cautioned them. ''Things've changed a lot in almost a hundred years. Roads have moved, buildings come and gone. He may have to look for a while to be accurate.''

Hampton nodded. ''Well, it may not be there anyway. But it will be fun to find out where he left it back then. If it's gone, someone might know who found it.''

Delafosse nodded and disappeared once more into the

back of the building to see if the attorney was ready to be let out of Wilson's cell. Hampton and Jessie went eagerly out the door, anxious to get to the museum. They had been gone only a few minutes, however, when Jessie came back.

"Shall we meet you here for lunch?" Jessie asked Alex. "You and Del plan to eat, don't you? We can all go, if that's all right with you."

"Sure, sounds..." he hesitated at the sound of the front door opening again and turned to find Sean Russell coming in.

"Where's Delafosse?" he demanded.

"In a meeting with an attorney."

"Said he wanted to see me, and I want to see *him*."

Jessie stood where she was, watching. There was something uneasy, almost disturbed in Russell's voice, and it was the first time she had seen Senator Russell's son.

"He should be out in just a few minutes," Alex told him, waving a hand at an empty chair. "Make yourself comfortable."

Russell's beige appearance was relieved this time by a blue jacket. It looked strangely as if it should have been worn by someone else, the hue an interesting contrast to his washed-out coloring and the rest of his clothes.

Russell frowned and walked past the chair toward Clair's desk. "Na-aw. I'll stand. Just have a question or two." He turned and paced back across the room to look out the windows on the west side, but not stopping there either, turned and walked back.

"Is it something important? Can I help?" Jensen asked.

He shook his head. "Nope. I'll wait to see Delafosse. What's he want anyway? I understand he has my assistant up. Why? What's going on? He the one that killed my father?"

"Better let him tell you."

They watched him fidget and move nervously around the room, looking at pictures and out windows. Something about the dis-ease of the man caught and held Jensen's attention. Russell couldn't seem to keep his hands still; touching things he passed, fussing with the fringe on a flag in one corner, rubbing at a spot on a windowpane.

"What's taking so long?" he asked, once again walking up to Clair's desk.

"He won't be much longer," she told him.

He picked up and put down the square stone penholder she had been close to using for protection several days before.

"They released my father's body yet?"

"I don't know, but the inspector will be able to find out for you, I'm sure."

She watched Russell straighten a pile of paperwork in a basket on her desk. Jessie walked across the room and sat down in a chair next to the door. While Alex watched Russell, she was paying close attention to him. Her alert expression said clearly that she was aware that something subtle was going on that she didn't understand.

"Let me tell the inspector that you're here waiting for him," Clair said, and started to rise from her chair.

"Hey," said Russell, when she was only halfway up. He reached across her desk to the items on the evidence bag. "My pen. How'd that get here? I must have dropped it in here the other day, huh? Wondered where I lost it."

He turned from the desk, holding the green pen in one hand, a pleased expression on his face.

Jessie sensed that Alex had grown very still. Clair, a startled look on her face, sat back down in her chair and pushed away from the desk with both hands. There was a moment of silence, then the sound of the door to the interview room opening.

"Mel will let you in to see Mr. Wilson whenever you want," they heard Delafosse tell the attorney.

"What makes you think it's yours?" Alex asked Russell, with elaborate casualness. "Lots of green pens." He made a small "hold it" motion with one hand to Delafosse, who appeared alone in the doorway.

"Not like this one," Russell enthused, examining the pen. "You can't get them here. I special-order them from the East Coast because they will write even in the rain, on wet paper. Great for outdoor stuff at the site. This is the last one I had and I didn't know where . . ."

He looked up, noticed the look on Jensen's face, and hesitated. "What?"

Delafosse stepped carefully into the room. "Sean. That pen's yours?"

The pleased expression faded slowly from Russell's face and a subtle, calculated cunning took its place. "Is it?"

"You said so."

Russell glanced nervously around at the four people staring at him. "It . . . it must not be mine. I've made a mistake."

"A bad one, I'm afraid. That pen is evidence. We found it at the place on the river where your father was murdered. You said you were never there."

Comprehension widened Sean Russell's eyes as he almost threw the offending pen back on Clair's desk. Panic replaced it. With one swift motion, he snatched a half-full bottle of soda from the desk and almost leaped toward the door. Before Jessie could move, he smashed the bottle against the wall, breaking the top of it and spilling its contents. Grabbing her from behind he positioned what was left of the splintered bottom of it just under her chin, sharp spears threatening her throat. Breaking the bottle had cut him, and blood dripped slowly from the fingers of his tense right hand onto the front of her light green sweater.

"Alex?" she said, in a small, whispery, disbelieving voice.

"Shut up," Russell told her, gripping her shoulder with the other hand. "Don't move. Don't even breathe."

She followed his directions, freezing in the chair. Only her eyes moved, first to Clair, who sat with both hands over her mouth, then to Delafosse, who half crouched just in front of the doorway, ready for anything, and finally to Jensen, where they met and clung to his, recognizing and sharing the fear that her life . . . their life . . . could be gone in a second.

His face was white, his lips stiff as he spoke, slowly and quietly, "Do exactly what he says, Jess. Don't move."

Chapter Twenty-seven

No one moved for another long minute.

"Stand up—very, *very* slowly," Russell told Jessie and began to guide her to her feet with his hand on her shoulder. "Don't!" he said to Jensen, who had involuntarily taken a step forward.

When he and Arnold stood to one side of the chair, he stopped and looked across at Delafosse. "Give me the keys to your truck."

The inspector hesitated, glancing at Jensen before reaching into his pocket for the keys.

Russell released Jessie's shoulder and grabbed a handful of the hair on the back of her head. Pulling her head back, he bared her throat and laid the broken glass against it. Carefully he applied pressure until a thin line of red appeared against the white of her skin.

Jessie's eyes widened and she bit her lower lip, but otherwise did not physically react to the sudden pain. The room was so still they could all hear her ragged breathing.

"Do it," he snapped. "Give them to *her*."

Delafosse moved toward him slowly and reached out to drop the keys in the hand Jessie raised.

"Back," Russell told the inspector. "Get back over there."

The inspector backed away.

"Now," he said, still holding Jessie by her hair. "You will all move over there by the windows. *We* are going out . . . *together*. If anyone here moves from where I can see them, she loses. Got that?''

"Listen, Sean . . ." Delafosse started.

Once again, Russell pressed the glass to Arnold's throat and a fresh line of blood appeared. Still she kept herself from reacting, afraid that if she moved, even a fraction of an inch, more damage would be done.

"GOT THAT?''

The two officers nodded.

"Then move. Over there, behind the desk, and face the windows.''

Delafosse and Jensen moved slowly and carefully across the room to stand with Clair, who had risen from her chair.

Jensen was seething with frustration and apprehension.

"Jessie," he said tensely. "Do exactly what he says. Move very carefully.''

"SHUT UP,'' Russell screamed. "No talking. Turn around and face the parking lot.''

They did.

He began to pull Jessie backward toward the door. She felt cold and as if she couldn't get enough air. Adrenaline seemed to heighten her senses. She could feel, but not see, that he had moved the bottle enough so that it no longer rested against her neck, but was still close, sharp and deadly. If she grabbed his arm with both hands, could she keep it away long enough for Alex to get across the room? she wondered briefly before discarding the idea. She didn't know Russell, had no idea how strong or quick he was, but he was obviously desperate. She was just a means of escape to him. He probably wouldn't hurt her unless he was pressured or forced. If she cooperated, there might be a safer opportunity to get away. Carefully, as Alex had told her, she moved back, step by step, not resisting the steady, hurtful pressure of his grip on her hair.

She heard the rattle of the doorknob as he bumped it.

Jensen started to turn his head toward them and Russell stopped.

"Don't even consider turning around," he said. "You've seen a sample of what will happen if you do.

"Stand perfectly still," he told Arnold.

She felt him let go of her hair to open the door and wanted to step away, but the broken bottle remained just under her chin. The knob turned and the door opened with a tiny squeal. It had a closing device that forced him to hold it with one hand to keep it open.

"Step back," he told her.

She stepped. The glass wavered and touched her.

"Again."

She took another step and felt the doorsill under her left foot. With care not to lose her balance and accidentally cut herself, she stepped over it. Looking at the back of Alex's head, she noticed a strand or two that stuck up from a cowlick and wondered if she was seeing it for the last time. If he cut her, could they get help fast enough to keep her from bleeding to death? Stop it, she thought, taking a deep breath. I won't pay attention to that now. She forced herself to focus on where her feet were going and what Russell was doing behind her. Two more steps and she was clear of the door, both feet on the porch.

Then, behind her, Russell made an odd, soft sound of air expelled and, suddenly, the glass was gone from her throat.

"Move away, fast," a voice told her, calmly.

Arnold lunged forward and whirled to see Russell struggling in Hampton's muscular grip. One arm, strong from driving canoe paddles through the heavy water of many rivers, was around the beige man's neck in a choke hold that almost lifted him from the floor. The other, like a vise, held his right wrist out to the side, the broken bottle still clutched in his fingers. With his free hand, Russell clawed ineffectively at the arm that restricted his breathing. The two of them looked almost as if they were dancing against the heavy door.

"Ugh," Russell grunted, his face turning red.

Almost methodically, Hampton began to pound Russell's right hand forward against the door frame. Three, four times he hit it, till the bottle fell, breaking on the hard wooden porch. When the hand was empty, Hampton half carried, half marched his choking captive forward into the office, leaving the door to close itself behind them.

Jensen and Delafosse both moved quickly to help, but before they could get around the desk and cross the room, Jessie acted first. Stepping forward, she whipped her fist into Russell's diaphragm in a punch that would have doubled him over without Hampton's unwelcome support.

"You bastard!" she spit at him. "You pitiful coward."

She hit him again with the other fist, then stepped back, ruefully shaking both hands, and turned to meet Alex.

"He deserved it," she said.

While Delafosse assisted Hampton, Jensen gathered her into his arms, where she was glad to stay, shaking slightly as the adrenaline rush and fear subsided.

In a minute, she looked up from the embrace to see a combination of love, relief, and humor on his face.

"Couldn't you just watch for a change?" he asked.

Clair, who noticed that Jessie's injured neck was bleeding on his shirt, went for the first-aid kit.

"That green pen. And we hadn't even had it checked for fingerprints." Delafosse shook his head regretfully and examined the pen in question, now in a new evidence bag.

"We did have a few more promising leads, you have to admit," Jensen reminded him. "Trash from the beach would have been a long shot and we automatically prioritize the most important stuff first. It was due to go down to the lab."

"I know, but . . ."

"And if you had sent it already, it wouldn't have been here for him to find and pick up. His alibi might have kept us guessing for some time—and looking at Charlie's lies."

"You're right, of course. Still . . ."

"Forget it, Del. Least said . . . Where was Mel while all that went on? I kept expecting him to walk in on it."

"In the back, keeping an eye on Duck Wilson, who wasn't too pleased with the representation the court sent him. We wanted to make sure he didn't decide to express his displeasure physically, so I told Mel to stick around.

He didn't hear a thing. It *was* actually pretty quiet.''

"I remember it as screaming loud."

"Well, you would. It was your Jessie, after all." He grinned. "Those were quite some punches she threw. Ever consider recruiting her?"

"Not a chance. One of us in the game is enough."

"Where is she?"

"I sent her back to the hotel for lunch and a nap. She said she was exhausted from standing in for police officers who did nothing but look out windows."

"She did, did she? You picked a good one, Jensen. That's where Clair went, too, I guess, home for a rest. I told her to take the afternoon off."

"Yeah, and Hampton walked over with them."

"What shoulders on that guy. If paddling a canoe builds that kind of strength, I think in a few months I'll get the whole post out on the river for spring training."

"Pretty impressive, all right. Sure glad to have him on our side. He took hold and hung on like Russell was a rag doll, thank God. I've never felt so helpless in my life."

"You were not alone, my friend. I could hardly tolerate standing there, listening to him take Jessie out the door."

"You happy with the way things turned out for the Kabanaks?"

"Very."

Sean Russell had replaced Hasluk and Kabanak junior in the cell. Knowing he had been caught was all it had taken to have them fall over themselves to tell what they knew.

After Sean left for Dawson, Hasluk, troubled that he had been told to lie or lose his job, had searched the village site and found where Sean had sunk the stolen boat and, hidden in the brush, the motor and the hatchet with Hampton's initials. Afraid that his word against Sean's wouldn't be believed, he had recruited Henry junior to help him make sure the hatchet got to the police in Dawson, hoping that it would be enough to incriminate Sean. They had followed Alex around town, trying to leave it where he would be sure to find it. Kabanak junior was the figure he had seen coming out of the hotel. They had made the tracks to the truck from the snow machine but, finding it ransacked already, decided to leave the hatchet on the back porch of the RCMP office. Unexpectedly confronted by Mel, they had maintained silence: Hasluk, afraid of being charged with Russell's murder; Kabanak, out of respect and fear for his friend.

Chief Kabanak had come in time to hear most of their story and take them both home.

"Yes, it was good to be able to let them go with Henry." Del smiled and sat up from where he had been leaning with both elbows on the table. "Well . . . it's over and the questions are mostly answered. I'm also glad to know Sean didn't mean to kill Warren."

"But he did mean to murder Will."

"Yeah. Too bad. If Charlie hadn't accidentally shot Will, it might have ended up differently."

"Lot of ifs in this one. If they hadn't stolen Jim's gear, for instance, Sean wouldn't have used it to set him up."

"Just chance that he saw Hampton's camp the night before from the Zodiac and recognized the canoe and those waterproof equipment bags."

"If Will and Charlie hadn't stolen that old man's RV, he wouldn't have died, and they wouldn't have come home to hide."

"And started stealing boats and stuff, getting Will killed by walking into Sean's attempt to hide his dad's body."

"If Duck hadn't beat up on Charlie, he wouldn't have tried to force Hampton to take him over the pass and frozen his face, hands, and feet."

"And Willard wouldn't have offered to teach you to spit tobacco."

"True. Now there's a real loss, but I think I'll stick to my pipe. Jess says she can put up with that—likes the smell of it, even."

Jensen stretched his long arms behind his head and yawned. The back of his neck ached from bending over the paperwork he had stayed to help the inspector complete. "We almost done here?"

"The important stuff. The rest can wait till tomorrow. I'll clean it up and get it sent down to Whitehorse."

"Good. I won't fight you on that. Well over an hour of interrogating Russell and at least that long shuffling paper. About time we got some of that potent Canadian whiskey you keep pushing. It's probably going bad in the bottle as we speak. Needs somebody to drink it before it's completely spoiled."

"My thoughts exactly. Let's get out of here. Clair's invited us all to dinner."

Chapter Twenty-eight

❦ AGAINST A HILL JUST SOUTH OF DAWSON, Clair McSpadden's small, well-built log cabin sat among trees, spilling a warm golden glow from its windows into the dark and highlighting the feather-large snowflakes that fell close enough to be caught in the light. Smoke from a wood fire rose from its stone chimney, dispersing a hint of evergreen and something deliciously redolent of onions and garlic into the air.

Though ravens fly back to communal roosts at night and do not usually remain near human habitation after dark, one cantankerous old bird with a damaged wing muttered and complained momentarily from high in the branches of a spruce, before settling into silence again, with a ruffle of ebony feathers over its feet. Between the tree and back door was a covered feeding platform fastened to a stump, where Clair made sure the old fellow could help himself to tasty items separated from her garbage: stale bread, scraps of fat, meat and vegetables.

The boots of several people had worn a path in the snow, which led to the front door, and the sound of voices, background music, and kitchen noises could be heard coming from inside, where most of those involved in the case had gathered at Clair's wonderful handmade house for dinner. It was a snug four rooms full of comfortable furniture, brightly colored curtains, books, and currently, six people enjoying each other's relaxed company. A fire crackled invitingly in the stone fireplace, fill-

ing the air with the scent of a handful of spice she had
tossed in.

"Hey, this is really well made," Hampton commented
from his seat on the raised hearth, as he examined a small,
handcrafted model of a birchbark canoe he had found on
the mantel.

"Like to build one like that full-size?" Alex asked,
from a place on the sofa next to Jessie, who sat with her
feet curled under her, leaning against him affectionately
and sipping from a glass of white wine. The turtleneck of
a white sweater covered the scratches on her throat and
her honey-colored curls shone in the light from the fire.
With frequent glances and a more than usual inclination
to stay in physical contact, he realized that he was still
just a little uneasy from Sean Russell's threat to her. The
continuing warmth of her thigh against his revealed her
similar need.

"Think I'll repair the one I have first," Jim grinned.
"Now that you guys'll let me take it home."

Watching him turn the canoe over in his hands, Jensen
remembered the clean, careful lines and finish work on
the remains of the smashed canoe, and decided that any
furniture Hampton made was probably put together with
a great deal of skill and pleasure.

"How're you feeling, Cherlyn?" Del asked, coming in
from the kitchen to set a basket of corn chips and a container of salsa on the old trunk that doubled as a coffee
table. "More wine?"

"No, thanks. I'm fine."

She smiled crookedly up at him from a cross-legged
position on the floor across from Jim. The bruises on her
face were still deep purple, and she was carefully sipping
from the side of her mouth, avoiding the pair of stitches
the doctor had put into her lip. Still, she looked happily
at ease in a pair of Clair's jeans and a bright blue blouse
that contrasted pleasantly with her blond hair.

"Glad to hear it," he told her, and disappeared back
into the kitchen, where he was helping Clair with dinner.

Though the others had offered assistance, she had
turned down all but Del, and Alex had already resigned

himself to the idea that if the meal took longer to prepare as a result, the developing relationship would certainly benefit. He was also perfectly contented with his second Canadian whiskey and the handful of chips he took from the basket and began to crunch one at a time.

He and Del had invited Hasluk and the Kabanaks, but the chief had thanked them and refused. His son's mother, he said, was anxious to have him back at home.

Hampton stood up to set the miniature canoe back in its place and picked up his bottle of beer instead, casting a look of anticipation toward the kitchen. "The smell of whatever they're cooking is driving me crazy," he said. "Hope there's more cooking than kissing going on in there."

"I heard that!" Clair called, as Del came back in, ferrying a huge bowl of green salad to a large, round dining table on the other side of the room.

"Come and get it," he announced. "Spaghetti's ready, and the garlic bread's hot. There's more wine."

In five minutes they were cheerfully settled around the table, making satisfied sounds and wiping clam sauce from their faces. By the time chocolate cake, ice cream, and coffee were served, they had all overeaten, but conversation had reestablished itself.

Hampton shook his head when Cherlyn asked a question about Sean Russell.

"What a combination of contradictions he seems to be," he said to Jensen. "I can't imagine what kind of anger or fear it would take to kill someone . . . especially your own father."

Jessie and Alex quietly held hands on the table between them, each satisfied for the moment with knowing the other was within reach. Alex leaned forward, an elbow on the table, pipe cupped in his other hand, to comment.

"Sean killed Will, all right, but he never meant to kill his father. In fact, he really didn't, but . . ." he glanced at Del, who was whispering something to Clair, sitting beside him, proudly making no secret of the fact that she was exactly where she wanted to be. "Let the inspector tell you. It's his case."

But Del shook his head.

"I'm tired of being in charge. I'm going to come to work in your detachment, where you'll have to make the decisions. You know as much as I do, go ahead."

Alex laughed. "Fair enough. Well, to begin with, Jim, Sean stole the Zodiac in Eagle because his own boat was useless and he badly wanted to have what he saw as a last chance to talk to his father. When he couldn't locate Warren's camp after dark, he decided to wait till the next day and camped alone.

"When he met Warren, just after noon the next day, they got into another argument. Russell refused again to help him buy a new boat. Sean started to leave, angry and frustrated. Warren reached out a hand to stop him and Sean shoved it away. A rock turned under Warren's foot and the older man lost his balance and fell, hitting his head on a rock on the beach.

"When Sean realized Warren was dead, he panicked. He had just gone up the bank into the brush to look for a place to hide the body when Will and Charlie showed up and got out of their boat. Warren's body was just out of sight behind the tent, and Sean knew if they came any farther they'd see it. He had a gun he carried for bear at the village site. He shot, not to hit but to scare them, but they didn't know that.

"They shot back. Will got in the way. Charlie hit him and escaped in Warren's boat, leaving theirs and what he thought was Will's body on the beach. He didn't know Will wasn't dead."

"What a run of bad luck," Hampton commented. "No matter what Sean did, it looked bad, didn't it?"

"Sure did and worse. But if he'd come to us then, we could have straightened the whole thing out. He might have been convicted of manslaughter, but not much else."

"But he didn't. He set me up?"

"Right. Now he was—he thought—left with two dead men, neither of whom he was responsible for. But he *had* stolen the Zodiac, and after all the disagreements with Warren, he was terrified that no one would believe he hadn't meant to kill him. He didn't care about Will, but he decided the best thing would be to get everything of Warren's off that beach and hidden somewhere else, where, hopefully, no one would ever connect it to him. And where?''

"My camp."

"Not yet. He was headed for the place he was most familiar with and could hide things easily—the village site down the river. He knew that Charlie had shot Will and, assuming he was dead, went down to see if he could drag him up into the brush and leave him out of sight. But Will came to with Sean looking down at him.

"Now he'd been seen. If he wanted to get away without anyone knowing he had been there, he couldn't leave Will alive. He questioned him and found out they had stolen your gear. Will offered it to him if he'd leave him alone— told Sean all about taking your stuff and shooting you. He assumed if he hadn't killed you, you'd drowned.

"Sean shot Will again, killing him this time, and dragged him into the brush, where he covered and left him. He then loaded Warren and his gear into Will's boat, finding all of yours in the process, including the hatchet. He used it to cut enough wood to take along to start a fire, in case he needed to burn anything incriminating. But he used it later, as we figured, to light your campsite as he set it up.

"Towing the Zodiac, he started down the river after dark, heading for the village site, where he thought he could get rid of the evidence and body.

"From the river, he saw your fire and thought it might be Charlie. He tied up and slipped along the shore to see. When he found you asleep and saw the condition of your camp, he realized you were the one whose gear Will and Charlie had stolen, the tourist they thought they had killed. Since it was easy to tell which was yours—those bags with your name on them—he decided to leave your gear—it would be easier than hiding it—figuring you'd be glad to get it back and might not go to the police over what was no longer stolen. He crept up and hit you over the head, so he could put it back without your knowing who had brought it. He hoped you would assume it was, for some reason, the thieves and, at the least, wouldn't be able to prove it was ever missing.

"Then, while he was unloading your equipment, he realized that he could set you up for his father's death just as easily. Since you were an unknown, from somewhere else, and not familiar, he hatched a plan to frame you. But because the bruise on Warren's head didn't look enough like violent murder, he used your hatchet to hit his body again. Sometime after that he found the shotgun and decided it would be even better. By now he was exhausted and totally irrational. He blasted Warren's head with the gun, over the hatchet wound, and placed the gun under the body, which he had carried into the brush above your reestablished camp.

"Making the hatchet wound and shooting Warren almost broke him. He really did love his father, but he hated him too. Miserable situation. He's going to need some help getting it straight in his mind. A lot of the anger he displayed came out of that, I think.

"He crushed your canoe, dumped booze on you and as much as possible down your unconscious throat, put Warren's gear in your tent, and left. Going back upriver, on the spur of the moment, he deflated the Zodiac and sank it by Kabanak's fish wheel. Another suspect wouldn't hurt—if only of stealing the inflatable boat. He took Will's stolen boat back to the village site with him, where he hid the motor and the hatchet, and sank the boat in a deep spot in the river. When the investigation that he knew would result died down, he intended to get the boat back, repaint it, and claim he had bought it used somewhere. He bribed his assistant, Hasluk—who didn't know about the murder, by the way—to give him an alibi, also threatening to fire him if he told anyone Sean hadn't been there all the time. Then he settled in to wait for someone to bring the news that his father was dead, killed by a stranger, a tourist with a canoe.

"The hatchet he kept, in case he needed an extra piece of evidence that pointed to Hampton, but never got around to using it—forgot and left it at the village site, where Hasluk found it later."

"So," Jessie asked, "he might have succeeded, if he hadn't come to Dawson?"

"Might. I'd like to think we're better than that and it would just have taken us a little longer. But he couldn't stand not knowing what was going on. He used waiting for his father's body to be released as an excuse to stick around. That led to his great mistake of claiming the pen we had picked up in the place Warren was killed."

"Well, at least it's over," Clair said. "It's good to know what really happened. Sean Russell's locked up, and Duck Wilson. Old wretch won't get a chance to know the joy of filth again for a long time. Poor Charlie will be tried as soon as he's well." She smiled up at Del. "You got them all, Inspector."

"*We* got them all." He nodded around the table, then smiled wickedly, laying his arm around her shoulders. "You ran the women's shelter and made coffee and ..."

"Hey!"

"Alex did a lot of investigating and learned to appreciate Canuck whiskey"—he lifted his coffee cup in a toast to Jensen—"even Jessie got more involved than she intended—could start classes in pugilism—but Jim actually *got* him at the last there. Thanks, Jim, for all of us."

"Especially for me," Jessie said, leaning to where he sat beside her, to give him a hug. "I ... well, you know. Thanks for being there." She sat back and Alex smiled at the glow on Hampton's face. She did have that effect on people, he thought.

"Shall we give him a strong-man trophy?" he asked her.

"No." She smiled. "I think we should invite him, and his friend Judy, to come up next summer. We could show them a lot of good canoeing and fishing spots."

"That invitation I'll accept right now," Hampton said. "I'll bring both Judy and her daughter, Megan. You'll like them a lot and I can hardly wait for them to meet you."

"Good. That's settled."

"Oh," Del remembered, "you can have the journal

back, if you want it, and the nuggets are yours. There don't seem to be any leads to his family.''

"Hey, thanks. Enough money for me to build a new canoe, I bet. But I had a talk with the museum curator and I think I'll leave the journal here with him. The museum's where it really belongs, don't you think?''

"Great idea, Jim,'' Alex said.

"I've got one more, I think. How would it be, Del, if we buried Addison Riser's bones back on the riverbank where I found them, and put a small marker there that gives his name and who he was? Would that be okay?''

Del nodded, obviously pleased. "I think that's the best one yet. If you'll come back up next summer, I'll help you do it.''

They all agreed it was exactly right.

"Hey, when are you coming back to Alaska, Del?'' Jensen asked. "We could do some fishing in the spring.''

"Sooner than that, I hope. I thought maybe Clair would like to go to Anchorage with me for Fur Rendezvous in February. I was there last year and it's a lot of fun. What do you think, Clair?''

"I think that could be arranged,'' she said. "If the boss'll let me take the time off.''

Their smiles almost matched the exceptionally pleased one on Jensen's face.

Jessie poked him in the ribs. "Matchmaker,'' she muttered.

"I have very good instincts,'' he said with mock dignity.

"And taste,'' she reminded him.

"And taste,'' he agreed, heartily. "*Very* good taste.''

"You may deserve, after all.''

As Hampton got up to refill the coffee cups, there was a knock on the front door. Clair opened it to reveal curator Robert Fitzgerald on the porch, thoroughly dusted with snow.

"You've got a *raven* in a tree out here,'' he said. "It scolded me with *quorks* all the way up the path.''

"That's Swiftwater Bill,'' she told him. "He's got a bum wing. Come on in. You're just in time for dessert.''

"Great choice," he grinned, stepping in and shaking the flakes from his fuzzy hair. "For the famous Klondike stampeder of the same name, I assume."

"Partly. But he's a mouthy—you could say, *billy*—bird. I know. Bad pun," she admitted at the groans from the group still at the table.

"Sorry to interrupt, but they told me at the RCMP office that Jim Hampton was here and I thought he'd like to know what I found."

"Found?" Hampton poured him coffee, as Alex pulled up another chair and Clair brought Fitzgerald a slice of cake. "You found it?"

"Found what?" Cherlyn asked.

"Where?" Jessie chimed in.

"Hold on," Fitzgerald cautioned, waving both hands to halt their onslaught of questions. His grin was amused, but they could see he was bursting to tell them something, but inclined to draw it out.

"Did you locate McNeal?" Alex asked.

"No, but I will eventually. No, it was that old map, you see, and one I had in the file that almost matched it. I enlarged and overlaid the important parts."

"Where was it?" Hampton was practically rocking in his chair.

"Where's what?" asked Cherlyn again.

"He's figured out . . . where Riser buried the gold. Right?"

Fitzgerald hesitated long enough to look around the table at the intensely interested looks on their faces, prolonging the suspense.

"Where, man? Where?" Alex demanded.

"Well . . . without a doubt . . . ah . . . the overlay shows that he buried it . . . ah. I don't know if you'll believe this."

"*Where*?" Unsynchronized shouts of frustration from everyone at the table.

"Ah . . . well, okay . . . he buried the gold on the lot where . . . It's really very unfortunate, and I'm sorry to say, will be impossible to ascertain, because—very soon after Riser buried it—Arizona Charley Meadows covered

the lot by erecting the most famous building in Dawson
... *the Palace Grand Theatre*!''

* * *

In the summer of 1994, a small block of granite was
placed by Charles Delafosse, RCMP, and James Hampton
of Denver, Colorado, on the east bank of a bend in the
Yukon River between Dawson City and Forty Mile, Yukon Territory, Canada. On it were these words:

> AT THIS LOCATION, IN SEPTEMBER 1993,
> WERE FOUND AND ARE NOW BURIED
> THE REMAINS OF
> **ADDISON HARLEY RISER**
> OF TACOMA, WASHINGTON,
> A STAMPEDER OF THE
> KLONDIKE GOLD RUSH AND VICTIM
> OF THE DESPERATE WINTER OF 1897.
>
> HIS TERMINATION DUST FELL EARLY.
> R.I.P.

Addison Harley Riser

The Account of My Journey
to the Gold Rush from Tacoma, Washington
to Dawson City, Yukon Territory, Canada 1897

SUNDAY, SEPTEMBER 5
STEAMSHIP AL-KI
HEADED FOR ALASKA TERRITORY

I BEGIN THIS ACCOUNT AS WE STEAM NORTH ABOARD A crowded ship, headed for Alaska Territory on the beginning of my great adventure to the gold fields, and on this day I am in a much more cheerful disposition. Upon departing Tacoma, the last of August on this steamer Al-ki, most of us, I think, felt a bit sad at the thought of leaving family and friends and embarking into the unknown wilderness. I was disconcerted and sad to leave my dear wife, Polly, and our children, Tommy and Anna, not knowing when I would be able to greet them again, and knowing that, until I can, she must care for all three. There were many of us on deck and all were quiet and thoughtful for a time, as we watched the island scenery slide by. But by the time we passed Vashon Island and docked briefly in Seattle, where we took on a few more passengers and a number of horses, a gayer mood prevailed and we were soon singing "Hot Time in the Old Town Tonight," and comparing our expectations of fortunes in shining gold in the future.

The Al-ki tied up at the Schwabacher dock, where the Portland came in from the Clondyke on July seventeenth with the two tons of gold that inspired this whole venture. I could not help but think of the headline in the

Seattle Post-Intelligencer. "GOLD! GOLD! GOLD! 68 Rich Men on the Steamer Portland. STACKS OF YELLOW METAL!" *And more than five thousand people waiting at six o'clock in the morning to see those ragged miners stagger off onto the docks with their strange assortment of bags and containers so heavy they could scarcely carry them. The handle pulled straight off one such case.*

Hopefully, less than a year from now, I may come back with such good fortune. How I long for that day. I know Polly has forgiven me for throwing over my employment at Jordan's Mercantile, and that she tries not to worry. I simply could not be a clerk forever, watching Polly and the children want for things they deserve to have provided. Had there been a position available for me to make use of my training as a newsman, things might have been different. The last few years of the country's depression have been desperately hard and this is my opportunity, the answer to our prayers. If I cannot find a rich strike, I can, perhaps, write down my impressions and sell them to a newspaper somewhere, possibly even a book.

Leaving Seattle, I took time to look about me and assess the company and surroundings in which I was to spend almost two weeks and travel more than a thousand nautical miles. This is a second Clondyke run for the Al-ki, which is not a large vessel, having a single smokestack, cabins and bridge toward the stern, and a rather long foredeck, where I have pitched a rain fly and deposited my bedroll between piles of cargo, wood for the steam engine, and the outfits of others going north. There are more of us without than with staterooms, since the boat was originally a freighter and not designed to carry the more than two hundred passengers that crowd its decks. I was surprised to find a few women and several families with children aboard. They are crushed into the few staterooms, while most of us single men camp on the deck, where we do our best to stay dry in the mist and rain that accompany us up the coast. Temporary bunks have been hastily installed in the hold, but the air is close and stale below, rank with the seasickness of many unfortunates. I am glad to be up in the fresh air and do not much mind the dampness.

I have no private place to write, the boat being so crowded with human beings that we all but ask permission to turn around, and eat in shifts in a small galley beneath the bridge on the upper deck. This is some way from the narrow dining room and the food is almost always cool before it can be carried down the deck, through the social hall, and reach the tables. There has been some humorous speculation that the food is prepared to condition us to the limited bill of fare that is likely to be available in the Yukon, for the biscuits are consistently underdone. It is predominantly starch and meat; we have very little in the way of vegetables or fruit, but there is plenty of what has soon proved repetitious. We shovel down our victuals and do not linger, for someone is always awaiting their turn at board.

A curious assortment of persons are passengers on the Al-ki, but most are decent, ordinary men, hoping for good luck and gold. They come from all parts of our country, Canada, and, a few, from Europe. I have met merchants, clerks, farmers, a banker, two lawyers, a photographer, a seamstress, railroad men, sailors, and a shoemaker, for example. There are a couple of sharpers, one of whom runs a card game in a corner of the deck much of the time but has caused no particular problems and is balanced off by the young woman who leads a few souls in singing hymns in another corner. One arrogant young man from New York complains incessantly and runs his hired man ragged in the attempt to fetch and carry for this Eastern polka dot. Needless to say, I think he will get his comeuppance on the Yukon, though I gravely doubt he will make it that far. For the most part, however, my traveling companions are pleasant enough and a polite camaraderie, strangely lacking in class-consciousness, prevails.

Much of my time is spent at the rail, enjoying the scenery, for the passage north is most amazing. Much of the time we steam along between the mainland to the east and islands to the west, which protect boats traveling this

*route from the unpredictability of the Pacific Ocean and
its storms. Often the landscape is shrouded with heavy
fog and mist, and the shrieks of boat whistles and fog-
horns resound and echo back from the veiled hills. But
the few clear days have assured us that the land is truly
unsettled and a complete wilderness. Like a motionless
ocean of dark green, the tree-covered slopes roll back
steeply from the dark waters over which we speed. Only
once or twice have we crossed inlets through which we
could view the Pacific. The rest of the trip we have
threaded our way through channels and passages that
twine between the islands like braided cords. Often eagles
soar overhead. Once we saw a bear. In one great open
sound, dozens of whales leaped from the water and blew
air and water from their spouts. How my little Tommy
would have enjoyed that sight! In the same place several
icebergs could be seen floating near the eastern shore.*

*Regularly we pass or are passed by other boats and
ships, coming or going to or from the north. Any kind of
vessel that can carry people and goods has been pressed
into service to transport the hundreds of stampeders and
their grubstakes to the Clondyke. Many are quite unsuited
to travel either the distance or on the sort of waterways
through which they are required to make way and a number have sunk or wrecked along the route, loaded to the
rails with passengers and cargo.*

SATURDAY, SEPTEMBER 11
DYEA, ALASKA TERRITORY

*Almost a week into the voyage, we stopped for a day in
Juneau, capital of Alaska Territory, a small, bustling community created by a gold strike more than ten years ago
and named for the miner who made it. It was a rather
industrious little town, huddled on a narrow strip of
land against mountains that rose straight up behind it like
a wall. As it was the last point from which to buy goods
for the Clondyke, I added a keg of nails and a whipsaw
to my outfit, at the suggestion of a friend I made on the
boat.*

A tall streetcar conductor from Tacoma, who used to give my son penny candy when we took him on the car, recognized me on the Al-ki. He is a bit unusual looking, with a red mustache and one wall-eye; his name is Frank Warner. The employees of his company organized themselves, pooled their ready cash, and elected men to go to the goldfields and stake claims for them all. Frank was one of the lucky nine. We became acquainted when he happened to bed down on the deck near to me and have decided to travel and partner together. He seems a good, God-fearing man, and I am glad not to be entirely alone in this hazardous venture. A strong, hardworking soul, he spent some time in a logging crew before becoming a conductor, so he knows more than I about building the boat we will need on the Yukon River.

The following day we left Juneau on the final leg of our journey here to Dyea, where we would disembark and start our long tramp to the Yukon. The mountains continued and became more rugged, interspersed with glimpses of blue and white glaciers hanging between the peaks. Traveling through the night, we arrived at our destination before noon, where we waited for high tide to take us as close as possible to the beach.

There are no wharves or docks at Dyea, though plans are under way to build them. We were, therefore, forced, at our own expense, to have our goods transported from the Al-ki to the shore, in small boats, or lighters, where they were unceremoniously dumped into the mud. Horses aboard were simply shoved overboard to swim through the icy water to solid ground, so I guess we should have been grateful not to be treated in similar fashion. We struggled valiantly to drag our outfits above tide line, piling all among many similar heaps of those who arrived before us.

I was disconcerted to find that my slabs of bacon, which had been shipped below decks, evidently in close proximity to the boiler, had gone rancid. Frank's were still good, and for this we were thankful since there is little possibility of replacement.

Dyea is like a hill of ants, with people moving con-

stantly in all directions, but mainly toward the Chilkoot Pass. Some, however, have no intention of traveling farther and are getting their fortunes by providing services to others. Teams and wagons can be hired to carry goods up the beach, but the teamsters charge twenty dollars an hour when the tide is falling and fifty when it is on the rise.

Buildings are being thrown together in a matter of days by opportunistic members of the carpenter's trade, bought and put to immediate use as mercantiles and restaurants by some who had the foresight to ship in whole inventories of stock, food and liquor. Tents and even temporary shacks are pressed into service.

Before this stampede there was only one store here, the trading post of a man named Healy. In only a matter of weeks, wilderness has been transformed into a jumble of log cabins, frame hotels, saloons and gambling houses with false fronts, but nothing appears permanent, particularly the hundreds of tents scattered everywhere. Structures have been built with wood which was used for passenger bunks and stalls for horses in the boats, then ripped out and sold as lumber. I saw a man yesterday asleep under a red and white checkered tablecloth he had rigged to keep off some of the rain.

Everyone slogs knee deep in mud. Wagons mire up to the hubs. Transporting our goods up to and over the pass will mean many trips back and forth to ferry it all to the top, where we are told we must camp through the winter, build a boat, and wait for the spring thaw to continue our journey to Dawson City by water. Opinion on this, however, seems to be somewhat divided. Winter freeze-up has held off so far and, with a little luck, we may be able to make it downriver before the passage closes.

Tomorrow will see us off. Warner went off over an hour ago to locate a miner who is said to have come into town from Dawson. He hopes to gather additional information about the route to the Clondyke and what we face on the trip we are about to undertake. Rumors from the sublime to the ridiculous abound among the stampeders. Level-headed and practical, Frank is anything but content to go *without knowing everything possible, or to let the future take care of itself. This does not displease me, though it makes me smile, knowing that the poor miner is in for a stubborn barrage of questions when Warner catches up with him, which he, with certainty, will.*

TUESDAY, SEPTEMBER 21
LAKE BENNETT, YUKON TERRITORY

A hired packer carried a letter from Polly up the trail to me with his load, giving me the news from home. How I miss her and little Tommy and Anna. It was generous of him, for he refused payment, saying that he had left his own wife in San Francisco two months ago. Forwarded one to her with him on his return trip.

I was glad to know that her mother sent good wishes, for she was opposed to this venture, along with the father. Perhaps he, too, will come around soon. They must realize I am only doing what I think best for our future.

We have reached Lake Bennett at last, after more than a week on the trail. All that time to travel thirty-five miles, but the longest miles in the world. In actuality much of it was traveled not once but more than a dozen times, as we brought our outfits ahead one load at a time, then went back for another. And it is impossible to walk any speed but slowly with sixty to eighty pounds of goods on your back, over mud, rocks, roots, and all uphill. From the beach to the top of the Chilkoot Pass the trail rises 3,740 feet in a series of steep, step-like ascents, interspersed with level areas.

We left Dyea on Sunday, September 12, and traveled for two days up the Taiya River with the help of Indian packers and their canoes. The first nine miles, to the head of the canyon, a temporary camp called Canyon City, were not easy and took us two days, but were nothing compared to what followed. As we were going against the current, the only way to move the loaded canoes was to pull them with long ropes from the bank. Frank Warner and I took turns pulling with the Indians and standing up in the canoes to guide them and exert leverage with a pole. Before we started, we had taken care to wrap everything in oilskin, which was fortunate when, halfway up, one of the canoes turned over. Collecting the goods, we repacked and continued with no real damage done. As we worked our way up the river, we could sometimes see those less fortunate, who could not afford to pay for helpers, packing their goods back and forth across the streams and over the bowlder-strewn, muddy trail.

Late on the second day the Indians left us and all our supplies on the bank near where a steep trail led from the river up the canyon toward the pass. I was a bit sorry we had not hired them to pack some of our goods on up the trail, though we could not afford it. Those fellows can surely pack. Some of them can carry over a hundred pounds in a single load, simply go up steadily, putting one foot in front of the other with never a hesitation. And they can do three loads to every two of mine. Even some of the squaws hire out as packers and do very well, though their loads are not so heavy.

Where they left us the real effort began. We divided our outfits into manageable-size loads and started early. It did not aid us that, after two days of good weather on the river, the skies opened and poured rain for the next three.

Horses, wagons, and packers all moving up the trail had turned it to a quagmire of mud and water. As bad as it was on the trail, it was worse off it where branches of spruce, cottonwood, and hemlock clawed at your pack and the rocks and mud were wet and terribly slippery. Without my rubber boots, I would never have made it and I was glad for the rubber-lined coat Polly insisted I bring. With the collar turned up, my broad-rimmed hat kept the worst of the rain from running down my neck and soaking me immediately. Still, we arrived at the first stop on that trail as wet as if we had been plunged into the river before starting our tramp.

Four miles up the trail we arrived at Sheep Camp. This spot consisted of a haphazard collection of tents, pitched in any available flat space, piles of outfits and goods, and a couple of rough frame buildings. We made the error of neglecting to set up our tent upon arriving with the first load and, by the time we made our final trip of the day, were so tired we elected to take advantage of whatever hospitality was offered by the so-called hotel, as one of the buildings was advertised by a hand-lettered sign painted directly on the outside wall.

One fairly large room held a curtained-off section for the family that ran it and a large table, where we took turns with others to sit down in relays for supper. Beans, bacon, and tea cost us seventy-five cents each, but if expensive and limited in scope, it was hot and surely welcome. For fifty cents, when the meal was over, we laid out our own blankets and, with boots hanging to dry from a rafter and my coat under my head, settled down for the night among as many men as could crowd onto the floor. I might have had trouble sleeping with all the sounds and smells of so many damp and filthy strangers had I not been every bit as distastefully dirty, myself, and so exhausted that I was snoring with the best of them almost before my head hit my makeshift pillow.

I awoke next morning so stiff that I needed help rising to my feet. Groans from those around told me I was not alone with my aches and pains. Frank was not much better off, but we walked most of it off on the way back to the river for our next load. Soon we had managed to complete the task of transferring all our possessions to Sheep Camp and set up our tent.

Beyond this stage it was almost impossible for horses, so most everyone on the trail carried their goods on their backs as did we. After a gentle rise for the first three miles, the last mile to an area directly below the pass called The Scales steepened to twenty-five or thirty degrees, taxing the energy of already tired men. Between Sheep Camp and The Scales was a stopping point named the Stone House because of a large rock with a generally square shape. Back and forth we trudged until we had all our gear together at The Scales, including one load of firewood, for until we reach the lakes there are only rocks on the treeless summit.

All along the trail we came upon piles of abandoned goods, where some had simply given up the fight and left

*what they were carrying to go back to Dyea to await the
next boat going south. I picked up two good wool blankets
and some nails from one such pile that had been left with
a scribbled note which read, "Help yerself if yer loony
enuff." I will not comment on the spelling or grammar,
though perhaps he went back for an education. In the area
below the pass many more looked at the steep wall ahead
and turned back, selling their outfits if possible. The lucky
few who could realized perhaps ten cents on the dollar,
for supplies were at no premium there.*

*As the weather was clear and quite warm for Septem-
ber, we did not raise our tent at The Scales, but spread
our bedrolls on top of our bags and boxes and, with the
two extra blankets, slept without the discomfort of cold or
rain. The morning brought us to the worst struggle of the
long hike. Though the distance to the top of the pass
looked close above us, the way up zigzagged back and
forth among the many bowlders to reduce the grade, so
it was more than twice the distance of a straight line and
took us hours. For two days we staggered up and down,
stepping cautiously, a time or two sideways, clutching the
stone face to assure passage.*

*The summit was a maze of heaped up goods that looked
like a city of low buildings with spaces between for
streets. Late afternoon, when we brought up the last load,
the wind, though not too cold, was howling. We could not
tolerate the thought of going back down to the shelter of
the U-shaped valley and, instead, found a place between
our goods and some others' where we put up a canvas
shelter and huddled for the night in the lee of our possessions. Frank chose to make his bed on sacks of flour,
while I preferred those of peas and beans, and both of us
slept in our clothes and boots.*

*At just after six in the morning, we were already up
and preparing to move off the pass toward the lakes when
we heard a thunderous roar from a glacier which hangs in
a high valley directly above The Scales. This glacier
had previously caught our attention and others' with its
beautiful colors: blue, green, and glistening white in the
daylight, a changing variety of pastel pinks, golds, and*

purples in the evening. Cannon-like reports had been heard from this river of ice for days, as it moved and shifted in a slow, downward journey.

Hastening to the lip of the pass, we observed that a huge block of ice had fallen from the face of it and crashed into the area below. Behind it flowed a virtual lake of water that had evidently built up, dammed by the ice, and was released when the block broke loose. It has evidently been unseasonably warm for September this year and rain combined with melting snow and ice had obviously weakened the front section of the glacier, allowing it to drop and free the water behind it. This poured into the valley, sweeping away anything in its path, goods, tents, anyone who had not run fast enough to higher ground, horses and wagons, in a wall of water close to twenty feet high, churning up mudslides as it went.

Farther down, the Stone House was picked up in the strength of the flood and moved almost a quarter of a mile. At that location it was possible to hear and see the water coming and many more escaped, but with little other than the clothes on their backs. It is amazing that only three people were killed, although a number were injured, and many simply reversed direction and began the trek downhill to the beach, wasting no time in a search for their belongings. Others salvaged what they could and went on.

I am astounded at the single-minded pursuit of the majority of these stampeders to make their way to the goldfields. They are absolutely determined and will allow nothing to interfere, sometimes to the point of callousness. I heard about a man who fell, breaking his leg, who lay by the side of the trail all day, while men passed him by, although he was obviously in pain and in need of assistance. A hired packer by the name of Linville finally went to his aid and carried him all the way down to Dyea and a doctor.

Arizona Charley Meadows and his wife, Mae, a couple I met earlier on the trail, had lost less and were more optimistic than those who quit and walked out. They were traveling with hired packers and horses, and had sent them on to the top of the pass the day before, so their outfit was spared and they lost mostly personal items.

He is a flamboyant character in buckskin jacket and high boots, with a pistol at his belt, who was once a star in Buffalo Bill's Wild West Show as a rider and crack shot with a rifle. His wife was a rider and chariot racer in Meadows's own show, which they had left to go to Dawson. Among other things, they were transporting goods for a restaurant, a saloon, and a general store. At each stopping place, he would set up the bar and sell liquor to the stampeders, at ever-increasing prices as they moved away from a source of supply. The flood carried off the saloon, her clothes, his favorite pistol and supply of western hats. She bought what clothing she could from those leaving for the coast and the two came on to the pass, through the knee-high mud, to join the rest of their party. I had to admire her, for she kept up with the men and always had a smile, no matter how steep the trail. Though I envy him the company of his wife, I would not have mine here in this rough country.

The steep side of the pass was not the end of our hard work. On the other side was a long, rocky, treeless valley sloping down to the lakes. This part of the trip seemed carved out of stone, and not all of it solid. Our legs and feet ached from the jarring effort of stepping down under heavy loads and, as I developed the habit of clenching my teeth before my foot hit the ground, at the end of each day I could not decide which ached more, legs or jaw. Had there been snow it would have been an easy task of loading everything on sleds and sliding off downhill. As it was we had to carry it, as usual, for we could not wait or risk losing essential time. Though there is little snow and the weather has been remarkably good, the temperature is rapidly dropping and soon the lakes and rivers will freeze.

Double quick, we moved our supplies past Crater Lake, around Lake Lindeman and to the shores of Bennett Lake, where we have made a good camp and are about to build a boat. We must make haste or we will fail to make Daw-

son this fall and be forced to winter here, waiting six or seven months for spring thaw. Toward this aim we have cut and hauled several of the largest trees we could find to saw up into lumber. We had to haul them some distance as everything close to the lake had already been cut by others with the same objective in mind. A whole town of tents has sprung up here on the lake shore and hundreds of people are working hard to avoid being wintered in.

Frank ran into an old acquaintance of his yesterday and brought him back to camp. His surname is Wilson and Frank calls him Ozzy, so I think his Christian name must be Oswald. They worked together in the lumber camps before Frank became a streetcar man. I am not sure that I would have joined up with him, but Warner took it for granted and I really had no chance to refuse. Since it will be easier and faster to build a boat with three of us, I think it will be fine, but this Ozzy is rather taciturn and perhaps a little sullen compared to the loquaciousness of his friend. I am probably just used to having only two of us and we will all soon grow used to each other, but time will tell how we shall fare. Ozzy is a large man, with arms and shoulders that show the results of swinging an ax.

Today we built a scaffold about six feet high, to hold the logs up off the ground for cutting. We will start tomorrow, with one man up and one down, to pull the whipsaw through the length of the log from one end to the other. An arrangement of this kind is called a strong-arm mill, for good reason, and Ozzy will come in handy in working ours. It is quite an efficient method of cutting boards, but the sawyer on the bottom gets a shower of sawdust on the downward stroke, which sifts into eyes, ears, and shirt-neck, and is a constant irritation. Again I will be glad for my broad-brimmed hat.

This sawing of lumber can cause disagreements as to who is and is not doing his share of the work. Yesterday at noon two fellows near us had such an argument they decided to split up their partnership. They carefully divided up their supplies, down to and including the half-

*built boat, which they cut exactly in two. One took the
tent, the other the stove. It rained like blazes in the night,
so the one with the tent was dry but couldn't sleep for the
cold and the other huddled by the stove all night, trying
to dry out his wet clothes. By this morning they had made
up their differences and put the vessel back together
again, giving us all a good laugh.*

*We have heard rumors that there are so many people
either in or headed for Dawson City that there may be a
shortage of provisions. Warnings are being given out that
no one should leave here without a sufficient amount to
last out the winter. Though Wilson has brought less than
Frank and I, combining our supplies should give us
plenty. Besides, there is word that supply boats are on
their way up the Yukon, bound for Dawson, and will probably arrive before us. There is also word that the Royal
Canadian Mounted Police intend to enforce a regulation
that no one can cross into Canada without at least a
year's supply of food, about twelve hundred pounds, and
everything else necessary to keep going in this country
without aid. Soon they will turn back anyone who reaches
the top of the Chilkoot with less.*

*As fast as we can put together a proper boat we shall
be off. Water on the lake is already looking slick in the
mornings and a rim of ice can be found where it meets
the shore. The temperature is dropping to well below
freezing at night, but every day boats leave for the Yukon
and so shall we in only a few more.*

*Ozzy went off for a bit this afternoon with his gun and
came back with two late ducks, which are now simmering
with three of our precious whole potatoes and a handful
of evaporated onion. We shall dine like kings before seeking our bedrolls, but what I wouldn't give for a slice of
Polly's apple pie.*

*Like almost everyone else, I am growing a beard. It is
not always convenient to shave and whiskers will keep my
face warmer this winter.*

*I found this page from a guide book abandoned in this
campsite by someone who must have felt it unnecessary*

to carry, or who lost it. Comparing the items it lists, I am well outfitted indeed, with almost everything required already in my possession—excepting the rancid bacon, of course. I have fifty pounds more beans and half again as much rope.

LIST OF ITEMS NECESSARY TO CARRY TO THE YUKON

Flour	400 pounds
Bacon	150 pounds
Split Peas	150 pounds
Beans	100 pounds
Evaporated Apples	25 pounds
Evaporated Peaches	25 pounds
Apricots	25 pounds
Butter	25 pounds
Sugar	100 pounds
Condensed Milk	1½ dozen cans
Coffee	15 pounds
Tea	10 pounds
Pepper	1 pound
Salt	10 pounds
Baking Powder	8 pounds
Rolled Oats	40 pounds
Yeast Cakes	2 dozen
4-oz. Beef Extract	½ dozen
Soap, Castile	5 bars
Soap, Tar	6 bars
Matches	1 tin
Vinegar	1 gallon
Candles	1 box
Evaporated Potatoes	25 pounds
Rice	25 pounds
Canvas Sacks	25 pounds
Wash Basin	1
Medicine Chest	1
Rubber Sheet	1
Pack Straps	1 set
Pick	1
Handle	1

Shovel	1
Gold Pan	1
Ax	1
Whip Saw	1
Hand Saw	1
Jack Plane	1
Brace	1
Bits, assorted	4
8" Mill File	1
6" Mill File	1
Broad Hatchet	1
2-qt. Galvanized Coffee Pot	1
Fry Pan	1
Rivets	1 package
Draw Knife	1
Covered Pails	3
Pie Plate	1
Knife and Fork	1 each
Granite Cup	1
Tea and Table Spoon	1 each
14" Granite Spoon	1
Tape Measure	1
Chisel, 1 ½"	1
Oakum	10 pounds
Pitch	10 pounds
20d Nails	5 pounds
10d Nails	5 pounds
6d Nails	6 pounds
⅝" Rope	200 feet
Single Block	1
Solder Outfit	1
14-qt. Galvanized Pail	1
Granite Saucepan	1
Candlewick	3 pounds
Compass	1
Miner's Candlestick	1
Towels	6
Ax Handle	1
Ax Stone	1
Emery Stone	1

Sheet Iron Stove	1
Tent	1
Personal Clothes, extra Boots	
Sled for Winter Travel	

SATURDAY, OCTOBER 2, 1897
WHITE HORSE CITY, YUKON TERRITORY

We arrived at what, with a questionable sense of humor, they call White Horse City yesterday. It is less like a city than anything I have seen so labeled thus far.

Lakes Bennett, Tagish, Marsh, and a section of the Lewes River are behind us. A difficult section indeed. By taking a great risk, we came through Miles Canyon, Squaw and White Horse Rapids without portaging, but in the turbulent and dangerous rapids of the first, which is for good reason called Dead Man's Canyon, we came close to losing all we have worked so hard for. I still take a deep breath when I think of how close we came to utter destruction. However, all's well that ends well, and we are here and sound, and I am relieved to know that the rest of the trip is reputed to be gentler to the intrepid traveler. According to our rough map, only one lake, La-berge, lies before the Yukon River, which will take us the rest of the way to Dawson with only a minor rapid or two along the way.

Aside from a few log structures, White Horse City is largely a tent-filled wide spot on the east bank of the river. As soon as the rapids are past, those who have come through by water, and survived intact, need to pull out and make repairs before the final stretch to Dawson. They are about to build a wooden tramway to run along the east bank, above the rushing waters, which will allow, for a substantial fee, goods to be transported in horse-drawn wagons around the dangers. For now, anything that doesn't come through the rapids in a boat is packed by hand along the full five miles. All day long the sound of hammering and sawing fills the air, along with the smell of pitch and oakum. You would think they were back in the boat building business, as some are.

The mood is exuberant relief for those who came through, but frustrated and sad for those who did not, or who lost members of their parties to the icy clutches of the angry river and its rocks. Even here some turn back, broken in spirit. It is said that when the ice broke last spring, and boats began to run the rapids in high water, over 150 boats were wrecked in the first few days and half a dozen men drowned. So it is with worry alleviated that we pause briefly with others in this place where they say everyone stops to wash their socks. Mine are clean, along with the rest of my clothing, and dripping dry over the cook stove we have fired up in the tent.

As we have decided to take one day here to recover from the excitement of the last two, I have time to catch up in this journal and describe the last part of the journey. Frequently we meet men coming from Dawson, on their way outside for the winter. When it sets in there will be complete isolation.

Back at Lake Bennett, by virtue of much hard work and long hours, we managed to complete our boat in a week. It is a queer-looking craft, almost twenty feet long, of rudely sawed planks, with a flat bottom. Though we strove to make the planks even and as smooth as possible as we sawed them from logs, all of us have numerous splinters acquired as we nailed them in place, or rubbed them into our skin on the way here. Our boat has a good bow and a flat, somewhat awkward stern. It is better than some traditional flatboats I have seen, with both ends square like boxes or crates. These are exceptionally difficult to maneuver, and slower, since they resist the water they should cut through were they more blade-shaped.

When all the work with wood was done and held in place with our precious nails, we had to seal the cracks, a hot sticky job. Boiling a pot of yellow pitch, we dipped the stringy fibers of oakum into it and forced them into all the seams. This was a miserable process that raised blisters on our hands as we attempted to hold the hot stuff in place and pound it quickly in with hammer, chisel, and caulking iron before it cooled. Heating and reheating that iron was a task in itself. Too hot and it sometimes melted

*out what we wanted left in place. Too cold and it would
not melt pitch and oakum enough to wedge it in properly.
Every slightest crevice must be filled carefully so as not
to leak and sink us.*

*During the final days of boat building, we added one
more man to our party, for a total of four. Edward
McNeal, Ned, as he prefers to be called, is a Scotsman
from New York, where his parents emigrated when he was
young. I fell into conversation with him one afternoon
when I was out scouting for more pitch for the caulking
pot and he trudged past on his way north, looking for a
place to start a boat of his own. He stopped for a breather
and assisted me in scraping pitch off several trees which
had been slashed by previous boat builders. He is a pleasant sort, with his head on straight and a calm, positive
way about him. I so enjoyed his company, and the hint of
rolling r's in the slight accent he retains, that I found
myself asking if he would like to help complete our boat
and join us for the trip downriver.*

*Frank and, particularly, Ozzy seemed reluctant when I
announced my invitation to them, but had to agree there
was room enough in the boat for him and his outfit. When
they knew that he had been a fisherman on the eastern
seaboard and was at home in a boat, they lost no time,
however, in welcoming him to the endeavor. When he also
sold some of his boat building materials and contributed
extra food and a little cash to the effort they were more
than satisfied. I do believe he saved our skins in Dead
Man's Canyon and, in so doing, more than earned his
place. He was quietly grateful, for it saved him the time
it would have taken to put together a vessel of his own
and, thereby, probably also prevented his being wintered
in at Lake Bennett.*

*I am glad to have him along for another reason. There
is something about Ozzy I can't quite cotton to, though
he has done nothing to me personally to cause me to
actually dislike him. He talks little and, when he does,
says almost nothing about his background or where he
came from. He has a temper and is unreasonably suspicious of others, seems to expect a slight or ill deed. There*

*seems to be a suppressed rage in the man for some un-
known reason. Midway through the boat building, he suddenly accused the perfectly honest pair of fellows working
next to us of stealing our nails. They, astonished, declared
their innocence, but Ozzy brushed it aside with an angry
retort and picked up his ax, apparently ready to physically
resolve the issue then and there, which concerned me
greatly. I resolved never to be in the way if he becomes
truly angry.*

*At that point, Frank called out that he had located the
missing nails in their keg under a canvas he had tossed
over our supplies. Ozzy immediately laid down the ax and
returned to his work, but never offered apologies to our
neighbors, which to me seemed in order. They departed
two days later, seemingly with relief, as they had watched
Ozzy rather closely following the ruckus, and kept an eye
on their goods.*

*It is, therefore, good to have Ned for company. Though
we work and travel together, Frank and Ozzy tend to keep
each other's company, while Ned and I are more inclined
to fall in together. I was the odd man out before he joined
us, now it is more even. Besides, he keeps us laughing at
his jokes and entertained with a mouth harp that he plays
rather well.*

*At last our feverish labor was done and the boat com-
plete and solid as we could make it. Launching and packing it with all our assorted bags and baggage, made
secure from water to the best of our ability, we spent one
more night upon dry land and embarked upon our voyage
early Sunday morning, September 26. I am inclined to
think that departure on the Lord's Day may have influ-
enced our successful passage through the rapids which
were to follow. Though I am sure others might say it was
simply excitement and a skill born of desperation, combined with an exceptionally large dose of luck.*

*We started down the twenty-six miles of Lake Bennett
on a sunny day with a smart breeze blowing the right
direction, and cruised along pleasantly enough for most
of the day, largely enjoying the sensation of being able to
relax after so much hurried labor and long hours. We*

took turns at the rudder, Frank found a space to nap on some sacks with his feet on a box, and Ned fired up a pipe that he clamped between his teeth and puffed at contentedly. As we glided along, he pulled a map from his pocket and showed us the route a returning miner had been good enough to sketch for him in Dyea. It gave no indication of the miles, but showed the rivers, lakes, and stopping places along the way. Of special interest were the rapids and things along the waterways to watch out for, or that were of particular danger. Ned related that it should require most of two weeks to travel the five hundred miles by water.

There were dozens of other boats besides ours, headed with all possible speed toward the far end of the lake. Everyone was uneasy at the thought of being frozen in and anxious to reach the river with its faster-moving flow. Throughout the morning I watched them, as they passed and were passed. Mountains capped with snow rose steeply from either side of the broad lake, with almost no place to land. We took the shortest route possible, which was down the middle of the almost currentless waters. Having been warned that sudden storms and winds were common on the lakes, we kept a sharp eye out for any indication of such, but the day remained warm and calm, with enough breeze to speed us on our way.

Late in the afternoon we spotted the narrow passage that would allow us through into Tagish Lake at a place called Caribou Crossing on Ned's map. We took out the oars and rowed perhaps half a mile from one lake to the other, passing a few Indians fishing from the banks, who watched us closely, but did not respond to my wave. I imagine they had seen so many other boats that it was no rarity to be gestured at by a white man. They must think our obsession with gold strange to say the least and would probably rather have fish.

Barely onto Tagish Lake, we stopped and made camp for the night, but the next morning we were back on our way before it was fully light. There was no wind at all and we were forced to take turns at the oars, two by two, spelling each other. We worked hard all morning, making *up for our sloth of the day before, until close to noon, when a breeze a little stronger than before sprang up and allowed us the luxury of resting again. I was glad of the respite as the sight of the cliffs to the east of the lake was spectacular. Rising thousands of feet straight up, they were more than impressive. Approximately a third of the way down the lake, they split to reveal an inlet called Windy Arm. This, Ned's cartographer had said, was one of the dangerous places, as sudden and violent winds were known to spring up without warning to howl over the waters of Tagish like a hurricane. Glad to reach the other side of this arm, we continued and watched the cliffs turn into lower hills, all liberally covered with snow, reminding us that soon it would fall farther down and we had better make haste while we were able.*

Midafternoon we rowed again, this time through the river-like channel between Tagish and Marsh Lakes. Tired with all the rowing, we camped about ten miles down Marsh Lake and all went to bed early. This lake certainly deserves its name, as it seems mostly swamp in spots.

Through the day we drifted slowly along close to the shore, with an erratic wind that came and went, at times lifting the sail, at others leaving it slack. We were all drowsily nodding after a cold noon meal, when a sudden crash and frantic splashing brought us up wide awake. A moose and her calf came leaping out of the reeds of the shore, splashed into the lake and began to swim, paying no attention to our silent passage very near to them. Some predator, wolf or wildcat, perhaps, must have pursued this mother, forcing her to take to the water with her young. As long as we could see they swam strongly, steadily heading for the opposite side of the lake. We were fascinated that an animal of such bulk could move through water with little or no trouble.

The last ten miles of the lake were soon behind us and we found ourselves on the Lewis River for the majority of the day. With a swifter current, our speed picked up considerably and the fifty miles of water approximately two hundred feet wide passed quickly in comparison to the time spent rowing the day before. It seemed no time at all until we noticed that the river had begun to narrow and gain speed. Then, suddenly, we noticed several men waving in exaggerated gestures for us to come ashore. Near them was a sign, painted in large letters which read, "WARNING! WATCH FOR CANYON!" Another close by simply read, "CANNON," and though I had to chuckle at the spelling, the intent was clear. We had reached the notorious rapids and, heeding the warnings, pulled with a will for the right bank.

The men who had waved us in offered to take us and the boat through Miles Canyon for a hundred dollars. When we hesitated, they came down to seventy-five, then fifty, but we were determined to see the rapids for ourselves before deciding on a course of action. From where we stood, we could hear the rush of water from around the next bend. We hiked up a trail which took us to the rim of the canyon and walked along until we could look down almost a hundred feet into a maelstrom of water below. Churning, white with foam, it roared through the narrow space between the rocks so loudly we had to shout to hear each other. Frank's face turned a sort of greenish-white. Ned clamped his teeth down on his pipe and frowned at the sight.

Two large whirlpools lay close against the cliffs, one with bits and pieces of what appeared to be parts of some broken boat that was being pulverized in its giant gristmill.

"Holy cow!" Ozzy exclaimed, shaking his head. "We'll never make it through this. I vote we pack around."

A flatboat appeared as we considered the wild current, hurtling along at great speed, tilting and turning, all but out of control against all efforts of the three men struggling valiantly to keep some kind of grasp on its course. Barely missing one canyon wall, the craft swung drunkenly toward a whirlpool and I expected to see them sucked down and demolished. Somehow they made it past, however, and we watched in awed silence as they disappeared around the next bend, still fighting for their very lives.

"That does it," Frank said. "I'm walking."

But Ned, still frowning, said he thought we could make it. He made us look at the path of the water and notice that, aside from the whirlpools, it was mostly just fast water with no apparent large rocks except the walls themselves. We walked the full length of the rapids to see exactly what we faced, and the only real problem seemed to be taking care to stay in the center of the channel as much as possible. By the time we retraced our steps, even Frank had decided he would give it a try.

Tightening down and covering our gear, we rode through like an arrow from a bow. There was no time to even think, once we were in the clutches of the current and headed downstream at a speed faster than we could have imagined. It seemed much worse from water-level than it had from above, but we were committed and, with only a stroke or two of the oars to put us in midstream, were swept away by the boiling waters. Faster and faster we sped down the corridor of stone, past the whirlpools that we closely missed, rocking and careening atop huge waves that pounded against the walls, rebounded and hammered the boat in their fury to escape the confines of the canyon.

Just as we were coming close to the end, the boat was caught by one tremendous wave and thrown around almost crosswise of the current. A torrent of water washed overboard and threatened to swamp us. Frank scrambled toward the stern and seemed about to abandon ship, but Ned quickly threw his weight on an oar and shouted loudly for us to "r-r-row, boys, bloody r-r-row." His efforts, and some of ours, straightened the boat enough to allow the bow to once again point in the correct direction. Then, with Frank and Ozzy bailing for all they were worth while Ned and I manned the oars, we remained afloat. By the time we miraculously flew out the far end into calmer water we were drenched by both sweat and water, and panting with exertion. Both my hands had blisters, when I could force my fingers to uncramp from the oar I had wielded. We made it to shore and sat in the boat, shivering like dogs from fear and cold.

Strangely enough, in the midst of all the confusion, I

remember clearly seeing the wreck of some vessel, splintered planks and shreds of canvas, sucked into a whirlpool as we passed it. What focused my attention was the white face of a man who was clinging to it, and the certain knowledge that he was a goner for sure, with no hope of rescue. When I had caught my breath, I mentioned it to Ned, who frowned and shook his head, but said nothing, for what could he have said?

After resting for an hour, and putting our trust in Ned, the other two rapids passed with no more than a like amount of difficulty, as he determinedly kept us off the walls and in midstream. Throwing all our combined strength into the effort, we followed his shouted commands frantically and without question. We scraped once on a rock at the last, where an underwater reef made out from the left bank, creating a wave three or four feet high to cover it, but made it through with little damage to the boat and naught but a drenching to ourselves. I have never traveled five miles so fast in my life. Another survivor told me that he had checked his watch before and after their non-stop run through the first two rapids and the elapsed time was eight minutes. Portaging would have taken at least two days.

Much of our outfit, like others who came through, is spread out around me, as I write, to dry. One poor fellow's whole supply of sugar was soaked. He dumped it, melting, into a tin dishpan and has been begging bottles and corks from anyone who could spare them to contain the resulting syrup. Hope his bottles don't shatter when they freeze, as they most assuredly will.

As I see Ned returning from a walk along the bank to stretch his legs, I shall end this account and assist him in returning some kind of order to our goods. His tobacco remained dry in its can, for he is puffing up plumes of smoke as he rearranges the canvas sacks, spread over nearby bushes. As the temperature is falling, I think they are more likely to freeze than to dry, though some thin sun is shining. Still, I huddle close to the stove, toasting my stockinged toes while my damp boots steam nearby.

I take heart at the thought that soon I will be in the

Clondyke where gold may be had for the taking. So far we go well and all the real difficulties are now behind us.

SUNDAY, OCTOBER 3, 1897
LEWES RIVER, YUKON TERRITORY

We left White Horse early this morning and made good time due to the swiftness of the Lewes River. Though sandbars kept us alert so as not to run aground, there have been no more rapids and the ride is quite smooth, taking us between light-colored cliffs a hundred feet high. Beyond them we could see rough mountains and timber-covered slopes as the sun came up. This is a young, broad-shouldered country with terraced hills rolling back massively where glaciers once worked their way. The river flows through a wide valley from which canyons branch deep into the wilderness.

The weather is perceptively colder and we now encounter ice at the river's edge even in the middle of the day. The days are also growing swiftly shorter. By mid-December we will have only four or five hours of daylight.

Over a quarter of the way to Dawson in miles, we should arrive at our destination in only a week or so, if we travel without delays or incidents which would slow our speed. We glide along, hardly needing to touch the oars, with others heading in the same northerly direction. There are not so many vessels, as many were lost or damaged in the rapids before White Horse. If repairs are not effected rapidly, they will not be able to reach Dawson before the river freezes. The thought of being frozen in somewhere along the river is not a pleasant one, although I imagine we could build a rough cabin and hold out with our outfits and food until spring. This, however, would mean missing the winter's mining on the Clondyke, so we proceed with all speed.

This evening we have made camp on a low bank east of the river and will reach Lake Laberge tomorrow. It is very cold, with a brisk wind blowing up the river. We huddle close to the fire, where Frank is cooking pancakes.

I will be glad of my extra blanket and we are all sleeping in our clothing and coats.

MONDAY, OCTOBER 4
LEWES RIVER, YUKON TERRITORY

Headed almost due north on the Lewes River, we were well on our way this morning, after an uncomfortably cold night, when we discovered a leak in the side of our boat. It must have suffered a brush with a bowlder in the rapids, for the pitch and oakum was missing along one plank which showed evidence of some scrapes. Pulling in to shore, we made a hasty fire and repaired the leak before it could let in enough water to soak our supplies.

All day we floated down the river, using our oars more in the afternoon as it widened and slowed somewhat coming into a broad valley of terraced hills. The soil must have contained a goodly amount of iron, for the riverbanks began to exhibit a reddish color, though they were much lower than those near White Horse. Gold must not be the only mineral in which these parts are rich, but certainly the one most sought after. Perhaps in years to come others will come with the equipment and means to extract less valuable ore, though I can't imagine this wild country cut through with the roads or railroads it would require.

To the east the panorama was an ever-changing picture of snow-covered mountains, set off against the green of the spruce. A range of these peaks runs north and south, paralleling our route but miles away. I wish we had the time to climb away from the river and see the entire valley spread out below us. It must be spectacular. As it is, we must make all speed possible toward Dawson. This day has seen many miles put behind us as, indeed, we traveled late, wanting to reach Lake Laberge.

This we did, after dark, at about nine o'clock, when the riverbanks suddenly disappeared to right and left and we realized we were afloat on the waters of a broader body of water. Campfires along the shore guided us to a spot suitable for the night and we made haste to build one of our own, wishing to warm fingers stiffened by our hold on the cold oars. Setting up camp, we made a quick dinner of pancakes and coffee, and set a pot of beans to boil for the morrow. We had kept them soaking all day in a pot in the bottom of the boat, so they were ready to cook with a bit of salt pork and some evaporated onion. It is the lake for us tomorrow and I look forward to seeing it in the morning light. As I write it is spitting snow, but only a little. Hopefully it will not increase during the night.

TUESDAY, OCTOBER 5
LAKE LABERGE, YUKON TERRITORY

What a wide and wonderful lake this has turned out to be! When the sun came up we were already on our way and could see for miles over the water. A large dark island covered with spruce trees stands out to the northwest and mountains rise all around it.

To a bird in the air it must seem a jewel in a sea of green that spreads out for hundreds of miles without the suggestion of a road or settlement. Such wilderness is almost impossible to imagine, and here we are in the middle of it, in a small shell of thin wood, floating along. The more I consider, the more I feel like an insect in a puddle, compared to the uninhabited space around me.

Some white men have been here for years, setting up temporary camps, packing their belongings on their backs and living off the land, searching for gold, though seldom finding it. In these far reaches, with such a tangle of rivers, streams, lakes, and so many hills, it seems incredible that any of them find it at all. Such men are deserving of respect, mad though they may be, but they seem to like it, to wish to live nowhere else. Some settle down with an Indian squaw, though I must admit I do not understand the attraction. Perhaps after so long a time away from civilization a woman of any nation would become acceptable. But these silent shadow-women, who watch without reaction and are not particularly clean, seem unlikely helpmates. Strange. Some of the prospectors are very Indian-like themselves. I can hardly wait to get what I came here for and go home to my dear wife and children. They seem so far away and I miss them.

All day we rowed over the mirror lake without a hint of wind or current and, luckily, no more snow. The cold remains, however. I have not been truly warm for days. We are camped on the shore again now, eating the same beans for supper that we ate cold at noon. Frank made some biscuits. What I wouldn't give for an apple, or a bit of boiled cabbage. A turnip? Well, as the saying goes, we are having a thousand things for supper, and every one of them is beans.

Shall reach Thirty-Mile River tomorrow.

THURSDAY, OCTOBER 7
THIRTY-MILE RIVER, YUKON TERRITORY

I must find a way to talk to Ned alone somehow. But whenever I suggest going for wood or leave the camp for any reason, Ozzy follows me, watches me. He knows I saw the watch fall from his coat pocket when he took out his mittens and that I know it is the Swede's watch and believe he stole it.

Late evening before last, when we were all but asleep, a boat full of shouting men pulled in, drawn by the light of our fire. Five Swedes jumped out and asked to camp with us as they desperately needed a quick fire. One of their number had accidentally fallen overboard while lowering the awkward sail they had contrived and was all but frozen. Stripping off his wet clothing and wrapping him in blankets, we built up the blaze and began to get hot liquid into him, along with a shot or two from Ned's whiskey bottle. Rubbing his extremities brought the color back to his skin and saved him from frostbite, but he was pretty well done in.

Ozzy wrung out the Swede's wet clothing and hung it to dry around a second fire. It steamed and was still damp yesterday morning in spots that had frozen as the fire burned low. The party elected to stay there another day, until all was dry and they were sure he was not to have pneumonia. They waved us off early yesterday.

I remember the victim of the drenching asking about his watch before we left to go on down the lake, and when they could not locate it, he decided that it must have been lost in the lake. Later, when we were well onto the Thirty-Mile, Ozzy pulled his mittens from his pocket and out fell the watch into the bottom of the boat.

I simply stared at it, and when I looked up, he was watching me. He picked it up and said it was his, but we both knew better without saying so. He even showed it to me and said something about having had it all along. I know it is a lie, for he has, several times on this expedition, asked me for the time. Would he have done so if he had a timepiece of his own? I think not, but cannot prove it. There were only the two of us, no other witness. Unless we meet up with the Swedes again there is no way to say positively. But I know. And he knows that I, at least, suspect.

What shall I do? Nothing, I suppose, for now. As I say, he has followed me everywhere, without seeming to. I have not been able to speak to Ned once in confidence. All last night, when we camped on the river, he was there, slyly close at my elbow. Either he stays with me, or with Ned, so I cannot speak to him alone.

Again today this continued and, I have to admit, I am somewhat afraid of him. There is his temper, which I have mentioned before, and he has a cruel streak, a way of expecting things to turn against him and, therefore, to feel the need to protect himself any way he can. I do not like this man Oswald, or trust him. But what can I do? Let him assume I have forgotten the incident. I will act as always and be cautious, but will tell Ned at first opportunity, for I think Ozzy could be dangerous.

We made our way through the outlet of Lake Laberge and into the rocky reaches of the Thirty-Mile River yesterday morning. We had been warned about the swiftness of the river and its many rocks and underwater bowlders, so we were ready for it and did not relax our vigilance while passing through it. The water was low and gave us a few problems, with Ned once again guiding us along with no major damage.

Another stream called the Hootalinqua soon came in from the east, adding much to the waters of the Thirty-Mile. By late afternoon we came to the celebrated Cassiar Bar, an area of many sandbars, where we saw fellows panning for gold, especially along one large space covered with sand and gravel. Miners found gold there more than ten years ago and many were still finding color washed down from some unknown source in the hills that no one has been able to locate.

We put in and camped just below the bar last night, having come approximately fifty miles from Lake Laberge, a good day's run. The cliffs there were once again very high, over a hundred feet I should think, and very colorful with white and coal-black bands in places.

Back on the river this morning, we traveled in similar country throughout the day. More than once we passed by cabins on the banks, several set back in the trees. They seemed unoccupied, but it was a good feeling to know others had spent enough time there to erect a log structure, perhaps to spend winters past.

For the last few nights we have witnessed the Aurora Borealis, or Northern Lights, in bands of glowing greenish-white in the dark sky. They move and pulse in swirls and curtain-like formations, and one can see the brightest stars through them. Almost ghostly in their silence, they yet seem almost alive in the rhythm of their movement. Beautiful and alien, one could watch them for hours, their fascination is completely compelling.

I write this in the boat, while Ozzy is taking a turn at the oars and cannot read over my shoulder. I have asked several questions about the route, so he will not suspect I am writing about anything but the traveling. I will keep watch, but give him no reason to feel threatened before I can talk to Ned.

SATURDAY, OCTOBER 9, 1897
BELOW CARMACKS TRADING POST, YUKON TERRITORY

The last two days have been as miserable as any on the journey. Yesterday we woke and got under way early, as usual, but it was overcast and much warmer. Just after noon it commenced to rain and was soon pouring so much water down upon us that we were forced to bail the boat. Even in my waterproof coat, I was soaked through in a short time, as was the rest of the party. Rain this time of the year is just short of freezing and seems colder than lower temperatures, however dry. We were chilled to the bone and shivered constantly, though we worked hard at rowing, hoping to make good time. My fingers lost all feeling and were like sticks on the ends of my hands.

Rain and mist made it hard to see what sort of country we were passing through, but occasionally we could make out high cliffs around us. The river ran swift and smoothly most of the time, carrying us rapidly along. Late in the afternoon, we came around a wide bend and there, to our ragged cheers, was Carmacks Trading Post on the bank ahead.

Having had enough of the rain, we pulled in and spent the night in one of his three small log cabins. For the first time in weeks we slept inside four walls, with a roaring fire in the stove to dry out our clothes and gear, and cook a meal on the rarity of a flat surface. What a luxury. I had almost forgotten what it is to be warm. We heated water and washed ourselves, then trimmed each other's hair and beards. Soon we will be among civilized people again and it seemed right to improve our appearance as much as possible. As a result, our spirits were also much improved, as if cleaning away days of filth lightened our outlook as much as the color of our faces. Snug in our wooden tent, we slept warm and well.

When we awoke this morning the temperature had dropped and the landscape was a sheet of ice. Freezing as it fell, the rain had covered everything in sight with a crystal coating that gleamed in the early sunlight like Pol-

ly's cut-glass bowl on the windowsill. Each tiny branch of the bushes and trees was encased in ice. Walking was treacherous, as at every step your feet threatened to fly out from under and hurl you to the ground without warning. We moved like decrepit old men, ferrying our belongings from cabin to boat half a load at a time.

On the next to last load, Ned lost his footing where the bank slopes to the river and, feet and arms up, slid down on his back to fetch up against the bow of the boat, his burden of dry clothing scattered the length of his wild ride. It was fortunate he was uninjured, for we doubled over with laughter at his sad plight and would probably have been unable to keep from doing so had he been broken in pieces. The helpless waving of his arms and legs, and his great howl of indignation, reduced us to knee-slapping roars. In two minutes, however, we were all sliding like children on pieces of sacking and having a gay time of it. Even Ozzie made a couple of trips down the incline, though he growled that it was nonsense and a waste of time, impatient to get under way.

Very late this afternoon, in half-light, we came through Five Finger and Rink Rapids, which were nothing compared to those above White Horse. Rounding a left-hand bend, we spied four enormous islands of rock ahead, which divided the river into five channels. As we had been warned, we rowed as fast as possible for the right-hand channel and hugged the cliff. That channel is supposedly deeper and has no underwater rocks, so we felt comparatively safe as we felt the boat drop with the rushing current and bound through what must have been two hundred feet of white water with stone walls on either side. It was over so quick we hardly had time to prepare, but were out on smooth water again in only a few seconds.

Rink Rapids came perhaps five miles later, but were little more than a series of ripples compared to the others we have endured. Soon after we pulled out on a tree-covered island near the shore and set up camp for the night. Tomorrow we will come to where the Pelly River joins this one and we are truly on the mighty Yukon at last. Fort Selkirk is there, which I am anxious to see.

I spoke with Ned today, when we stopped to make coffee at noon and Ozzy went off for firewood, and told him about Ozzy. He thinks I did well to keep silent and pretend the incident of the watch was forgotten. Reminding me that there is absolutely nothing to be done, he suggested that we wait until we arrive in Dawson. The Swede will catch us up there, he says, and it may be possible to have a word with him about the lost timepiece. I agreed. There is nothing to be gained by confronting Ozzy now. Neither of us, however, wants to work with him in Dawson. We must make sure that he is not included in any partnership we make. In Ned's mind this also includes Frank Warner, for he and Wilson seem to be an obvious twosome. So we wait and watch, but I feel better for his knowing what I witnessed.

Twice this evening I have heard the scream of a wild cat in the woods along the west bank. Frank says it may be a lynx. I would like to see one, but it seems unlikely. We never see the wolves we frequently hear howling in the dark.

We are not far from the end of our journey now. Two or three more days will see us in Dawson City ready to claim our fortunes. I cannot imagine what it must be like and can hardly wait to find myself a claim and dig up some gold. We are all excited in anticipation. It has been a long and hazardous undertaking, but is soon over. What ho!! for Clondyke!

SUNDAY, OCTOBER 10, 1897
YUKON RIVER, YUKON TERRITORY

Fort Selkirk is not a fort at all, or is not one now. According to the proprietor of Harper's Trading Post, it was burned down over forty years ago by Chilkat Indians who were angry that the Hudson's Bay Company was taking the fur trade away from them. Only the trading post is left, though its builder, Arthur Harper, has contracted consumption and gone to Arizona for a cure.

Departing Fort Selkirk, we were on the Yukon proper, which was much swelled with the waters of the Pelly. It grows ever-wider and speeds us along as if it was as anxious as we to reach Dawson City. It is almost dark, as I write this in the boat, but we are reluctant to put in and make camp with our objective so close. Ned has spotted a good campsite, however, so we will pull in, but I wager we will be up early tomorrow, for the last day of our journey.

I can scarcely contain my excitement at the attainment of our objective. My cheeks ache from the grin which keeps stretching my face. I notice the same from Frank and Ned. Even Ozzy is in a more positive mood. We have made it all the way before freeze-up and I am sorry for those back on Lake Bennett, whose boats will not be completed in time to make the voyage and must wait until spring. We have the jump on them. Perhaps by the time they arrive we will all be rich men and ready to return.

This trip itself has been worth something, however. To have overcome all the obstacles in our path, the Chilkoot, the lakes, the rapids and rivers, carried all our goods and outfits this incredible distance, seems worthy of recognition. Whatever we find in the gold fields, there will be a sort of anticlimax at the end of all this traveling through the wilderness. We will move on into another part of the venture, which does not include the wide, beautiful, ever-changing reach of hills and valleys that has been our daily experience up to now. I, for one, will miss them. I like this country, rough and rude though it may be, and will not mind remaining in it for a time, though it will soon be blanketed with snow.

Ice is frozen so far out from the bank that we must break through it to make any kind of landing. Chunks of it slip past or accompany us along with a kind of rustling sound as they bump into each other. We must make haste to reach our destination before we are completely frozen in.

TUESDAY, OCTOBER 19, 1897
DAWSON CITY, YUKON TERRITORY

Over a week since I last opened this journal, and I hardly know what to write. Dawson City is not at all what

I had imagined, nor does it compare with the visions of my traveling companions, I am sure.

The once mud streets of this so-called city are now frozen into ruts and ridges. Hundreds of men walk up and down them, most with nothing to do and nowhere to go. They simply cannot stay still in one place after so many miles of moving ahead as fast as possible to reach this place. All of us are feeling an incredible anticlimax.

Every inch of ground remotely suspected as gold-bearing has long been claimed and staked. There is no gold to be had for the taking in or around Dawson and little even to share work for. All the claims were filed long before any of us left on the long, difficult passage that brought us here. Indeed, Bonanza and Eldorado Creeks were completely staked, by men already in the territory, six months before the steamer Portland tied up at the Schwabacher dock last summer.

The city is packed with people, over four thousand of them, without hope of making a strike, and more pour in every day, though the river is freezing fast and will any day be impassable. The expected steamboats with their cargoes of supplies for the winter will not reach us before spring. Captain Hansen of the Alaska Commercial Company left early in September to find out what was delaying five steamboats supposedly bound for Dawson. He returned on the twenty-sixth with the news that they were, and would remain, four hundred miles downstream, near a place called Fort Yukon, marooned by low water in the mud flats. Within hours, over a hundred open boats full of people had left to go downriver, hoping to reach them. A number of others headed south, afoot or by boat. We saw some of them, only one day out of Dawson, and should perhaps have heeded the cry of a man walking south on the bank with a pack on his back, "There's no food in Dawson. You will starve. Turn back. Turn back."

Many stampeders came here with little or no food goods, expecting to buy what they needed here with the gold they would certainly find. But there is nothing to buy, or what little anyone is willing to part with is more valuable than the gold coming out of the ground. Even salt *is worth its weight in gold. The A.C. Company has locked its doors and will only allow one man at a time inside to purchase a limited amount of provisions. They line up fifty deep outside, waiting for a chance to buy. It is a desperate situation that can only grow worse when we are wintered in and isolated for the long cold months. Thank God we brought our winter supplies with us and have enough to survive. We have had dozens of offers for what little we have and two days ago caught a blackguard attempting to steal from our cache, so we now keep a firearm handy at all times and watch through the nights.*

The Swedes came in three days behind us. Ned and I meeting two of them on the street asked about their companion who fell overboard. They were sad to inform us that he had indeed contracted pneumonia and died, despite all they could do to save him. Ned gave me a long look, at which I did not mention the watch. We have discussed it and decided to leave well enough alone. There is nothing to be proved and only trouble in accusations. I hate the thought of Ozzy's getting away with the theft, however. He has become almost impossible, since we arrived and found our hopes dashed. Ill temper and contempt seem his natural state. Even Frank leaves him alone for the most part. Ned and I stick together in town, for Frank and Ozzy have hiked off to search for some opportunity in the goldfields, but the venture seems all but hopeless.

At last we have split with them, to my relief. We have divided our goods, but I am sure that my bag of flour has been opened and part of my supply of beans is missing. I made the mistake of mentioning it when Ozzy was within earshot. He growled that I should take better care of my goods and that I'd better not be accusing him. I dropped the subject, but I am convinced he took them, more glad than ever to be without his company.

FRIDAY, OCTOBER 22, 1897
DAWSON CITY, YUKON TERRITORY

Three days ago McNeal and I moved into the rough cabin of a Scotsman that Ned met on the street in Dawson.

Very low on supplies, he has gone with a small party to attempt the long journey from here to the coast, where he can catch a ship out for the winter. In exchange for this winter shelter, we have promised to burn a shaft for him during the cold months.

We have already begun this effort and it will be a miserable one at best. Its one redeeming feature is that it will require finger-warming fires to melt the frozen ground as we must first heat, then dig out as much as we can, making a deeper space to build another fire. Between times, we must walk miles to cut timber for those fires, since every close tree was long ago reduced to ashes in the shafts of other claims. We must quickly get sufficient wood hauled and cut before the snow buries it all too deep to find easily.

All the rubble we dig out is piled around outside the cabin to await sluicing when the spring melts enough water to allow it. The melted earth immediately refreezes into solid lumps. The claim will be a mire when warm weather returns.

The cabin, if it may be called one, is minimal shelter at best; so low is the roof that we must stoop rather than stand when inside it. Little was done to chink the spaces between the narrow logs that form its walls, so the frigid wind whistles through like a sieve, whipping heat away from my stove, which we have set up in one corner, as fast as it is produced. We spent one day collecting moss and cramming it in the spaces with mud. Now it is somewhat better, though nothing which could be identified as cozy.

We have hopefully seen the last of Warner and Oswald, who have found a place of their own somewhere close to Dawson. What they are doing, I have no idea and care not. I am still furious that Oswald somehow contrived to make off with portions of my beans, sugar, and rice, as we separated our outfits. Damn his eyes.

There will now certainly be no boats full of supplies for the winter. The river is frozen. Word has come with a trapper who came in by dogsled that the riverboats Weare and Bella battled heavy ice in their attempt to make the three hundred and forty mile run down the river to Fort Yukon. The Bella froze in once at Forty-Mile, but a warm chinook wind melted the center ice, allowing him to clear a channel and escape to Circle City. The Weare, which had reached that place earlier, headed on, only to be solidly halted by ice, forcing its passengers to trek over fifty miles to Fort Yukon, where food was also dangerously low.

We carefully guard what we have, for without it we would not survive the winter. Food is the foremost subject on everyone's mind.

The temperature dropped alarmingly and has held at fifty degrees below zero for several days. We huddle in our tiny shelter, taking turns going for wood, trying to keep warm. I shudder at the thought of those on the long trail back to the Chilkoot Pass, for they must be suffering terribly.

Still, depressingly, too cold to write, though we have reached eight feet in burning our shaft. Ned and I stay close to our cabin, except for trips to find wood.

Walked into Dawson today, where on the street I saw Joaquin Miller, the "Poet of the Sierras," sent to the

Clondyke by the newspaperman, Hearst, to report on the gold rush. He had attempted to make it to Fort Yukon on the Weare, but after being stranded in Circle City, he and another man turned back to Dawson on foot and finally made it, though Miller suffered greatly, losing his left ear, part of a toe and one finger. He came in on November fifth completely snowblind with both cheeks frozen. He is a tall, gaunt, unusual figure with a white beard, and is dressed in fur and reindeer skin. At almost sixty years old, it is remarkable that he survived to reach Dawson and is to be hoped that he lives through the winter.

On November 29, the temperature dropped so low we spent two whole days wrapped in our blankets, shivering though the fire was never allowed to subside. We know now that it was sixty-seven below and trees cracked like gunshots in the cold.

Thanksgiving night two dance-hall girls reputedly had an altercation which ended in one throwing a burning lamp at the other. The resulting fire burned most of Front Street in Dawson, leaving people on the street in fifty-eight below zero weather. McDonald's saloon, the site of the lamp-throwing, burned to the ground, but has already been replaced and is once again open for business, which is brisk.

We toil doggedly on, alternately building fires and digging out the thawed soil. At fifteen feet, we hit a rock too large to raise and dug around it. There, we began finding nuggets of gold, which we pick out of the dirt when we see them. Ned's friend will be pleased, if he ever returns, for there are now over forty such nuggets in the tin under my bed, a few as large as my thumbnail, others half that size. Obviously, others lie in the piles of dirt to be sluiced in the spring, for we pick out only what we see easily.

SATURDAY, DECEMBER 25, 1897
DAWSON CITY, YUKON TERRITORY

Christmas Day. I think of my family, Polly and the children, so far away and wish I could see them. In recognition of the

*day, we cooked up a good batch of beans and ate them with
a hare Ned shot last week when we went for wood. It was
tough, but wonderful to have fresh meat.*

TUESDAY, JANUARY 4, 1898
DAWSON CITY, YUKON TERRITORY

---

*I am heartsick and frightened. McNeal is dead. His head
crushed in the shaft by a large rock rolled in on him,
certainly by Warner and Oswald. I came back to the cabin
with a load of wood and found Ned crumpled and half
buried in the shaft, his bright blood frozen on his clothes
and broken skull. There I left him and walked to the next
claim for help. We pulled him out and wrapped him in
his blanket, but the two fellows who helped gave me odd
looks and mentioned cautiously that two friends of mine
had found him earlier and gone to Dawson for the law.
Their description matched Frank and Ozzy, and I recognized their tracks in the snow.*

*So I am now hiding with a friend in Dawson, whom I
will not name for fear this journal may be found. He has
determined that Frank and Ozzy told the authorities they
saw me leaving the cabin just before they found him dead.
I could assure my innocence and provide witnesses of my
character, but would I be believed? The deciding factor,
however, is that I know they intend to kill me as surely
as they killed Ned, and why.*

*They came to our camp last week, asking to share and
claiming rights as our partners. When we refused, they
insisted they would have it, one way or another, that the
owner would not return and the claim would be ours and,
therefore, theirs. Ned showed them the shooting end of his
rifle and they left, making threats.*

*They will not leave me alive to witness against them,
when my death would make all easy. I expect that if they
had the chance, they would kill me and tell the authorities,
such as they are, that I attacked them, tried to escape, or
some other such nonsense. Whatever they said, it would
be two against none, with me dead, and two against one,
if I were to go to report it myself.*

I have decided that my only course is to attempt to head down river for Forty-Mile. My friend agrees and has made me the loan of a wolfskin coat, beaver-fur mittens and hat. We both know it is more of a gift. Probably I will not make it, but, who knows? God being just, I may, and can return his coat next spring. It is better than waiting here for their nefarious and certain judgment. The first time it snows to cover my tracks, I will be off with a small sled and only enough goods for survival, probably tomorrow. I have buried most of the nuggets here in Dawson, in the best place I could think of that could not be easily located, and have drawn and hidden a map.

Dearest Polly, If I perish and this is found, know that I love you and the children. All I can leave you is this record and the gold, which does not really belong to me. If you will remember where you secreted the letters I wrote you before we were married, you will know where the map is hidden. I am only sorry things did not turn out differently, but it was not a bad idea to come here, all being considered. Events simply conspired against me, and against Ned, certainly. If we had been wintered in at Lake Bennett and forced to wait until spring, it might have been advantageous. But one can go crazy saying what if. Just know that I would never leave you with two children to raise unless it were as necessary as it seems to be. Either I die here, or try to make it there and perhaps die on the way. I like my chances better in not waiting here. Whatever happens, I send you all my love. In haste. Your loving husband, Addison Harley Riser.